NAKED
CONFESSIONS
BY TRACEE HANNA

AUGUSTUS
PUBLISHING

WHERE
HIP HOP
LITERATURE
BEGINS

AUGUSTUS
PUBLISHING

This is a work of fiction. Names, characters, places, and incidents are products of the author's imagination or are used fictitiously and are not to be construed as real. Any resemblance to actual events, locales or organizations, or persons, living or dead is entirely coincidental.

© 2013 Augustus Publishing, Inc.
ISBN: 978-19358833-8-8

Novel by Tracee Hanna
Edited by Lauren Tannenbaum
Creative Direction, Design By Jason Claiborne
Photography by BigAppleModels.com

Augustus Publishing paperback September 2013
www.augustuspublishing.com

TRACEE HANNA

CHAPTER ONE
FACING REALITY

There are many truths in life, this is mine. I married the best fuck I ever had in my life, and with time I learned to love him, even adore him. I protected our sensuous flame for as long as I could, as it weathered many storms. My shameless mantra, a brief statement of facts which lacked candor. The heartfelt truth is, I married for love.

In the beginning, Jack took care of me when I had no one else. We met quite by chance within three weeks of my moving to town. I studied Spanish in Phoenix, over a thousand miles from home. He was the most beautiful man I had ever laid my eyes on. Instantly I was crazy about him. Our passion was limitless. The sex was hot, borderline savage and I loved it. Faithfully, I waited for Jack to marry me. We had a lovely intimate family wedding on the tenth anniversary of our first date. Jack was my husband and the father of my children. I was in it for life. Time passed quickly. My love never faded—for fifteen years I firmly believed that Jack was the love of my life and I was his.

I treasured our life together. I had it all. I cherished my family. I enjoyed being a wife and mother. I even liked my job. Everything in my life was perfect, except for the fact that Jack had lost interest in our marriage shortly after our fifth wedding anniversary. I took notice however I did not take it to heart, as marital highs and lows were to be expected. Jack came home every night and we made love on a regular basis. I was not worried. Although there were good and bad times, we were still a family—husband, wife, and two beautiful children.

We had a happy home, at least that was the lie I told myself over and over again. As the years passed I found activities to involve my daughters and myself in, to better occupy our time. Gone were the days of playing dress up and having tea parties. Little did I know that such innocent diversions would change my life forever.

One Saturday afternoon Jack took the children to a ball game. Nothing was special about that afternoon save for the fact that it was the first Saturday in October. I accepted the invitation to an event in South Phoenix, The Coalition, a monthly patrons' appreciation luncheon held at The Post, a hip hop club located on the south side of town in a predominately African-American neighborhood.

I arrived just after two in the afternoon. I drove around, searched for an empty parking space to no avail. There was nothing available in the main lot or the overflow lot. I was about to leave when a woman who had just exited the establishment stopped me, and offered her parking spot.

My truck rolled slowly across the gravel. The rocks crunched under the weight of the Ford Ranger XLT as I followed her to her car. She started the engine, put her car in gear, and hit the gas. I saw her coming at me fast, too fast, but there was nothing I could do.

I screamed, "No!" That tank, a nineteen eighty-six Buick Regal, slammed into my vehicle hard. The force of the impact pushed my brand new pick-up truck sideways over four feet, demolition derby style. "No, no, no, this cannot be happening…"

Gripping the steering wheel, I closed my eyes, and pressed my body against the back of the seat. Before long it was over. I opened my eyes and took a deep breath. Unfortunately for me, the airbag deployed in that moment, late, punching me in the chest. "Oh God," I cried. I was in a lot of pain. I closed my eyes again. I pressed my hand against my bosoms as I gasped for air.

"Are you okay?" the woman asked. Shouting, and stumbling out of her car, she came staggering towards me.

"This bitch is drunk!" I yelled, incensed. An adrenaline-fueled rage deceptively cloaked my pain. I wanted to hurt her but the driver side door would not open. I climbed out through the passenger side. "Oh, I'm going to beat her drunken ass," I declared. However, the moment my feet touched the ground I was overcome by mind-blowing pain. A gut wrenching cry forced its way past my lips. I fell back onto the passenger seat.

"Tia!" Tammy shouted, her voice panic stricken. I saw my friend running towards me, clearly worried. "Stay still! I'm coming with help."

Before she arrived, I attempted to stand again. That was a mistake because I became dizzy and felt like i wanted to faint. The earth was spinning, and I saw stars. Immediately, I sat back down in the passenger seat of my truck. Then I leaned my head back, and closed my eyes.

"Tia, are you alright?" Tammy asked.

"Tammy please call my sister. She has to bring my pain pills." I looked into her eyes, " Oh God this really hurts." I cried. "Oh my dear God, I'm in so much pain."

"Okay Tia! I'm on it."

I thought to myself, who gets hit by two drunk drivers? Me. A drunk driver ran a red light four months ago and now this. That particular afternoon was my first time out on the town in months. I had just completed my rehabilitation therapy the day before. Before too long, the police were on the scene. My sister Nicole arrived shortly thereafter, with medication. I refused to go to the hospital. I truly believed that all I needed were my pain meds and some rest. Everything would be all right by Monday morning. All I wanted to do was get my vehicle towed home and get into bed. Alas a simple solution was not to be had. Suddenly I could not breathe. I began coughing up blood. My sister immediately drove me to the emergency room.

"Nicole, please call Jack," I said then collapsed.

Several hours later I regained consciousness in a hospital room. My family stood around me. My husband was not there. Jack arrived twelve hours after I was admitted, at three o'clock in the morning.

"Jack, what took you so long to get here?" I asked.

"I was changing out my muffler so my car was down."

"You couldn't have borrowed a car from someone and gotten here sooner?"

"You're here with your family. It's not as if you're alone."

I was lucky he came at all. Yeah, that's love. They kept me overnight for tests and observation. My diagnosis was dire: spinal damage, bulges in my lower back and neck, scar tissue, inflammation, severe nerve damage, my pelvis was tilted forward on the right side, and my left arm needed to be rehabilitated as well. I could not walk without acute pain—even so I refused to get into a wheelchair. I was terrified I would never get out again.

Less than twenty-four hours after being released from the hospital, Jack wanted sex. I was home recuperating. I lay in bed on a fluffy mound of pillows. Heavily medicated, I weaved in and out of drug induced sleep. I was alone for most of the time, as I needed my rest. Late Monday evening Jack climbed into bed next to me.

"Tia, I want to make love to you tonight," he said.

"I can't, I can barely walk. How am I going to be able to make love to you?"

"Take an extra pill. Hell, take as many as you need but we are making love tonight. Here I'll prop you up on some more pillows and get you a drink. Get ready for me."

"Please don't do this to me, Jack."

"You are my wife and I have needs."

"Please Jack," I begged.

I could not stop him. Sadistic pleasure danced in his eyes as I suffered relentless agony. I prayed I would faint. I cried, I begged, and I called upon the Lord. An hour later it was over, and I lost consciousness.

Day by day my pain became more intense. I could not return to work. The vicodin was not effective, in bed I lay all alone, breathlessly still and engulfed in misery.

Jack accompanied me to my next doctor's appointment. I asked for stronger pain medication. I confided in my doctor. I told him that the pain after sexual relations with my husband was worse than childbirth. He prescribed seven point five milligram Oxycodone, a powerful muscle relaxant as well as anti-inflammatory medication. He advised my husband about the risk of further injury and strongly recommended that Jack give me time to heal.

"Why did you have to tell the doctor that I hurt you during sex?" Jack hissed the moment we left the doctor's office.

"Because you did," I replied.

"You are my wife."

He wrapped an arm around my back and held out the other for me to hold on to as we continued down the hall.

"Jack, the pain was completely unbearable. And so is your cruelty."

"So I'm supposed to suffer."

"Would you like to trade places?"

"No. I wasn't trying to hurt you, Tia."

"You're hurting me now. Please slow down, you are pushing too hard."

Jack seemed genuinely remorseful and concerned about my wellbeing but that was before we entered the main corridor. He stopped abruptly. I looked up to see why. He stepped away from me, leaving me standing helplessly in the middle of the hall.

"Mary Jo!" Jack exclaimed.

I looked from him to the approaching woman, white trash with unwashed hair. Their matching smiles told a tale that my heart could not bare. She stopped in front of us.

"Hi Jack," she said cheerfully.

"Hi Mary Jo! Wow. I haven't seen you in a long time. How are you?"

"I'm fine! You look great."

I stood there oddly trying to decide which hurt worse, physical pain or heartache. That was it—in that very instant my love for Jack sustained a fatal blow and slowly began to die. I made my way over to the wall, held on to the railing and walked away.

Two weeks later on November sixth, at exactly eight fifteen p.m., Jack began to gently make love to my body. By eight nineteen he had completed his task. He tried again, however erectile dysfunction had settled in. I smiled. Not wanting to admit defeat, Jack made attempts from time to time however he was unable to sustain an erection. On the rare occasion when he could, he ejaculated prematurely. I endured it because I could not fight him off and he knew it. This naturally led to a few heated arguments.

"You know what Jack, I'm so tired of you making me suffer from your abysmal sex. It's not worth taking a pain pill for this shit and I get ninety of them for ten dollars."

"Why you got to be so damn bitter and mean?"

"I'm just telling it like it is. Your sex sucks, your dick can't even stay hard for more than thirty seconds at a time."

"Tia, you know damn well that shit isn't true."

"What? Your dick can stay hard for a whole forty-five seconds? How dreadful. Excuse me if I left a couple of seconds out. The plain fact is you can't fuck worth a damn." I glared into his eyes as I continued, "We don't make love anymore. I would gladly accept you if I thought for a moment that you still loved me."

"All I wanted was..."

"What?" I interjected. "All you want to do is fuck! No more, no less. You left me here alone. Look at me. I have pimples and blackheads all over my body. My skin is rough and dry. You can't be bothered to help me to the toilet. You can't be bothered to help me with my bath or my hair. So please don't do me any other favors."

"I can't lift you anymore."

"That's because you are the asshole who feeds your crippled wife cellophane wrapped vending machine food instead of cooking healthy meals. Why don't you go inflict this shit on someone else? I don't want you." I took pause and smiled sadistically before continuing, "Oh I know, go call Mary Jo."

"What?"

"I hate you!"

Jack walked out as usual. All I could do was pray. Please God help me overcome this. Please take the pain away. My husband is cheating on me. He could be exposing me to AIDS but there is nothing I can do to fight him off. He won't wear a condom and he won't help me to clean my body. Help me please! In Jesus' name I pray Lord, amen.

That night I crawled to the bathroom, pulled myself up and sat on the side of the tub. I wrapped a washcloth around a silver plated decorative toilet brush, which made it possible to reach every part of my body. I caught the water with a Seven-Eleven Big Gulp cup and bathed. The smell of Japanese cherry blossoms filled the air. It felt so good to be clean. I never knew that something which was ordinarily inconsequential could be so perfect.

The following morning I decided to crawl around the floor for a few minutes several times a day. The days passed, and I slowly regained more strength. Within two weeks, I could stand without falling. My left leg supported most of my weight, and I was able to lean on the walls as I attempted to walk independently. The following month, I was strong enough to begin physical therapy. Within thirty days I could walk. Although I had to use a cane, I no longer had to crawl to the bathroom. There was no more holding onto the walls for support. Gone were the days of eating cellophane wrapped vending machine food. I did not have to be alone anymore. I was not bound to Jack and his whims.

I had a lot of work to do. My muscles had atrophied. I gained sixty pounds over a three month period. I looked into the mirror and saw that I had gained so much weight my face had changed, a complete stranger stared back at me. I did not want to be her. That jolt of terror gave me determination and drive. I had to eat four times a day in order to take my pain medication. I tried not eating. I tried eating less but the medicine made me nauseous. I had to eat.

I made a plan to eat healthy. I went grocery shopping with my daughters. For the first time in my life I noticed that there were electric shopping carts at the grocery store. I thanked God. I finally had pain-free mobility and better food choices. I adopted the low-carb lifestyle. I smiled brightly as I drove around the store.

My oldest daughter pushed a cart behind me. I filled my shopping cart with fresh fruit, vegetables, meats, cheeses, and eggs. The store had a low-carb food section filled with pasta, breads, prepared meals and condiments. I was like a kid in a candy store. The second cart began to fill up quickly. I purchased a few of my children's favorites before checking out.

I enjoyed being in the kitchen again. I prepared every meal fresh from scratch every day. I maintained a twenty carbohydrate per day regimen. Although I enjoyed the American favorites as time passed I began to venture out. I added frittatas, omelets, no crust quiches, to my breakfast regimen, my daily salads became gourmet creations, and culinary masterpieces were served for dinner at least once a week. My daughters joined me in the kitchen as often as they could. I loved cooking alongside them.

Pretty soon the end of January was near, my birthday was coming up. My sister, Nicole, visited. She asked me to take a ride with her as she ran some errands. I got in her sports car, but the seatbelt could not buckle. I was too fat. My heart dropped. I really had no idea that I had so much girth. I was more hurt than embarrassed. I had worked so hard to lose the weight.

Before that moment I was proud that I lost twenty pounds however in that moment reality became clear. Twenty pounds was just a drop in the bucket, I had a long way to go. Still, I wanted to tag along with her. Although I sat in the car for most of our outing, it was good be out of the house. When we got home, there were a couple of cars in my driveway, one belonging to my mother and the other to my second cousin.

"Damn, I really don't feel like company today," I said, instantly irritated. "I don't want anyone to see me like this, Nicole."

"Tia, don't be that way. It's only Mama and Helen," Nicole replied.

"I know, but I just don't feel like being bothered. They've stayed away this long."

I did not want to hear people comment on my weight or the pimple scars on my face or the condition of my hair. I had suffered enough. My heart could not bare their well meaning insults and total disregard of my life changing injuries.

"Come on Tia, I'll help you out of the car."

We walked into the house. Everyone screamed, "Surprise!" My brothers and sisters were there along with my nieces, nephews, and cousins. I was genuinely surprised.

"Oh my God I had no idea, thank you!" I cried with joy.

"Tia, if you would've looked down the street you would have seen everybody's cars parked on the next block," Nicole said as she laughed.

"Oh Nikki, thank you..."

"It was not my idea. Your children threw this party for you," Nicole corrected.

My heart filled with happiness. My daughters, who I had rarely seen since the accident, planned a surprise birthday party. I thanked my girls profusely. I hugged them tight. The party was such a spirit lifter that I did not notice Jack's absence until he came in to sing happy birthday. Jack took his cake to go. No one seemed to notice, therefore I refused to care. I was happy.

February was uneventful, other than the fact that I moved into a separate bedroom. Valentine's Day of that year was nice and sweet. My children were my Valentines. We ordered pizza, made mint tea, popped popcorn, filled a bowl with Hershey kisses and enjoyed a movie marathon. Their father quietly joined us hours later. He lay on the floor in front of the couch. Jack's birthday was a little over two months away. By the first of May I felt and looked a whole lot better.

I decided to throw an eighty's themed house party for Jack's birthday. I invited Jack's car club buddies, coworkers, friends, and family. Everyone arrived in costume except for the car club people, only two of the twenty-five car club members I invited were in attendance. Everyone else was there. We sang karaoke, danced, drank, talked, laughed, and ate good food. The next day that bastard had the nerve to complain about not getting a gift or card. I spent hundreds of dollars throwing that cheating ingrate a party and that was the thanks I got. I was crushed. Regrettably, I soothed my hurt feelings with deliciously fattening food.

Stupid me, I still wanted my marriage. I held on to my commitment to family. I worked even harder in physical therapy and planned for the next occasion. Our anniversary rolled around. I sent our children to my mother's house in hopes of Jack and I sharing a little romance. I grilled two porterhouse steaks, roasted fresh vegetables, whipped up a batch of garlic mashed potatoes, and baked fresh bread. The house was illuminated by nothing but candle light. I chilled a good bottle of champagne. I thought that Jack and I could try to find our way back to one another, maybe even make love again. I was wrong. He came home well after midnight. I blamed myself. The heartache was too much for me to bare alone yet I could not share such humiliation with any living soul. I began keeping a diary on my laptop.

"I've got to do better. I was way too fat," I said to myself.

CHAPTER TWO
SOCIAL BUTTERFLY

Eight months passed since my accident. My weight yo-yoed up and down. It was mostly up. I was now wearing size 3X. I'm only five feet and two inches tall. I was a ball of lard. I went to physical therapy three days a week. I still needed to be heavily medicated for any and every thing that I chose to participate in so I started taking ephedrine to stay awake.

The next month my dear friend, Javier, invited me to a birthday party at one of the local clubs. I use to braid Javier's hair back in the day. I accepted the invitation with stipulations: a guaranteed seat and consent to bring my pillows. He agreed right away. Nikki accompanied me. That was the night Nikki and I met Jerome, the man to which she would later become engaged. I was sitting alone on a bed of pillows when he walked up to me curiously.

"Hi," Jerome greeted me with a smile.

"Hi," I responded in kind.

"Are you all right?" Jerome sincerely asked.

"Yes, thank you."

"Do you need me to fluff your pillows or get you anything?"

"No, but thank you all the same. Why don't you have a seat, and keep me company for a while?"

He sat down and before too long we were engaged in a deep conversation. I listened mostly. I got a good feeling about him. I decided to play matchmaker.

"So tell me Jerome how old are you?" I asked to lighten up the conversation.

"I'm twenty-seven."

"Really, I've got a little sister and you seem like good people. Have you caught sight of that pretty young lady in red?"

"Yes, why?" he asked.

"That is my sister Nicole. Would you like to be introduced?"

"Hell yeah," he exclaimed.

"I'll call her over here for you."

Nicole was a social butterfly. She had learned from the best and that was me. I sent her a text, and before long she appeared.

"Nikki this is Jerome, Jerome this is my baby sister, Nikki."

"Hello Nikki, would you like to dance?"

"Yes," she said. She smiled. We hugged as she whispered, "He is fine as hell."

That was the start of their relationship. At the end of the night he walked her to her car and kissed her goodnight. Two weeks later Nikki had a house party to celebrate her birthday. Nikki and I spent the day before, and most of that day, cooking. By the time we finished I was tired and in pain. I went home, took my medication and a nap. I grabbed a quick shower before the party. Just when I was leaving Jack stopped me.

"Tia, where are you going?" he asked.

"I already told you, Jack. Nikki is having a birthday party at her house tonight."

"Who are you meeting there?"

"A whole lot of people, friends haven't seen me since my accident."

"A bunch a men, huh?" he asked accusingly.

"Yeah," I said, shrugging my shoulders.

"I'm going with you! You're not going to leave me behind like you did two weeks ago."

"First of all, I didn't leave you behind. You decided at the last minute that you didn't want to go. So I went without you," I said, glaring at him. "What, you expected me to stay here with you...? Ain't no way in hell! If you want to go, you know where my sister lives. You can meet me there."

"I can't ride with you?"

"Hell no. I'm ready to go now, and I refuse to wait. Bye."

About an hour later, Jack met me at the party. Every step I took he was right there behind me. I could not move fast or far away from him. Jack was like a dark shadow. He was not only hostile, but also argumentative.

"You and Nicole know all of these men don't you?" Jack asked.

"Yes," I answered curtly.

"Who came here to see you?"

"All of them, except for about one or two of Nikki's co-workers. Pay attention, and you will see what genuine care, and concern looks like."

Not even a minute later a beautiful, well groomed, nattily attired, deep-chocolate man walked up to me, arms extended. He gathered me up in an affectionate hug, and I gladly accepted his embrace. I stayed in his arms for a moment too long on purpose. The hug ended, the embrace did not.

"Hello Tia darlin', it's good to see you out again," he said.

"Thank you, Darrious. How have you been?"

"You know me baby-girl. I am always about making money. You are still beautiful Tia. You'll find your way back before too long."

"Thank you. Go find Nikki before you make me cry."

"Take care of yourself, baby."

The moment Darrious walked away, I turned my attention back to

Jack. The look on Jack's face was all worth it. I let my innocence showed when I looked into his eyes. He was displeased.

"What?" I coyly asked.

"Who the fuck was that?"

"Darrious, didn't you hear me say his name?" My voice was sugar sweet. "Jack darlin', please don't make a scene. After all, this is a party. The last thing you want to do is make any of these men think that I am in distress."

"Who is he to you?"

"Just a person I know. Why?"

"I'm your husband, and you didn't even introduce me to him."

"He knows who you are. Everyone who knows me knows who you are."

"Well I don't know who the fuck all of these damn men are, who just so happen to know my wife," he said loudly.

"Lookey here Jack, start some shit if you want to. I can have any one of these brothas up in here kick your ass for me. Would you like me to introduce you to Xavier?"

I pointed to a six-foot-seven, three hundred pound man. He looked like he could snap my husband like a green bean. After that, Jack found somewhere to be other than up under me. Jack stood six-one, and weighed about one hundred and eighty pounds. He was very handsome, which meant nothing to me anymore because he was a bully, an asshole, and a cheater.

A few hours had passed. I began to feel some pain. I had no choice but to sit down for a while. Little did I know that Jack had taken all of my pain pills out of my car and purse while I showered, in an attempt to get me to leave the party sooner than I wanted. Luckily for me when my pain got to be too much my home boy Big John walked in the door. I got up and greeted him.

"Hi John, I'm so glad you could make it."

"It's been a long time, Tia. How are you?"

"My back really hurts right now, and ol' asshole took all of my pills. I took an overdose of the over the counter stuff, but it's not touching this pain."

"Put 'em on me, Tia," John requested.

I reached up and wrapped my arms around his neck. I put my breasts high on his chest. He reached down, placed his arms around me and lifted me up. Vertebrae by vertebrae my back popped relieving the pressure. After a few shots of vodka I was good to go for another few hours.

The next few months passed without incident. As a matter of fact, other than hitting me up for sex once a month, Jack left me alone all together. My therapy continued, my children's birthdays came and went. Before I knew it, the holidays were here. Jack spent Thanksgiving with the family. However he was nowhere to be found on Christmas. Between Thanksgiving and Christmas holidays, I finally got it together. I dropped twenty-five pounds. I wrote the following line in my diary.

I'm trying soo hard to get Jack to notice me again. I need to get the hell out of dodge before he completely breaks my heart.

I had planned to go to St. Louis to bring in the New Year with my home girl Linda, however, Jack freaked out about it. He even accused me of meeting a lover there. It had become common place for him to accuse me of cheating, especially since I was losing the weight in the winter. When a cheater is cheating they always point the finger.

To keep the peace I changed my plans. I sent for Linda instead, and she arrived the day before Christmas. Linda called me the minute she touched down. I drove like a speed demon all the way, arriving within fifteen minutes. She didn't recognize me when I pulled up. I opened the sunroof, and waved her over. I popped the trunk before getting out.

"Hi Linda girl," I shouted.

"Tia? Hey," she exclaimed.

"I can't help you with your luggage, but he will," I said as I pointed to a man in uniform.

"No, I got it."

"All right," I said as I rolled my eyes to the sky. I firmly disagreed with Linda's attitude. "Lets go."

"I like your ride. But Tia girl, you are looking rough."

"I know. I'll look better tomorrow."

"Well I'm here now, and you've got to look good if you are going to hang out with my fine ass."

I busted out laughing. Linda followed suit. It felt good to laugh. The next day I relaxed my hair in preparation for Christmas dinner at my sister's house. There were four females in the house, a frenzy of showers, blow dryers, and curling irons, not to mention the clothes. Everyone was ready by two that afternoon. When I walked into the living room Jack was sitting on the couch playing video games as usual.

"Hey Jack, we are finally ready but I think we are going to have to take two cars so everyone can fit comfortably." I began. "Linda is going to take the children in the truck which leaves you and me," I smiled. "Are you driving or shall I?"

"I'm not going."

"All right," I replied cheerfully.

I walked away thinking of how tired I was trying to reach out to this man. I planned on having a good time even if I have to create one for myself. If a man wasn't spending the holidays with his family he had to be creeping with someone else.

We arrived at Nicole's house at about two thirty. She was still putting the finishing touches on dinner. I rolled up my sleeves, washed my hands, and pitched in. Before too long Jerome's family began to arrive and our family dinner turned into a nice little party. After dinner we played a game of spades. Nikki and I were up against Jerome and his brother, Paul. The girls were winning.

"Paul, I think we just set y'all asses," I said.

"Oh, okay Tia. You want to talk shit now that you're just a little bit ahead. But we're going to see who will win this here game," Paul replied.

"Bring it on baby. Show me. It's your turn to deal so let's see if you can do right by yourself."

"We're goin' to bid in the dark. We'll take seven."

"All right now, Paul. Don't hurt yourself."

We laughed and drank tequila shots until the wee hours of the morning. I was so glad to be in their company, so glad that someone could take my mind off of my crumbling marriage; even if just for a little while.

New Year's Eve, I took the liberty of taking our children to my mother's house. Jack made a point of saying that he wanted to go with me to ring in the New Year, however at the last moment he cancelled. I immediately stopped getting ready. Jumped into a jogging suit and walked out. When I returned I glowered at Jack as our daughters ran over to him and hugged him tight.

"Jack, darlin', I told the children you wanted to bring in the new year with them. I even stopped by the store and bought a bottle of sparkling cider. They are so very excited." I beamed as I thought, checkmate baby. He just looked at me like, 'no that bitch didn't.' All I could do was smile. I continued getting ready.

That was the first time I had ever gone out for New Year's Eve. I was so excited. The hotel's grand-ballroom was decorated in silver and black. The music was a mixture of hip-hop, R&B, and reggae. There was a soul food buffet and complementary champagne. Nicole, Jerome, Linda and I found our table and ordered drinks. Nicole whipped out her camera. We laughed together, genuinely enjoying one another's company. I danced with three different men, and at the stroke of midnight I kissed one. When we returned home Linda went straight to bed. Jack and the children were still awake watching a movie in the living room. I looked at them and smiled.

"Hello family," I said.

"Hi mommy," the girls said as they waved, still focused on the movie.

"Tia, I need to talk to you," Jack calmly stated.

"Come to my room," I said. Once we were in the room he closed the door behind him as I took a seat on the bed and began undressing. "So what's on your mind?" I asked distractedly.

"Did you kiss anyone when the ball dropped?"

"Yes."

"On the lips?" he inquired.

"That's generally how it works. If you really cared you would have been there."

"Was there any tongue?"

"No."

"Who was it?"

"Guy."

"Who is Guy?"

"A stripper I know."

"A stripper…?" Jack exclaimed.

"Yes. What?"

"You don't see anything wrong with that?"

"Nope," I replied.

"Nope?" he asked loudly.

"What? I said no. How many ways do you want me to say it?"

"You're sleeping with me tonight. I'm going to make love to my wife."

"All right..."

"Come on, we're going to my room."

"Okay," I sang.

Jack was jealous, and I was tickled. My back felt better. I needed some passion. I could care less if it was fueled by anger. And then I felt it, my husband nestled between my thighs. Flesh to flesh, his hard dick pressed against my pussy lips. My body trembled in anticipation. We began to make love. My heart filled with hope. That was before everything suddenly ended, a mere two minutes after it all began.

"Jack, don't ever touch me again. You truly are a disappointment."

I picked up my clothes and left the room. Then I went to my room and took a shower before bed. I masturbated with my handheld showerhead until the room began to spin. After regaining my composure, I climbed into bed naked, satisfied, and exhausted.

Linda kept me company for two weeks. A week after she left I went to my physician to get the results of my latest MRI. I felt healthier. I had lost a total of fifty pounds however the pain had not subsided. My routine MRI led to a prediction of imminent death. Doctor Commack's eyes filled with tears as he informed me that my spine was producing blood.

My heart was not producing enough blood to sustain my life. He handed me a piece of paper. The prognosis was one of three blood cancers: leukemia, lymphoma or myloma. My doctor apologized repeatedly. He took the liberty of making my initial appointment with a top oncologist. He stated that it was very important for me to go in for a series of blood tests. I was overcome with fear and utter hopelessness.

On the drive home I was so lost that I did not see the red flashing lights at the railroad crossing. I continued through and the brilliance of the train's light caught my attention. I pressed the gas, avoiding the train by mere inches. I made it home safely. At first I kept my prognosis to myself. The last thing I wanted to do was burden anyone with a maybe. Although I wrote in my diary, everything kept weighing on my mind. I decided to confide in my husband. I found him in the living room.

"Jack there is something that I need to tell you. Can you come into my room and sit with me for a while?"

"What's wrong, Tia?"

We went to my room. I sat on my bed. Jack chose to stand. The tears began to roll down my face before I uttered the first words. My voice was normal, my face was expressionless, yet tears streamed. "Jack, I went to the doctor last week to get the results of my MRI. They told me that my heart was not producing enough blood to sustain my life therefore my vertebrae were producing blood to compensate. I might have leukemia, lymphoma or myloma. They sent me to a hematologist/oncologist. I had my first blood test today. They said at worst, I might need a bone marrow transplant."

"What?"

"I might have cancer Jack. I have to go through a few months of blood testing. I might need to have a biopsy within the next six months if my condition worsens."

He looked at me. I looked at him. I saw no compassion. He did not reach for me. He did not cry out to God. I could see that he was reflecting on the information. I thought he might have been in shock, as I was when I was told. He stood there quietly for a few minutes longer. He took so long I decided to stretch out on the bed. I never in a million years expected him to say what came out of his mouth next.

"Well, I know you are unhappy in this marriage so if you do have leukemia then..." He paused for a moment. I sat up, dried my face, and looked into his eyes. "I won't hold you back. You can do what ever you need to do to make yourself happy."

Damn! I thought you would make me happy, Jack.

CHAPTER THREE
BIRTHDAY BLUES

Fifteen months had passed since the accident. My diary was filled with heartache and painful disappointments. I was told that I would never again be able to walk without a walker or a cane. I knew God would not do that to me. I continued to try and get to as close to one hundred percent as possible. I woke up on the morning of my birthday in a very cheerful mood. I sprang out of the bed and stepped on the scale. I had lost an additional twenty-five pounds. I was down to a size fourteen.

"Yes, I've exceeded my goal!" I shouted.

I washed my face, brushed my teeth, took a shower, and got dressed. I came out of my room expecting breakfast to be ready but no one was awake. I cooked my own birthday breakfast. One by one my family came out and made themselves a plate. No one even said happy birthday. I was shocked that my children did not remember. Before I could get out of the house my mother called.

"Hello."

"Happy birthday, Tia," she exclaimed.

"Thank you Mama. You're the first one to call."

"What do you have planned for today?"

"I don't know yet but I'm going to have fun."

"Enjoy your day baby."

"Thank you again, Mama. I love you."

"I love you too."

"Happy birthday, mommy," my daughters shouted the moment the call ended.

"Thank you, pretty babies."

Jack said nothing. I smiled brightly although my heart was shattering into a million pieces. I prayed, God help me to get through this day. My mind was filled with questions. What is this, leave the dying woman alone to die? Don't I even exist anymore? I guess Jack really meant it when he told me to do whatever it takes to make myself happy. Oh God, let me get the hell out of here before I break down and cry. Just as I was walking out of the door Jack stopped me. I held it together. I did not look back.

"Hey, where are you going?" Jack asked.

"To run some errands…" Although tears pooled in my eyes my voice was steady. "Why?" I said.

"Do you mind if I ride along with you?"

"Nope," I said, reaching for door knob as I batted back my tears. "Come on."

Once we were in the car and on our way Jack leaned in, and kissed my cheek. A glimmer of hope instantly returned.

"Happy birthday, honey," he said.

"Thank you."

"So, where are you on your way to?"

"Well, seeing as no one has any plans for my birthday, I thought I might go to the store and get a few things. Why?"

"I'm sorry. I forgot."

"You would have to care to remember. I know you don't love me anymore so don't worry about it."

"I love you, Tia."

"Okay."

"I do!"

"Okay."

All the while he tried his best to convince me, but the only thing I heard was his bottomline.

"Do whatever it takes to make yourself happy."

I remembered the pain of that verbal knife to my heart. I was lost in that memory. The doctor cried and hugged me, but not my husband. Jack never touched me. He never tried to console me, and I could never forget that.

We returned home just after the noon hour. I went on into the house, leaving Jack to bring in the bags. My oldest daughter, Elli, greeted me at the door.

"Hello mommy," she smiled.

"Hello baby."

I took a few steps into the house, and there was my baby girl, Alexi. "Hello mommy," she smiled.

"Hello baby. Okay, what are y'all up to?"

"We have something for you," Alexi said as she and her sister took me by the hand.

"Really…?"

"Yes. Did you think we forgot about your birthday?" Eli asked.

"Well, uh, yes," I replied honestly.

"Wrong!" they shouted together.

"Daddy wouldn't give us any money or even take us to the store to get you something," Elli said.

"Yeah, we had to walk to the Dollar Store to get your cards," Alexi quickly added.

"It's alright girls. The best gifts come from the heart not the store. This is beautiful. I can tell that the two of you put a lot of effort into making this special book. You have everything including my hospital band. Your efforts made this gift even more special. I love both of you so much."

"We love you too mommy," they said together.

My beautiful daughters each bought me a card and created a picture-scrapbook chronicling my recovery. It was lovely. It was also the highlight of my day, with my family. I knew that my children loved me. I cherished their love. I bought my own dinner and cooked it. I bought my own cake as well. Stouffer's lasagna can make any occasion special. Just as dinner was coming out of the oven Jack ran out.

I sat in the dining room with my daughters awaiting his return. He bought me a balloon and a card. It was so nice to be an afterthought. I felt so special—ah good times. After dinner and cake everyone went back to doing whatever it was they were doing. I sat in my room alone. I wrote in my diary, 'It's my birthday. I have exceeded my weight loss goal. I need to celebrate being alive.' I decided to call my best friend Tammy.

"Hello."

"Hey Tammy,"

"Hey Tia, what's up, girl?"

"I have no birthday plans."

"Oh girl, you ain't said nothing but a word. Get dress, I'll be there to get you in an hour."

It is always good to have friends who are down for whatever. No one is as down as my girl, Tammy. I got ready as quickly as I could manage. Just when I was applying my makeup Tammy called.

"I'm almost ready," I answered.

"Good, I'm coming around the corner as we speak," she replied.

"Okay, I'm on my way out the door. I can do the rest in the car."

I grabbed my things and headed for the door. Just as I was leaving

Jack got up and blocked my way.

"Where the hell do you think you're going?"

"Out," I retorted.

"You can't stay at home with your family?"

"Well let me see now... Hell no! It's my birthday, and I really don't know if I'll live long enough to have another one. Sadly, I had to buy my own dinner and birthday cake. I am not about sit here, and watch you play video games as well. I am going to enjoy myself tonight. So please, get the hell up out of my way. I'm out."

He stepped to the side, and I walked right out of my front door. Tammy had already arrived.

"Wow, Tia you are looking nice," Tammy said as soon as I opened the car door.

"Thank you," I replied, getting in the seat. "You know damn well you're always put together."

"Thank you, girl. How much weight have you lost?'

"I've lost fifty pounds since Thanksgiving."

"I love your shoes."

"Thank you. I was told a year ago that I would never be able to walk without the assistance of a cane or walker, but today I am walking in ruby red high heels."

"Girl, do the damn thang," Tammy looked concerned. "Just don't do too much."

"No worries I have some ballerina slippers in my purse," I smiled brightly. "So tell me, where are we going?"

"To party downtown," Tammy replied, smiling back at me.

"I'm not ready for that. I need to lose a few more pounds before I will be ready to go back down there. You remember how I use to do it."

"Girl, please... You know for a fact that you are beautiful. I don't want to hear any of that. It's your personality that keeps them, just smile and be you. It will be alright." Tammy looked into my eyes before continuing, "After all, I have never seen any man walk away from you."

"Yeah, that's it," I grinned. "Pump me up. It's exactly what the doctor ordered. Oh, by the way, I need to stop and get some cigars. Jerome's brother Paul got me hooked."

"That's cool we'll stop when we get closer to downtown. Tia, get ready to have a lot of fun tonight, after all today is your birthday," she sang loudly.

"I'm ready. I took my pills and drank my coffee. I'm straight for at least four hours. The only thing I can't do tonight is operate heavy equipment or make any important life changing decisions."

We both laughed. Then Tammy said, "Girl you need help."

"I know, right… Tammy I really do need you to keep an eye on me tonight, okay? I'm ripe for the picking. Someone just might slip under my radar."

"I doubt that."

I loved the way Tammy saw me. I wanted to be that beautiful, brash and sassy woman again. However all I felt was vulnerable and unsure.

We stopped by the store for lollypops, cigars, and gum. I was elated to be out and about downtown again. I didn't even think about the extra weight. We had such a good time. Men sent drinks to our table throughout the night. I even danced—twice! I was asked more than twice, however, because of my leg, I declined. I did not want to fall. The men were handsome, tempting little devils dressed in designer suits. There was one individual, who I hadn't seen since before the accident. He sought me out. I was sitting at my table when he walked up to me.

"Tia?"

"Dietrich?"

"Stand up girl and give me a hug." While we embraced he spoke in my ear, "Hey baby, it's been a long time. I heard about your accident."

NAKED CONFESSIONS

"Yeah, it took a toll on me."

"Is it true you couldn't walk?"

"Yes."

"Well Tia baby, you're definitely look good."

I ended the hug and sat back down. He sat with me holding one of my hands in both of his.

"You must have heard about how big I got."

"Come on now, Tia. I heard that you were hurt really bad, and that you were determined to overcome it all."

"Who told you?"

"John, he said he saw you at Nikki's party. He also told me about what your husband did to you."

"John talks too much."

"Tia, you know that shit was foul."

"I know, but I don't want to talk about it," I smiled. "So tell me handsome, how have you been?"

"Sexy, single, and still waiting for you," he said in a charming way, and really warmed my heart.

I was tempted. I wondered, how many pills would I have to take to get with him tonight? I smiled at his words as well as at my thought. I looked into his eyes and I saw his appreciation for my beauty—sexual attraction. They weren't just sweet words. The way he looked at me, his admiration had not changed.

"You're still sexy, Tia. Baby, it's all in the right places."

"Thank you, Dietrich."

"When are you going to leave that nigga and give me a chance?"

I took a deep breath and closed my eyes. I exhaled slowly as I thought— Ooh Dietrich! Truth be told, you could have a chance tonight, if I didn't think I would have to overdose to take you on as a lover. Mm-m, he'd be worth it. Well, maybe not. If I haven't slept with him by now there has got to be a reason. It's just not coming to mind at this moment, but I know it's something. Hmm...? Ah yes, I'm married. I opened my eyes.

"Stop that now or you will have me running off with you tonight," I replied teasingly.

"My car is valet parked. I can have them bring it around right now," Dietrich coaxed.

I laughed nervously; temptation filled my veins like a shot of morphine—numbing my sensibilities. "Stop that, Dietrich."

"Come dance with me, Tia."

"I can't. I was out there on the dance floor already tonight, trying to pretend like there was nothing wrong with me. I'm afraid if I chance it again I just might fall. I have a trick leg, it just stops working on me with out any notice."

"I got you, I won't let you fall."

"All right then, yes."

It was wonderful to be in his arms. He held me close, making me feel practically weightless, as we danced. Dietrich was a beautiful man, he looked like a younger version of my husband, but with fuller pouting lips. He had a wonderful personality, a successful professional life, and no children. I thoroughly enjoyed his attention.

I imagined if I ever took a lover he would be the exact opposite of Jack. He would have chocolate brown skin like mine. He would be young, a well built country boy, a southern man with the gift of gab. He'd be charming, bold, and quick witted. Someone that was not trying to keep me forever, just enjoy me for a while. In that moment the old adage, 'be careful what you wish for', popped into my mind. I took pause.

What the hell was I thinking? Knowing me, I'd probably get right down to the wire then chicken out at the last minute. I was way too fat to have a lover. There was no way in hell I was about to take my clothes off in front of anyone, especially with all of this extra fluff on me. Not only that,

I was too old and crippled to do any tricks. Who would want to be with an old, fat, crippled girl anyway? Dietrich was sweet, but he couldn't possibly mean what he said. This fat girl looked better in her dress. At the least I could still flirt.

CHAPTER FOUR
HARMLESS FUN

Nikki called the following evening Friday, the last day of January. Little did I know that one inconsequential phone call would lead me into temptation and further still.

"Hello Nikki."

"Hey Tia, whatcha doin' tonight?" Nicole asked.

"Nothin', why?"

"Well, I was thinking about going out to happy hour and maybe even singing a little karaoke."

"That sounds nice."

"Tia, why don't you come along with us?"

"I'm tired of being the third wheel, Nikki. After New Year's Eve, I just haven't had it in me to go out anymore, other than for my birthday last week, but that was just me, and Tammy."

"Don't be that way, Tia. Don't let Jack do this to you. You're beautiful, and you can sing. Come on, it'll be fun. Besides which, I didn't get the chance to celebrate your birthday with you. I was hoping we could do a little belated celebration tonight."

"Okay Nikki, I'll meet you there."

"Are you really gon' go or are you just saying yes to get me off of the phone?"

I needed to live my life, and enjoy whatever time I had left. If Jack wouldn't give me the attention that I needed then another man would. I needed to touch and be touched. If I was turned on and came home then this could be Jack's lucky night. I just needed a couple of oxycodones and wash them down with a little Irish coffee, and I'll be good to go.

"I said that I was comin' didn't I?" I responded lackadaisically. "Hang up so I can start gettin' ready."

I dressed in black: turtleneck, long slacks, and square heeled ankle boots. I needed to feel desirable without dressing like a winter wonderland whore. I was a voluptuous size eleven/twelve, thick in all of the right places. I looked good. I knew it. My hair was slicked back. My makeup was flawless, smoky gray eye shadow accentuated with silver and black, mulberry blush, and cherry red lipstick—a lady villain for the night. Low self-esteem has never been an issue for me. My mild case of insecurity had cleared up quickly enough.

I drove to the urban dance club in downtown Phoenix on Central Avenue. I really hated being a tag along however staying at home would have been even worse, or so I thought. I wanted to be naughty, have fun. I arrived before Nikki and Jerome. As I made my way through the club several men stopped me to say hello. I parlayed just long enough for a quick introduction before moving along. I found a table, ordered a drink, and before I knew it the rest of my party had arrived. We sat together at a round table for four, with Jerome sitting between us sisters. I could not help but notice the chair next to me was empty, as usual. The night started off a little slowly but after a while I really began having a good time, so much so, I had completely given up the notion of flirting. The three of us talked, laughed, and drank as we waited for karaoke to start.

"Tia, what song are you and Jerome going to sing first?" Nicole asked.

"Unforgettable, the duet: why don't you sing with us Nikki?"

"Girl, you know I can't sing, but I'll write it out for you, hand me one of those little paper forms and a pencil, that way I'm a part of the group too, ya know, a silent partner," Nikki said, pressing her lips together.

We all laughed. It was nice to be silly and lighthearted.

"Here's the song book and paper but I don't see a pencil," I said.

"It's okay Nikki baby," Jerome interjected. "I'll go get you one," Jerome said, leaving the table.

"Nikki, while Jay is gone I wanted to say thank you for inviting me to tag along with y'all tonight."

"Girl please, I know what you're going through at home. It was my pleasure to ask you to come out with us. The last thing you need is to be up in that house with a man who doesn't love you anymore, feeling rejected and unappreciated. I don't know why you married him in the first place."

"I married him because I loved him—we have children together—a family Nikki."

"He goes out with his friends, right?"

"Nikki…" I paused for a moment before continuing on. "Hell, you know damn well he goes out."

"All right then, at least you're out with me, not some so-called friends."

"Shit, more like dogs."

At that moment Jerome returned. "What are you two talking about?" he frowned as she shook the pencil at Nicole and I.

"Nothing!" we chorussed, smiling brightly.

"I know you two," he said skeptically.

Jerome sat down. He looked back and forth from me to Nicole real fast, acting goofy, as if he was watching a ping pong game, which made us sisters laugh out right. I stopped laughing a little too soon. All of a sudden I just wasn't feeling it. Yearning mixed with sadness filled my heart as I watched Nikki and Jerome laugh together. I could not remember the last time Jack and I laughed together. Jerome took notice right away. He never liked Jack. What's more, he loved me as a sister.

"Tia, your sister and I are going to make sure you have a nice time this evening," Jerome announced. "I don't even want you to think about Jack tonight. I wanna see that pretty smile of yours all night long. Ya hear me girl?"

"Yes, I hear you," I said contentedly however I did not smile.

"Don't make me get up! I'll start dancin'!" Jerome animated his body as he spoke. "I will dance like a Brady." He began to snap his fingers and wiggle around in the chair off beat. "I can feel the music," he grinned as he wiggled his eyebrows. "I think I might have to get up! Hell, I'll act like the whole damn bunch."

"No, please don't do that, especially not the father!" I begged as I laughed out loud. "I'm smiling. See?"

My sister chuckled until she was out of breath. Jerome danced around in his seat a few more seconds for good measure before collapsing into hysterics himself. Although I enjoyed living in that moment my mind would not let go of my loneliness. My smile never quite reached my eyes. I wished I had somebody to enjoy life's best moments with, someone special. I needed someone to help me through my reality, as well as fulfill a few of my sexual fantasies. After all, I was knocking on death's door.

As the night continued on, the weight of my world slipped away. I enjoyed singing along to 'Hey Mickey,' at the top of my lungs, along with the rest of the crowd. The evening was going great, innocent enough. That was before the moment I saw a particular young man. I just so happened to look up and there he was, walking towards me. He was a tall, beautiful, brown man with a sexy smile. His eyes were fixed on me. I watched intently as he walked across the floor. His long legged stride was a smooth sensual glide in my direction. I wanted to slowly unwrap his mouth-watering chocolate as a belated birthday present—sweet, succulent, and decadent yet seemingly appropriate. I had always been taught that the devil had many tantalizing talents. Who would have thought one of which was a master chocolatier? I was tempted. I do not know how that man got so close to me so quickly however there he was, smiling down at me.

"Hello pretty lady, my name is Tyrique," he said with a deep, dirty southern brogue.

"Hello Tyrique, I'm Tia. It's nice to meet you."

"I heard you singing. You really do have a lovely voice."

"Thank you," I smiled brightly.

"And a beautiful face." His southern drawl was captivating.

"Why thank ya," I nearly gushed. My voice was soft and girly, a timbre I barely recognized.

Tyrique made it incredibly easy to give into temptation. He was a terribly sexy, sinfully debonair, country boy wish granted. I would have never dreamt in a million years that one teeny tiny indulgence would be the catalyst for a whole new existence. From the moment I spotted him walking across the dance floor, his incredibly expressive eyes never left mine. His desire was blatant. His gaze was enticing. His eyes teased and enchanted me. I missed that kind of attention. I decided to thoroughly enjoy it, oblige myself if you will. I flirted shamelessly with him. He was exquisite, charismatic, and confident. I felt like a woman. I felt sexy. I felt alive.

"You don't mind if I sit in this here chair, now do ya?" he asked ever so politely.

"No not at all, by all means have a seat," I said invitingly.

"Thank ya ma'am," he drawled.

"May I buy you a drink, Miss Tia?" Tyrique inquired.

"Yes, thank you," I said. "So tell me Tyrique where are you from?"

"Atlanta, Georgia. Born and raised..."

"What brings you out here?"

"The U.S. Department of Defense, I'm in the Air Force," he responded with pride. "And where are you from Ms. Tia?"

"St. Louis, Missouri."

"I thought I heard that Nelly twang."

"You aren't exactly accent free ya-self."

"Oh, I know I'm a country boy."

I saw a kindness in him, a gentleness, which was very alluring. I could feel myself wanting him, however I fought the feeling. There is nothing like a sexy, charming, southern man. I do not care what nationality, a country boy is like a black stallion—sexy as hell, strong, rugged, and untamed. Tyrique stayed next to me for a while. He looked on appreciatively as I sang, so I sang to him. I was turned on, however that was before I asked his age. Once I learned that he was only twenty-three years old, I was done with him—or so I thought. I still wanted him although I could not admit it, even to myself.

All I could think was, oh Lord I'm sitting here playing with some woman's child. Who in the hell let him out of the damn sandbox? Damn it, he is so young I'd have to hold his hand while he crosses the street. "Sweetness, I'm way too old for you," I stated emphatically.

"You can't be no older than twenty-five, twenty-six at the most," Tyrique protested.

"Try again," I said unmoved by the conspicuous complement.

"What, twenty-eight? Five years, ain't really no real time," he said, continuing to plead his case, to no avail.

"Tyrique baby, I am thirty-two years old and that makes it nine years, not five, and um, nine years is definitely some time," I replied patiently yet firmly before saying, "And I'm not Stella."

My mind raced—please go away little boy. Trouble was stamped all over your fine ass. I knew, damn well, that if I don't stop now I'll be in trouble. Or trouble would be deep inside of me. Damn, that shit sounded good. A little sample, perhaps. I was thinking nasty thoughts, and couldn't quit looking at him.

I turned my back to him and continued on with my evening as if he was not sitting next to me. I went to the stage. I sang another duet with Jerome. We laughed at the fact that we were so off key. We were definitely tipsy, acting silly, and having a wonderful time. After the song was over I returned to my seat. The young man was still standing there, looking at me with those invitingly expressive eyes. I could not help but to look into his eyes again. My pussy pulsated. I quickly turned away. The moment I did he placed his hand on my shoulder. I looked back at him.

"Tia, I'll be right back."

"Okay Tyrique," I said, turning away again.

I was relieved. I had no doubt in my mind of my exceptional beauty. Pullin' in a twenty-three year old was such a coup. I felt so good I decided to make it Jack's lucky night as well. Alas, Satan was working overtime—who else could make a faithful Christian wife regret doing the right thing?

About thirty minutes later, I spotted Tyrique while I was on my way to the bathroom. He was talking to another woman. I wished for his attention. I battled with myself as I walked on by. I couldn't have him so why waste time? I wish I had not sent him away so quickly. Even if I was young enough to play with him, I was still married. Two wrongs didn't make a right. The hell it didn't! That young devil looked like he would make it, feel right, if nothing else. Oh Lord, I needed to quit. I had to be more careful with my wishes. No, Tyrique was not my birthday wish, he was a coincidence, I concluded.

I returned to my seat, smiling at Nikki and Jerome, but my smile was forced, and my perkiness was gone. Slightly disappointed, I downed the rest of my drink. I thought about Tyrique. Damn, I should have let him touched me somewhere other than my shoulder. A nice tight hug or even a dance would have been fantastic. Oh well, I enjoyed the way he looked at me more than anything else. I just needed to let the rest go. At least that was what I told myself. I attempted to throw myself headlong into having a good time.

"I'm ready to sing again y'all," I abruptly said. "Nikki hand me the song book." My movements were stiff and perfunctory. "Maybe I'll sing that song that the donkey sang. How does it go? 'I'm so all alone, there's no one standing here, beside me...'" My shoulders slumped momentarily. "Just kidding. I'm having a good time tonight, really."

"Nikki, Tia, I'll be right back." Jerome said suddenly as he stood.

"Okay Jerome baby," Nikki responded a little confused.

"Wait a minute Jerome," I stopped him as he was rounding the table. "Let me give you some money, I need another drink."

"Girl you know you don't have to give me no money, so quit playin' and put your purse away," Jerome said. He kissed Nikki's cheek before leaving us. He was only gone for a short while. When he returned he brought drinks for everyone.

"Thank you baby," Nikki said.

"Thank you Jerome," I seconded.

"You're welcome ladies," Jerome replied.

I became a bit giggly, everything seemed funny. I resolved not to give Tyrique another thought, moreover, I was more than happy with the company I had. To my surprise, Tyrique returned to our table. He sat down next to me, as if the seat belonged to him. My heart skipped a beat.

"Hello again, Miss Tia," he greeted gallantly.

"Hi," I replied completely surprised.

I didn't know what else to say. He smiled. I smiled. I was glad he came back. All we could do was to stare at each other for the longest while. I was lost in thought, damn, he is gorgeous. I wonder what he tastes like, what he feels like. I had never cum for another man before. Just Jack. I wonder if he could make me cum... Stop it Tia! Stop it right now! Where were these thoughts coming from? I need some help here, 'cause we were not talkin'. We are just lookin' and thinkin'. I bet his thoughts were just as naughty as mine. No, he was a man so they had to be worse. He was probably picturing me in every sexual position he knew. Wait a minute. That was a nice thought.

A little while later Jerome's brother, Paul, came over to the table. Finally, I was able to look away.

"Hey sister-in-law," Paul hugged Nicole before coming around to greet me. "What's up, Tia?"

"Hey darlin', I didn't know that you were go'n be out tonight," I said slightly too enthusiastically.

"I decided to come out at the last minute baby, it wasn't planned."

I introduced the gentlemen to one another. Then Tyrique excused himself once more. Paul stood in front of me. We chit-chatted for a while. Paul had a magnanimous personality. He was the homeboy at the club that was always a little bit too loud, yet never embarrassing. We got along fine. However, there was absolutely no attraction on my part. Paul was my homey. Although he had deep, dark, cocoa skin, and was very handsome, well groomed, and impeccably dressed, I could never go there. Hell, I never even thought about it.

"Can we have Tia to the stage please?" the Karaoke host announced.

"Okay y'all, they're callin' my name. I'll be right back."

I was in the middle of a singing a song about pleasure and pain when Tyrique returned. He caught my attention instantly. I could feel him without him touching me. His eyes were locked on mine from the moment he entered the karaoke area. He stood at the back of the room watching. I continued to sing as he held my gaze, only this time I was perfectly on key. I sang the hell out of that song, damn it. I sang my heart out to him. Alas, I instantly filled with regret. After the song ended I walked back to my table. I kept an eye on Tyrique as I enjoyed the company and conversation of our group. The moment his attention was occupied I made my move.

"Hey y'all I'm go'n go on upstairs for a little bit to dance."

"Okay Tia, Jerome and I will come up later. We are going to sit here with Paul for a while," Nikki replied.

"Save me a dance Tia," Paul interjected.

"I think I can do that for you, Paul," I happily said.

CHAPTER FIVE
CAUGHT UP IN IT

I left the karaoke area, ran up the steps, sat at the farthest end of the bar and ordered another drink. "Hi, brandy straight up please."

"Coming right up ma'am," the bartender said with a smile.

"Thank you."

I was so focused on escaping that I forgot my drink downstairs. There was an older gentleman sitting a few seats away. He watched me with his head tilted sideways, pensive. As I waited for my drink he turned to me.

"Brandy straight up…?" He asked his voice filled with pseudo-surprise. "Woo, now that will put hair on your chest."

"Well…" I paused as I turned to look at him. "I've been drinking it this way for over ten years and um, I haven't grown one single solitary hair on my chest to date, but thanks for the warning," I said good-naturedly.

"Can I buy that for you?"

"Sure, thank you."

"So, what's your name?"

"Tia and yours?"

"Sterlon. Tell me Tia, who did you come here with? Do you have a man?"

God help me, I thought. It took everything in me not to roll my eyes up to heaven. Instead I gently smiled

"I came out tonight with my sister and her fiancé. And yes I do have a man. As a matter of a fact, I have been faithfully married to him for fifteen years."

"You can't be that old."

"Really, I am."

"What is your secret?"

"I have really expressive eyes therefore I don't make any facial expressions unless I'm having really, good, sex. I get fewer wrinkles that way," I said, and immediately realized that it was wrong of me to say, but I already did.

"You bad," he commented, completely turned on.

"Yes, I am."

"How can a man like me get a woman like you?"

If you sold your soul to the devil for one last hurrah, maybe you could. Then again, maybe not.

The thought made me smile. I talked with the gentleman for a short while. Just as the little old man was asking me for my number, Nikki and Jerome sat at the table that was closest to me. I excused myself. I walked over to the table, however I didn't sit.

"Hey, I see y'all finally made it up here."

"Hey Tia, whatchu up here doing?" Jerome asked. His eyelids fluttered teasingly.

"Nothing Jerome, I'm just having a little bit of fun."

"What, with the geriatric?"

"He's a cute, old man that lacks game, so I kept him company for a while. I made him smile."

"That's not all you made him do."

"Shut up Jerome, you're so nasty. Nikki girl, how do you put up with this nasty man?"

Nikki bounced in her chair and smiled.

"Ooh Nikki y'all both nasty. I'm gon' go get my drink before the little ol' man slips me a mickey. Y'all want anything?"

"No, we're straight," Nikki replied.

"Okay then."

"Leave the old man alone, Tia," Jerome exclaimed.

"Shut up, Jerome."

We all laughed. It was at that moment of lightheartedness that Tyrique appeared again. I looked up and there he was looking at me with those wonderfully sexy talking eyes. I turned away, went to the bar, and ordered another drink.

"Hey, I left this unattended. May I have another one, please?"

"Sure," the bartender agreed. "Brandy straight?"

"Yes, thanks."

I stood at the bar waiting, and Tyrique walked up behind me. He stopped so close I could feel the heat of his body up and down my spine. My pussy beat like the rhythmic pounding of a racing horse running at top speed. My knees were weak. I slid onto a barstool simply to escape the intensity of the pain. I situated myself, and took a calming breath before turning to face him. As I looked up into his eyes, he smiled. I decided to play with fire.

"Hello again, Tia," Tyrique crooned.

"Hello Tyrique," I all but sang. My voice was husky and laden with desire.

"May I sit next to you; talk with you for a while?"

"All right."

Tyrique sat very close to me, too close, well within my personal space. He gazed deep into my eyes. There it was again, that look, it was not a predatory look per say, it was a look of pride and confidence; a mixture of male strength, bravado, and mischievousness—incredibly sexy, sensuous, and extremely inviting. He knew beyond a doubt what he had to offer as a man and I had no doubt in my mind, I would thoroughly enjoy him. He made me very aware of my body, my femininity. He was the kind of man that, at first sight, a woman thinks to herself, 'This will not end well.' Still, knowing that, I helplessly tempted fate.

"Tia, you really do have a beautiful face," he touched me as he spoke. "A sweet smile," he said, caressing my bottom lip with his thumb. "And a lovely voice."

I was used to compliments. They didn't sway me one way or the other. However his touch was electrifying. Still, I persevered as if I was unaffected.

"Thank you. Why are you interested in me, Tyrique? Don't you think I'm just a little bit too old for you?"

"I think you are a beautiful woman. I enjoyed talking to you downstairs, and I would like to get to know you."

"Know me or kno-o-ow me?" I asked provocatively.

"Know you, all of you," his response was laden with innuendo.

"Hmm..." I took a sip of my drink. "All right, I'm always up for a good seduction. You are a very attractive man. I really don't have anything to lose. Let's play a game. If you can get me to say the word, 'yes', you can have me. I'll go wherever you want me to go."

The older man, who had been listening for a while almost fell out of his seat.

"That's all I have to do in order to have you tonight?" Tyrique asked skeptically.

"Indeed. Just make me want you, be irresistible. I want to forget that the word 'no' even exists. I'm all yours if you can do just that."

"That's all?"

"Yep, that's all. But you have to do it right here tonight. Before I leave the club."

"All right, sit still so I can get atcha. I'm goin' ta make ya want me. You'll be sayin' a hell of a lot more than yes to me tonight, but you have got to stop runnin' away from me."

"I won't run. I'll face you head on. Good luck, Sweetness."

"I have a feeling that Lady Luck is already on my side tonight," Tyrique confidently said. "I want you, Tia."

"Do you, now? And what's in it for me?"

Ooh Jack, I could take all of this out on you when I get home. I had a feeling that I was leaving here horny, and hell bent on fuckin'.

I convinced myself that Tyrique didn't have a snowball's chance in hell. He asked me to sit at a table with him. Once we were secluded the games began. He was relentless in his pursuit. His soft words, and knowing touch along with his warm breath lightly brushing my flesh with every syllable he uttered, sent goose bumps traveling all over my body.

"Tia, I can satisfy your every need."

"Can you? You know what I need?"

"Yes, you need to relax. Let your hair down every now and again. You need someone in your life who you can trust, truly be yourself with."

"Umm-hmm, I really do."

"Tell me something, Tia?"

"Anything..."

"You calculate the risk of everything before you do it, don't you?"

His words made me think. He was reading me like a book, now that was definitely a first. I was going to have to keep on my toes if I was going to win this game. I'll be aloof. Respond damn it.

"Not everything," I said with a smile.

Most men saw that I was flirty and took the shallow route by telling me that they could sex me like no other. They get downright explicit with it, turning me off. It was easy to say no. Tyrique was a far cry from most.

"When you first saw me tonight, you thought that you'd entertain yourself with me for a little while, and then send me on my merry way, now didn't you?"

"Something like that," I said, and still believed.

"You need someone to tickle you, make you laugh... thoroughly pleasure you again and again."

"Hmm, I really do."

"I know you're a passionate woman. I saw it in your eyes when I first said hello. You need someone to bring your passions to the surface, someone to make you surrender unequivocally, beyond a shadow of a doubt, with no shame or guilt," Tyrique said with conviction, before whispering, "I am that man, Tia," he whispered, and his lips floated like a feather across the pulse of my neck.

I closed my eyes and leaned into his body. I allowed myself to take in his every word. He had me for a moment. I relished the thought. I want you to be that man for me, Tyrique. I want you to... STOP! I needed to think. Oh damn! I mean damn, hot damn! That shit sounded good, real good, but I've got to be strong. Let the moment pass, Tia, before responding. I was telling myself. Okay, one, two, three, four, five — now sit up, look at him, and smile. You are in control.

"You don't say?" I replied.

Tyrique was a little taken aback by my response however he was a man on a mission. I enjoyed his efforts.

"Come dance with me, Tia, let me hold you close so I can show you what I am workin' with."

"Show me what?"

Tyrique pulled me by the hand to the dance floor. It was as if I got caught up in his momentum, like he had spun a web to cloud my mind. This was someone's baby, some woman's child that I was kicking it with. I knew that. However, the moment he took me into his arms and pressed me close to him all I could feel was one hundred percent man. Even so, I had to fight it.

"Tia, when was the last time a man laid you down and took his time pleasuring every part of your body?" Tyrique asked tenderly.

"I cannot recall."

"When was the last time you were kissed like this?"

Tyrique stopped dead still. He looked into my eyes before slowly moving in for the kiss. I had been kissed many times before. I had been kissing for twenty-five years which was longer than Tyrique had even been alive. However, you would have thought I had never been kissed before by the way my body reacted. His kiss stirred my libido. I felt the effects of that kiss to my core. My pussy quivered, a shockwave of desire shot straight through me.

When the kiss was over, I had no choice but to hold on to him for support. As my eyes fluttered open, I looked up into his. Once I saw his expression, I knew I had given away too much, but I just couldn't help myself. I could not hide the effect he had on me. All I could do was close my eyes, lay my head on his chest, and keep on dancing.

"Tia?"

"Hmm?"

"You won't regret it..."

Only Satan could seduce this well. Damn it, I had to stay strong! He stopped dancing again, tilted my head up and looked into my eyes. In that instant I knew he was right. All I wanted was to say, 'yes, take me sweet baby, take me now! I'm yours for tonight'. However, I needed to sober up a bit before I made that decision. I had to know that I made the choice, and not the alcohol.

"Tyrique darlin', I need some water. Can we go sit for a while?"

He led me back to the table. He kissed my cheek, before going to the bar. I had a moment's reprieve. I tried to get my thoughts together however as soon as he brought back my water, my will wavered. He stood close to me. He leaned in closer as he whispered in my ear. He caressed my back as he spoke.

"Tell me that you want me, Tia."

I didn't respond, hell, I could barely breathe. His hands moved to my neck, where he massaged gently. "I'm going to do everything you need me to do. I'll give you every pleasure your body's been longing for. I'm going to take my time with you…"

When I felt the moisture of his lips on the nape of my neck, I had to go. I wanted to leave. Tyrique was in hot pursuit. He was winning the battle, and the war. He whispered softly into my ear again.

"Tia?"

"Hmm…?"

"Don't you want to go home with me tonight?"

He sounded so southern, so alluring, so damn hard to resist. I looked into his eyes; he looked delicious—more than just sexy—completely irresistible, so much so, I just had to tell the truth—to hell with being aloof.

"I really do..."

"Then come on over to my house for some hot passionate sex."

"Alright..."

"It's goin' ta start off a lil' bit like this..."

Tyrique took me into his arms. Now to everyone else it looked as if he was just giving me a hug however that was simply not the case. He gently bit my neck three times dragging his teeth across my skin, setting my soul on fire.

Aaw damn! I couldn't take this anymore! I wanted him soo bad. I wanted to know… Right damn now!

"Tyrique, I have got to go. Now," I said, my voice was a whisper.

He appeared disappointed, yet he was still polite and personable. Conceding, he bowed his head for the briefest of moments as he spoke.

"Can I at least walk you to your car, Tia?" he asked before looking into my eyes again.

"Yes."

I gazed at Tyrique. My eyes were filled with passion. My smile was laden with desire. I licked my lips as I caught his hand, stopping his whimsical caresses on my thigh. I slid out of my chair, turned and walked away. I could tell by the gracious gentlemanly expression on his face he had not realized that he had won our little game. On my way out, I stopped by my sister's table. I sat down for less than a minute. As I looked at Nicole and Jerome, my face was completely expressionless.

"Hey," I began flatly. "I really don't feel like being here anymore so, I am going to just go ahead and go; bye Nikki, bye Jerome, bye y'all."

I didn't wait for Tyrique. Hell, I didn't even wait for my own sister to say goodbye to me much less anybody else at her table. I simply walked away. I didn't look back.

Catch me Tyrique! No sooner than I thought it, he appeared. Tyrique caught up with me just outside of the club. He walked with me over to my car, without physically touching me once. There were no words exchanged between us, just gazes.

His eyes asked, 'Did you really say yes?' My eyes replied, 'Damn skippy I did.' then there was his look of, 'Do you really mean it?' My eyes sparkled, 'Hell yeah!' We reached my car. Tyrique took me into his arms, he searched for a hint of uncertainty yes all he found was passion. He smiled triumphantly, 'Let's do the damn thang!' And I concluded with a gaze of, 'Yes Sweetness, just lead the way.'

He opened my car door and held my hand as I settled myself behind the steering wheel. He smiled as he closed my door. As he walked to his car he looked back several times to make sure I hadn't changed my mind. I smiled at the thought of just peeling out, but for some reason I stayed.

CHAPTER SIX
MY SWEETNESS

I firmly believe that every woman has a sex diva inside of her. Unfortunately, mine had been in a coma for quite some time. I remembered her, thought of her from time to time. I missed her. She thoroughly enjoyed the sexual pleasures a man could provide. Regrettably, for ten years no one had been able to entice my sexual diva to come out and play but the night Tyrique revivified her.

Tyrique pulled around in front of my car and got out. As he walked over to my door, I let my window down. I took a real good look at him and thought: Hot passionate sex with him? Hell yeah!

"Follow me," Tyrique instructed. "I just have to make one quick stop then we'll be on our way."

"All right," I replied sweetly. Tyrique turned to walk away. "Purr…" He turned back quickly. I smiled playfully, "Lead the way."

The next thing I knew, I was tailing Tyrique down the street. I waited for him as he made a quick stop at the convenience store, after which, I followed him on to his place. Once I was parked he opened my door and helped me out of the car. Tyrique held my hand as I followed him up the walk, into his house, into his room, and into his bed. That young southern man had me so weak with desire—all I wanted was him. Nothing else was important or even registered in my mind for that matter.

"Lay back, Tia," Tyrique said in a voice that was so perfectly calm. "I will take care of everything."

Okay, my pleasure was in your hands. I couldn't believe I was really here. I couldn't believe this was really happening. A new lover, after all these years. Stop thinking, Tia. Just feel, and let him do you like you need to be done.

I laid my body down. Tyrique began kissing me haphazardly here and there while peeling away my clothing. His touch sent shock waves of heat coursing through my body. He was really good with his hands, so knowing, strong, and absolutely capable. I allowed my eyes to flutter shut as I relaxed. I gave him complete control. He awakened my flesh with his every touch, his every kiss.

"Hmm Sweetness!" My purring had become second nature.

Oh hell yeah! Do that shit! Oh sweet, sweet, sugar babe, I didn't want to be disappointed. This just had to be right! The anticipation was driving me up the fucking wall. Oh, help me please! I was not use to all of this attention. The sensations… The suspense… Please, please, please, oh please be good! No, be better than good. I needed him to fuck me, until I just couldn't take no more!

I was in a strange man's bed almost completely naked and more excited than I had been in years. My pussy was sweltering, steam pot hot. I took deep, slow, calming breaths. Tyrique paused. I opened my eyes. He looked at me as if to make sure I was for real. Maybe it was just to make sure I didn't pass out—I don't know. I checked to see if he was properly covered before I let him continue however there was no condom in sight.

"Wait, I didn't see you cover yourself."

"You are not ready for me yet, don't worry, everything will be right by the time you are," he smiled wantonly as he spoke. "After all, your thong is still on."

"Why did you stop?" I asked genuinely confused.

Tyrique smiled patiently before responding. "Tia Baabay, I have a feeling that you really do need some special attention tonight so, I am goin' ta take my time with you. I'm goin' ta make sure that every inch of your body is either touched, caressed, kissed, or licked. Just to let you know, some parts will get all four, like this breast right here."

"Hmm!" My reaction to his lips on my flesh was honest and immediate. "Oomph, oomph, oomph!"

He sucked my breasts one by one before pushing them together and suckling both nipples at the same time. That was it, he found my super enhanced erogenous zone, and really turned me on. He kissed his way down my body and lingered between my thighs. He nibbled every inch of flesh around my pussy, concentrating on my inner thighs all the while expertly fingering my pussy. He brought me to the brink of orgasm over and over again, what sweet torture.

"Tia baby, are you comfortable?"

I closed my eyes before I responded. "Yes Tyrique."

"Are you sure you want to do this?"

I opened my eyes and looked directly into his then said, "Oh yes, I'm sure."

"Close your eyes, baby. Relax yourself."

"Make it hot, Tyrique."

"Oh, I will Baabay. You can count on that."

As my eyelids fluttered closed, Tyrique began entering my body. The first thrust took my breath away. His dick stretched my pussy. I gasped for air, squealed and squirmed all over his bed. The pleasures were intense. When the first orgasm rocked through my body I could barely breathe much less talk. He slowed his stroke until my body calmed. Once my body settled and my breath returned to normal. I looked into his eyes. It was as if my whole body smiled at him.

"Are you alright?"

"Hell yeah, hmm-hmm… Hmm!"

"I can see the pleasure in your eyes."

"Can you now?"

"Oh yeah."

"Wonderful."

Tyrique made me insatiable. All I wanted was for the pleasure of him not to end. The more he gave, the more I craved. His hot kisses and passionate touches were all that I desired.

My back arched instinctively as he slid his dick into my flesh again. I exhaled slowly as I wrapped myself around him. Stroke for stroke, we moved in unison leisurely enjoying fucking just for the pure pleasure of it. Tyrique fucked like a champion. My body responded to his with unabashed excitement. Pure ecstasy took me over and over again.

Sweat ran down our skin as we were striving together for climactic pleasure. Thrust for thrust, grinding, gripping—pushing one another to the edge of sanity—our primal dance. My orgasm soared. Juices rushed out of my body sending titillating pulses through my being. We needed to switch positions. It got buck wild during doggy style. Hair pullin', ass slappin', thank ya for doggy style. We were wild. As the pace increased all words were lost, all that could be heard were the physical efforts of two people trying to reach a common goal.

We fucked as if it was going to be our last fuck on earth—unbridled passion. Switching positions, it was as if we were acting out a Prince song. And when it was all over there was no guilt, there was no remorse. All I could think of was doing it again, yet all I could do was lay there like a crash test dummy and smile. He was completely exhausted. I was spent yet my pussy pulsated as if it had a heartbeat.

We both struggled to catch our breath. He gathered me in his arms. He stroked my hair, as I lay on his chest. We rested like that for a while, silently waiting for our bodies to settle.

"Baabay, I knew you had an untapped passion deep inside of you."

"Tyrique darlin', I'm so glad you found it."

"I could get used to this, Tia."

"Oh really now," I said, shocked to hear his words.

"Yeah, really."

So could I, but I know this is only for tonight. No promises, no second thoughts, just us basking in the taboos of an amazing moment in time—one night. I was fully aware of that fact. I could admit how I feel right now without the risk of any future repercussions. I told myself that I was gon' go fa broke. Damn it!

"Truth be told, Tyrique. I could get used to this too."

"I did promise you hot passionate sex."

"Oh yes you did, and man oh man did you deliver."

"So did you," he said, looking at me, and smiling. "No woman has ever..."

"I know, baby," I interrupted.

At that point we both had caught our breath but for some reason my pussy didn't want to calm down. I craved more. I decided to start it all over again. I was impassioned. I was so hot for that man I could have shook the devil's hand and not gotten burned. It was my turn to return the favors he had done for me. It was my turn to really let my hair down, to ride that sexy young hard body like a rodeo cowgirl—Bodacious the Bull style.

"You ain't seen nothing yet, Sweetness. It's my turn now. My turn to show you what I got!"

Although my voice sounded innocent, my actions were not. For the first time in my thirty-two years I boldly gave of myself, without being asked. I allowed my desires to dictate my every move. I explored his body with all of my senses. I breathed in his scent. I looked at every inch of Tyrique's body, committing it to memory. I gently touched him, caressing his flesh. I kissed, licked and sucked his velvety soft skin, placing tiny little wet kisses ubiquitously, from one head to the other. I rejoiced as I listened to the sounds of his pleasure.

"Did I mention that I have a tongue ring?" I asked before I opened my mouth and engulfed his dick, slathering it with my tongue—feasting as if I was licking the dessert spoon.

"Girl! Oh shit!" Tyrique cried out; the sound was half moan half roar.

"I know," I said, pausing for a moment. "I don't get to do this at home. And I'd like to thank you in advance for letting me have my way with you. Lay back and relax. I'll take care of everything. You don't have to move a muscle, unless you just can't help yourself."

I lingered, licking and sucking his dick for a while longer. I played with the head until he cried out for my pussy. I kissed my way up his body. He slipped into his magnum just before I straddled him. I began riding his dick reverse doggy-style. He gripped my hips with both of his hands, driving deeper. He pulled my hair, hard. Once my cum washed over his balls it was time to switch positions.

My pussy gripped his dick tight as I spun around to face him. I smiled as I held my hands up for him. He laced his fingers between mine, intertwined in a death grip. I began to move and he quickly followed—took control. I love it when the man bucks like a Morucha bull. I held on tight, riding his hard dick while waves of cum flowed out of my body. I gripped him with my thighs until my muscles grew weary, springing up and down, as I rode and rode my bucking bull on home. He cried out as he came. We collapsed: tired, sweaty, smiling, and still connected as I lay on his chest trying to talk and catch my breath at the same time.

"Hot damn that was just so fucking delicious... Oomph, oomph,

oomph! Thank you, thank you, thank you! Tyrique, Sweetness, that right there was definitely hot! Whoa!"

I knew damn well if I died right now I would go straight to hell.

"Anytime, Baabay," he said between gasps. "Anytime you feel the need just call on me."

"Oh, I definitely will."

If I had your phone number, but that's okay. This was nice. No, better than nice. This was exactly what I needed. I actually came for another man over and over again. I openly enjoyed everything about him. Hot passionate sex…? Hell yeah!

"Tia Baabay, I didn't see that tongue ring when I was talking to you earlier."

"I know."

"But uh, I kissed you several times."

"I know, but I didn't want you to know that I had it so, I didn't letcha reach it."

"Right, right."

"Did you like tonight?" I asked timidly.

"Hell yeah," Tyrique exclaimed.

Enough Tia! No more talking, no more getting to know each other, no tomorrow. Look him in his eyes and say goodbye. Smile Tia. Release him from any obligations, spoken or unspoken.

"Good, so did I," I replied politely. "I really had a very good time but I have to go."

"Okay, I'll help you get dressed. After all I did take all of your clothes off."

Tyrique dressed me excluding my stockings and my boots, my skin was too moist. He gave me a pair of his shoes, which were way too big, to wear outside. He walked me to my car, carrying my boots. I unlocked my door with the remote. He opened it for me. I sat in my car and started the engine. I let the window down before closing the door. I looked up and smiled at him as I handed him back his shoes. He smiled at me as he handed me mine. I put my boots on the passenger side floor of my car before turning on my headlights.

"Wait Tia," he exclaimed. "I don't have your number. Do you have a cell phone?"

"Yes."

"Let me see it for a minute."

"Here you are," I said, handing him my phone.

He didn't leave getting the correct number to chance. He programmed his number into my phone and then called his. I must admit, it was a cute way of making sure I didn't give him the wrong number.

"Tia Baabay, call me. Let me know you made it home safely."

"All right," I acquiesced.

"Good night, Baabay. Drive safely."

"Good night, Sweetness."

He leaned in and gave me one last kiss, only that time I let him touch my tongue ring. That night as I drove home, all I could do was smile. Every part of my body tingled with the delight of his thorough dickin' down. After I pulled into my driveway, I smiled a very satisfied smile, I beamed. I was sexually satisfied for the first time in years. I reached for my cell phone. I called my young lover to let him know that I had made it home safely as promised. My pleasure rang clearly in my voice, after all I did have several orgasms. Being multi-orgasmic was a blessing when you have the right dick to share it with. When he answered the phone I could hear the sexual aftermath in his voice as well.

"Hey, pretty lady."

"Hello, Sweetness."

We sounded like two purring cats.

"Did you make it home already?"

"Yes, I did. I'm sitting in my drive way right now."

"How fast were you going?"

"Fast enough to make it home by now; I don't live too far from you, it's mostly freeway."

"Are you alright?"

"Hmm! Yes, I am just fine."

"No regrets?"

"Oh no, none at all. I feel too damn good to regret the time I spent with you."

"I tried to make you happy, do more than just satisfy ya. I wanted to make you want to come back for more."

"You did, let me tell you that much. Damn it, Tyrique. I can still feel you."

"We can do it all again whenever you want."

"Don't threaten me with a good time."

"You can always come on back, hell; you really didn't have to leave."

"Yes, I did. Hey, I'm go'n go in now, before you have me driving back over there tonight, call me tomorrow."

"Oh I'm goin' ta call you alright. Good night, Tia Baabay."

"Good night, Tyrique."

Baby? I have got to get used to him calling me that. Wait a minute, no I don't, we had our night. It's over now.

Dear Diary, I was a bad bad girl tonight, yes that is the perfect first sentence for tonight's entry.

CHAPTER SEVEN
TWISTED REVENGE

I called my sister to let her know that I made it home. Before I dialed her number I got my story straight. I sure as hell was not telling the truth.

"Hello?"

"Hey Jerome, I just called to let y'all know I made it home."

"Where have you been? You left the club a couple of hours ago."

"No whur'."

"Did you leave with Tyrique?"

"Who?"

"Tyrique, the man that ran out of the club after you," Jerome clarified.

"What?"

"Right after you said goodnight, he came over to the table, and said he was leaving. He missed every dap, he was running after your ass so fast, not only that he was looking at you walk away the whole time he was trying to say goodbye to all of us."

"Really?"

"Hell yeah, he even forgot Nicole's name. He said, 'I'm sorry that

NAKED CONFESSIONS

I forgot your name but it was nice seeing you again, I got to go bye.' Then
he turned and actually ran out, and I'm not talking about that homeboy trot
either, he really ran. What did you do to him?"

"Nothing. What do you mean do to him?"

"All I'm sayin' is you should have seen that brotha run."

"Ha, ha, ha! Really?"

So, my Sweetness ran after me. Well, well, well, I was glad he did.
It would be nice to see him again, even touch him again, to taste him again,
and to be fulfilled by him again. Stop!

"You had to do or say something, dog, because I had to shake his
hand goodbye after he missed the second dap with me. I was like, okay dog,
you in a hurry, so don't worry about it. After that he just waved at every
one else, said what he said to Nikki, then took off. And I know damn well,
he was running after you because not even ten seconds went by after you
said goodbye to me and your sister. He came over and started saying his
goodbyes too. He walked up to the table right after you left. Like I said, at
first he watched you walk away then he just sprung into action."

"I didn't do anything to him, all I said was I had to go, then I came
over to say goodbye to you, Nikki, and Paul. I do remember him asking me
if could he walk me to my car but I wasn't about to wait for him to do so."

"Well did he catch up with you?"

"Yes, he did. He walked me to my car but that's about it; besides
which he is just a little boy, I would break him. Hell, I didn't even remember
his name until you said it just now."

"Tia, you're off the hook."

"Well Jay, I truly am tired, more like worn out, so I am going to get
on off of the phone now, okay?"

"Oh, you went to another club?"

"No, more like a small house party."

"What, a little get together?"

"Yeah, something like that, you know not too many people, but I had a lot of fun."

"All right then, I'll let your sister know that you made it home. Good night, Tia."

"Good night, dog."

The night air was cold. I rushed inside and turned up the heat. I thought about Tyrique undressing me as I disrobed. I bundled up in my robe, sat on the bed and rested my head on my pillow. I reminisced as I waited for the shower to warm up. Tyrique sought me out, I thought that was phenomenal. I rolled around in my bed giggling like a schoolgirl. That cold night in January I felt like a hot sex goddess, instead of a crippled woman. It represented the final break of emotional ties, which already became imminent the day I informed Jack of my cancer prognosis. I had finally seen the good in Jack's suggestion. I found my own happiness, sweet revenge. I sat up in bed.

The notion of revenge began to take seed and grow. I decided to postpone my shower. As I made my way though the dark to Jack's room my mind filled with devilish inspiration. The thought of my husband licking my pussy just after it had been thoroughly fucked by another man oddly appealed to me. After all, I mused, turnabout is fair play.

"Jack, are you awake?"

"Tia?"

"Yes, Jack."

"Come get in the bed with me."

I tiptoed close to the bed. Out of the blue, compunction hit me like a ton of bricks. I froze before whispering, "No thank you."

It did not matter how much he deserved it. I simply could not do it. Revenge would have been perfectly justified in that moment. Nevertheless, my sense of self would not allow it. My secret night was good enough. After all, it was one to remember. I did not want to turn a pleasurable evening into

NAKED CONFESSIONS

a nightmare. In the end it was mine. Jack had nothing to do with my night. That was before Jack took the bull by the horns.

"Then what the hell did you come down here for?"

"I don't know. I'm home early. I thought you'd be up. I'm going to just go ahead and go." I took a step back. "I'm sorry I woke you."

"Hell no," he bellowed as he grabbed my wrist. "You're not just going to come down to my room, and wake me up for nothing."

"Like I said, it's early so I thought you would still be awake. I came down here to talk to you about our marriage. The fact that the most joyous moments of my life are spent with other people hurts. But I can see that you have already gone to bed. As soon as I realized you were asleep I thought better of it. Since you are in bed for the night I'll go and let you sleep."

"No Tia," Jack said, his voice was kind and gentle. "Stay." He released my arm. "Come lay next to me."

"Why?"

"So we can talk."

"There's no use. It's too late anyway."

"What do you mean it's too late?"

"It's after ten. I woke you up."

"Is that what you really meant?"

"Yes, I had a wonderful night. You were sleeping so peacefully. There's no sense in ruining everything by bringing up our issues. I'll just leave."

"You're not going anywhere," he shouted. Jack leaped out of the bed. "I'm your husband." He grabbed me and threw me down on the bed.

I fought back, at first. "Stop it, Jack. Please don't do this."

"You're my wife."

"You don't act like it so why should I?" I said, kicking at him.

"You're going to act like it tonight," Jack said, grabbing my legs.

"No," I cried.

"Don't make me hurt you, Tia."

"I don't want you anymore."

"You need to stop fighting, and give in. Just let me have you."

"No."

I kicked free and got to my feet. I made a mad dash for the door, and then I felt it. Agony filled my senses as Jack wrenched my injured arm. I cried out in pain. In that moment my heart and my mind changed. I thought to myself, why go toe to toe with this man when I came down here to inflict a little revenge anyway? If he wanted me that badly, who am I to say no to the twisted pleasure of doing my wifely duty?

"Fine," I consented.

"Get into the bed!" Jack ordered.

"Okay, Jack. But no bullshit, just fuck, and get the hell on. I don't want you touching me in the first place. Damn it."

I was too tired to fight, and my arm was hurt. I avoided further injury. I averted rape. I fell onto my own sword. The thought of revenge was entertaining until I actually faced what it entailed. Jack had other ideas. He tried to kiss me but I turned my head. He kissed my neck, and massaged my breasts. My body refused to respond. He caressed my pussy as he kissed his way down to my belly button. I grabbed his head stopping him.

"I'm not in the mood for any of this. Just get some lubricant, and get on with it. Besides, I've been dancing tonight so I am not exactly fresh, and I won't be returning the favor."

Jack wouldn't listen, he was hell bent. I stared out into the darkness waiting for it all to end. I was stuck there with the lick and stick king. I was thankful that his pornographic tactics would end quickly, or so I thought. Regrettably, that night he licked and tongue fucked my pussy relentlessly. I felt sick.

My body began to repeatedly involuntary retch. Jack mistakenly took my dry heaves for an orgasm. Shortly thereafter he pushed his dick into my vaginal canal, flesh to flesh, dry uncomfortable sex. I could not understand how my pussy could go from juicy to dry so quickly. However before I could give it much thought Jack was finished. He stood over me panting.

"I made you cum."

My body retched again. I grabbed the trashcan just in time. The contents of my stomach staged a revolt. I wiped my mouth, glared at Jack and said, "No, you made me sick!" I turned my back on him. "The only thing your sex evoked was vomiting." I left the room, slamming the door behind me.

"Fuck you, Tia!" Jack shouted.

Somehow his words angered me to my core. I wanted to hurt him back. My best weapons were words. I opened the door just enough to be heard.

"You tried and failed. I'm thinkin' it's time to trade you in for a younger model."

"Who else is going to want you?"

"I'm sure I could find a willing participant."

"You can't do no better than me."

"Sure I can. After all, you're just another old man needing Viagra."

"I don't need no damn Viagra!"

"Admit it, Jack. You have erectile dysfunction."

"That's a lie," he hollered.

"Okay, baby. What ever you say."

"Ain't nothing wrong with my dick."

"Of course not dear," my voice was sugar sweet. "After all, there's absolutely nothing wrong with having sex in two minutes or less, especially since you can get it up again so quickly."

"Fuck you, Tia!" Jack said, his voice was low, and filled with emotion.

I laughed bitterly, and sarcastically asked, "How long does it take Jack, about a week or two?"

"Fucking bitch…"

"That four minutes of sex per month is all I can stand anyway."

"Fuck you, you fucking bitch!" He said, struggling against his tears.

"Remember you said that. It will come back to haunt you."

"Whatever."

"A bitch fucks what she fancies. So maybe I'll take you up on your suggestion."

"Oh so what, now you're going to go out and cheat on me?"

"Why would I do a thing like that, especially when you are such a sexual virtuoso? What more could a woman ask for? Oh no, I am perfectly happy, no, grateful for the one minute lick and the two minutes of dick that I get now." I peeked my head in before continuing. "It is not cheating if I tell you in advance."

"Go to hell, Tia!"

"Being subjected to your horrific sex is my living hell."

I closed the door. I was lost in thought as I walked through the dark. What did I do to deserve this kind of marriage? I wanted him to be my husband too badly. For ten years I couldn't see the forest for the trees. All I wanted was a family. No matter what the cost.

I was gripped by the Christian notion of washing away my sins. I washed thoroughly with extremely hot water and antibacterial soap. I took the longest shower of my life. I felt like a stranger in my own body. The fact that I had sex with two men in one night made me feel dirty. I told myself to forget everything, nothing that happened that night could ever be repeated. Yet there was a part of me that still wanted it all.

"It would be nice to be able to cum for Tyrique again, my Sweetness." I said aloud as I crawled into my bed.

I lay in under the covers with my eyes closed waiting for sleep to take me over. As I waited vivid flashes of the night's activities zoomed through my mind's eye, as if I was watching a slide show. I allowed myself to be seduced by the memory. My pussy became wet. My hips began to rock. I pinched my nipples, rolling them back and forth between my fingers. I opened my legs and masturbated with both hands until I came. Even still, the images would not subside. I needed to tell someone. I called Tammy. I got her voicemail. I left a message.

"Hey girl, it's me. Call me when you get this message. I have lots to tell. All I can say is his name is Tyrique. Bye."

Finally, I drifted off to sleep. I slept well, a little bit more peacefully than usual. The next day I woke up early.

CHAPTER EIGHT
FINDING TIME

The morning after, I didn't get out of the bed right away. I rolled over onto my back and stared at the ceiling. I was lost in thought from the moment I opened my eyes. More accurately, I was absorbed in an internal debate. I questioned everything that took place the night before. I wondered how I had allowed myself to have sex with another man. I was an adulteress. I wanted to blame the devil. I wanted to blame my husband. Alas, no matter what temptation Satan had placed in front of me and no matter what Jack had done, I knew what I had done was wrong. Two wrongs never make it right.

Even still, I somehow felt justified. After all, Jack had left me to face cancer alone. I was bleeding to death, very slowly. My heart was far too busy trying to keep me alive. It no longer had any consideration for Jack. Too late now—what's done is done, was the thought in the forefront of my mind. I could not change the past therefore I refused to feel shame or guilt. My night with Tyrique did not involve a lot of thinking, it simply felt good. I had my one night, my secret to keep me going without dwelling so much on how I was wronged. It was a fabulously pleasure filled night. I do not have to worry about him telling anyone about our clandestine night because he is military and I am married.

Married? For the life of me I could no longer understand the meaning of the word. I abruptly scrambled out of bed and ran to the mirror. I stared at my reflection. A tear rolled down my cheek. I smiled as I wiped it away. It was in that moment that I realized that I was no longer in love with my husband. I quietly mourned the death of my marriage..

Saturday morning, I had to get going. I had way too many obligations, all family. Now that I was a functioning cripple I became my family's go-to-girl. I was all booked up from early that morning to about two am the next day. By and by my life was going to go on as usual, with the thought of imminent death still looming in the back of my mind. There was nothing I could do to rid myself of the feeling of doom. However, the thought of Tyrique put a much needed smile on my face.

I quickly showered and dressed. I had taken to dressing in animation themed jogging suits as I spent most of my time with my children, nieces and nephews. They loved it. I started breakfast, bacon first. Before long, my children appeared.

"Good morning, Mommy," Alexi said. She hugged me and kissed my cheek. "I'll make the eggs."

"Good morning, Mommy," Elli said, following up. She gave me a hug and kiss on the cheek. "Pancakes, waffles, or cinnamon rolls?"

We all paused, and looked from one to the other. "Waffles," we shouted one by one.

"Mommy, can you teach me how to make your butter pecan waffles?" Elli asked.

"It's easy, just add a half of teaspoon of butter pecan extract to the waffle batter. Do not add the crushed pecans to the mix. Instead, pour the batter onto the waffle iron and place the pecans on top of the batter just before you close the lid. They will sink in as it cooks."

"Wow Mommy, that is easy."

We enjoyed our morning together, just the three of us. After breakfast I tidied up the kitchen while my daughters prepared for the day. Just as I placed the final dish in the cupboard Jack entered the kitchen. He sniffed the air as he looked around. He stood in front of the stove, opened the oven and peeked inside.

"Is it in the microwave?" Jack asked.

"What are you talking about?"

"Breakfast, the bacon?" he said.

"What bacon?"

"I know I smell bacon."

"That's the new air freshener," I said, barely stifling my laughter.

"You didn't save me any, Tia?"

"I have to go," I said, softly giggling while walking away.

"Tia, what are your plans for today?" Jack called after me.

"I have to take the children to the library," I said, stopping. I didn't want him following me to my room. "After that, I'm going to babysit for my brother. Tonight, I'm going out to a new blues club, they're supposed to be just as good as the ones in St. Louis. Why?"

"Who are you going with?"

"Nikki. Did you want to come with us?"

"No, I already have plans for this evening," Jack said, squaring his shoulders.

"Oh okay, bye."

"What time are you leaving?" Jack asked.

"I've got to leave in five minutes," I answered nonchalantly.

I turned and walked away. The second my back was to him my sinful smile returned. I wondered how long I would be able to hold on to the feeling. I felt so sinfully delicious.

"That's it?" he asked, a bit taken aback.

"What?" I glanced over my shoulder.

"You don't have anything else to say?"

"Nope, okay well, bye," I said.

My thoughts were rushing me to get the hell out of this house before I slip up. The gratification of last night was still fresh in my mind. Jack appeared dumbfounded as he stared at me. All traces of my insecurity vanished into thin air. I realized that fact only after I was on my way to the library with my children. I knew that I had to treat him in the exact same manner as I did before my night with Tyrique. Any change in my attitude would be an, all too obvious, clue of infidelity.

It didn't matter what the change was. I could look too happy, maybe too much attitude, too distant, too quiet, or be too affectionate, it did not matter. Jack would zero in on any change and wonder what brought it on. He would dig until he figured it out. I knew him well. He had been looking for a change in me for years. He had done too much dirt, and he knew I had found the courage to get even. Jack had been waiting on edge for the other shoe to fall. Karma was about to slap him in the face.

If the only difference in my personality was my thought process and a few smiles, I would have been home free. Unfortunately, Tyrique weighed on my mind like no one ever had before. I tried to calm myself and keep as busy as possible but nothing really worked. I smiled so much my cheeks hurt. I went to my sister's to pick up my niece first.

"Good morning, y'all. Is Birdie ready?"

She flew out of her room, and said, "I'm sorry Aunt Tia, I'm almost ready."

"Don't worry about it baby, I'll sit and wait."

Everybody stopped dead in their tracks. Their heads instantly snapped in my direction. Their reactions tickled me to death. I laughed a little bit, took off my shoes, walked on into the living room, and sat on the couch. My smile lingered. Nikki walked over to me with a knowing look on her face.

"So Tia, did you get some this morning?" Nikki asked.

"No, I left the house before Jack could piss me off."

"Oh okay, I knew it was somethin'."

I smiled, thinking that I was not gon' tell her what. Damn, had I really been that bad—that angry?

Later while I was in the library helping my daughter with her science project, my cell phone rang. *"You're All I Need to Get By,"* echoed through the building. I quickly muted the ringer. I had no choice but to let it go to voicemail. Before too long my daughter went off looking for more reference material. I took that moment alone to check my messages.

"Hey Tia Baabay, give me a call when you get this message. I hope you are having a good day. By the way this is yo boy, Tye."

I walked outside, and immediately called him. Tyrique answered welcomingly.

"Good afternoon, lady."

"Hello Tyrique, I got your message."

"What are you up to today?"

"Well, right now I'm at the library with the children."

"I would really like to see you at some point today."

"I'll be at the Silver-Blue Moon tonight."

"I haven't heard of that one."

"It is fairly new. It is a blues club downtown."

"Well I wasn't really planning on going out tonight."

"You don't like the blues, now do you?"

"Naw, not really."

"That's all right darlin'. Why don't you touch base with me throughout the day and I will try my very best to get away. If push comes to shove I can just leave the club early."

"All right, Baabay. I'll talk to you later."

I could not believe that I was being pursued by a twenty-three year old. I had always attracted older successful business men. I thought Tyrique was supposed to be 'one night only' but then I remembered. He insisted on getting my number before I drove off. My curiosity peeked. I wanted to know how far things with Tyrique would go. Although I had moral issues my need to be needed and to be wanted, naked, superseded my principles. I had been the good responsible sacrificial lamb for far too long. I took care of everybody's everything. This was for me. I decided to have a weekend fling and repent on Monday.

All Saturday I tried to get together with Tyrique however, it was not meant to be. I had too many family obligations. Later on that night I had plans with Nicole, Jerome and my home girl Tammy. When we got to the club everything seemed as if it was all right. Tyrique called and I told him I would try to sneak away. But no, that wasn't going to happen. Jerome began drinking heavily right from the start, which angered Nicole. He wanted to dance but she didn't want to dance with him while he was acting stupid. To make matters worse Jerome and Nicole began arguing at the table. I tried to talk some sense into them.

"Why don't y'all just go home?" I begged.

"Tia, Nikki is the one with the problem," Jerome said, unashamedly pointing at Nicole. "I'm just trying to have a little fun."

"Drinking yourself silly isn't fun for me to watch, Jerome," Nikki interjected. "Tia will tell you, our father was an alcoholic, and I just can't stand it when you drink to the point where you lose control."

"Well, how the hell did he get so drunk so fast in the first place?" I asked dumbfounded.

"I'm not drunk," Jerome exclaimed.

"He started drinking before we left home," Nicole replied, ignoring Jerome.

"Well damn. I have a phone call to make. Excuse me, I'll be right back."

I went to the ladies room, and called Tammy.

"Hey Tia," Tammy happily answered.

"Where are you?" I asked abruptly.

"I'm in the car on my way, girl. What's wrong?"

"Nikki and Jerome are arguing at the table, and I'm supposed to meet up with young Tyrique tonight. So please hurry up."

"I'll be there in a few minutes."

"Thank you, that's Tyrique on the other end, I'll see you when you get here."

The moment I clicked over my whole demeanor changed. I sounded like a sex kitten.

"Hello," I purred.

"Hey Baabay."

"Hello Tyrique."

"Are you having fun?"

"No."

"No?"

"Not at all…"

"Come on ova hea and I'll put a smile on yo face."

"You just did."

"Am I going to see you tonight?"

"God, I hope so."

"What time does the club close?"

"Two thirty but I'm leaving at one no matter what. You go'n wait up for me?"

"Hell yeah!"

"If I can I'll sneak off earlier."

"You do that."

"Okay, bye Sweetness."

"Bye Baabay."

Tyrique had a wonderful calming effect on me. I was ready to go back out there and deal with my sister and her man. Although, all I wanted to do was leave. There were other things, sexy things I would rather be doing right in that moment. Even so, Nikki was my sister and I was not about to leave her there, especially with Jerome acting a fool. When I returned to the table Nicole was sitting alone.

"Where's Jerome?" I asked

"Out thur' on the dance floor acting like the damn godfather of soul."

I looked over to where Nicole was pointing, and saw Jerome. He was moving like the king of pop, the godfather of soul, the king of rock n' roll, and a one man boy band, all rolled up into one. I looked back at my sister as she looked at me. I pressed my lips together as tight as I could to keep from laughing but my eyes gave me away. We looked over at Jerome again and then back to each other. We both held it in for as long as we could. We busted out laughing. We laughed so hard that tears ran down our faces. We could barely speak, but we tried to talk anyway.

"Nikki," I exclaimed, laughing. "Look at him go!"

"I..." Nikki could barely breathe. "I, I know," she cried with laughter.

"Is he that way in bed too?"

"Tia, girl…" Nikki nodded as she smiled so big I could see her wisdom teeth. "Hell yeah, girl," she yelled.

"Well damn," I said.

Any other day, I would have been thoroughly pissed off and embarrassed. I would have acted like I was Jerome's mother and made him get off of the dance floor. He would have gotten the lecture of his life. Apparently I had lost my sense of humor, and my carefree love of life years ago. I welcomed that side of me back. Nikki and I calmed down, smiling as we watched Jerome for a few more minutes. At the end of the song, Jerome dropped down into a split, popped up again, and went immediately into a spin.

"I hope he didn't slap his balls on the floor with that move," I remarked earnestly.

"Tia, I hope he didn't either. Good God, that would really hurt a lot. Ouch." We started laughing again.

"Nikki, go dance with your man. Deal with your issues tomorrow," I suggested.

"There's somethin' different about you Tia," Nicole commented as she eyed me curiously.

"I haven't been home all day," I smiled. "Go dance."

"Okay."

Good dick was not the reason I was acting better. There was no revenge sex. I had completely forgotten about Jack by the time I found myself saying yes to Tyrique. The truth of the matter was quite simple, for the first time in a long time my heart was not hurting. Infidelity coupled with cruelty and emotional abandonment really did a number on me. Moreover, the fact that Jack had nothing to do with my new found happiness, made it all the better.

With Tammy on the way and the whole Nikki and Jerome situation, I couldn't just sneak off. I was finally able to escape at one in the morning as promised. However, when I called Tyrique, all I got was his voicemail. Damn! That was bad timing. Maybe this sexcapade wasn't meant to happen tonight. I didn't know what the hell I was thinking in the first place. Oh well, I was just going to have to carry my ass on home, take a shower, and go to bed. I guess after tonight it's definitely over, so much for my weekend fling. A feeling of disappointment overwhelmed, me and my heart sank. Maybe everything could be possible in another life, but now was all I had.

I was a very busy woman. There was always something that needed to be taken care of, but that was the life I had chosen, and would not have had it any other way. I loved my family dearly. I wanted to always be there when

I was needed. After all I did not know how much time I had left. My Sunday morning started with a phone call just as I was stepping out of the shower.

"Hello?"

"Tia, this is Nikki."

"Why are you up so early? I know you and Jerome left the club after I did."

"One of Mama's uncles died, her favorite one, and I was thinking we all should get together for breakfast, that way she has the support of her children, which is what she needs right now. I'll cook here at my house," Nikki said.

Whenever my sister starts talking fast without taking a breath or a decent pause I know that there is something that she wants from me. I began to dress.

"So that means I have to go and get her, right?"

"Well it's on your way."

"What time?"

"Now, she's distraught."

"I'm on my way."

"Thank you, Tia."

"Is there anything I need to bring?"

"No, I have everything here."

"Is she ready?"

"Yes."

"I'm walking out of the door right now."

Oh God in heaven please let my mother be okay. In Jesus' name I pray. Amen.

I drove to my mother's house, which was about five minutes away, and for the first time ever she was actually ready to go. When I pulled up she was already outside waiting. She got in, and we were on our way.

"Good morning, Mama."

"Good morning, baby."

"How are you holding up?"

"I'm doing okay I guess. Where are your children?"

"Still sleep."

Poor Mama. Okay, I couldn't argue with her today, no matter what she said to provoke me.

"Tia your phone is ringing."

"It's probably Nikki, making sure we are on our way."

I was almost to my sister's house when my cell phone rang. I was concentrating so hard on getting my mother to Nikki's house that I did not hear it. It was just before nine in the morning. I looked at the call screen and then back up at traffic. I smiled. My heart skipped a beat. My heart rate increased as my breathing became shallow. My whole demeanor changed to one that I almost did not recognize. A barely familiar feeling began to settle over me as I became painfully aware of my femininity.

"Hello," I answered.

"Good mornin', lady."

"Good morning."

"I'm so very, very sorry I missed your call last night. I fell asleep."

"It's okay."

"There's always today."

"Yes, there is."

"What are you doing right now?"

"Taking Mama to Nikki's house for Sunday breakfast."

"Oh, do you want me to call you back?"

"Yes, please. Better yet, I'll call you from Nikki's house. My cell phone doesn't get good reception over there."

"Okay Baabay, call me after you finish breakfast."

"I will."

"Bye, Baabay."

"Bye."

Just the sound of his voice made me want to do thangs. I closed my eyes for the briefest of moments as I brought my car to a stop at a red light. I had no choice but to end the call shortly after saying hello. After all, the last thing I needed was my mother asking questions. I put the phone away, and drove on down the street like it was nothing. My mother looked at me inquisitively however she didn't say a word.

All I had to do was figure out how to get to his house. It dawned on me that I did not remember where he lived. I began to question how much Brandy I had to drink that fateful Friday night. I wondered if Tyrique was indeed as handsome as I remembered or if I only thought he was good-looking because I had been looking out of liquor soaked eyeballs. How could I trust an alcohol tainted memory? I would have to wait and see.

CHAPTER NINE
MAKING TIME

My siblings and I arrived at Nikki's house within minutes of each other. We catered to our mother's every need and comforted her as best as we could in her hour of need.

"I can't believe that my favorite uncle is actually dead," my mother tearfully said. "I want to go to the funeral but I can't afford it right now. He was my favorite uncle, my favorite for sixty years. I can't believe I'll never talk to him again. Every summer Mama and Daddy would take us down to Mississippi to visit."

"Didn't you get to see him at the family reunion back in July?" Nicole asked.

"Yes Nikki. I just can't believe I have to say goodbye after sixty years, sixty years is a long time to love someone and to have to let go, just like that."

I saw how sad my mother was, and how much she wanted to go to the funeral. I knew that money was not the real issue. We could all just pitch in to send her, and she knew that fact. Mama didn't want to go alone.

"Mama?" I began.

"Yes?"

"I was going to ship my truck to St. Louis this month, but I guess I could drive it there, and we can swing by Mississippi on the way to the funeral."

"You will drive me?"

"No, you will drive my truck and I'll ride with you. I can drive a little bit, but not too much because of my back. However, I'll be able to keep you company."

"Really Tia?" my mother asked, surprised.

"Yes Mama. Just let me know when you want to leave."

I could kill two birds with one stone, and save a little bit of money as well. Mama seemed to be in better spirits. Oh my God what did I just agree to do? We couldn't get along for two hours. How in the hell was I going to handle being in her exclusive company, in a locked vehicle no less, for a two day road trip? About two hours after I arrived at Nicole's, I went into her bedroom, and called Tyrique.

"Hello?"

"Hey Tyrique," I said, trying to be cool.

"Good mornin' again, Tia," he crooned.

"Good morning."

"Did you enjoy your breakfast?"

"Yes."

"Good, so when do I get to eat mine?"

"Did you need me to bring you a plate?"

I thought that his asking me feed him was his way of getting me to come over there but, I was wrong, which seemed to be the case a lot with him.

"No."

"No?"

"I was planning on having you for breakfast."

"Well damn!"

Now that was a very good way of asking me to come over there. He was downright sexy. It went on from there. He tried every way he could to get me to come to his house. After a great deal of coercion I agreed to meet him at his place by noon. I already had my whole day planned. Although squeezing him in was going to be a chore, I believed he was well worth the effort. All I had to do was some creative juggling. I thought about it for a little while.

I need to take a thorough shower, dress in something sexy but sporty which will camouflage my true intentions from Jack. But first, there's the tricky part, I need to get the hell out of here without taking Mama with me. Okay here goes nothing.

I didn't address anyone specifically; I just started talking the minute I got to the living room.

"I forgot to shower with all of the chaos of this morning so, I'm going to go on home right now and take care of that before I start to smell bad, but I'll be back before y'all miss me."

I smiled at everyone in the room, turned, and walked on out of the house. I went home, took another shower, and fragranced in my favorite kiwi scented body spray and lotion. I dressed in a blue cotton hooded dress that stopped just above my knees. I curled my hair then brushed it up into a ponytail. Finally I slipped on some matching blue mules. I walked right out the front door completely unnoticed, as always.

Once I was on my way I let my hair out of the ponytail. I combed it out, so that my light fluffy brush curls hung over my shoulders and down my back, after which, I started applying my makeup. At the first stop light I applied lipstick and a little bit of eyeliner. At the next one I put on my mascara and a dab of blush. At the following light I rubbed a little bit of body shimmer on my breasts. By the time I got to Tyrique's house, I was all put together.

While my conscience screamed, 'Tramp!' I pressed forward. I

justified my actions. I was slowly bleeding to death and my own husband could care less. First, Jack was so focused on his video game he did not say a word to me when I came back home. He didn't even take notice of the fact that I not only showered but changed clothes. Last, he didn't bother saying goodbye when I left. I was hell bent on enjoying my little weekend fling. I rationalized that I would have a secret which would leave me with just enough guilt to be good to Jack. I smiled as I thought; I have never had a one night stand in my life so why would I start now?

I pulled into his driveway and there he was standing outside waiting for me. At first glance he was not disfigured. Tyrique greeted me by opening my door and helping me out of my car. I took my time. I had to get out of the car without hitting my head, stumbling, or doing anything else that might be embarrassing. I took his hand as I stepped out of the car gracefully. I concentrated so intently on being smooth that I did not have a chance to take a good look at him.

"Hello Tia." Tyrique's voice was sexy yet slightly uneasy. "You're looking beautiful. It's nice to see you again. I'm glad you were able to make it."

I could not help but to smile modestly. It was good to know that he was nervous as well. I liked that he talked a lot when he was nervous, something we had in common.

"Hello Tyrique, thank you." I looked into his eyes. "It's nice to see you again as well."

My, oh my, he was very attractive. I thought he was nice looking when I pulled in but after getting a good look at him, he was hot. I thank God he did not have that alcohol induced beauty.

"Come here," Tyrique demanded as he gathered me in his arms.

He gave me a warm hug and kiss hello, before leading me by the hand from the car through his front door. I could not believe I was actually there, at his house with him, sober. I made every attempt to play it calm and cool. Although I tried to relax, the excitement had not diminished. In fact the thrill of it all increased by the moment. He let go of my hand after we were just past the threshold. I watched him as he closed and locked the door. Even with his back turned to me he was sexy, the shape of his head, definition of his back, the curve of his body and the strength of his legs all triggered my blatant desire.

I stood there in the entryway of his home wearing a dress, bra, and some shoes, nothing more nothing less. I could feel my body temperature rise with every passing moment. I did not know what to do. It was my first time. For the life of me I did not know what to expect or how bold I could be. All I could do was stand there quietly looking at him as I waited to see what was going to happen. Anticipation was a powerful aphrodisiac. The moment he turned back around, Tyrique looked at me with so much appreciation I began to blush. Tyrique took me by the hand once more and pulled me into his embrace.

"Now that we're inside, I can give you a proper hello," he said.

He wrapped me up tight in his arms. He kissed me until I was absolutely breathless. All I could do was hold on. His kisses trailed down my neck as his hands pressed me closer to his body. When he finally released me I was a bit unsteady, in the mind.

"Oh my," I sighed.

"Come on in, Tia." He took me by the hand again and led me into the kitchen. "I was just watching a movie in my bedroom. Would you like to join me?"

"Sure?"

He looked back at me and smiled before asking, "Can I get you something to drink?"

"Water please."

"That's all you want?"

"Yes, thank you."

He kissed me again, a nice soft peck on the lips. He smiled at me once more.

"Go on in the room and get comfortable on the bed, Tia. I'll be right in with your water."

"All right," I sighed. I smiled into his eyes before sauntering off to his room.

I was convinced that if I could be with Tyrique while I was stone sober and the passion was still mind-blowing then it was real. If what I felt was genuine, I wanted to keep him for a little while.

My conscience screamed at me again, "Oh now it's a little while. First it was a one night thing. Then it was a weekend thing. What the hell happened to repenting on Monday?"

My mind was made up, after all I did not exactly say which Monday I would ask for forgiveness. Hot, passionate sex, stone-cold sober, I haven't had that indulgence in years. I pretty much forgot what consciously making the decision to have sex was like. I wanted to remember everything. I needed to enjoy every moment of the process while I was fully aware of all of my inhibitions. I wanted to bask as my reticence was wooed away, replaced by passion, instead of it being drowned out by alcohol.

I sat comfortably, in the middle of his bed, attentively watching the movie previews. Tyrique walked in. I glanced up at him. He handed me a glass of water, took my face in his hands, and planted one hell of a kiss on me. When the kiss was over all I could do was blink, as I stared into his eyes. I was becoming very fond of his lips. Sexual stimulation was more intoxicating to me than booze.

I took a drink of water as I watched him get into bed. He sat close to me and wrapped an arm around my waist. I realized that I did not know much about him.

"Tyrique darlin', tell me a little bit about yourself," I suggested.

"What do you want to know?" he asked.

"Well, do you have any children?"

"Yes, a son, he's three."

"Have you ever been married?"

"No, no one will have me."

"I find that very hard to believe."

"Really?" he asked.

"You are a very attractive man. I find it hard to believe that some woman hasn't tried to snatch you up by now."

"Yeah well, I'm single. It's just me"

"I'm looking forward to that day."

"What happened?"

I told him a brief synopsis of the past year of my life. He offered to be the passion that I needed so desperately and I accepted.

"I need to put my glass down. Do you have any coasters?"

"No, just put it down on the top of the headboard. It'll be all right."

"Okay."

As I stretched back to put my glass down, the hem of my dress began to rise. I twisted to the side a bit to get the extra inch I needed to reach his headboard. I put the glass down before I righted myself. That's when I saw him watching me. I looked into his eyes. I saw a look, the look I wanted to be there, I needed to be there. The hem of my dress rode high on my thighs. I pulled it down as I smiled at him sheepishly. Tyrique stretched himself out in the bed. He asked me to join him, I did. We watched the film in comfortable silence. About an hour into the movie I had to go the restroom.

"I'll be right back," I announced.

"Okay Baabay, I'll pause the movie for you."

"Thank you."

I returned. I hiked my knee up to climb into the bed with him, which was uncommonly high. The top of his mattress was even with my pelvis. As my knee rose, so did my dress. Tyrique was facing me, watching me. He took a double take as my knee landed on top of the bed, after which his eyes never left me. I climbed in, on my hands and knees. I stretched out beside him, smoothed my dress down and pretended as if everything was normal. I looked directly at the television.

"Okay I'm all settled. Press play please," I casually uttered.

"Uh, Tia, what's under your dress?"

"You looked under my dress?" I asked as I continued to gaze forward. I briefly glanced in his direction. "Start the movie, please."

Tyrique spoke slowly, "Are you sitting next to me wearing nothing but a dress?"

"No," I said as I reached in the opposite direction to retrieve my water. After I took a sip Tyrique took the glass from me. I finally looked into his eyes and innocently stated, "I'm wearing a bra," I smiled politely. My eyes fluttered enhancing the facade of wide-eyed naiveté.

Tyrique looked at me with primal intensity. His glare declared that he was done playing at being polite. He kissed me passionately before looking into my eyes once more. My mind grew heady with desire. The excitement, mixed with a little bit of fear, coursed through my veins. My pussy became down right demanding, watery—like a babbling brook. When he slipped his hand under my dress, I slowly parted my legs welcoming him. I craved him, my body was on fire. I felt as if I was going to go mad from the intensity, the anticipation, the longing. His touch was gentle, feather soft. My body trembled as he undressed me.

"Get under the covers, Tia," Tyrique instructed.

In the time that it took for me to fold back the covers, he was out of the bed and completely naked. I slowly looked him over. There we were, nude and looking passionately at one another. I slipped under the covers. I held them open as I smiled up at him.

He crawled into bed and took me into his arms, rolling me on top of him. From the first touch to the last we were in a sexual frenzy, we lost all control. I couldn't account for everything we did to, with, and for one another, but this I remembered. We were stone cold sober, yet completely inebriated—high on lust, drunk on passion, and fucking like wild cats on the Serengeti. Hair pulling, back scratching, ass slapping—our fiery cries reverberated throughout his home. In the end we were both cum-soaked and out of breath. We wound up in each other's arms, in deep pillow talk.

"Tia, Baabay, you make my toes curl and ain't no woman ever done that to me before."

"I'm glad to be of service."

"I'm serious."

"Me too... That was thorough dicking down and I really do mean thorough."

"I like the way your body responds to me."

"There's nothing like completely loosing control to unabashed passion, giving in to perpetual longing while trying to satisfy an insatiable craving. When every sound, every motion, even every breath is dictated by sexual desire, it is absolute ecstasy."

"You do lose control, now don't you?" He asked as he smiled a proud smile.

"Yes, and so do you. I love the way we set each other on fire."

Please let him understand that this is a weekend affair not a relationship. This is strictly physical. No love or feelings, just lust and the pleasure of sexual decadence. Something I can repent for on Monday. Who am I kidding? I'm hooked on his dick like a crack addict.

I smiled up at him. My face beamed with sexual satisfaction. I sighed. Tyrique smiled as well. He gathered me close. He ran his fingers through my hair. It was wonderful living in that moment. I wished every day of my life could have had a moment like that so that I might die a happy woman.

"Tyrique Sweetness, I need to shower and get back to my sister's house."

"Oh alright, I guess I gotta letcha go. I'll get you my robe and put some towels in the bathroom for you."

"Thank you, Tye," I said, stretching up. Placing my hand on his cheek, I gave him a gentle kiss on the lips before turning away.

CHAPTER TEN
COMING TO AN UNDERSTANDING

After showering, and getting dressed, I walked out to the living room. Tyrique sat on the couch watching a sports show.

"Tia?"

"Yes, Tyrique."

"Do you really have to go right now?"

"I really should."

"Come sit down next to me. Talk with me for a while."

"All right."

"You are so agreeable."

I smiled. I sat next to him, faced him, and said, "So what should we talk about?"

"I think we should really get to know one another."

"I agree. I'll tell you anything you want to know."

We talked about our childhoods, the good times and the bad. We talked about past relationships without dwelling on anything or anyone precisely. It was more like a matter of fact conversation which stated how we had gotten to that specific point in our lives, respectively. We were open, honest, and very candid, or so I thought.

"Tyrique darlin', there's nothing you've told me at this point that would run me off. I have only one request. My request is very simple. I always begin by treating people the way I want to be treated, however, after a while and I do mean a very short while, I will start treating you the way you treat me. Please, treat me the way you want to be treated."

"That sounds fair."

"I'm glad you think so. Do you have any stipulations?"

"Just one," he said with a mischievous sparkle in his eyes.

"What?"

"Always be wet and ready for me."

I grinned. "You mean like earlier?"

"Oh yeah Baabay, just like earlier."

"All right."

"Tia?"

"Yes Tyrique."

"What do you want?"

"What do you mean?"

"Baabay, what do you need me to be to you?"

"Well, I already have a husband so I'm thinkin' I need a lover."

"A lover?"

"Yes. I don't need you to be my man. You do what you have to do and so will I."

"So um, how often can you come see me?"

"Whenever you call. I will never be more than fifteen minutes away."

"I'm just letting you know from the start, I like a whole lot of sex."

"Good, so do I. Oh, and just to let you know, I firmly believe that good dick for good pussy is an even exchange. I don't want you trying to date me."

"I like the way you think."

"Why thank ya."

"Please feel free to dress just like that every time you come to visit me. As a matter of a fact, just show up in a robe, and some slippers. Hell, you really don't need the robe because you have tinted windows, but seeing as it is winter, you really should cover your feet. I don't want you catchin' a cold or nothin'."

His statement tickled me to my core. We both fell over laughing. I looked at him. He looked at me. We beamed with happiness laced with concupiscence.

"I'll tell you what, Tyrique," I began. I touched his face as I said, "I'll always keep it interesting."

"You know I haven't been able to stop thinking about you."

"Really?" I asked, genuinely surprised.

"What did you do to me last Friday night? Did you put something in my drink?"

"I'm thinking it was you that slipped me a micky. Because, ever since I let you walk me to my car that Friday night, I have been acting completely out of character."

"Sometimes you just have to let your hair down."

"My hair was more than just let down, hell, as I recall, it was pulled."

"Did you like that?"

"Yes, I did."

"Tell me what else you like, Tia."

"I like going with the heat of the moment. I love to be caught up in a passion that's so strong that, I simply can't help myself. I love to be tempted, seduced. Tyrique darlin' you do all of the above very well. So tell me, what do you like?"

"I like it when a woman responds to me without hesitation; when a woman gives her all without being embarrassed afterwards. I like the way you look at me, Tia."

"How do I look at you?"

"Like you want me… Like you thoroughly enjoy me..."

"I do want you. I enjoyed you, tremendously. Tipsy or not, you had me coming back for more."

We laughed and talked for two hours. I had never been more comfortable in a man's company. I really did not want it to end. "Sweetness, it is time for me to go."

"Can you come back later?"

"Yes, just call me."

"I love it when you say yes to me."

"I really can't think of one single solitary reason to say no to you."

The notion of adulterous sin popped into my mind however I no longer allowed myself to care. I needed someone in my life to take away the pain. Post coital endorphins had such a magical way of doing just that. I negotiated an arrangement that I thought would be really easy to live with and enjoy. I had a secret that was willing to stay a secret. I firmly believed that making an agreement in the beginning would prevent the situation from getting twisted, however with experience comes knowledge. I needed to hurry home to take my pain meds before I began to fall apart. I made a mental note to place a few pills in my purse. Once I was on the freeway I called my house. Jack answered the phone.

"Hello."

"Jack, please get the girls ready to go."

"Are you still at Nikki's house?"

"No, I'm in my car on my way home. Tell the children to dress nice for the party at Irene's. Are you still going?"

"No, I'm not in the mood to deal with your family."

"Okay, just have the children ready by the time I get home. I'll be there in fifteen minutes, bye."

Let me call Nikki.

"Hello Tia. Where have you been?"

"I told you I had to go home and shower."

"That was almost four hours ago. Did you and Jack get into it again?"

"I don't want to talk about it. Are you going out to Irene's?"

"No, my car ain't running right but the kids want to go. Is Jack going?"

"No."

"So y'all did get into it?"

"I said I don't want to talk about Jack!" I yelled.

"Okay Tia. I'm sorry. Hey, can you come back by to pick up ya niece and nephew?"

"Sure, if you can get Mama to ride with Cory."

"Okay."

"I'll be there in about a half hour."

My oldest sister, Irene, planned a sobriety party for her husband Ronald. She wanted us to celebrate his one year mark as a family. I picked up my daughters, swung by Nicole's house to get her children and then continued on to my oldest sister's house. It was nice to see Irene and Ronald happy again. After the party I dropped my children off at home first, just in case I got a call from Tyrique. I wanted to see him again however I did not want to have to come up with an excuse to leave my house. I took Nicole's children home.

"Hey Nikki girl, I'm not going to stay."

"I understand. You look a bit worn out."

"Yeah, these children can be a handful. Well, I'm on my way home now, goodnight."

"Goodnight girl."

I was disappointed. I waited for his call with heightened anticipation. I was beguiled by the way my body anticipated his sex. I hungered for him to ravish my body again. My shoulders slumped as I walked to my car. I turned on some Saint Louis style hip hop music and sped away. Shortly after I left Nikki's house my cell phone rang. I looked at the call screen and smiled. It was Tyrique.

"Hello darlin'," I answered sweetly.

"Hey Baabay."

"How are you?"

"I'm fine. How was that party at Irene's?"

"It was nice. She cooked a lot of food. We all enjoyed each other's company."

"Would you like to enjoy my company tonight?"

"Yes, as a matter of fact, I would."

"I need your body in my bed right now. Come on over here Baabay."

"I'll be there in fifteen minutes."

I reached in my purse, grabbed my prescription bottle, fished out two pills, and swallowed them dry. I was good to go. I took a two hour detour which proved to be absolutely delightful, nevertheless, utterly depleting. By the time I left, I was exhausted.

I have always loved a magnum sized dick, regular or XL. Tyrique's was no exception. Plus he had youth and dexterity on his side. We shared more than just a forbidden fuck. We were engulfed with rapture. It was an uninhibited experience fortified with emotional passion and carnal indulgence. Our bodies intertwined, flesh to flesh, stroking, grinding, and moving as one. We were intimate, as if I had known him for years. Tyrique made me feel perfect. In his eyes I wasn't broken.

As I drove home that night, I still didn't feel guilty. I did however struggle with the fact that I was committing a sin against God. I questioned myself. What have you done? Who are you? Me, alone and dying. It was Sunday night, and I had made it through the weekend. I sincerely doubt if he'd call me anytime soon. We had our fun. We said things in the heat of the moment, but that was that. I was still scheduled for that Monday morning repenting session. I needed to bask in my afterglow for as long as possible. I needed to enjoy the memory of this experience as much as I can, in view of the fact that my life was a living hell. After all, it had been over fifteen years since I had good reason to be a damn heathen.

Monday morning marked the end of our clandestine affair. I was ready to ask God for forgiveness. The problem was I was not sorry. I erroneously assumed that with time, regret would begin to fill my heart. I patiently waited for that to happed for quite some time. Tyrique called me Monday night, and Tuesday night. The latter night we engaged in phone sex, which only made Wednesday's activities even hotter. Our evening of passion started off with a phone call. Tyrique called during his break on Wednesday afternoon.

"Hello Tyrique."

"Hey Baabay, what are you up to today?"

"I'm packing to leave town for a few days."

"Thanks for letting me know."

"Oh I'm so sorry." I stopped what I was doing. I sat down on my bed. "I was going to call you later on today and tell you."

"Umm-hmm," he uttered disbelievingly.

"Really I was. I have to take my mother to Mississippi for a funeral. After that, I'm going on to St. Louis to drop off my truck to my best friend. She is having a tough time of it. I have an extra vehicle so I thought to myself since I'm already going to be out that way, why not just drop it off to her."

"You are a good friend."

"Always," I proudly stated.

"So, you are driving all the way to Mississippi then to Missouri?"

"I'm not strong enough to make the drive. My mother will be doing most of the driving, so in reality I'll be riding along to keep her company."

"When will you be back?"

"We fly back on Monday afternoon."

"My break is almost over, but I'll call you later on tonight."

"All right."

"Bye Baabay."

"Bye Sweetness."

Tyrique always put a smile on my face. I quickly finished packing. Later on that evening, I was relaxing with a glass of wine when my cell phone rang.

"Hello Tyrique."

"Hey Baabay, come see me before you go. Are you free now?"

"Yes, I can be there in fifteen minutes."

"Come on."

"Alright, I'll see you in a few, bye."

I took an extra loratab. It was fifteen minutes brfore I had to get there, plus another ten to fifteen minutes before we got naked. So, I'd be good. I drank it down with a little wine. Hmm, maybe a half a glass more. That was it. Now I could get ready.

Jack was home which made getting out of the house was a little bit tricky but not impossible. I had just showered about a half an hour before Tyrique called. All I had to do was slip out of my panties and into a dress, slide into my shoes and leave the house. As I walked past my husband, who was sitting in his favorite spot in the living room playing video games, I started talking.

"I'm going to the store for some toiletries and other things I need for this trip. Okay, bye."

"Bye," Jack replied, eyes glued on the screen

I walked out of my home wearing a little burgundy turtleneck dress. The matching satin high heel shoes alone should have given me away. I knew Jack no longer paid attention to me.

Our marriage had been passionless for quite a while. Nonetheless, a part of me thought that Jack would notice or feel something if I started having an affair, which would mean he cared a little bit. But then I remembered his response when I told him that I was being tested for three different blood cancers. I knew deep down that Jack was no longer in love with me. It was painfully obvious that ill-fated day. His cold, calm demeanor, and heartless response burned into my soul forever. He did not care one damn bit about me, no matter how much I wanted him to. I told myself to quit hoping for something that was never going to happen and enjoy my time with Tyrique.

When I arrived Tyrique was standing outside waiting for me as usual. I liked that. He opened my car door. He helped me out of the car but before I could get my bearings, he took me into his arms and kissed me as if I was going off to war and he didn't know if he was ever going to see me again. The thought of us fucking on the hood of my car flashed through my mind. My succulent pussy throbbed with need. I thanked God I took that extra pain pill.

"Hello Tia," Tyrique said oozing sex appeal.

"Hmm, hmm…" After that kiss, all I could do was whisper, "Hi."

I could tell by the look in his eyes he was very satisfied by my response to his kiss. He took me by the hand and led me straight to his bedroom. I stepped out of my shoes, pulled my dress over my head, and stood there before him completely naked, smiling. He jumped out of his clothes in a flash. He gathered me up in his arms.

"You are so beautiful, Tia," Tyrique said, gazing into my eyes. "You make sure you drive carefully and come back here to me. This is only the beginning."

I did not know what to say to that, thankfully there was no need for words. As soon as Tyrique stopped talking he began kissing me again. He held me tight as he walked, pushing me backwards, to the bed. He lay me down, taking complete control. All I could do was react. His dick was hard as steel with precum dripping from the tip down my leg. I spread my legs as we scooted into the bed. My body was hot with need—primal expectancy. I anticipated the sweet pain of the first thrust, his dick entering my flesh filling my delta inch by inch. He kissed his way down my body to the folds of my pussy. Tyrique licked my clit, and tongue fucked my pussy until I came all over his face.

"Are you ready for me, Tia?"

"Hell yeah, Tyrique! Fuck me, Sweetness! Fuck me now!"

Scissor position, tucked in tight, we fucked like animals in heat. My head was thrown back, my fingernails dug into his right bicep, and his left butt cheek. With labored breath I toiled, moving my body with his until orgasm after orgasm gripped my body, and carried me away. Each climax was more powerful than the one it followed. We were lost in sexual decadence. I felt his hot cum explode inside my body. After he was done all I could do was lay there staring up at the ceiling.

"Tia?"

"Yes Tye."

"Are you alright?"

"Umm, hmmm."

"You haven't moved a muscle since we finished."

"I can't."

"I didn't hurt you, now did I?"

"No, Sweetness, you didn't hurt me," I said, although I thought, at least not in a bad way.

"Then what is it?"

"You make me weak. I'm too tired to move right now. My bones and muscles feel like jelly." I looked over to him my eyes gave emphasis to my feelings. He looked at me. He was very proud of himself, yet not cocky. I said, "Can't you see that even my eyelids are droopy?" Then my face beamed with a huge smile.

He gathered me in his arms so my head could rest on his chest. He stroked my hair, the way he did the time before. Only this time, he kissed the top of my head every so often, as well. Feeling his genuine affection hurt my feelings I immediately wondered how a stranger could show more care and warmth than my own husband. I refused to cry. I looked at everything realistically. One day at a time. No regrets.

My diary was my best friend and confidant. Tyrique was a temporary lover.

CHAPTER ELEVEN
THE PERFECT LOVER

The next week passed so fast that there was no telling where the time went. Most of my time was spent on the road. By Monday morning I was so looking forward to flying back home. I missed Tyrique. I thought about him often while I was gone. I called him the moment I arrived at my house.

"Hey Baabay, you home?"

"Yes I just got in."

"You go'n come see me?"

"Hell yeah!"

He let out a little sexy laugh, and said, "All right then Tia baby, I'll be home by six."

"I'll be there by six-fifteen."

He laughed again then said, "I knew that there was something that I liked about you, Miss Tia."

"All right, Sweetness," I said. A little sexy throaty laugh escaped. "Get back to work. Call me later."

"I'm go'n do more than just call ya girl."

"Hmm, don't threaten me with a delightful time."

"Delightful?"

"Oh hell yeah. Don't I sound absolutely delighted the whole time we're together, doin' what we do?"

His voice grew deeper, and sexier when he said, "Ah yeah, you do. Especially when I have your left leg crossed over my left shoulder."

"Yeah, I do like that."

"You know what I'm go'n go to you first?"

"Tell me baby." I said. I sat back and closed my eyes so I could picture everything that he said as he said it.

"First I'm gone take every stitch of clothes off of yo body."

"Mm-hmm…."

"Then I'm go'n ta have ya stand in the middle of my room with your legs spread really, really wide."

"Really?"

"Oh yeah, really."

"Why would you have me standing like that?"

"So I can get atcha. I'm go'n lick your click until you can't stand up no more."

My click…? Did he just say click? He was definitely country but I liked it. "What if I loose my balance?" I smiled.

"Oh, no need to worry 'cause I'll catch ya then carry you off to my bed where I can really… Oh shit! I gotta call you back. Look at what you got me doin'. I'm sitting here like I'm at home talking to you. I've got everybody up in here looking at me like I'm crazy."

I could not help but laugh a little. My vivid imagination created a clear picture of Tyrique looking up just to find everyone staring at him like he had gone and lost his mind. Tyrique was air traffic control, small space, no privacy.

"Hang up the phone, Tyrique. I'll see you tonight."

"Yes you will."

I had hours to kill therefore I took my time getting ready for the evening. I pampered myself with a personal spa day. I began with a Brazilian wax. I arched my eyebrows, washed my hair, medicated, and lay down for a nap. I woke up refreshed. I took an effervescent bubble bath. The bubbles tickled my skin. I wiggled my toes and giggled like a child. I sat at my vanity swathed in my dark red plush cotton robe. I wrapped a heat pad around my left shoulder before I painstakingly fashioned my hair in spiral curls. I applied my makeup, perfectly highlighting my eyes with hues of gold and black. The weather was uncharacteristically cold. I wanted to wear something warm but sexy and really easy to take off. I chose a black Baby Phat cold shoulder velour jump suit, no panties, and a pair of black strap chain high heel booties.

I arrived at Tyrique's house promptly at six thirteen. The look in his eyes was surprisingly desirous. I looked down at myself to see what he was actually looking at. After all I was wearing a fancy jogging suit. I followed his gaze to the apex of my body. The black velour fabric accentuated my pussy perfectly. I allowed my eyes to roam his body. We looked up into each other's eyes. I smiled at him. It was nice to know my efforts were appreciated.

"Come on over here, Tia, and give me my hug. Girl, I have missed you."

"I missed you too."

He held me tight. He led me by the hand into the house. As soon as the door was locked he grabbed me by the front of my pants and pulled me into his bedroom. He turned and yanked me to him. My body collided with his. He wrapped his arms around me as he bent me backwards. I held on tight.

"I hope you're ready for me Baabay, 'cause I'm go'n show you just how much I've missed you."

"Hmm Tye. Let's strip down, and get started Sweetness."

He righted me. The moment he turned me loose I stepped back, taking my shoes off with each step. I smiled at him all the while. I jumped out of my clothes like they were on fire.

"Well damn! Now that's what I'm talkin' 'bout," he exclaimed.

A laugh escaped me before I replied, "I learned it from you, Tyrique. I've never seen anyone get naked as fast as you do."

"Well you know everybody's got a skill or two."

I smiled brightly as I thought: you've got more than a skill or two, that's for damn sure. You've got gifts and natural talent. I giggled a little as I climbed up into his bed. Before I could get myself situated he was naked and slowly walking towards me, like a predator. I was so very excited. I smiled and then licked my tongue out at him playfully. I lay back. I opened up to him and all of the pleasures I knew we would share that night.

Tyrique began nibbling my inner thighs and soon there after I was lost. His every touch quietly whispered I missed you. Every part of my being answered back I missed you too.

"Stop," I said abruptly.

"What's wrong Tia?"

"Let me… After all I have missed you too."

"Okay Baabay."

"Lie on your stomach."

He looked unsure but he did as I instructed. I let my hair glide over the posterior of his body. He loved it. He cooed with delight. I caressed his flesh calming his goose bumps before telling him to turn over again.

"Tia…" Tyrique all but purred, reluctant to move.

"Turn over. This is about to get really good," I coaxed.

"What do you have in mind?"

"I am going to do some sweet things to your body followed by a wicked thing or two, but you'll like it, all of it. Trust me."

He did. That night we took things very slowly. We overindulged in sexual pleasures, basking in naughty decadence. I poured spumante over his balls and licked them clean. I bathed his dick with my tongue until it was distended. Once I felt the pulsating hum of his engorged dick I knew it could not get any harder. It was time to ride. I straddled up lining the head of his dick perfectly with my pussy. I pushed my kegal muscles out as I lowered myself inch my inch until he was deep inside of my flesh. I squeezed tight closing my vaginal walls on his cock like a death grip. He cried out which only spurred me on. I rode his dick hard. I put his body through its paces—sexing him with amorous greed. I fucked him instead of being the one who was fucked. He tried to take control however I would not allow it. The moment my body betrayed me he began to dominate.

Damn my hip! I hated what that drunk bitch did to me! Oh my God this hurts. My pills should have kicked in by now. I needed a break. I couldn't let him know I was in pain. I couldn't allow our paradisiacal fantasy life to be ruined.

"Tye," I said, slowing the pace. "I can't cum anymore. I'm too dehydrated," I said, dismounting. "Will you pour me some more wine, please?" I asked as I stretched out on the bed.

"Sure Tia," Tyrique said, filling my glass before handing it to me. "I'll eat your pussy while you take your little drink break."

Tyrique licked my pussy gently, lulling my body until the pain subsided. My gratitude could not be measured. With my libido reprised my orgasmic bliss climaxed quickly. I came. I reached for Tyrique's dick gobbling it up like I was starving. I couldn't get my fill of him—ravenous greed—sexual gluttony. I sucked and sucked, keeping his dick hot and wet. He came in my mouth. His dick was deep in my throat. I swallowed every drop as he bucked wildly.

When all was said and done we both looked at each other sheepishly. I could tell that Tyrique's feeling of taboo outweighed mine. We showered together for the first time. He gently washed my body, all the while deep in thought. After our shower he asked to talk. I agreed. I took my time dressing. I found him in the kitchen. He was in his boxers.

"Tia, I poured us a drink."

"Thank you."

He handed me a cognac neat, his was with cranberry.

I did not understand why we needed a drink as we had already finished a bottle of wine with our sex and I needed to drive home.

"Come on into the living room and have a seat with me."

"Okay."

I noticed that he brought the bottle of cognac in with us.

"So, tell me about your trip Tia."

"Most of my time was spent on the road. My mother and I took a lot of pictures. All in all we enjoyed the trip. We even stopped in Louisiana for some crawfish."

"That sounds nice."

"What's really on your mind?"

He started to look sheepish again. I could tell he was thinking about our bedroom antics. I waited for him to broach the subject.

"I was just thinking about earlier."

"What about it?"

"We did things."

"Yes we did."

"I know that we got caught up. I just want to make sure you are alright with everything that happened. I want to make sure I didn't make you do anything you didn't want to do."

"You didn't."

"Are you sure?"

"Yes, I'm sure."

Tyrique's look of disbelief spoke volumes. I imagined that he thought that I was too unaffected. That I was just biding my time with him until I could get the hell out of there and never see him again. He kept refilling our glasses. On the third refill I had to speak up.

"You know that I have to drive home."

"You are not leaving right now, are you?"

"No, not right now but I do need to be sober by the time I do decide to leave."

"You will be." He held my hand. "You could always stay here."

"Is there something else on your mind?"

"You just seem to be a little bit too calm."

"Calm, about what?" I asked satisfied that I had him pegged.

"Tia, we did get a little bit freaky."

"A little bit?"

"See I knew that you had a problem with it. You don't have to be ashamed."

I smiled as I looked into his eyes. "I'm not ashamed or embarrassed. Why would you think that?"

"It's just that we got carried away."

"We missed each other. Let me put your mind to rest. If I wanted you to stop I would have said so. I have been with the same man for fifteen years. There's nothing that I have not done at least once. Throw in some gadgets and handcuffs, and then it would have been really freaky. Am I making myself clear?" I smiled a lusty she devil smile as I lifted one eyebrow for emphasis.

"Very. We're going to have to try some of that gadget and handcuff stuff."

"Yes, we do."

"You are a naughty girl."

"Yes, I'm very naughty—kinky even. The best part is I'm not the least bit ashamed about it."

"Really?"

"Really," I assured him. "So, could you please stop looking at me like that? A little bit of kinky sex is not going to run me off. I licked wine off of your balls, my idea not yours."

He laughed. It was more a laugh of relief than anything else. I was glad he was not worried anymore. We decided to watch a movie. I stretched out on the couch laying my head on his lap. I fell asleep almost immediately. I woke up just before the movie ended.

"Hmm," I purred, stretching in satisfaction.

"Hello sleepy head."

"I'm sorry I dozed off. I guess I was really worn out."

"You must have been."

"Just one question…"

"What?"

"Did I fall asleep with your friend on my cheek or did he come out to say hello after I fell asleep?"

"You kept moving your head so he peaked out to see if you were trying to play with him or what. He didn't know you were sleeping."

I spoke directly to his dick. "Is that true? Are you ready to play with me again? Come here."

What started as a little playfulness, turned into a sexy wrestling craze on the living room floor. We fucked hard and fast changing positions like wrestlers making every effort not to get pinned. We both had a few carpet burns by the time we were done. They were really vivid the next day. How the hell was I going to explain these? I wondered.

Three days before Valentine's, we had been lovers for all of eleven days. My diary had developed into the beginnings of a novel manuscript, the naked confession that none of my friends and family would ever believe.

CHAPTER TWELVE
VALENTINE'S DAY

The icing on the cake was definitely Valentine's Day. I had spent every holiday since Thanksgiving, including my birthday without my husband. It had only been two weeks since my affair with Tyrique began. I decided to make plans with my home girl Tammy. Jack walked into my room the minute he heard the shower go off. He had been home for about two hours, yet nothing was said, not even a hello. But wouldn't you know he found his tongue when I was getting dressed to go? At first he just stood there watching me dry off, perfume, and moisturize, however the minute I reached for my red g-string the shit hit the fan.

"Where the hell do think you are going?" he asked, hostility filling his eyes.

"Out," I replied casually.

"With who?" he asked as he stood there gawking.

"Tammy."

"It's Valentine's Day, the day for lovers."

"I know."

"Oh so what is she, your lover now?"

His insult fell on deaf ears. I knew he wanted to hurt my feelings. However, I instantly thought about Tyrique and I smiled. I no longer carried my heart on my sleeve.

"No Jack, she is not. If I ever chose a lover he would be about half your age."

Everything in me wanted to crack up laughing but somehow I held it all in except for the tickled smile which was plastered all over my face.

"That shit ain't funny." He retorted, not knowing what else to say.

"Neither was asking me if Tammy is my lover. I keep telling you to watch what you say to me or you'll get your feelings hurt. I'm dying Jack. I have nothing to lose."

"I made plans for us today."

"Really?"

"Yes, I want to spend Valentine's Day with my wife."

"Why?"

"Because you are my wife… I thought I'd take you to dinner then we could come home and go to bed."

"Oh sweet Jesus, how romantic I just don't think I can turn down such a well thought out evening. I mean damn, you must have put a whole lot of thought and planning into your night of magic."

"You don't have to be so damn sarcastic all of the time."

"Really? Then let me put it like this, I am not sleeping with you just because you take me dinner. You must have me confused with someone else. What did you think? Did you really believe you could insult me every chance you got, ignore me for months on end, wait for Valentine's Day to roll around and then what; buy me a twenty dollar dinner and I'd fuck you again? You know damn well that kind of shit will never work on a woman like me. I don't get all mushy just because of a pissy ass holiday."

"I just thought today would be the best day possible to try again with you."

"What?"

"I know I've been treating you wrong, Tia. I want to make up for it."

"Let me tell you what I hear. 'I want some pussy tonight so I will play nice, yet, do as little as possible to get some. Tia should be super horny by now.' Well guess what, you are soo sadly mistaken."

"What, do you have plans to meet someone else besides Tammy?" he shouted. "Is the new man you've been fucking going to be at the club? I'm going wherever you are going tonight!"

"No, no, and suit yourself."

I took the wind right out of his sails. He was practically dumbfounded. He stood there fuming. I continued to dress. I wore a white angora and wool sweater dress which clung nicely to my nee figure and accessorized in red.

"Will you go to dinner with me first?"

"Sure, as long as you are buying for the entire night."

He took me to dinner at an Italian restaurant. However it was completely unremarkable. After dinner, he wanted to go back home, and have sex. I refused. Instead, I drove to a popular club downtown. Although I prayed that Jack would not embarrass me, I took precautions.

"Tia, why are we sitting in the corner? Do you always sit in the corner when you come to the club?"

"Jack, my love. Please give it a rest."

"What are you hiding from or should I ask who?"

"No one. As you can see, this is the only available table. I could have sat somewhere else if we had gotten here earlier."

"Why is that man looking at you?"

"What man?"

"The one in the blue suit."

"Where?"

"Quit playing games, Tia, that man right there," Jack hissed.

"I don't know I am beautiful, men are bound to look."

"Do you know him?"

"You mean in the biblical since? Uh, no. As a matter of fact, I do not."

"You know damn well what I mean."

"No, but I see someone that I do know so, if you'll excuse me I'll be right back."

"You ain't going nowhere," he said loudly.

"Fine, I will just wave him over."

"Him! Who the hell is he?"

"You really do need to calm the fuck down or get the hell on away from me. I will not sit here and let you embarrass me at the club." My voice was calm yet chastising. "You are worse than a woman coming up in here in her yellow polka dot house coat, pink hair rollers, and green house shoes looking for her baby daddy and his new bitch, talking about her baby need some new shoes."

"I know for a fact that you, are or werc, meeting someone here tonight."

"You are right. I've already told you I'm meeting Tammy. We were going to have a girls' night out. What?"

"We have been here for thirty minutes and I don't see Tammy." Jack accused.

"She must be running late."

"We could have stopped by home for some quality time."

"Don't you mean two minutes worth of sex? I really don't think so... That shit ain't quality."

"There has to be someone else."

"I'll tell you what, if you behave tonight I'll give you some pussy the minute we get home. But I'm telling you this for the last time, stop trying to make a scene or I won't fuck you for a month of Sundays. I'll be right back. I have to go to the ladies' room."

I was mortified. I called Tammy the moment I walked into the ladies' room.

She answered the phone, and immediately said, "I know, I know, I know. Before you say anything, Tia, I'm sorry. But you know it couldn't be helped."

"That's not why I'm calling."

"What's up girl?"

"Jack is here."

"What?"

"Yes, girl. He said he was going wherever I was going tonight then jumped into my car."

"Girl, no!"

"Um-hmm, so if you still want to come..."

"Hell yeah, I ain't gonna just leave you in the lurch."

"He already thinks I'm lying about us having plans for a girls night out. He is scoping out the club trying to see who's looking at me too hard or for too long. That bastard has been commenting about each and every brotha who allows his eyes to wander in my direction."

"Oh no," she exclaimed.

"Yes, please believe me."

"I'll be right there."

"Thank you Tammy. I just hope Tyrique doesn't show up."

"Don't say that or it will happen."

"You're right, but it is too late. I have already put it out there."

"We can play it off no matter what."

"True, true," I said as I nodded my head in agreement.

"Alright girl, hang up the phone so I can hurry up and get there."

"Okay, bye."

"Bye."

I guess I must have taken too long because the moment I walked out of the bathroom there was Jack, standing close by. All I could think was, you have got to be kidding me. I took a calming breath before I walked over to him.

"Hey Jack."

"What took you so long?"

"It's the ladies' room, there is always a line. Look there's four women going in at once right now."

"Well do you want another drink?"

"Yes, please. I'll have an Amaretto sour."

"Okay baby."

"Thank you. I'm going to go back to our table and wait for Tammy."

"Stay right here, we can go together."

"Alright."

Thirty minutes after we returned to the table Tammy showed up. At first Jack was polite and civil, but within an hour he was back to being raunchy. He had the nerve to start talking about me not wanting to suck his dick. He spoke loud enough so that anyone near by could hear every word.

"Jack I already told you I will never suck your dick ever again because you cheated on me. I meant that. We were free and clear of anyone else's germs and you know damn well that we got downright freaky all over the house but after my accident you would not accept my limitations. I tried for you but I just wasn't enough, now was I?"

Besides which, I have a new dick to suck whenever I want. Oh and what a nice young dick it is. A nice fresh twenty-three year old dick that stays hard for more than two minutes at a time.

"That's not what I'm talking about Tia and you know it."

"You cannot talk about your desert dick without me talking about your wayward dick. Ask me again in ten years... I just might say yes."

"Damn it Tia!"

"I'm going to the ladies' room."

I couldn't think of a better excuse to leave and I didn't care if he believed me or not. I got up, walked away, went out to the patio and bummed a cigarette from a friend of mine. He is a Jamaican man in his fifties that I had known for almost three years. We used to work together before my accident. Wouldn't you know, before I was even half way finished with my cigarette, Jack walked up to me.

"This doesn't look like the ladies' room to me," Jack said, his hostility was obsessive.

"I'm done with you and your attitude, Jack. I'm leaving."

I apologized and said goodbye to Tammy. When we got home I went to my bedroom and locked the door. I couldn't believe that I was at home at eight thirty on a Friday night. I undressed and got into my bed. My cell phone rang at nine. I answered it without looking at the call screen.

"Hello."

"Hey pretty lady, happy Valentine's Day."

I cheered up instantly. "Hello Tyrique. Happy Valentine's Day to you as well..."

"So Miss Tia, what do you have planned for tonight?"

"Absolutely nothing; as a matter of a fact I'm already in bed."

"I bought you a present."

"Did you?" I smiled brightly.

"Yeah Baabay."

"I got you something as well," I lied.

"Aaw, you go'n have me thinkin' that I'm special."

"You are."

"Do you think that you can come see me tomorrow?"

"Yes, that would be nice."

"I'll call you."

"All right."

"Good night, Tia."

"Good night, Tyrique."

I should have taken the hint and went over that night to get my present, but I just could not get out of the bed. However, the next day would be a whole different story.

CHAPTER THIRTEEN
MY JOURNEY BEGINS

The day after Valentine's Day I regretted not getting out of bed and making the most of Valentine's night. As I sat in his bed waiting for him to bring me a drink, I was thinking. This was what I should have been doing yesterday. I took my meds forty-five minutes before I arrived in an attempt not to have a repeat of the pain I experienced last time we were together. I was ready when he made his approach.

"Here's your drink Baabay."

"Sweetness, I said Jack on the rocks, not ice tea." He smiled a sheepish smile. I thought, damn that glass is kind of full, however I said, "Oh so you're trying to get me drunk?"

"Naw, I just want to make sure you don't get thirsty."

"Aw okay. But just to let you know this won't get me drunk or even tipsy. I have an unusually high tolerance. You'll go broke trying to get me drunk. That's why I drink water when I'm over here."

"Really?"

"Oh yes. You want me to show you?"

"Go for it." I downed the whole glass. His eyes widened as he exclaimed, "Damn! I'm scared of you."

"You aught to be," I declared.

Being with him was amazing. I could barely believe how much my outlook on life had changed in just two short weeks. We fucked for over an hour, ending in doggie style. I came fifteen times. Our love making was more than just satisfying, it was quickly becoming mind-blowing. He gathered me in his arms intertwining his legs with mine. I rested momentarily.

"Okay it's time for my shower. Let me untangle my legs and get up."

"No, don't get up yet."

"All right."

"Tia?"

"Yes Tye?"

"I'm leaving in ten days."

"Where are you going?"

"Back home to Atlanta."

"How long will you be gone?"

"Oh about three and a half weeks."

"Damn, I'll miss you."

"I'm gon' miss you too, boo." Tyrique held me tight. "But we can make the most of the next ten days."

It's too bad I started my period the very next day. Alas I had to face reality. Leukemia, lymphoma, myloma, leukemia, lymphoma, myloma… So sorry Tia, I didn't know how else to tell you this… Leukemia, lymphoma, myloma… Cancer. My doctor was sorry but my husband wasn't. My daddy cried however my husband didn't show any emotion. Today was the beginning of my journey, my first visit to an oncologist. Leukemia, lymphoma, myloma… God help me. I called my daddy.

"Hello?"

"Hi Pop, I'm leaving the house right now. Are you ready?"

"Yeah, come on."

"Thank you for going with me."

"You're my baby, there's no place else I'd rather be."

"I'll see you in a few minutes."

As I drove I kept telling myself that it was only a test. I had not been diagnosed with cancer. The tests were for elimination purposes. I had my daddy going with me. I was not alone. I needed to simply go and do what I had to do. I had to stay calm, be still. With a still heart, calm emotions, and a clear head I could handle anything. I prayed that everything would be all right. I picked up my father. He walked slowly towards the car, looking intensely worried.

"Good morning Pop," I greeted him cheerfully. "Seatbelt."

"Good morning child. How are you holding up?"

"I'm fine daddy." I looked him dead in the eye for emphasis. I turned forward, put my car in gear, and drove on down the road.

"Well it's a shame that your husband could not take even a half day off of work to go with you."

"Yes it is, but I'm not faithful to him anyway so it doesn't even matter."

"What?"

"Yes Daddy, I'm a bad-bad girl."

"Now you know—"

"Wait a minute now, Pop. Before you get started, think about the last fifteen months of hell that I've gone through. I've had to endure a whole lot, so please don't ask me to let go of what little joy I have, especially in such trying times. Just pray for me. Okay?"

"Okay, but you know—"

"I know, but let's just recap the last ninety days. Shall we?" I took a deep breath. "On Thanksgiving, he spent a whopping two hours with his family. Christmas, he was a no show all together. New Year's Eve, I got stood up at the last minute. My birthday, nothing, no plans, presents, or flowers and I paid for my own frozen lasagna dinner. Valentine's Day, he followed me to the club and started more than one argument." I gripped the steering wheel. "Then of course there's today. Do you see him? Because I sure don't. Not only that, please keep in mind that when I told him about this six weeks ago he didn't care. He cold heartedly told me to make myself happy, so that is exactly what I did."

"How long has this been going on?"

"Three weeks. He was my belated birthday gift to myself and my Valentine last week. He gave me the sweetest card, a large box of Belgium chocolates, that stuffed animal right there in my window, and these garnet earrings."

"I see."

"No, I don't think you do. I was hit by a drunk driver fifteen months ago. Now I am permanently disabled. While I was doing my level best to get my body rehabilitated my lying cheating husband hurt me every chance he got. Now I am facing a cancer prognosis. He has turned his back on me completely, when I needed him the most. The new man in my life is my happy thought in the midst of all this heartache and sadness. He has no idea how much he means to me right now."

I stopped talking before I slipped up. My father's health was not strong enough to help me through. I had no one else to cling to. No one else cared. My heart ached with despair. I desperately wanted to cry on my father's shoulder however I could not. I focused on the road, refusing to allow a single tear to escape my eyes.

"Just be careful." My father advised.

"I will."

The appointment went quickly, thank God. My father looked as if he was heart broken and seconds away from stroking out the whole time we were there. I chose to speak with the doctor alone. She went over my MRI and explained that it would take several months and many blood tests to get a handle on my condition. We started with HIV, anemia, and multiple myloma testing. After the appointment I drove my father to his house. I smiled happily as I lied about what the doctor said. I showed him a prescription for iron supplements and stated emphatically that I most likely had acute anemia, which seemed to calm his heart. The moment after I dropped him off tears began to stream uncontrollably. I pulled over and wept. I have no idea how long. I was on my way home when my phone rang. I answered it without checking the call screen.

"Hello?"

"Hello pretty lady."

"Hello Tyrique."

Oh God, how did he know that I needed to hear from him right now? I didn't tell him about my appointment today.

"How are you today?"

"Wonderfully well now that you have called."

"Were you having a bad day?"

"No, my morning was trying however I don't want to talk about it. How's your day darlin'?"

"Oh Baabay, they are working me like the first African slave."

"Hmm, you seem to like it when I work you like a sex slave."

"Now see that's different. Hell, you be there working hard right along with me."

"Well you know... I do try. I mean, I figured if we're both working towards the same goal then I should be working just as hard as you do."

"I knew that there was something that I really liked about you."

"What, my work ethic?"

"Yeah that's it."

We both laughed.

"Tia, what are you doing Saturday?"

"You?"

"Good answer. Come by for lunch. I'll cook you some crab legs and shrimp."

"That sounds lovely. What do you want me to bring?"

"A steamer for the crab legs, if you've got one, or I'll just boil them."

"I have one. I'll bring it with me."

"Okay good. I have to go. I'll see you Saturday."

"Yes you will."

I continued driving home smiling the whole way. Saturday morning rolled around. My period was over just in the nick of time. Tyrique called at twelve forty five.

"Hello darlin'."

"Hello Baabay. Come see me."

"I'm on my way."

All morning long Jack had been gone 'grocery shopping.' It took him six hours to buy about a hundred dollars worth of groceries. Jack walked in the door as I was on my way down the hall. I stepped into the bathroom until he turned into the kitchen. The very minute I heard him put the bags down; I scurried on down the hall and out the door. I was well on my way down the street by the time Jack realized I had left the house. I laughed like a schoolgirl. I snuck out of the house for the first time in my life. I was thirty-two years old. My cell phone rang and rang but I didn't answer. Tyrique met me at the car as usual.

"You look lovely today Tia."

"Why thank ya. The steamer is in the back, it's open."

"All right, let me get that." He quickly grabbed the pot before taking me by the hand. "Come on in and get comfortable, I just started cooking."

"Do you need any help?"

"No, I got this. All I have to do is put the crab legs in the steamer and turn down the heat on the shrimp a little bit," I followed him into the kitchen and watched him work. "Okay, perfect. Now we can work up an appetite."

"You ain't said nothin' but a word." I could barely contain my excitement.

"Come on to the room." Tyrique invited, he lead the way.

I giggled and all but ran right behind him. I began undressing while he closed the blinds. He turned around just as I was bending over, sliding off my ice pink thong.

"Well damn! Look at all that ass! Girl!"

I giggled again as I glanced up at him. I righted myself. I ran the bottom ball of my tongue ring across my lips before climbing into the bed. Tyrique lit a candle and turned on some music. He was naked in a flash, as usual. Tyrique had a way of making me want to give as good as I got, no matter what. That day was no different except I gave a bit little too much. I could not move at all, I was in so much pain. I closed my eyes and smiled in an attempt to mask my agony. He kissed my cheek.

"Go shower darlin, I'll be right there," I said.

He was in no hurry to go. I prayed that he would leave before a tear rolled down my face. I could not bear for him to see me as a cripple. A moan escaped me. I rolled over onto my stomach and lay with my face turned away from him.

"Baabay, are you alright?"

Hell no! I was a thirty two year old cripple trying to act like an eighteen year old gymnast. I was doing well, until I fucked up on my dismount. Damn it! I should have taken an extra pill before I left the house. The pain was getting intense, but I concentrated on sounding sexy and pleasure filled.

"Oh yes, I just need to catch my breath, and stretch my body for a moment. So go on and take your shower, I'll be right there."

"Okay, because I'm hungry."

"You should be."

My mind was screaming get the hell out! Get the hell out! Get the hell out! Why the hell won't you just leave?

"The robe is right here on the back of the door," Tyrique said unsure. "I'll leave the towels laid out for you on the bathroom sink."

"Hmm, thank you Tyrique," I purred. My thought was saying, now get out! You can't see me cry, damn it.

Up until the moment I heard the door close, I had not realized that I was holding my breath. I exhaled slowly, wiped the tears from my face, took the meds I retrieved from my purse and began my stretches. After a few minutes the pain began to subside. I was naked in the middle of my last stretch when he returned to the room.

"Well damn," he all but shouted.

"Why thank ya."

"You had better get the hell up out of that bed before I get back in there."

"Oh shit! Let me get up. I'm already hungry and weak." I let my leg flop back down onto the bed. "Damn it," I smiled.

"Come on, baby. I'll help you up. I left the shower on for you."

"You are soo good to me, Tye."

"I'll go to the kitchen and make our plates."

"Thank ya darlin'. I'll make it quick." After my shower, I walked into the kitchen. "Hey sexy man. Everything smells so good."

"It tastes good too." He licked his lips and wiggled his eyebrows at me. I could not help but smile up at him sheepishly. He dished up our plates. "I set everything up in the living room and picked out a movie."

"That sounds nice."

"Follow me."

Tyrique put his plate on the floor and started to sit down beside it. I placed my plate on the loveseat behind me. He was halfway between the couch and floor when he sprang back up to sit on the couch. I smiled.

"Go ahead and sit, get comfortable." I encouraged. "I'm sitting down on the floor with you. I just didn't want to put my plate on the floor." Tyrique smiled at me as he relaxed on the floor. "I keep telling you that I'm not snooty."

We shared a wonderful meal. We laughed as we watched a movie about not drinking juice in the hood, thoroughly enjoying each other's company. My heart felt at peace. I knew if I was not careful I would fall for him. He wrapped his arms around my waist and kissed my cheek.

"Hmm Tye, I could so easily get used to you."

"And I you," he chimed in perfectly. There was a knock at the door. Tyrique got up and helped me up as well. He looked at his watch as he walked to the door. I sat in the overstuffed chair. "Oh shit I forgot I had friends coming over. I was supposed to go play basketball."

"Oh okay, I can go now. I'll come back for my steamer another day." I got up. I reached for my purse and keys.

"Whatchu doin'? Fuck them niggas, I can play basketball anytime. You ain't goin' no where."

I sat back down. Tyrique opened the front. In walked two of his friends. Before they could say as much as a hello Tyrique said, "I ain't going."

The men were immediately agitated. They bellowed, "What do you mean you ain't going?"

"I've got better things to do," Tyrique said, looking at me, they followed his gaze.

"Hi," I said, looking up at them innocuously.

The fellas warmed up to me right away. They didn't wait for Tyrique to make introductions. They walked up to me and introduced themselves. One of the men was looking at me a bit too intently. I excused myself.

"I'm going to step outside for a smoke," I announced.

His friends stayed for a short while. When they left Tyrique joined me out on the terrace.

"My friends like you, Tia."

"Really? I like them too, but not as much as I like you."

He smiled at me. I wiggled my finger for him to come closer to me. He looked behind himself and then back at me. He pointed to himself as he mouthed, 'me?' I smiled.

"Yes you. Come on over here."

Tyrique did a baby-trot halfway then he stopped. "Come on, I've got somethin' for ya."

He took a few more baby steps my way, stopping just out of my reach. I took a step towards him closing the distance between us. I grabbed him by the front of his pants. I took a step back and returned to my seat, pulling him along with me as I sat. I looked up into his eyes and smiled deviously.

"Let's play a little game," I suggested.

"What kind of game?"

"Let's see just how quiet you can be."

He looked a bit confused, however he understood the object of the game the moment I began to unzip his pants.

"Look at what you got me doing." He looked around nervously before looking back at me. "For real, Tia?"

"Oh yeah, don't get us caught. Ready, set, go." I took the head of his dick into my mouth savoring the taste of him. I paused. "Don't forget, you're the look out Tye." He moaned his pleasure. "Shush, you are supposed to be trying to be as quiet as possible. You can be quiet, now can't you?"

"Yeah."

"Okay good. Do that."

I continued, however, I wanted to see just how much he could take. He spoke fast gibberish. His voice was loud and high pitched. I watched his toes curl in his socks. I felt him sway a little bit. I'm more than sure that a feather could've knocked him off kilter all together. I felt sexy, powerful. He grabbed the wall topping as the palm of his other hand hit the window. I stopped. "That's not being quiet, Tye."

Tyrique began as he knelt down before me. He wrapped my legs around his neck and gripped my ass before he said, "Let's see just how quiet you can be, Miss Tia."

Oh hell yeah, was the first thought that entered my mind, yet I calmly replied, "I can be very, very quiet my dear."

He skillfully ate my pussy, sucking my clitoris and tickling my g-spot. The only noise that escaped me was the soft sugary sound of my passion filled breaths. The pleasure was undeniable. Although I might have emitted a squeak or two as I climaxed, I was far quieter that he. I wanted to scream, more than once.

"I love the way you cum, pretty lady."

"You have to stop before my pants are too wet to wear. Hell, my thong is already a lost cause."

"I don't see the problem."

"Say what?"

"I have a washer and dryer. You need to come one more time before I take you back to the room, soo."

"Wait." Tyrique swirled his tongue around my clit once more. "Ooh Sweetness, there you go…" I had to keep quiet. My heart quickened. My breath became short. A sweet teeny tiny moan escaped me as I came once more. It took my every effort not to scream out his name. "I told you I could be quiet."

"You were not quiet."

"Oh I was quiet, compared to you. Hell, I'm surprised you didn't break the damn window," I laughed.

"Hell, I wouldn't've cared." He took me by the hand pulling me up out of the chair. "You were sitting the whole time Tia. You had a death grip on my arms as you were making your pretty little noises. I was standing. But that's okay, 'cause uh, we go'n see just how quiet you stay."

Tyrique's lusty stare was followed up by wonton action. He slid his two fingers into my pussy, as if I was a fleshy bowling ball, and turned his back to me. He guided me to his room pulling me by my pussy all the way. A mixture of fear and excitement coursed through my whole being. My pussy walls greedily gripped his fingers. I almost came. He fucked me with his fingers. He fucked me with his tongue. He fucked me with his dick. I cried out as orgasmic raptures ripped through my body.

When the time came for me to go, he walked me to my car. We embraced, he held on to me so tight that I didn't want him to let me go; however, I knew I had to be on my way.

"I have to go, Sweetness."

"I know Tia."

"Hurry back to me Tyrique. I'll truly miss you."

"Not as much as I'll miss you."

CHAPTER FOURTEEN
DISTANCE

Oh my God, this is turning into more than an affair, I realized as I drove home. Tyrique had developed feelings for me. I chastised myself for not seeing the signs before. He had become affectionate. He offered me a drawer to keep my toiletries at his home. The tender look he gave after he kissed me goodbye touched my heart. He watched me drive away.

I believed that his leaving came at the perfect time. If what I saw in his eyes was real, he was trouble. I needed to end it. I am slowly bleeding to death yet the doctors have no idea why. I need fun, not a relationship. I was lost in thought for most of the drive home. I needed advice. I called my best friend.

"Hey Tia."

"Hey Tammy, how are you?"

"I'm good. How are you?"

"I don't know. Are you busy now?"

"No. Why? What's wrong?"

"I'm knee deep in a situation that I have no idea how to handle. I cannot figure out how to put the whole thing into perspective."

"What have you done Tia?"

"Bless me sista girl for I have sinned."

"Ooh Tia! What kind of sin have you committed?"

"Adultery."

"What! You? With who!"

"Tyrique."

"But I thought Tyrique was just a friend. I know you two flirt audaciously with each other," Tammy sighed, "I'm at home. Get over here."

"I'm already on the road. I'm on my way."

I got to Tammy's house ten minutes later. She opened the door talking.

"Tia! Get in here. What have you been up to and how long has it been, has this shit been going on?"

I walked in responding, "Hello to you too, Tammy. I have been having sex with that twenty-three year old young man for about three weeks. The problem is I think I'm falling for him."

"What?"

"I just left his house."

"No wonder your hair is all fucked up. How in the hell did this get started?"

I told Tammy the kinky details of my affair.

"Be careful Tia. You are new and exciting to him therefore he is going to say and do whatever it takes to keep you."

"You are right. I forgot all about the ninety day rule."

"What ninety day rule."

"My grandfather said that people can only keep up a façade for about ninety days. After that their true personality will start to show."

"Up until Jack, none of my relationships lasted over ninety days.

They'd piss me off. I'd dump them. Hell, even Jack showed his true colors before the ninetieth day, but I was pregnant by then."

"What did he do?"

"Who, Jack? He locked me in his apartment before he went to work on the weekends. He made me lose my job; all kinds of neurotic stuff."

"You knew he was crazy before you married him?"

"Yes, however he was the father to my children and I wanted us to be a family."

"Be careful what you wish for."

"You've got that right."

Tammy and I talked for a while longer. She was a bit upset at me for keeping it all a secret for so long, but she got over it. After I left her house I reluctantly drove home.

The day after Tyrique left Jack went ballistic. I was lying in my bed watching television when he entered my room livid.

"Who are you fucking?"

"What? What the hell are you talking about?"

"You ain't fucking me."

"So what, what's your point?"

"You're going to give me some pussy tonight," he hollered.

"No the hell I'm not." Jack attacked me. His hands were around my neck so fast that any other woman would have been shocked and overwhelmed. I, on the other hand, calmly kicked him in his balls and pushed him up off of me. "What the fuck is your damn problem? Never forget who you married. You know damn well not to put your motha fuckin' hands on me, you sap sucking son of a bitch."

"I know that you are fucking someone Tia! If I didn't know before I damn sure know now. You have never acted this way before," he screeched.

"What way was that?" I defended myself. "How dare you come up in my room and attack me? You fucking pussy. You motha fuckin' bitch made nigga! You weak-ass bastard! Only a pussy-ass mothafucka would attack a crippled woman!"

"Who is he?"

"Who is who?"

"I've seen you leave this house and come back in a muuuch better mood. I know damn well we haven't had sex in weeks. You have to be fucking someone."

"I have sex with you once a month or so. It hasn't been a month yet."

"And your moods?" he pressed.

"The less time I spend in your company the happier I am. Valentine's Day proved that. If I was fucking someone I wouldn't be laying here in my room alone watching these damn dating shows. I would be out fucking him right now."

He dove at me again, catching me by the throat but this time he was positioned so that I could not kick him in the balls. My hand was close enough. I grabbed them bad boys and held on for dear life.

"My neck, your nuts," I said with ultra calm. "Get your mothafuckin' hands off of me, now."

"Okay." He released me. "Let go, Tia," Jack cried.

"Oh hell naw, not yet! You need to know that if you ever touch me again, I'll be forced to kill you. Don't let my education and social refinements fool you. Always remember who I am. I was born and raised in the hood. Killing you would be easy." I didn't let go of his balls until I saw tears swell up in his eyes. "Get the hell out of my room, now." When I finally turned him loose he cupped his groin, and slowly walked out, closing the door behind him. I relaxed once more.

"What the fuck was that?" I asked aloud.

The following Saturday I finally heard from Tyrique. He called bright and early, seven thirty in the morning. We talked for a little while however the conversation ended abruptly when Tyrique told me that I was special but I did not reply. I did not know what to say. Tyrique called me later on that night. I was happy. We talked and flirted.

Our endearments quickly turned into phone sex. I undressed, lay in my bed and pictured everything he said as he said it. I masturbated over and over again. I fell asleep holding my pussy. I woke up early Sunday morning to my phone ringing again.

"Hmm, good morning Tye."

"Good morning, pretty lady. How are you this morning?"

"I'm doing well, and you?"

"I woke up thinking about you this morning. I waited as long as I could to call."

"It's never too early for me to hear your voice."

"Really?"

"Yes really. I went straight to sleep after talking to you last night."

"You didn't go out?"

"No. There was no need to. I was completely contented by you."

"I like the way you respond to me. It's so easy being with you. I really do miss you Tia. I didn't expect to feel this way."

"Neither did I..."

We shared that moment in silence.

"Tia?"

"Yes Tyrique."

"I really do miss you, Baabay."

"Not as much as I miss you."

I heard his door bell ring and then a lot of background noise.

"Tia, could you hold on for a second?"

"Do you need me to let you go? It sounds like y'all just got a lot of company."

"Yes, my cousins just got here, but I'll call you back later on tonight."

"All right have a good day."

"You too, Baabay."

Tyrique called me later on that night. He told me about his day. He sounded happy but tired so we kept the conversation short and sweet. I enjoyed listening to his voice. That was the first weekend in two months that I didn't go out to any clubs or house parties. I didn't want to play with anyone else. All Monday morning I lay around thinking about him, especially after his hot sexy phone call. There's nothing like starting your morning off with naughty thoughts. The second time he called he was happily watching his son ride the merry-go-round. The third time he called me was different.

"Hello again, Sweetness."

"Hey Tia."

"What's wrong?"

"I'm on my way back to Florida."

"Why? You've only had your son for four days."

"I know."

"I'm soo sorry, Sweetness. What happened?"

"Everything was fine at first. She called me Sunday night, right after I finished talking to you."

"Um-hmm."

"She started with that 'let's make a family for our son,' bullshit."

"Really?"

"Yeah, but when I tried to tell her it would never work out she got mad. When I explained to her that it was her who put doubts in my head about my little man being mine she hung up on me."

"Damn."

"She called about a couple of hours ago and said I needed to bring back her son to her before she calls the police on me. She said, until I had proof he was mine I had no right to see him."

"When do you take the test?"

"Next Monday."

"Is there anything I can do?"

"Not really, but I do wish you were here."

"So do I."

"Thank you for listening."

"Any time..."

"I'm not in the best of moods Tia, so let me call you back later."

"Okay Sweetness. Be careful on the road. I wouldn't want anything to happen to your dick, I mean you baby. I wouldn't want nothin' to happen to you."

He heartily chuckled then said, "Thank you for making me laugh. Bye Baabay."

"Anytime, Sweetness, bye."

About three hours later he called back. He had gotten tired and needed a little company. His son was fast asleep in the back seat. His tone was bitter as he spoke more of the child's mother. I gently changed the conversation. Before long we laughed. We finished up our conversation with a little steamy phone sex. I lay across my bed smiling at the thought of him. My mood remained lighthearted, that is until Jack came busting into my room, which scared the shit out of me.

"What the hell are you doing home?"

"I've been home. I got off early."

"What did you come busting in here for?"

"Who the fuck is Tyrique?"

"Who?"

"Tyrique Carter!"

"Where the hell did you get that name?"

"Your e-mail! Let me see if I can quote it right. "I miss you boo. I'm looking forward to seeing you again."

"Oh Tyrique..." I smiled briefly before frowning. "Wait a minute what the hell are you doing hacking into my e-mail?"

"I knew something was up. I knew you were too happy lately."

"Oh please. Ain't nothin' up, damn it. No man in this state has had sex with me other than you. There's no man in this state I was fuckin', have been fuckin', am currently fuckin', am thinking about fuckin' or wanting to fuck. And that my dear husband is the honest truth. I can swear it on my last breath."

I smiled as I thought: after all, the man in question is on his way to Florida.

"Then who the fuck is Tyrique Carter?"

"Tyrique is Chris, remember my friend you just hated because you thought he liked me too much?"

"Yeah, I remember that bastard."

"Well, he moved out of state remember?"

"And? What does that have to do with Tyrique being Chris."

"Well, every month Chris e-mails me using a different name. Generally it is someone that we both know. He knows how much you don't like him and we really are the best of friends, so he didn't want me to have to deal with any bullshit, however, he wanted to stay in touch with me, so we decided to do it like this. I always know when it is him but I never remember the names he uses. Hell, he has used some of everybody's name including yours."

Chris was a man I had met a few years back. He was absolutely beautiful and charming. However, back then I was too much in love to cheat. After seeing each other out a few times we started a friendship which has lasted for years. He was one of the nicest people that I had ever met and I cherished his friendship.

"Do you know Tyrique?"

"Yes."

"When was the last time that you've seen him?"

NAKED CONFESSIONS

"I've seen him out at the club once, and at a house party once, in the last year."

"And that's it?"

"The last time I saw him at the club was in January, the week after my birthday. The house party was six months prior to that. Before that, who knows? You have no business in my e-mail in the first place. It's not as if there's anything inappropriate said."

He went into a rampage. I have no idea what he said. I tuned him out.

"Tia!"

"Hmm?"

"Did you hear a word that I said?"

"How could I not? Hell, you are screaming at the top of your lungs."

"I want to know what the fuck is going on!"

"Nothin'."

"Bullshit!"

"Looky here, it's obvious I'm not fucking this man, after all he is out of town, and I've never met a man with a two thousand mile long dick, so uh. Why the hell else would the e-mail say I miss you?"

"I don't want you having any contact with that brotha. None whatsoever!"

"Too bad."

CHAPTER FIFTEEN
DRAMA

The next morning, after Jack went to work, I logged on the internet just to find that I had no access. Jack had broken into my email, changed the passwords and secret questions. Little did I know, Jack had also sent Tyrique an e-mail telling him to leave his wife alone using the vilest language possible.

Tyrique called to check on me. He stated emphatically that I meant a lot to him. He offered me the use of his apartment but I refused. We talked about Jack's new interest in me yet neither one of us could figure out what sparked it. I assumed, because I was no longer miserable, Jack wanted to steal my happiness. Tyrique agreed. We spoke or chatted online almost everyday. Each conversation ended in phone or cyber sex.

I called him the morning of the DNA results. I immediately wished him well. He had a lot on his mind. He was nervous and wanted to talk for a little while.

"How you have come to mean so much to me so quickly, Tia?"

"Yeah, I know. You mean a lot to me too."

"It's more than just the hot passionate sex, and your dirty mind."

"Ditto, although I love the fact that we think alike."

"We do now don't we?"

"Yes."

"Too bad you are not single," Tyrique challenged.

I rolled my eyes to the heavens as I thought, here we go. "Let's not talk about that today."

"How's the weather?"

"Lovely."

We laughed. We talked comfortably, as if we had known one another for a long tine instead of a little over a month. Tyrique's insecurities surfaced. He asked if I would have given him the time of day if the sex wasn't hot. I lied at first but then, after Tyrique would not drop it, I told the truth.

"I wouldn't have ever spoken to you ever again," I stated, my voice sugar sweet.

"You wouldn't have given me a second chance? What if I was nervous?"

"Nervous? After the way you got me to go to your place, promising me hot passionate sex and all, you had better not have had an off night. Man, I would've had to kick yo ass," I stated only half jokingly.

"Oh damn, she's violent."

"Yes, I am. Damn it!"

"You ain't got no sense."

"I know. You keep fucking my brains out," I joked, and we both laughed.

"I'm gon' make damn sure you never think straight again." We laughed uncontrollably for a while. Tyrique took a deep breath. "Tia, on a serious tip, I don't think that I could have made it though this shit if I didn't know you. You have a way of making me feel like everything is go'n to be all right."

"It is you know. You're gonna feel what you feel, there's no controlling that, but you can control the way you react to those feelings.

When things are at their worst, separate yourself, emotional detachment is hard but worth it. Never dwell."

"You keep telling me that. Being in this situation has made me believe it."

"I'm glad I can be here for you."

"If it wasn't for you I wouldn't be laughing right now, hell I wouldn't even be smiling. Thank you for that. You are a wonderful woman Tia."

"And you are an amazing man Tyrique. Any woman would be lucky to have you in her life. I know I'm very happy I know you."

"The feeling is mutual, Baabay. Never change on me."

"I won't."

"Even if we have a disagreement?" he asked.

"I don't argue. I say what I have to say once, so you know where I stand and I leave it at that. We will either agree or agree to disagree, either way, no argument."

"I like that. What if I make you mad?"

"I don't stay mad for long."

Tyrique had grown more curious about my marriage and what led me to his bed. Our conversation turned into a question and answer session. I began to grow weary of the process.

"Before I allowed myself to be seduced by you I had been faithful to Jack from the moment we first met. Both of my children are his. I am an excellent mother. My children adore me." I took a deep breath before listing the rest in quick succession. "I cooked, cleaned, fucked and sucked. I never used sex as a bargaining tool. I never rejected his sexual advances. I never argued or threw past mistakes in his face."

"What the hell was that man thinking when he let you go?"

"I have no idea."

"That's a dumb-ass nigga."

"Yes, he is."

"Tia, would you ever take him back?"

"It's too late now."

"Why is that?"

"I'd have to tell him about you, and in great detail."

"No you wouldn't."

"Trust me when I tell you, I would. Jack would most likely confess and ask for my forgiveness, so I would have to do the same. I could not, in good conscience, be able to try with him again without telling him the whole truth."

"Do you think he'd forgive you?"

"No."

"Why not?"

"I'd be smiling brightly as I confessed."

"Say what?"

"Oh yes. Think about the things that we do and tell me the thought doesn't bring a smile to your face. I would undoubtedly say that 'I've been having hot passionate sex with the young sexy Tyrique, a twenty three year old hot body, every chance I got. I came for him again and again. Can you forgive me, please?'"

Tyrique laughed for all he was worth. I patiently waited for him to finish. "I see your point," he said still chuckling.

"I would add... 'I'm not sorry. I have no guilt or remorse and I would do it again.'"

"Well damn! That kind of confession could get you shot."

"He'd shoot you first."

"What? You would point me out?"

"No, never that... He just might shoot something vital, then where would I be? No more hot passionate sex for Tia."

"We can't have that, now can we?"

"No."

"Let's just forget about him killing me or paralyzing me. The most important thing here is your sexual pleasure." He didn't sound amused, however, I laughed and laughed. I could barely breath I laughed so hard. "Tia, breathe." He was not amused.

"Tyrique darlin' I was joking. I enjoy having you in my life."

"'It's nice to know you don't want me just for my body."

"How could you say that I want you solely for your body?"

"Well that's what it sounded like to me, at least for a minute there. I was starting to feel like I was just an object for your sinful pleasure."

"What?" I cracked up laughing again. "How could that be true when you are the one who seduced me? When you are the one who calls me over to see you?"

"I'm vulnerable to you."

"Vulnerable?"

"Oh yes!"

I laughed again. We talked and laughed for hours. Tyrique did not hang up the phone until he had reached his destination. I wished him well. I expected to hear from him later on that day, however, I didn't hear from him until the next morning. After the DNA confirmed the paternity of his son he was allowed to visitation. He was overjoyed. He told me that there were so many things he loved about me, after which he thanked me for being me. There was no misunderstanding, I did not believe his statements of love meant he loved me, and rightfully so.

As his trip progressed we spoke less and less. Absents did not make his heart grow fonder. Out of the blue, his care and concern of late began deteriorating. Our conversations quickly shifted from greetings to either cyber sex or phone sex. One night I could have sworn he said, "Take that bitch," however he was breathing heavily and whispering. I could not be sure. It bothered me. The next morning was pretty much the same but he did not say bitch. I figured I might have been wrong before. Tyrique was a bit talkative after.

"Has there been anymore trouble at home?"

"No, Jack calmed down after I swore there's no one in this whole entire state that I had ever had sex with or was even remotely interested."

"What?"

"Are you here now?"

"No."

"Well then, I was telling the truth."

"True that. What else have you been up to since I left?"

"I went out last night."

"You need to keep ya fast ass at home sometimes."

"I haven't gone out to the club since you left, until last night."

"Really?" he asked.

"Yes really. For some reason I just didn't feel like going no where."

"Oh Baabay, have ya missed me that much?"

"Yes."

"You act like I'm special or something."

"You are very special to me. Damn it."

We talked for a little while longer, ending the conversation just shy of saying, I love you, which was truly spooky. I didn't hear from him for next day and a half. I left a voicemail on the third day, just before noon. He instant messaged me that evening. He announced he would be returning the following day. He had decided to return a few days earlier. Our orgasmic chat was hot as hell on judgment day. I climaxed three times before he came.

Tyrique had been in town for three days before he called me, although I left a voicemail asking if he had made it safely. The mood of our conversation lacked the usual luster. Tyrique seemed to have grown distant. I told him that I was happy that he was back. He claimed he would have called me sooner had he not had to take care of a few things first. Little did I know Tyrique was hiding life changing secrets. He waited for me to question him, one of the things I said I would never do.

"You goin' out tonight?" Tyrique accusingly asked.

"No."

"Really?"

"I just don't feel like being bothered by anyone. There's only one person I want to spend time with right about now."

"You don't say."

"Oh yes."

"Tia, let me call you tomorrow."

"Okay. Have a good night."

There was definitely something different about him. The next morning my sister came by for a late breakfast.

"Hey Nikki girl, come on in."

"Hey Tia, whatchu up to this morning."

"Nothin'. I just ate a little something and took my meds. I haven't showered yet this morning." I said as I pressed my arm close to my side. "What brings you by?"

"I started work at six this morning so it's my lunch time."

"Oh okay. Well let me take a shower real quick. I'll be right back."

"You got any coffee made?"

"Yeah, help yourself." Just as I stepped out of my shower Tyrique called. "Hello?"

"Hey, pretty lady."

"Hey Sweetness. How are you this morning?"

"I'm still adjusting to the time difference. What are you doing right now?"

"Truthfully?"

"Yeah!"

"I just stepped out of my shower. I am standing here butt naked, dripping wet, holding my towel."

NAKED CONFESSIONS

"Throw on a sundress and meet me at my place."

"Right now?"

"Yeah, are you busy?"

"No, I'll see you in fifteen minutes."

"That's my Baabay."

I hung up the phone, half ass dried off, sprayed on some peach after bath splash, rubbed on a little lotion, snatched a sundress out of my closet, and threw it over my head. I took a swig from the vodka decanter on my dresser, grabbed my shoes, and ran out of the house barefoot.

"Tia where are you going?" Nicole asked, running behind me.

"I have an appointment. I've gotta go!"

"What appointment?"

"An appointment damn it! Lock up my house please. Bye!"

I left my sister standing in my doorway with her mouth wide open, in shock. I jumped in my car and peeled off. As I was speeding down the road my phone rang.

"Hey Baabay. Are you on your way?"

"Yes. I'm headed your way right now."

"Drive quickly, but carefully."

"Okay Sweetness. I'm getting off the highway as we speak. I'll be at your door in three minutes."

"I'll be waiting."

For the first time Tyrique wasn't standing outside waiting on me. I parked my car. I walked up the drive. Just as I was going to knock the door it opened. I walked in. I didn't see Tyrique. The door shut startling me. I turned quickly. He was there leaning up against the wall holding his robe wide open with dick swinging. I smiled my appreciation as I let my eyes take in every visibly naked inch of his body.

"Now I know why you didn't meet me at the car as usual. This is definitely a wonderful way to greet a girl."

"I figured if I was already naked when you got here I could get at ya a lil' quicker. I didn't want to waste any more time. I have truly missed you, Tia. Come give me a hug."

"Just a second, I need to catch up."

I grabbed the hem of my dress and pulled it over my head in one swooping motion. I tossed it to the ground. I opened my arms wide wearing nothing but my high heeled shoes.

"Oh damn! Look at you," Tyrique said visibly impressed.

"I'm all for conserving time," I announced. Tyrique was on me in two steps. He took me in his arms and kissed me as he pushed me backwards to his room. The minute I felt the bed behind me I pulled away from the kiss, turned and jumped in. "Come on over here Tye, and take that robe off."

"Hell yeah," he exclaimed. He was disrobed and in bed within seconds. "I should've called you over here the minute that I landed."

"I'm here now so stop talking and lay that sexy-ass body still for a minute. I have a few treats in store for you. I'm in a giving mood."

We lavished one another with oral pleasures. Tyrique was enthralled. His body bucked wildly.

"Come here now!" Tyrique demanded.

"Condom?"

"It's on, Baabay."

He took complete control. He fucked like a mad man. It was all I could stand, but not more than I could take. After he came I sucked his dick until he roared. I smiled triumphantly as he stumbled out of the bed.

"Baby are you alright?" I asked.

"Uh…" He smiled reassuringly. "Yeah..." He turned to leave the room. He staggered.

"Are you sure you're alright?"

"I, I…" He turned to me, poked his chest out and replied, "I'm fine."

"Okay, just checkin'."

After we showered and dressed he hugged me tight. He asked if I would come back later. I agreed.

"Damn, I really did miss you girl." He kissed me before I could respond. He continued. "All right Baabay, it's time to go. I'm tellin' you that I feel so good right now I actually don't mind going to work. For that I thank ya."

"Any time, Sweetness. Any time."

"I'm not playin, I'm go'n sit at my desk and just smile. Bet not nobody ask me to do shit, not even think 'cause I ain't go'n be able to do nothin' but smile and think about you. If a plane crashes today I'm sorry 'cause I ain't go'n be able to pay attention to a damn thang especially those little ass dots on the radar."

"Why go back to work at all?"

"Its Uncle Sam, Baabay, I gotta go back."

We walked out together. I waited for him to lock the door. He dropped his keys. The second that they hit the ground he looked at me.

"Are you sure that you are okay?" I asked for the third time.

"Trust me, I'm all right." Tyrique walked me to my car, opened the door, and helped me settle in. He gave me a soft kiss before saying, "I'm go'n getcha, Baabay."

"I know Tye, I'm looking forward to it. Call me later if you still want me to drop by."

We rolled out together. As we drove down the street he smiled in his rear view mirror and waved at me. I smiled as I sped past him and waved goodbye. Although I was happy in his company, something was very wrong. Everything felt different. We did not have affectionate sexy sex, we fucked. The mental note, Tyrique is just a lover, soared to the forefront of my mind. I got home undressed, showered, and went straight to bed. There was not a damn thing I wanted to do or was going to do, other than ice my pussy and take a nap. I was truly worn out, sexually satisfied but emotionally empty. Tyrique and I had finally come full circle.

"Where do we go from here Tye?" I asked aloud before drifting to sleep.

CHAPTER SIXTEEN
WHEN FEELINGS CHANGE

I woke up from my nap to my phone ringing.

"Hello?"

"Tia, it's Linda."

"Hey girl, how you doin'?"

"Not too well. I lost my job and I don't have enough money to pay my rent."

"What do you need me to do?"

"Well you said that I could come stay with you for a few months until I get back on my feet."

"Yeah, in July once you've paid off your bills."

"Well I ain't go'n have a place to stay by the end of this month and I don't want to move back in with my parents so I was thinking that I could just come now."

"All right, I can be there on Wednesday."

"Really Tia? Thank you so much! I didn't know who else to call."

"It's all right, Linda. You were coming here anyway. It's just goin' to be sooner than later."

"How's everything between you and your young lover?"

"Juuust fine! As a matter of fact I was just over there for lunch. The non calorie kind, if you know what I mean?"

"You need help, girl."

"I got all the assistance I needed, today. As a matter of a fact, I was asked to come back later on tonight after he gets off of work."

"You had better be careful. The last thing you need to do is get caught."

"I won't get caught, Linda. I'm far too good at this." I immediately frowned. Why does she have to be a kill joy? I mused. She must be jealous. No, Linda has been my friend since seventh grade. How could I doubt her? Maybe she doesn't quite understand. "He gives me exactly what I need and there's no way in hell I am goin' to do a damn thing to fuck that up. As a matter of fact I, other than the first night we spent together, I have never gone to his house after ten o'clock at night."

"What's that got to do with anything?"

"Well let me break it down for you so that you understand. That first night was a Friday night. Jack didn't expect me back from the club until sometime after one; however I came home shortly after midnight."

"Yeah and...?"

"He was happy that I came home early. He assumed I came home for him. Then there was that following Sunday when I saw him. We hooked up in the middle of the day then again at nine that night. All the while Jack was at home, not wanting to go to the family functions which were planned for that day. I used his attitude against him. Since he wasn't in attendance I came and went as I pleased."

"All I'm sayin' is to be careful," she said with a note of disapproval.

"I'm always careful, Linda. Like I said, I never see him during normal booty call hours. I don't treat Jack any differently. What I have with Tye is for me, not revenge. Self-reproach shows, I have no guilt or shame.

I'm just doing a little somethin' to make myself smile. There's no better feeling in this world than having multiple orgasms."

"You ain't nothing but a freak."

"That's not true."

We laughed and laughed. I blanked out for a few seconds. I was overcome by the feeling of not wanting my childhood friend in my home. I was not ready to put on my cape and boots and play captin' save a hoe, but a promise was a promise. I decided to look on the bright side. I needed a whole lot of endorphin releasing sex. With Linda living in my home, I would have an airtight alibi.

"Tia! Tia!" Linda yelled.

"Hmm?"

"I was talking to you. Where did you go?"

"I'm right here."

"Then why didn't you answer my question?"

"What question?"

"I asked if Jack would mind me living in y'all's house. I don't want to cause any more problems between the two of you."

"No problem, girl." An uneasy feeling crept up my spine. I shrugged it off. "He will be happy to be able to pawn me off on someone."

"Say what?"

"Oh yes, he'll be oh so happy to have me being watched by someone who he thinks has a strong moral fiber. It's a good thing he doesn't know what a slut puppy you really are."

"Slut puppy! What the fuck?"

"Aren't you the woman who have four lovers at this juncture in your life? How did you say it went?"

"I have a homey lover friend, a boyfriend, a guy that I kick it with, and my club man."

"See what I mean? But Jack thinks I'm far worse than you."

"He don't know shit, now do he?"

"Hell naw and that's the way we are go'n keep it. Lookey here, I'll see you in a week."

"Alright then, bye girl."

"Bye."

I believed that having Linda living in my home would make life fun and interesting. I booked a one way flight to Saint Louis, Missouri. What began as Christian goodwill towards my dear friend led to the utter destruction of my family.

After dinner my children and I were in the middle of playing a board game when I wondered why Tyrique had not called me yet. Although it was nice when he said that he cared about me and loved things about me while he was gone, I quickly pushed those thoughts out of my mind. I was unwilling to play along. I wished I knew what had happened to make him change. I went from being introduced to his friends to not getting a call back. I trusted that whatever he went through in Atlanta was the culprit. I was wrong. Again, I didn't talk to him for two days.

"Hello," I answered dispassionately.

"Hey pretty lady."

"Hello Tye."

"How are you on this fine Sunday afternoon?"

"I'm just chillin'. How you doin'?"

"Well, I can't complain now that I'm talking to you."

"Why thank ya. So tell me what's goin' on witcha?"

"Not much, I was just thinking about you. I tried to get a hold of you yesterday."

"I know, I got your messages, but when I called you back your phone went straight to voicemail. I left replies. I guess you must have been too busy to talk," I mused.

"Where were you?"

"I was at a barbeque out in Goodyear. My phone doesn't have good reception out there so all I could do was check for messages and return calls."

"Oh okay. Who's barbeque?"

"Tammy's."

"I don't think that I met her."

"She was at my sister's house party. But then again she passed out kind of early so maybe you didn't get the chance to meet to her, but you will."

"Tia Baabay?"

"Yes?"

"How would you like to come over here and have a night of hot passionate sex? I mean all night long."

"All night long?"

"Oh yes! The things that I want to do to you will definitely take all night to do."

"Oh really, now?"

"Really!"

"All right. What time should I be there?"

"I'll call you around seven."

"Sounds good."

"Okay Baabay, until then."

He never called. I did not hear from him for two more days, the day I was leaving. Whatever feelings I had begun to develop for him simply faded away. He was nothing more than a fuck buddy.

"Hello Tyrique."

"I'm sorry that I didn't call you…"

"Don't worry about it. You don't need to explain. I'm sure it couldn't be helped."

"Really?"

"Really."

"So, where are you on your way to now?"

"Back to St. Louis."

"What time are you leaving?"

"Nine tonight."

"Can you come see me?"

"Sure."

"Okay Tia, what is it? Are you mad at me or what?"

"Why would I be mad? You don't owe me any explanations about what you do with your time. That's one of the best things about being what we are to one another. Now, if you feel the need to explain then, go right ahead, but it's really not necessary."

"You serious?"

"Yes. We both have to do what we have to do darlin'."

"I'll be home by six, can you come then?"

"Yes, just call me after you get home."

"Okay Baabay."

"I have a few more things to do before I leave town so, I'll talk to you later."

"Okay Tia."

I enjoyed the fact that he sounded a bit uneasy. I had always been there when he needed me to be. However, I wasn't getting the same consideration. We were supposed to be there for one another no matei what. We were supposed to share our moments, good or bad. I shared, however he had begun to clam up. I closed my heart to him. I went on about my day trying to prepare for my trip. At exactly six p.m. my phone rang. I looked at the call screen and smiled. My smile reflected in my voice during the whole conversation.

"Hello."

"Hey pretty lady, I'm home can you come see me?"

"Yes, I'll be there in fifteen minutes."

I heard him take a breath of relief, which made me smile even more.

"Okay Baabay, I'll see you when you get here."

"I'm on my way, bye."

I arrived within twelve minutes. I listened to music the whole way. I didn't think about anything noteworthy, other than how fast I could get there. When I arrived Tye was standing outside waiting for me as usual. He opened my door, took me by the hand and helped me out. The second I was standing upright he took me into his arms and held me tight. We stood there for the longest while, embracing. The message of that hug was lost on me. I allowed him to hold on to me for as long as he wanted. After the embrace ended he took me by the hand and led me into his home.

He took a hold of me, kissing me like his very existence depended on it. I got the feeling that he needed me to be there for him, to erase whatever he went through. Passionate desperation, I knew that feeling all too well. He stopped kissing just long enough to pull my dress over my head. He tossed it to the floor without missing a beat. He removed my bra as he kissed my décolletage. I stood there wearing nothing but high heeled shoes. He stepped back, taking a good look at me, and smiled.

I sat on the bed watching him as he undressed, my lust and appreciation showed clearly in my eyes. He took a predatory step towards me. I was his prey. He kissed and touched my body as if I was his and his alone. I relished his every attention. I was almost lost in the affectionate way that he was caressing my body. It was more than our regular hot passionate sex. He licked my pussy slowly, deliberately, coaxing cum from my body. He didn't just fuck. It was as if he was making love to me. He held me tight as his dick moved in and out, deliberately—passion and desire mixed with demonstrative emotion. It had never been like that before. In the heat of the moment, I almost said I love you.

When it was all over I looked into his eyes. I just needed to know if what I felt was real. However, before I could get a good read he closed his eyes and kissed me gently. I tried to talk to him.

"Tye?"

"Hush Tia, let me just hold you."

There was so much raw emotion in his voice. I did what I was told. He scooped me up so that my whole body lay on his. I lay with my head on his chest and our legs intertwined. He stroked my hair, rubbed my back, and kissed the top of my head in between giving me very tight hugs. Although I loved the affection, I didn't really know how to take it. I did not know what to think. I lay in his arms and took it all in. It was just us. No candles burning. No music playing. The television was not on. Nothing could change between us. I had to end the moment as I could never trust it.

"Sweetness?"

"Yes?"

"May I have some water please?"

"Sure," he replied disappointed.

I slid off of him, looking at him the whole time, hoping to get a glimpse of his eyes. I had no such luck. He swooped in a little too quickly, kissed me, turned, got out of the bed and left the room, naked. I knew he was hiding something however I refused to care.

"Here's your glass of water, Tia."

Okay, I thought, I need to open my eyes, sit up, and just smile.

"Why thank ya. I really do need this." His eyes finally met mine as he smiled. I took a really big swig before putting it down. I licked my lips as I looked up at him. "Ding-ding, round two... Sorry, I forgot my bikini and sign, but I can put my heels back on if you'd like."

He leaped, yes leaped, back into the bed. I closed my eyes and squealed as he snatched me up in his momentum. When we settled I was straddling him, as he held me close, holding my head to his. Somehow during the landing, his dick slid inside of me.

Now I wasn't exactly sure how that happened. I replayed that moment over and over in my head, many times, and still I was not precisely sure. All I knew was his dick was ramrod hard and deep inside of my body without a condom. The moment that I felt him inside of me, my pussy muscles tightened around his dick, which spurred him on.

"Oh Tia baby, don't make me stop! Please trust me! Oh Baabay, you feel soo good."

"Tye…"

As soon as I said his name, he took a hold of me by the back of my head, capturing my lips in a deep mind numbing kiss. He fucked fast and hard, lost in desire. I was mystified by the sensations of every orgasm. At that point in time all I could do was to hold on to his shoulders as tight as I could, while he fucked me relentlessly. For the first time ever we stayed in the same position the whole time.

I didn't know what kind of price I would have to pay for such injudiciousness. For it was far more than just a faux pas. This one act could change my whole life forever. When it was all over, the first thing that he did was kiss me oh so gently before he began talking. He talked and talked about how good we were together as he held me tight, pressing me to him.

"Tia, don't be mad at me."

"Why would I be?"

"I…I didn't stop. I talked you into something that you know… I knew damn well, you wouldn't voluntarily do. I knew that you wanted me to stop but I couldn't bear hearing you say it."

"What's done is done."

"That's all you have to say?"

"Yes. What else is there?"

"You have to say something."

"All right then. I cannot get pregnant. I got that baby maker thing fixed thirteen years ago. I just got tested last month and you are my only lover. I know that I am disease free. Are you? You're okay on every front.

What about me?"

"Tia, I would never do anything that would put your life or health in jeopardy. I was a little worried about you getting pregnant though."

"That wasn't gon' happen."

"I get tested every six months like clockwork. I was just tested earlier this month. I'm clean. I always strap up. I had one break six months ago, but I had her get tested, and she was okay too."

"Oh really now?"

"Yes, Miss Tia, really."

"Sweetness, what time is it?"

"Almost eight."

"Oh damn! I've got to go my flight leaves at nine."

"Are you sure you gon' make it?"

"I have to."

"Call me and let me know if you made or not."

I got up and jumped into my clothes without showering for the first time since our first time.

"I'll let you know."

"Can you take a later flight?"

"No, I booked myself on the last flight out."

"Do you have to go home to get your luggage?"

"No, I told Jack that I was going to go to the airport to do an early check in to save time. You know security and all, so my bags are in the car."

"What about your car?"

"I will just have to leave it at the airport. I can call someone to pick it up."

"I'll take you. You can leave your car with me."

"Why thank ya. Let me use the bathroom right quick."

Once I was alone I wanted to freak out. I silently cried out to God. I stared into the mirror searching for answers. I closed my eyes, took a deep breath, and let it go. There was nothing I could have done to change it. I immediately made up my mind to get tested again. I turned my attentions back to the task at hand, getting to my gate on time. I freshened up a little bit, put on a panty liner and got on with it.

"I'm ready," I said, exiting the bathroom.

During that time, Tyrique transferred my luggage to his car, and parked my car in his garage. It wasn't until we were on our way that he started talking again.

"Tia?"

"Yes Tyrique." My cell phone rang before he could say another word, it was Jack. "Hello."

"Where are you?"

"I told you where I was going."

"You should have been back by now."

"Not necessarily, they are searching cars now, remember?"

"So what does that mean?"

"That means that I had to leave my car in secure parking, because there was not enough time for me to make it back. As a matter of fact I'm riding to the airport right now."

"So, you're just gong to leave your car parked there?"

"Yes, it's safe where it is. Is there anything else you need to know?"

"No."

"Okay bye."

Tyrique looked over to me and smiled. Then he said, "I love the way your mind works."

"Why thank ya."

"He actually thinks that your car is at the airport, and you've been there this whole time?"

"Yes, although I didn't tell him that."

"So how long are you going to be gone?"

"A week. I'll be back on Tuesday."

"I want to see you the minute that you get back."

"Okay. What time is it?"

"Eight forty."

"Damn! Just drop me off at departures."

"You don't want me to wait to see if you made your flight?"

"I'll make it."

"Call me, and let me know."

"Okay."

The minute we pulled up, I jumped out of the car and so did he. He got my bags, handed them to me, and then kissed me goodbye. I'm disabled so I was able to get a ride to the gate. I made my flight with one minute to spare. After I was settled in my seat I called Tye.

"Hey lady."

"I made my flight. I'm sitting on the plane right now."

"Okay, call me when you land. Have a safe fight."

"Thank you for getting me here in time."

"You're welcome sweetie."

I have a lot to add to my diary during this flight, I kept thinking. However the minute the call ended, I fell asleep. I slept the whole flight. I didn't even wake up during the landing. The flight attendants woke me up after everyone had exited the plane. Mixing alcohol with my pain medication was beginning to take a toll on me.

CHAPTER SEVENTEEN
HELL WEEK

Linda lived in a rundown apartment building adjacent to the freeway. It was a place where her cat served as pest control. As she went on and on in an attempt to rationalize her living conditions I thought to myself, wow. How in the hell did she really end up here? How was it possible for a single college educated woman with no children to mismanage her life to the degree of homelessness? I could have never foreseen that the truth of her life's journey would be more shocking than the current result.

That night I lay in bed thinking about Tyrique. I wondered about his angle. Was he trying to make me fall in love with him or was he just running game? Whatever his intentions, I had my own agenda. However I did not know if I should reach out or run. I knew there was more to Mr. Carter than met the eye. I pondered my willingness to wait and see how things played out. I refused to allow myself to get drawn into a situation that could hurt me.

As a neglected wife with a philandering husband I was easy prey. However once permanent disability and a cancer prognosis was added, my disposition changed. I had nothing to lose. I chose to look at my time with Tyrique logically. We had some laughs. The sex was hot. Nothing more, nothing less. The decision was made. I chose to run. If only I had chosen a less slippery road.

The two days that I spent in Linda's home turned out to be quite revealing, which should have served as forewarning. The nicest things I could have said about my visit were, she kept a tidy home, she loved her cat, and she had impeccably styled hair. Everything else about her was a hot mess. Linda suffered from a ghetto mentality. She blamed the Man, the system, and skinny bitches for everything that went wrong in her life. In truth she had poor taste in men, lacked money management skills, and basic social graces.

Linda boasted about the many lovers she had managed to juggle at the same time. Her social life, as she saw it was one for the record books. The ugly truth of the matter made me want to cry for her. Linda had loaned money to men who showed their gratitude by giving her sex. There was always an excuse as to why she had never been able to recoup one dime of those funds over the years. She rationalized it all away with one simple statement. "Life ain't easy for a black man in America."

Linda called every man in her little black book to say goodbye, many of whom never returned her call. She asked the ones who did call back to help her pack up her apartment. One man visited her late Thursday night. I helped her cook a lovely meal for him before I made myself scarce. I later discovered that he was her part-time lover and her pusher. He sold her marijuana which he helped her smoke. He gobbled up most of the food and asked Linda to pack what was left in a doggy bag. He sexed her up, collected the leftovers, and kissed her goodbye. Of course he apologized in advance for not being able to help her move, as he had to be on his hustle. Sadly, the only man who showed up to help her move was her brother.

Linda spent thousands of dollars converting her bathroom into a fully equipped beauty salon, which included every instrument save for the chair. There was a wall of wigs, drawers of department store makeup, and shelves of high end beauty products. She shopped for her clothing at specialty boutiques for plus sized women and at department stores for her shoes. The aforementioned would not have been an issue had her income not cried out for dollar store.

Linda admitted to me that she was not a certified teacher with full-time employment as she had led me to believe. Instead she substituted at different schools in the metropolitan area. She also went on to explain in detail how the principles of the city schools had conspired to blackball her. Apparently after stealing a female principal's man, lies about Linda's job performance had begun to spread. Within thirty days she was no longer employed. I firmly believed that Linda failed a drug test however she was my oldest and dearest friend therefore I did not challenge her story.

Linda's mother, Lilly Mae Johnson, was a sweet woman whose personality was rich with traditional southern charm. Yet, none of her social graces managed to rub off on Linda. Mrs. Johnson had loved me since I was fourteen years old. She stopped by to personally thank me for taking her daughter out of Saint Louis. She had high hopes that the change in scenery would also bring about positive changes in Linda. After all, her other daughters were living happy productive lives.

Linda and I got on the road Saturday evening. Linda drove like a turtle. It took us forever to get to the Missouri state line. That woman drove forty-five miles an hour from her door all the way to the Oklahoma border. Once I saw the sign that read, 'Welcome to Oklahoma', I made her pull over to the side of the road. I truly could not wait until we got to the next gas station or rest stop. I drove through the night across Oklahoma, and half of Texas. We got to Dallas Sunday morning just after ten. I have relatives in Dallas therefore I always made stopping there a priority. When we arrived my cousin Missy was waiting outside.

"Hey Tia, girl," Missy exclaimed as she ran towards me with open arms.

"Hey Missy," I said, hugging her tight. "This is Linda. Linda this is my cousin, Missy."

They shook hands and said their hellos. My cousin immediately turned her attentions back to me, beaming.

"Tia you are looking so much better. How much weight have you lost?"

"About sixty pounds so far."

"How are you doing it?"

"I have a twenty-three year old personal gym."

"How do you know that it's twenty-three years old? Where did you get it, the secondhand store?" Missy asked, confused. I laughed. The minute I did, she caught on. "Ooh girl, you cheating on Jack?"

"Every chance I get," I admitted proudly.

"Come on in this house and tell me what is going on out there in Arizona. Are y'all hungry?"

"I'm not, but maybe Linda is."

"Yeah, I could use some breakfast," Linda chimed in.

"I cooked some sausage, eggs, hash browns, and biscuits. Wash your hands and help yourself," Missy offered.

"Thank you," Linda accepted graciously.

"Tia, you had better eat something, after all this food that I cook," Missy said.

"Yes ma'am. I'm on a protein diet. I'll have some cheese eggs."

"What about some sausage?"

"You know I don't eat pork."

"It's beef! Smarty pants."

"Then I'll have some sausage too. Thank you. Missy, I hope you don't mind but I'm gon' wait a little bit before I eat. I need to take a shower, and brush my teeth."

"Okay girl, you can use my bathroom. There are fresh towels in the linen closet."

"Thank you."

I showered, brushed my teeth and combed my hair. After I was all perfumed, moisturized and dressed I returned to the living room, where Linda and Missy were chitchatting.

"Ah! I feel so much better," I declared as I reentered the room.

"Go make yourself a plate Tia," Missy instructed.

"I was just about to."

"Good, that way you can come on back on here and tell me what's been goin' on."

I returned with a full plate, and asked, "Where did Linda go?"

"To take a shower, at my suggestion," Missy said, sounding displeased.

"Okay..."

"We're family. You should never share too much of your business with friends, you know that. I wanted us to be able to speak freely."

"She knows about Tyrique, but not the details or my feelings for him. She just thinks I am wilding out, but I'm not."

"I know. Jack had to have really hurt you for you to take on a lover. You must have really needed someone to save you."

"He did hurt me, Missy. It hurt so bad I almost didn't survive it. I kept blinking in and out of reality. It was if I was running on auto pilot. Some days, time would just pass and I had no idea where it had gone. I couldn't account for what I did. I drank a whole lot. Hell, at one point I started putting whisky in my coffee. On the surface I looked normal. No one knew what I was going through. I refused to cry anymore."

"Tia, why didn't you call me?"

"I just shut down. I did what I had to do for my children then drank myself to sleep. I tried to pick myself up on my birthday. I tried to have a good time but it was all a façade—a charade that I could not continue with for one moment longer. I locked myself in my room with my decanters of liquor. A week later, I ran into him at the club after Nikki begged me to go out with her. I was on my second or third brandy straight when he walked up to me that night. As a matter of a fact, I had a couple more before the night was over."

"You met him at the club and left with him the same night?"

"I vaguely remember meeting him at Nikki's party six months before that. I remember him talking to Irene because he had the same name as the little boy that she cares for, her foster son. But that's about it. I remember thinking that he was handsome."

"And you didn't see him anymore until the night that you left with him?"

"No. And truth be told, I didn't remember him from the party until after I thought about it for a few days. As a matter of a fact, and this is a truth that I haven't told a soul, I didn't even remember his name until after he programmed his information into my phone. By then I was… I was freshly fucked, in my car, and trying to drive off. I would have left without knowing, if he had not insisted on giving me his number. I looked at my phone, thought to myself, oh so that's his name. The next day I could not even remember where he lived."

"Damn! You were truly lost."

"Yes, I was. At first I thought I had my night, a secret that could at least help me get through the shit I was dealing with. But then, he called. We started talking and by that following Sunday we decided to be homey-lover-friends. The only problem is I'm falling for him."

"No, you are not. Before we get into that tell me what the hell Jack did to you."

I told her every detail. By the time I was done Linda returned to the room.

"I don't what to interrupt y'all but can I use your phone?" Linda asked.

"Go right ahead."

"Thank you."

Once Linda left the room to make her phone call, Missy and I continued our conversation.

"I'm so sorry, Tia. You told him that you were facing a cancer prognosis…" Missy fought back her tears as she continued. "How can you tell that story without shedding a tear?" Missy asked.

"His reaction killed all the love I had for him. What is there to cry about? Tyrique, he saved me from falling into an abyss. He made me feel sexy, not fat, whole, not crippled, and alive, instead of dying. The other two cancers have been ruled out. Thank God. It's bad enough that I'm fat, and crippled, but leukemia is a death sentence if I can't find a bone marrow match. Remember that's what granddaddy died of."

"I remember."

"I can't believe that you are facing all of this alone."

"I would be alone if I didn't have Tyrique. He's so easy to talk to. He's been a good friend when it counts. I can confide in him."

"So what's the problem?"

"I don't know, he won't tell me. All I know is whoever he is dealing with or whatever he's going through, it's taking him away from me. I think it's time for the friendship portion to come into play."

"So you and your homey-lover-friend are just going to be friends, huh?"

"Yes. We have to before I get hurt."

"He's still go'n want to hit it."

"That's fine. I never had a problem with the sex. I can love him all I want to as a friend. I can't love him as my only lover or I'll undoubtedly fall for him and start acting bad."

"You haven't been sleeping with Jack?"

"I use to, about once a month, but that stopped."

"Don't get shot."

"I know."

The day before I got home I logged on to the computer to check my messages. Within minutes Tyrique logged on to chat. I told him that I would be home the following day. I asked him to drop my car off at my sister's house. He agreed. I promised to call him when I returned. I drove for sixteen hours straight trying to make it home. The only time I stopped was to get gas. I shouldn't have been driving but my home girl was not a good driver and I wanted to make it home in one piece. I called Tyrique the moment I hit the city limits, but I only got his voicemail. I left a message.

"Hello Sweetness. I'm back. I'm about forty five minutes away from my house. I have yet to hit a little old lady, just to let you know. I'm going straight to bed when I get home, but I'll call you when I wake up."

By the time I made it home I was exhausted and sore. All I could do was get out of the truck, take a shower, and lay down in my bed. I fell asleep the moment my head hit the pillow. I slept for about an hour before my cell phone rang. Who the hell is calling me now? I wondered before answering, eyes still closed.

"Hello?" My voice was laden with fatigue.

"Hey honey, I was just callin' to see if you made it home yet?"

"Yes Jack, I'm home. I'm really tired so if you don't mind I'm going to go back to sleep."

"Call me when you get up, okay?"

"Okay, bye."

I couldn't fall back to sleep. After about a half hour I gave up the idea of rest all together. However, all I could do was just lay there. I decided to watch television. Later on, early evening, I finally got up. I picked my car up from my sister's house.

On the way home I called Tyrique however he didn't answer. I left messages telling him that I was awake and missing him, however, I didn't hear from that brotha until five days later. There was no doubt in my mind anymore. He was just a fuck buddy. I was sitting in my room on the bed working on my manuscript when my phone rang. I looked at the call screen and smiled. I was relieved to hear from Tyrique. I needed our affair to continue. I suffered through enough heartache. I did not want to lose my lover on top of everything else I was facing, and I liked the character that I created based on the best parts of his personality.

I refused to rationalize his behavior away. I forced myself to cling firmly to reality. There was no use in hanging on to any feelings that might have been developing. Instead, I enjoyed our conversation and looked forward to his sex. He was my happy place. A few minutes after I hung up the phone, Jack walked into my room.

"Hey baby, Linda took the children to the mall."

"Okay."

"We are all alone, Tia. I want to make love to you."

"No thank you."

"Come on, Tia. We haven't made love in months."

"Really, I hadn't noticed."

"Please?"

"No. Excuse me I need to get a drink of water."

As soon as I stood up, he lunged at me, taking me by complete surprise. He grabbed me by my shoulders and threw me back onto the bed. I recovered quickly. The moment he tried to get on top of me I kicked him in his chest, and then sprung up off of the bed.

"Get yo muthafuckin' hands off me, you son of a bitch! What the hell is your damn problem? In the fifteen years that we've been together you have never raised your hand to me but now that you have gone and lost your mind over some bitch think you can take that shit out on me?"

"You are my wife, and you are refusing to make love to me."

"Lookey here damn it, you didn't give a rat's ass if I lived or died when I told you that I might have leukemia, lymphoma, or myloma. Not only that, from the minute that you started seeing that whore, your dick ain't worked right anyway. So why should I suffer through bad sex just because she's on her period or y'all ain't getting along this week?"

"Who?"

"Whoever the hell you've been fuckin' for the last eighteen months. Didn't it start a month after my accident? What? You think I'm stupid? You thought I didn't know? Fuck who ever the hell you go'n fuck. But keep your dirty ass paws off of me!"

"I ain't fucking nobody."

"What, right now? Anymore? Is it over now? I done told you, as long as you pay these bills, and take care of your children, I don't give a damn what you do. Cheating is a common thing. Hell, people make mistakes. I can understand having a weak moment. That is, if the bitch was pretty. But she is ugly man. U-G-L-Y! How the hell did you get your dick hard for that beastly looking bitch? No wonder your dick is confused."

"Tia…"

"Be quiet! I'm not finished yet. When you love someone and they love you as well, you just have to work through it. But you've already proven to me that you don't give a damn about me. Just try to remember what you said to me when I came to you with my health issues, I'll never forget. 'Do whatever it takes to make myself happy…' You didn't cry out to God, you didn't shed a tear for me. Hell, you didn't even give me a hug. You proved to me, that day, that you really didn't love me at all. I'm thinking you never did. I can't go from making love to you to just fuckin' you, at lease not without a divorce. Now get the hell out of my room!"

He turned and left without saying another word. There was no piety left in our marriage on either side. Once the adrenaline rush subsided, I was in agony. I rolled out my heat and massage mat, took my pain pills, and took a shot of tequila. The only thing on my mind was divorce. That was the last thought that I had before drifting off to sleep.

Tyrique called me from work the next day while he was on break. He said he missed me and he wanted to see me but he didn't make any plans to. I called him the next day, but he didn't answer the phone. I left him a voicemail and then deleted his number. I was tired of whatever game he was trying to play. I had enough drama in my life without him adding more. Tyrique called, as if on cue.

"Hello?"

"Hey pretty lady."

"Hello Tyrique."

"Is everything okay?"

"Why yes it is. It's been a nonstop party since my home girl got settled in."

"Really...? What you two been up to?"

"I took her to almost every club that I know."

"Really, where did ya take her?" His accent deepened as his displeasure increased.

"Well, let me see. Monday night we played pool. Tuesday night we went to that R&B lounge, you know the one with the live band. Wednesday we went to that soul food restaurant and bar for their karaoke night, the one that turns the restaurant side into a club after nine. Then on Thursday, we went to the Southside Suga Shack. I ain't gotta say no more on that. Now Friday night was off the hook, we went to four different spots. It's a good thing we started at happy hour. We club hopped all night long."

"You don't say?" Tyrique's voice was borderline sour.

"Oh yeah! Talk about having a ball...? We worked the club scene like it was a part-time job. We painted the town red. Did you enjoy your week?"

"Not that much."

"Oh I'm sorry. I'm so glad my home girl is here. Since she's been here I've had more than my fare share of a good time, that girl really knows how to party. Linda has a way with men, like a magnet. They can't help but to come to her," I lied.

"Well it seems like you have been thoroughly entertained."

"I have been. What have you been up to?"

"Just work and playin' ball." He didn't sound too happy.

"Well, I would love to chitchat with you for a while but today is my nephew's birthday and I have a lot more errands to run. As a matter of a fact I was just in your neck of the woods."

"You were?""

"Yes, I had to pick up a piñata at that little store right down the street from your house."

"You were two blocks away. Why didn't you call?"

"Somehow your number got out of my phone, but I got it now."

"Somehow? Okay."

"Oh Tye," I laughed, but just a little bit. I knew damn well that that conversation was not going the way he thought it would. "I'm sure it was accidental. Anyway I really do have to go so, I'll talk to you later, okay?"

"Okay, bye Tia."

"Bye."

I was not willing to tolerate anyone playing with my heart. I considered ending my liaison with Tyrique altogether. The next afternoon I was online and low and behold there was Tyrique. We chatted for a little while. He asked about the piñata. During our chat my phone rang. I was a little bit too preoccupied to look and see who was calling.

To my surprise it was Tyrique. Our lighthearted conversation continued over the phone. He told me that he missed me and wanted to see me again soon. As I was ending the call he asked me to call him back the next afternoon. I called. He did not answer or call back. I decided to occupy my time as usual. I treated Linda and my girls to the movies. I took my children shoe shopping and out for pizza. I stayed busy from three to six. In that time I came to a decision. I called Tyrique again.

"Hello pretty lady."

"Hi Tyrique."

"What's goin' on witcha, Baabay?"

"I need to bring back your stuff tonight."

"Let me call you back in ten minutes."

"Okay, bye."

Ten minutes came and went, which just made me more convinced I was making the right decision to end this now. After an hour had passed I called him back.

"Hello Tia."

"Hi. Lookey here I just need to return your things tonight and that's that."

"I'm at Target right now."

"Okay…"

"I'll be home by eight."

"Call me when you get home, bye."

CHAPTER EIGHTEEN
BREAKING IT OFF

"Hello," I answered my phone at eight p.m. sharp.

"I'm home," Tyrique unhappily announced.

"I'm on my way, bye."

"Bye."

I took an extra pain pill just in case. Goodbye sex is almost always raw and primal. When I arrived he was not waiting outside. I got out of my car and walked up the drive carrying his things. Just as I reached the door, it opened. I did exactly as I said I would and handed him his things the minute he opened the door. However, something went very wrong with my exit. He grabbed me by the arm and pulled me into the house.

"Stay for a while," Tyrique said, locking the door then removing the key.

I looked at him in total disbelief, but only for a split second. I smiled nonchalantly and said, "All right…"

I sauntered to the living room thinking, this ought to be good. I'll play along for a while. I took a seat on the couch.

"I'm just putting this surround sound system together. I'm almost done. Do ya want something to drink?"

"No, thank you," I replied ultra politely.

"Okay."

Tyrique stared at me. His intent was very clear. He was a man hell bent on getting his way no matter what. Rape was never my concern. What troubled my heart and mind was much worse, ownership. His gaze clearly stated, you can be mad if you want to but that pussy is still mine and you are going to give it to me willingly.

"Tia do you know anything about electronics?"

I instantaneously thought, you know that I do, however I said, "Yes. Why?"

"I can't get this damn thing to work. Could you take a look at it?"

"Sure." I took a look at it. He stood to the side, watching me.

"I can't see that you did anything wrong. All of your connections seem to be right. Let me see the instructions."

"Let me get them, they are in the box right there behind you."

He brushed up against me as he walked by. I recognized his game. I decided to stay out of his reach. As Tyrique returned with the instructions I held out my hand as far as my arm could extend. He looked at me and smiled as he handed me the booklet. We stood there quietly as I took my time reading all of the instructions. When I was done I walked around him to get to the system.

"I'm going to take it all apart. Please make sure it's unplugged."

"Yes ma'am," he said as he looked at me smiling.

"Alright, I'm going to read the instructions to you as you put it back together."

"Ma'am, yes ma'am," he quipped. Tyrique looked at me with vivid mischief. He saluted before getting into position in front of the television. "Ready for instruction ma'am."

I looked at him. Everything in me wanted to crack up laughing but

I held on to my resolve. With every instruction I gave somehow he found a reason to come my way. I leapt out of his way left and right. I almost tripped over the box trying my best to stay out of his reach.

"Are you okay, Tia?"

"Yes, I'm just fine."

"Well, you seem to be a little bit jumpy."

"Is everything connected?"

"Yes, unless there's one more instruction book."

"All right I'm going to check all of your connections to make sure that they are tight. After I'm done, you can turn it on." I checked everything. It seemed to be right. "Okay, plug it in."

Tyrique plugged it in, however the surround system didn't work.

"Ain't that a bitch!" Tyrique griped.

"I'm a sit back down. If I were you I'd take that thing back to the store. It's only half past eight. If you need me to go so that you can take care of it tonight I will."

"No, I'll go after work tomorrow."

"Okay."

I sat on the couch in the corner closest to the door. I took my shoes off, tucked my feet under me, and folded my hands on top of my lap. I watched him repack the box.

"I can't believe this. I spent my hard earned money and wasted all my time puttin' this thing together for nothin'."

I laughed a little bit. "Poor baby," I cooed.

"I'm gon' tell them a thing or two when I get there tomorrow." I laughed a little more which started him on a whole rampage. "I have half a mind to call the president of the store right now, and tell him about the piece of junk that they sold me today."

"You are soo funny."

"Now the damn thing won't even fit back in the box."

"It's just not your night. Ha, ha, ha…"

"I need a drink, damn it. But I don't have anything here."

"I can leave so that you may go get a drink."

"Naw, that's okay. I'll get something later."

"Okay."

He sat in the oversized chair to my right. "Ooh, I'm tired. I had a long ass day at work. I stopped by the store on the way home. I spent all that time unpacking the damn thing, puttin' it together twice then taking it apart and repacking it. Man…"

"Well, I can go if you need to relax."

"No, I'm not that tired."

I watched him as I wondered what he was up to. I saw him reach down to untie his boots before I returned my attention to the news. I peeked over at him again. He sat there in nothing but his green and brown camouflage military pants. I could not help but gawk. If I was that cartoon wolf my tongue would have rolled out of my mouth and my eyes would have been popping out of my head, as my heart pitter pattered through my shirt. He caught me staring. It took everything in me to finally look away. The moment I did, Tyrique stood directly in front of me. I tried to focus solely on his eyes and sound, as unaffected as possible, however I failed.

"Excuse me. I can't see the TV, Tyrique."

He unbuttoned his pants and slowly unzipped his zipper. My focus zeroed in on what he was doing. All I wanted to do in that moment was join in somehow. My eyes were glued to him. I blinked really hard and refocused. I cocked my head to the side in an effort to see around him. He began taking off his pants. My eyes locked on him again. I looked away almost immediately. My eyes seemed to have a mind of their own. They darted back for a few seconds longer.

"I'm not looking at you," I adamantly stated. He walked closer to me, so close I could feel the heat of his flesh. I could not see anything but him. He stood there dressed in red boxers, my favorite. I snatched my glasses off, and threw them down on the couch next to me. I threw my head back and stared up at the ceiling. "I'm still not looking at you. I cannot see a damn thing without my glasses on so, you are wasting your time."

He walked away. I sighed in relief. I put my glasses back on and continued watching television. I was so engrossed in the news that I didn't even see him reenter the room. The next thing I knew he was standing next to me, tapping my cheek. How odd, I thought as I slowly turned my head towards him. I could not believe my eyes. His dick was less than an inch from my mouth. I looked up at him. He was so very sexy, standing there in fully erect decadent splendor. The assured look of, 'I know you still want me,' was plastered on his face.

"Oh damn," I stomped my foot on the floor, grabbed a hold of his cock, and lustfully kissed the head. I sucked his dick as if my very sanity depended on it.

"Hmm… Tia, let's go to the room."

"Sweetness, let's make this the night we talk about forever. I want to thoroughly enjoy you, to not be able to look you in the eyes without blushing."

He took me to his room, lay me down and fucked me like he was getting paid for it. There were points where a third of my body was hanging off of the side of the bed in a back bend. We switched to a naked hand stand. He long stroked my pussy until cum splashed everywhere. He crossed my legs.

"Flip Tia," Tyrique said.

I pushed off of the night stand which made me swing around into the perfect flip. Tyrique dropped down onto his knees, spread my legs and licked my pussy from behind. He savored my flesh like a desert spoon. I came hard. My pussy spurted cum reminiscent of a water fountain. He gripped my waist. I dangled off of the side of the bed. Tyrique fucked long and hard. Blood rushed to my head as I climaxed in rapid succession. A feeling of euphoria fell over me. I was too delirious to stop.

"Arch your back, Tia. Come back up here on the bed," Tyrique instructed. He pulled me up. He sat on the side of the bed and positioned me on his lap, reverse doggy style. "Ride Tia!" he commanded. I reached back, grabbed my ankles and bounced off of his dick as if I was trying to win first prize at a rodeo, cum splish-splashing with every stroke. After a while we changed positions again. "Lie back, Tia," Tyrique directed. He rolled us both over. "Crawl forward, Tia."

We sexed it up, doggy style. When we finished the mattress was twisted and hanging off of the bed. We both lay there completely out of breath, panting as if we had just run a marathon. It took a good fifteen minutes for us to calm down enough to even talk.

"Tia?"

"Yes…"

"I really did miss you."

"I missed you too."

"I'm glad you made it back safely."

"Thank you," I said as I sat up. "I have to shower."

Tyrique looked over at me in total disbelief. I looked at him as nonchalantly as possible, considering.

"No," Tyrique obstinately stated.

"Okay," I said, lying down.

"This isn't over."

"Okay."

He sat up in the bed. He looked at me. His expression was intense, very serious. My expression never changed. He began kissing me, softly. He caressed my face after which he touched me gently, stroking my already over sexed pussy. He looked into my eyes. He was so impassioned, so intense that I could not help but to get caught up. He took his time, slowly making love to me. It felt so different, close like we were connecting body and soul.

My heart opened unexpectedly. I fell in love with him. I almost cried. I struggled with the emotions that filled the room, both his and mine. I knew that I could not fight the love that was growing in my heart. I knew that I could never tell him the depth of my affections. I quietly lay in his arms, deep in thought.

It doesn't matter how I feel. I cannot allow anyone into my everyday life. I cannot allow my emotions to control me. I came here to end this afffair and that's exactly what I'm going to do. I can't really be in love with him. I was just caught up in the moment. This is not real.

He kissed the top of my head. "Tia, this is just the beginning," Tyrique stated.

Damn! Nothing else entered my mind. I didn't respond. I let his statement stand for the time being. I let him hold me. I let him bathe me and help me get dressed. I could tell that he didn't want me to go so I stayed.

"Are you hungry, Tia? Did you eat dinner yet?"

"Well, I wasn't hungry before I got here however I'm starving now." I smiled at him, a coy little smile—almost awkward, as I looked up and batted my eyes at him. He smiled at me then laughed. I laughed too.

"Come on, Baabay. Let me feed ya."

"Are you cooking?"

"Unless you want to go out or order in." he inquired.

"No. I like your cooking. What are you making?"

"You want some crab legs and shrimp?"

"Ah, your specialty, yes I would love to have some. Do you need any help cooking?"

"I got this. You just come on out to the living room and have a seat. I can put the TV on the news for you if you would like."

"Oh so now you have jokes."

"Well, you did seem to be really interested in what was going on in the world."

"Did I now?"

"Yeah you were staring at it hard enough."

I cracked up laughing, so did he.

"You got me there. I didn't know that you were so strong and agile."

"Did I shock you Tia?

"Yes," I exclaimed.

"Good."

I followed him into the kitchen instead of going to the living room.

"I have a question for you Tye."

"What is that, Baabay?"

"What were you thinking earlier in the living room when you did that to me?"

"Did what...? Block the TV?" Tyrique did his best to look innocent, but he couldn't control the smile which started to spread across his face.

"You know what you did."

"I did a lot so, what exact moment are you talking about?"

"You know what you did. When you were standing there naked in the living room tapping your dick on my cheek?"

"Oh that? Well you know that he likes you. He just wanted to come out and say hello since he hasn't seen you in a minute."

"So it was his idea, not yours?"

"Yeah, you know how he gets."

"I did enjoy saying hello to him."

"He likes the way you say hello."

"Mm-m..." I was immediately lost in thought. God help me! This man is just too much for me to deal with. I don't understand how I got so damn twisted over him. He's far too young. No matter what, I have to say goodbye, tonight.

"Where did you go just now?" Tyrique asked.

"What do you mean? I didn't go nowhere."

"You were thinking about something that took your smile away."

"I had a hunger pain." I lied. "I really worked up an appetite doing something or other, whatever it was; I really need to eat right now."

"Something or other?" he asked teasingly.

"Hmm-hmm… As a matter of a fact, I might have lost a pound or two in the process."

"Well then let me feed ya."

I sat at the bar, and watched Tyrique cook. All I could think about was how I was going to say goodbye to him as a lover without making him mad enough to end our friendship. I heard Tyrique's voice.

"What did you say?" I asked lost.

"I asked you about your girl."

"Who?" I asked still confused.

"The one that you just brought back with you."

"Oh her!"

"You didn't hear a word that I said to you, did you? What are you over there thinking about so hard?"

"Nothing really."

"Tia, talk to me. I got you."

"There's nothing to talk about."

"Okay sweetie, but it looks like whatever it is, it's making you unhappy."

"Well maybe after we eat your friend can cheer me up."

"Yeah, he was just thinking the same thing."

"Oh really now?"

"You know that we are in constant communication."

"I know one of y'all is crazy and I'm thinking', it ain't him, seeing as his head has no brain."

We both collapsed into laughter. Tyrique walked over to me. He hugged and kissed me tenderly.

"Go on in the living room, Tia."

"Do you need any help bringing in the food?"

"No, I've got this."

"Okay Sweetness."

We were both starving. We blessed the food, and quietly ate as we watched TV, until the last morsel was consumed. We looked at each other and smiled.

"Well Tia, it's time to cheer you up," Tyrique said as he stood. He helped me up, took me by the hand, and led me to the bedroom.

"Yes lets!" I agreed. "I really do need you to make me happy. Let me have my way. I need to…" To say goodbye to you properly. I finished silently with just a thought.

I took the lead, watching him the whole time. I vied desperately to commit everything to memory. He watched me too. We had sex on just about every viable surface in his house including the kitchen sink. We fucked for the third and last time in the shower. It was definitely a wild night. He washed my body, concentrating on cleaning his cum from my vaginal canal. I helplessly came again during the process. We talked as I got dressed.

"Tyrique, Sweetness, I'm definitely all cheered up. I knew that there was something that I liked about you."

"Oh really now?"

"Oh yes!"

"Are you on your way home?"

"No."

"Where are you going?"

"I'm going to that little club that has a live band."

"And?"

"And I'm going to go hear them play. They play the blues. You know I'm a St. Louis girl. I love listening to the blues." It's the perfect ending to a bittersweet night like this, I mused.

"So, you tellin' me that you're going to go listen to the blues after I did all that work cheering you up?"

"Yes."

My response sounded a little bit too serious. He noticed right away. Although I tried to smile my way through it, I couldn't have been less convincing.

"Tia?"

Damn! He was on to my tatics. My thoughts were moving faster than my actions.

"Yes?"

"I want you to call me when you get to the club."

"Okay."

"Call me when you get home too."

"I will."

Tyrique walked me to the door. He gave me a long tight hug.

"Don't forget to call me."

"I won't forget."

I stepped backwards across the threshold.

"Drive carefully."

"Always."

"Good night, Tia."

I reached for him. I had to hug him one last time. I had to let him know, without actually having to say it, that our affair was over. I wanted to convey my message without hurting him. I did not want my words to come back and bite me. I needed plausible deniability just in case I had remorse and wanted to go back to him. I never burned any bridges that I may want to cross again. I looked into his eyes and said goodbye; one very simple word which spoke volumes. I turned and walked away. My feelings were hurt.

I attempted to leave without looking back. However I made the mistake of looking up into his eyes just before I put my car into gear. I knew immediately that he understood what my goodbye really meant. It was written all over his face. He stood there, in his robe, watching me the whole time. He continued to watch me as I drove away. All I wanted to do was cry yet I considered drinking until I could not feel anymore. As I drove to the club I settled on drowning everything out with music. I called as promised. He invited me back over. The band was good. The music and ambiance was exactly what I needed. I called Tyrique just before one a.m.

"Tia…"

"Go back to sleep, Sweetness. I'll call you after you get off work," I said then hung up the phone. He didn't call back.

CHAPTER NINETEEN
JUST FRIENDS?

In the wee hours as I drove home from my favorite after hours club, my phone rang. At first I thought, who the hell could be calling me at four o'clock in the morning? However when I looked at the call screen and saw that it was my sister, Nikki, my heart sank.

"Hello Nikki, what's wrong?"

"I had to take Jerome to the emergency room."

Oh thank God that it was not one of the children, I thought to myself. Then I quickly asked, "Is he going to be alright?"

"I don't know. The doctor wants to admit him, but Jerome doesn't want to be admitted into the hospital."

"Is there anything that I can do?"

"He will listen to you. Can you come to the hospital right now?"

"Sure, which hospital?"

As it turned out the hospital was only two miles from my house. I got there in no time at all. Once I found my way back to Jerome's bed, I peeped though the curtain.

"Hey y'all, what's goin' on?" I asked.

"Hey sister, how did you get back here?"

"Have you ever known anybody to say no to me or not let me have my way?"

"You've got a point."

"So tell me Jerome, what's goin' on witcha, dog?"

"Nothin'."

"Don't lie to me. Where's the doctor?"

"I'll go and get him, Tia," Nicole said.

I had already been informed that alcohol poisoning was the cause of Jerome's medical condition. While my sister was away he and I had a little conversation, which I dominated from the first word to his final acquiescence. I took a very firm hand. I told him that if he did not admit himself, I would make sure that he returned home to his apartment, instead of to my sister's house. I went on to say that I would keep my sister occupied so that if he did take a turn for the worse he would die alone. Somehow between a lost cell phone, and a sudden flat tire, Nicole would not make it to him in time.

"That's some cold-ass shit, Tia."

"I know. I wouldn't be so insensitive if I didn't have to be. But it seems to me that if I don't use a little bit of tough love, you wouldn't do what's right."

"Tough love?"

"Yes, if I did not love you I wouldn't care one way or another if you lived or died. I wouldn't be making sure that you got the medical help that you need. Now, stop giving my sister a hard time and do as I'm telling you."

Just at that moment the doctor walked in. Jerome agreed to be admitted. I stayed for two hours, until he was settled into his room. Within that time Jack called and visited. I wasn't at all shocked to see him walk into Jerome's hospital room. He stayed just long enough to verify that I was telling the truth.

"Nikki, I'm going to go on home."

"Tia, how soon can you come back?"

"I'll take a cat nap, and a shower. I'll be back, ASAP."

"I need you to do me a favor?"

"What?"

"Jerome left his cell phone at home so, can you call Devon or just give me his phone number so that I can call him myself?"

"I don't have Devon 's number."

"Tyrique does."

"I really don't talk to him that much. I broke up with him three days ago."

"Please Tia? I wouldn't ask if it wasn't important."

"Fine. Lookey here, I have got to go and get some rest before I fall down flat on my face."

"Thank you, Tia."

"Don't thank me yet. Although I talk to him every now and again, I don't know if he'll even answer my call."

"Please!"

"Fine! Bye."

I turned and walked out without saying another word. I went home then straight to bed, clothes and all. I woke up three hours later. The first thing I did after brushing my teeth was keep my promise to my sister.

"What's goin' on, pretty lady?"

"Good morning Tye, I need a favor."

"What is it, Baabay?"

"Do you have Devon 's phone number?"

"Yeah, hold on, let me get it for ya."

He gave me the number no questions asked. However, I offered an explanation along with my thanks.

"Anytime Tia. I'm here for you whenever you need me to be."

"Thank you, Sweetness." Oh damn I called him Sweetness. I had

NAKED CONFESSIONS

ot end this call right now! "Bye Tye."

"Bye Tia."

I called Devon before I took my shower. I reached under my pillow, threw on my sleep shirt, the football jersey that Tye gave me, and a pair of shorts. By the time I got back to the hospital Devon and his wife, Jennifer were already there. The moment I walked in everybody looked at me like there was something that they knew about me that I didn't want them to know.

"Hi y'all. What's goin' on?" I asked.

"Hi Tia girl, how are you doing this morning?" Jennifer responded.

"Fine Jenny."

"Come give me my hug, baby girl," Devon said.

I hugged Devon, before taking a seat. They continued to stare. I suffered from sleep deprivation. I was not in the mood for a guessing game and I made that very clear.

"What's goin' on between you and Tyrique?" Jerome asked boldly.

"Nothin'. What do you mean?"

"Tell her Devon," Jerome demanded.

"Just before you walked into the room Tia, Tyrique called," Devon began.

"So...?"

"He sounded all casual."

"About what?"

"He's coming to the hospital."

"Say what?"

I've got to get the hell out of here. I need to go home and change my clothes now. I didn't realize my sister was playing along the whole time until after she spoke.

"Tia, is there something wrong?" Nicole asked.

"No!" Thank God you kept my secret Nikki.

"Is there a problem with him coming here?" Nicole probed further.

"No, I just would like for Devon to finish telling me the significance of Tye acting nonchalant on the phone."

"Well Tia, he acted like he didn't just talk to you about Jerome being in the hospital."

"What do you mean?"

"He called and asked what we were doing today. So I told him that I was at the hospital with Jerome. He asked me which hospital, got directions, and said that he was on his way."

"Really?" I was shocked.

"What did you do to him?" Devon asked.

"Nothin.' Why do y'all think that I did something to him?"

Jerome spoke up again, and said, "He sure as hell ain't coming to the hospital to see me."

Damn! I thought, but asked, "Why the hell else would he be coming here, Jerome?"

"Well now let me think. I know him just as well as you know Jenny, so uh I'm thinkin' that he's coming here to see you, playa."

"Yeah sister, so uh you might as well just tell the truth. Spill..." My sister chimed in. I must admit that she played her part very well.

"Fine, we've been lovers since the week after my birthday. Beginning that night we all went to the club. However, I just ended our affair a little over three days ago, seeing as it is Saturday morning."

They were all in shock and all exclaimed, "What?"

"Oh yes, we had an affair for about two and a half months without any one of y'all knowing. How the hell do y'all think that I dropped thirty more pounds so quickly? Anyway, I broke up with him last Tuesday night, after which, we had hot passionate sex, then I went to the club and then I went on home. I haven't spoken to him since, that is until my dear sister asked me to call him."

"Damn! How the hell did you keep all of this a secret, from your own sister, no less?" Jerome asked, flabbergasted.

"It wasn't any of her business. He was exactly what I needed and wanted. I enjoyed our time together. Now it's over."

"Obviously it's not over for him," Devon quipped.

"What do you mean, Devon?" I asked.

"He wouldn't be coming here if it was really over between the two of you. I've known him for years and I have never seen him act like this over no woman. So why don't you tell us what you did to my man."

"I haven't done a thing to him that he didn't thoroughly enjoy. As a matter of fact, when it was over, I made our breakup drama free."

Just at that moment Tyrique walked into the room. All eyes were on Tyrique from the moment he entered the room. I looked at him for a brief second before I turned my head in the opposite direction. I peered out the window as I tried desperately to control my impish smile. God I cannot believe he was here. Tye was actually here.

Tyrique walked over to the bed and talked to Jerome for all of thirty seconds. He walked over to me. I had just gotten my smile under control.

"That jersey looks good on you," Tyrique said.

I looked up at him, and said, "Why thank ya."

"This is the first time that I've seen you in it since I gave it to you."

"That's because it's my sleep shirt, and we don't sleep together."

"Ya sleep shirt?"

"Yes. As I recall, I was asked to wear it to bed so that I would think of you. I'm wearing it now because I slept in my clothes last night and it was the first clean shirt that I grabbed."

"You look sexy in it."

"Oh please, I look like shit."

"Well if that's how you look right out of bed with only a few hours of sleep you don't have a thing to worry about."

"Aaw," I smiled. "You gon' make me think that you still want me."

His eyes said, 'You know damn well know I do or else I sure as hell wouldn't be here.' Yet his response was very different. "You look tired Tia."

"I am. I came from after hours straight to the hospital."

He walked pass me and took a seat in the chair that was perpendicular to me. His concern showed clearly in his eyes.

"You need to get some rest, Tia."

"I know but my sister needs me to be here."

"Why don't you close your eyes for a while right now?"

"Can I put my legs up on your lap?"

"Of course you can."

I stretched my legs out across his lap, leaned back in the chair and closed my eyes. I was too tired to care about the curious stares from everyone in the room. Tyrique gently stroked my calves as he carried on a conversation with the others. Unbeknownst to me, the four of them watched the two of us like they would the final seconds in a double overtime ball game. I rested for about thirty minutes. I was sure I could've rested longer if Nicole wouldn't have had questions. I knew that my sister had been curious all along. She saw her opportunity to get some answers, and she took it.

"So tell me Tyrique, what exactly is going on between you and my sister?" Nikki asked.

"Pay attention to your own man Nikki. After all, he is sick."

"He's going to be okay. I'm more interested in the two of you. You two look awfully comfortable over there."

Tyrique picked up where I left off. He said, "Not as comfortable as the two of you look laying together in the same hospital bed."

"This is my woman, playa," Jerome chimed in. "What we want to know is what's going on between you and her sister."

"Yeah Tyrique, Jerome does have a point. You've been rubbing my sister's legs for the past half hour, nonstop."

I opened my eyes only to see four pairs of eyes staring at us for answers. For the life of me, I couldn't understand why. I had no choice but to put an abrupt end to the whole inquiry.

"All right everybody, just for clarification, what goes on between Tyrique and I is our business, and none of yours. So uh, drop it." My voice was a little harsher that I wanted, however my point was made clear.

"On that note, I'm going to take my wife, and get out of here," Devon announced.

Devon and Jennifer said their goodbyes to Tyrique and I first. As they were saying goodbye to Nikki and Jerome, Tyrique and I settled into a private conversation of our own.

"Thank you for letting me rest a while," I said.

"Are you feeling better?"

"Yes."

"You know, I've never done it in a hospital before."

"Neither have I."

"You have enough energy to meet me in the bathroom?"

"You leave first."

I smiled that special smile of sexual anticipation. Tyrique slid his hand up my thigh. I watched as his hand disappeared under my shorts. I gasped as his fingers graced my thong. I smiled a little bit more as I slid down in my chair and opened my legs a little more. He slid his fingers past the rim of my underwear. I gasped again. He pressed his index finger against his lips. I wondered if anyone had heard me. I looked around. I thought, wait a minute, look at what he has me doing in a hospital room with four other people up in here. I loved his game. I played along quietly. I licked my lips and gapped my legs just a little bit more as I slid even further down in my chair. He scooted his chair closer to me. I focused solely on him and he on me.

What we didn't know was, by then everyone else was staring at us.

We didn't notice that the conversation and goodbyes were over yet nobody left the room. We didn't realize that we were being watched until my loving sister called out my name as if she was in shock. Tyrique slid back slowly, as if he had done nothing wrong.

"Tia...!"

"What?" I answered perturbed.

Why in the hell couldn't she just mind her own damn business? She could have 'see and not say. Tyrique stood up and offered to walk Devon and Jennifer out. The moment they left the room Nikki started in on me.

"Tia, what are you doing?"

"I'm going to the get something to drink from the cafeteria," I said, getting up an walking out. As soon as I stepped one foot out of the door, I was grabbed by the arm and dragged off. "Tye, where are you taking me?"

"You look like you need help using the bathroom. After all you are my little, crippled lady, and I would hate it if you were to slip and fall trying to take your thong down."

"You are so sweet and thoughtful. I would like to thank you in advance for helping me with my thong."

"You are more than welcome. Anything for you, Tia."

He took me to the part of the hospital where they were doing remodeling. Amazingly enough no one saw us duck under the yellow caution tape or into the deserted bathroom. He removed my clothing and laid them on the counter. I stood there wearing nothing but socks and tennis shoes.

"Turn around, hold on to the sink with one hand, put your other hand up against the wall and your foot up on the toilet. Hold on tight. I'll do the rest."

"That's more than one thing."

He spun me so that I faced the toilet. I put my foot up.

"I suggest that you hold on tight 'cause it's gone be a bumpy ride. We have to be quiet Tia. We don't want to get caught."

"All right."

He kissed my neck and back as he donned a condom. He caressed my body, resting his hands on my waist, as he entered my pussy with one powerful thrust. I couldn't be quiet. I have never been able to be quiet while fucking—at least not with him—his dick was too good to remain silent. He covered my mouth with his hand which made the whole episode seem even more erotic. He was quick yet shocking—thrilling. We cleaned ourselves up before exiting the bathroom, without being noticed.

"Wait, I said I was going to get a soda from the cafeteria."

I'll go get it for you. Just stay up here, go on back in and tell them that you ran into me and I offered to get it for you."

"Okay."

I returned to the room. The minute I entered, my sister had something to say. The first thing she asked about was the soda. She questioned me as if I had never caught her and Jerome in a compromising position. I told her to get over it. She should have looked away. Nicole pressed the issue further still.

"I thought you said that you broke up with him."

"I did."

"Well, it didn't look like it to us."

"Just because I broke up with him doesn't mean that I stopped liking him. And it sure as hell doesn't mean that I stopped wanting him. He's an excellent lover, a man who I can't seem to say no to at the moment, so..."

Tyrique walked in. I could tell that he heard my last statement. He smiled proudly. He handed me the soda.

"How in the hell did you get that soda so quickly?" I whispered in his ear.

"Nurses lounge," he whispered back before taking his seat.

"Thank you, Tye."

"You are very, very welcome."

Our undertones and subtext got me riled up again. I was still taken aback by the hot passionate sex in the bathroom of this hospital.

"Tia you really do need to go home and get some rest."

"Oh so now he's telling you what to do," Nicole interjected.

"Yes he is and you know what Nikki I'm going to obey him."

"Really...?" Nicole asked. She was definitely amazed.

"Yes, really. I don't think I've ever refused any of his suggestions to date. Why the hell would I start now?"

Jerome joined the conversation at that point, addressing Tyrique. He said, "You got it like that dog?"

"Why don't y'all talk about something else? After all we're here to visit you Jerome, ya know, keep you company and in good spirits. How you doin'? How you feelin'?" Tyrique said, without answering thr question.

"I'm feelin' better," Jerome replied in earnest.

We all talked and laughed for a while. However, after Tyrique left my sister, and her man attempted to grill me about the nature of my relationship with Tyrique. I did not know what got into Nicole or why she was so hostile. I refused to dignify any of their questions with a reply. I simply stood up and walked out. I needed sleep.

I called Tyrique a few hours later. I thanked him. Our conversation was nothing more than sexy reminiscing. At the end of our conversation he suggested that I not spend so much time at the hospital. I agreed, however I took my portable DVD player and some movies and went back to the hospital. I didn't return home until about eight that evening. I cooked dinner. After dinner Jack wanted to talk.

CHAPTER TWENTY
RESCUE ME

"Tia, can we talk in private?" Jack asked.

"Sure," I replied.

"Can you come down to my room? This is very important."

"Okay," I said, and followed him down to his room.

"Have a seat, Tia."

"No thank you, Jack."

"I'm not going to attack you. I just think that you should be sitting down."

"Okay."

I sat down on the corner of his bed. He pulled his desk chair up. and sat directly in front of me. Then he cleared his throat as he brought his gaze to meet mine. "What's on your mind Jack?" I asked.

"How would you feel if I moved out?"

"Overjoyed," I said, beaming with happiness.

"I'm serious, Tia."

"Ecstatic," I exclaimed.

"I'm moving out next weekend."

"Okay."

"I'm serious."

"Good, I'd hate to think that you were just joking."

"You really would like it if I were gone?"

"Hell yeah," I cried out.

"Who the fuck is he?" Jack asked irately.

"He who?" I asked. "Oh you are leaving me for another woman but Lord forbid, if I had another man waiting in the wings."

"Well do you?"

"No." I paused long enough for Jack to sigh in relief. "I just broke up with him last Tuesday." I couldn't help but to giggle a bit after sharing that tidbit of truth.

"Quit playing, Tia. I am serious. I need to have a place of my own. We're in separate bedrooms, living separate lives, so we might as well have separate homes. I don't feel like I'm at home here, Tia."

"Okay. Are you looking for a different reaction from me? You keep staring at me like you are waiting for something. Why don't you just tell me what it is, so we can address it?"

"You just seem to be a little bit too calm."

"I'm more relieved than anything. I've been praying to God you would leave. I know God did not put us together or we would not have fallen apart. We never became one. You are not in love with me. I'm not in love with you. The only difference is you felt compelled to treat me with cruelty where as I just simply want to move on with my life."

"You act like I don't matter."

"In the big picture you really don't."

"Damn, Tia."

"Well let's look at it from my point of view, shall we? I'm only thirty-two years old which means I still have over fifty years more to live. If cancer doesn't take me out prematurely. In that time my children will grow up, marry, and have children of their own. I might even have a great grand baby or two. At this time in my life, I'm approaching my sexual peak so dating will definitely be on my agenda. Who better than a string of young hard-bodies? I am going to fuck my ass off for the same number of years I wasted with you. Hell, I don't look my age as it is, so, I'm thinking I'll start to look for someone to settle down with shortly before I turn fifty."

"It sounds like you have this all figured out. You act like I'm in your way."

"Well, when you spend as much time alone as I do, you have time to think out life's what ifs. Our children are social butterflies, they are never at home. You are forever working late, shopping, or having some kind of car trouble in a twenty-five thousand dollar sports car that you have only had for three years. So…?"

"Tia, I don't want to argue with you," he said defensively, squaring his shoulders, and frowning at me.

"A statement of fact is nothing to argue about," I smiled up at him knowingly. "I have had a lot of time on my hands. I had to fill it somehow. I look at it this way; most women my age are not married. Hell, they have never been married. They are still dreaming about their wedding day, looking for that ring on their finger, their name to change, that first baby, well the first one within wedlock anyway, and all that other shit. I have already been there and done that. My children will be adults in four short years. I'll be the perfect catch. Oh, and the icing on the cake is I cannot get pregnant."

"What about love, Tia?"

"What about it? I loved you. What good did it do me? Never again will I allow my emotions for a man to change my world. I'm sure I can love someone so much that it hurts, and still, not include them in my everyday routine. I can make time. However, no one will ever interrupt my life ever again."

"Is that what I was, an interruption?"

"Yes. I had goals. I had a plan, but when you came along all of that changed. If whoever else comes along can't simply get in where he fits then he has no place in my life. I will not change my goals, alter my plans, or leave my dreams unfulfilled ever again. It's just not worth the disappointment."

"Not everybody leaves, Tia."

"Sure they do. They either die or walk out of the door."

"Did I make you this morbid?"

"I'm not morbid. I'm realistic. I'm the one facing cancer, not you. I'm the one living with fifteen years worth of regret, not you. I am the one begging God for another chance to make something of my life, every moment of everyday, not you. So excuse the hell out of me if I don't paint life in pastel colors any more. I can't afford to. First and foremost, I have to survive for my children, and then I am going to experience every happiness that this world has to offer me. You really aren't a factor in my life anymore."

"You use to love me so much."

"No I did not. I loved having a family. I loved how much the girls adored their daddy. I never fell in love with you," I lied. "I was so busy going after the big picture that I overlooked that one detail. The children came before either one of us was really ready. You got me pregnant on purpose so I wouldn't go off to college and leave you. I know now that you were not in love with me then because if you truly were you would have let me go."

"I was in love with you, Tia. I couldn't stand the thought of you leaving."

"No Jack, you were obsessed with a beautiful girl with a multi-orgasmic pussy. If you were truly in love you would have married me before the first child was born, not after our children turned nine and ten. You left me before, Jack and I guess, deep down, I knew you'd leave me again. I only took you back because you came back with a marriage proposal and I desperately wanted my girls to have a family."

"Why haven't you walked out on me?"

"Once I became a mother, my feelings ceased to matter. All that matters is my children's happiness."

"What about all that dating you said you were going to do?"

"I'll never do it in front of my daughters. My children don't need to know grown folks business. I'll date when you have them, when they are at school, or if they have plans for the evening."

Just like I do now... I was thinking. Jack was gone. I was free. Within a week of Jack's departure, Jerome came home from the hospital and my book was published. I called and e-mailed everyone I knew to let them know the good news.

I went to Nikki's house to tell her the news face to face. I rang the doorbell then waited on bated breath for her to answer. She opened the door. I shouted out, "I'm published!"

"Really?" her voice squeaked with surprise.

"Yes!"

"Congratulations, girl." We embraced. "Come on in the house."

"Can you believe it?" I asked.

Jerome sat in the living room watching basketball when I came in. He stood up, walked over to me, and gave me a big hug.

"Congratulations, Tia! We should have a party," he said.

"Ooh Jerome, now that's a good idea! Let's have a barbeque."

"The only day I'm off is Sunday, so let's plan it for then," Nikki chimed in.

"That's perfect," I agreed.

We spent the rest of that week getting ready for the barbeque. We invited everybody we could think of including Tyrique. She bought the food, marinated the meat, and gathered chairs and tables. The night before my barbeque Jack decided to stop by while I was out. Linda and I were at the grocery store getting the last few things we needed for the party. My daughters were home. When I entered my house carrying a bag of groceries he was sitting in my living room.

"Girls, go help Linda get the rest of the stuff out of the car."

"Yes ma'am," they said in unison, and then got right to it.

"Hello Jack, what brings you by?"

"I called your cell phone, but you didn't answer so I called the house, and my children told me that you were gone."

"As you can see, I went to the store. Didn't they tell you?"

"You were at the store?"

"Yes, don't you see the groceries?"

"Why didn't you answer the phone?"

"I was at the store down by Nikki's house. You know that there's just no reception down there."

"Why did you have to go shopping all the way down there?"

"Because the store by her house was having a grand opening sale, and I had to drop the meat off at her house anyway for the barbeque tomorrow."

Jack just stared at me like I was lying through my teeth. Being at the grocery store was one of his favorite cover stories. He always made a big show about the long lines filled with food stamp, and food voucher recipients, and their bad ass children. He would go on and on about them paying for food with fake looking money. His lies were pathetic. The electronic benefits card replaced the paper food stamps before the new millennia. Sadly, that was the lie which brought the truth of his infidelity to light.

"What barbeque?"

"Why do you care, Jack?"

I busied myself putting the food away. Linda and the children walked in carrying groceries. My oldest daughter began speaking the minute she entered.

"See daddy, I told you mommy went to the grocery store."

"Oh, so they did tell you where I was."

"They said you were at the store."

"I was."

"That's where you were, hmm? No where else?"

"Did you come here to pick a fight with me?"

"No, I came here because you left my children home alone."

"You mean our high school age children, right? So you are telling me that a freshman, and a sophomore in high school cannot be left at home alone while their mother goes grocery shopping?"

"Grocery shopping, hmm? Tia, who the hell are you fucking!"

I looked at him like he had just lost his damn mind. I turned to look at my children. They looked just as shocked as I did. I saw Linda standing there bug-eyed and mouth wide open.

"Girls please go to the playroom," I instructed calmly. I turned my attention back to Jack. "You're not going to do this in front of my children."

He wouldn't even wait for his daughters to get down the hall before continuing on. "I know your game, Tia," Jack shouted. "I know that you are fucking somebody. You couldn't wait until I moved out."

"Where the hell did that come from?"

"You could've had your good friend Linda drop you off, so that you could fuck while she did the grocery shopping, and then pick you up later!"

He was progressively getting louder and louder. It was as if he wanted our children to hear his accusations. My voice remained serene— dispassionate. I refused to rise to the occasion, more like debase myself for a fracas.

"What? Are you on drugs? What the hell is your deal? You left me, remember? Aren't you happy on your greener pastures?" I looked over to Linda. "Take my children to get something to eat. There's a twenty in the center console of my car." Then I turned back to Jack. Although I was seething I spoke just loud enough for him to hear me. "Don't you say another mothafuckin' word in front of our children, damn it."

He stayed quiet until after he heard the front door close. Then he said, "I know…" Jack began.

"Shut up," I said, my voice was low and smooth yet filled with strength. "Who in the hell do you think you are? Don't you ever speak that way, to me or about me, in front of my children, ever again."

"I know that you are seeing someone Tia. I know you've been fucked by someone since I've been gone."

"No I haven't."

I was getting my brains fucked out the day before you left, but not since you have been gone. The thought made me giggled.

It was an almost fatal mistake. In all honesty, I could not help myself. The memory of Tyrique and me in a bathroom at the hospital flashed in my head as clear as day. Jack instantly became incensed.

"You're laughing!" He bellowed. "You're lying."

Jack grabbed my neck with both hands and squeezed hard. I saw the murderous rage in his eyes, his furrowed brow, and turned down mouth. His face was red, his breath heavy. I was shockingly calm. I immediately kneed him in the groin with all of the might I could muster. He let go of my neck. I rushed over to the knife block, retrieved my largest carving knife and then started his way.

"Ooh you sap sucking son of a bitch," I spoke deliberately as I advanced towards him. "You ain't nothing but a lil pussy with nuts. Now I'm go'n have to kill you."

"No Tia!" Jack loudly pleaded as he bagged away. "Please." He held his hand out. "Stop," he shouted. "You already kicked my balls."

"You choked me," I said calmly. "Again… Now you have to die."

"Stop Tia, you don't want to go to jail."

"You threatened my life first. This is just self-defense. I already have my story worked out in my head. You came over here accusing me of cheating. You were irate and vulgar therefore I sent our children away. I tried to calm you down. I told you that I had not begun seeing anyone since you left, which is the truth, but you didn't believe me. You lost your mind and grabbed me by the throat. I struggled, tried desperately to save myself. I reached for the knife that was left on the counter. I began stabbing you with it. I just kept on stabbing until you let go of my neck."

"Tia no!"

"You are in the kitchen and my throat hurts. I'm sure my story will check out between you laying dead on the kitchen floor and me having evidence of stress on my larynx or whatever little things you hurt in my throat by squeezing it. I doubt if the police would even take me to jail. I'll do the news then the talk show circuits promoting my book as well as telling this tragic story. I'll write my second book giving all of the gory details, which will no doubt be a best seller. Women just love that, battered woman killing her husband, shit. And I'm a disabled battered woman to boot. Maybe the second book will get published by one of the top ten publishing houses." He turned and ran out of the house through the back door. "Bitch nigga," I shouted.

I laughed until I could not stand anymore. The look of terror on his face was priceless. The next morning I woke before six a.m. I had planned to take all of the party paraphernalia to Nicole's house as early as possible. I walked outside just to find a car parked in front of my driveway.

"Hey! You are blocking me in," I shouted angrily. The next thing I know, a man started running away from my car. I didn't see his face but I recognized the type of car that was blocking my driveway. "If I see you on this property again I'll shoot you right in your ass or in the balls, which ever is facing me at the time."

Jack sent one of his car club friends to take my car. He never expected me to be awake and out of the house at that hour. I thanked God that I was too excited to sleep. Unfortunately, I had to hide my car. Linda was starting her new job Monday morning therefore we could not share the truck. I had no idea what I was going to do about transportation. I took the first load of food down to my sister's house. As soon as Nikki opened the door I started talking.

"You will never believe what happened this morning."

"I can't believe you're up this early."

I completely ignored her statement and continued on with my story. I explained everything that happened before I got to her door.

"Why would he do that?"

"Because he thought I was going to stab him last night."

"What?"

"Can I put my car in your garage and then continue on with this conversation, please?"

"Girl, yeah!"

Once my car was safely tucked away, I asked my niece and nephew to bring in the food. I filled my sister in on the gory details of the night as quickly as possible.

"How are you going to get back home?"

"Linda. She's on her way with my children and the rest of the food. She'll be here by noon. I came early so that I can start the meat."

"Jerome was going to barbeque."

"Ha, stop playin'," I said. "He can stand next to me to see how it's done but uh, this is my barbeque and other than daddy, no one can grill Saint Louis style like I can."

"Truc that."

The best thing about barbequing is that it's a leisure activity. It's all about technique. I pierced the meat thoroughly and marinated it in a beer based marinade three days before the barbeque. I soaked chunks of hickory in water and seasoned the meat the night before with a rub I made from scratch, just like my father taught me but with a touch of cayenne pepper. I placed the wet wood on the hot charcoals so that the ribs could smoke and cook at the same time. All I needed to do was sit back, relax with a cold one, and let the meat cook.

People began arriving at about three; everything moved along very nicely. The food was great, we had the game tables going—spades and dominoes. We had the music bumping and the game was on. Just after six that evening I entered the kitchen carrying the last of the barbequed meat. The house phone rang. I placed the platter down and answered.

"Hello?"

"Anna May, what you doing answering the phone, Anna May?" Tyrique yelped.

I smiled immediately. I spoke with the innocence of a child, "I was in the kitchen when it rang."

"Whatchu doin' in the kitchen Anna May?"

"I was butt naked, on my hands and knees scrubbing up the floor."

"Butt naked," he shouted.

All I heard was his laughter.

"Yes. You see, I spilled some sauce on the floor, and I didn't want to get that nice new dress that you bought all dirty so, I took it off along with my bra, thong, thigh-highs, and shoes. I didn't want to get them all dirty either."

"You actually said butt naked! I knew that there was something that I liked about you."

"How are you doing, Tyrique?"

"I'm doin' just fine, thank ya. How's your barbeque going?"

"We're having a good time."

"Give me your sister's address again. I think I remember where her house is, but I'm not for sure."

I gave Tyrique the address. Just before I finished the call I felt someone's warmth on my back. Powerful arms wrapped around by body from behind. A denim clad penis pressed against the arch of my back. I closed my eyes as my heart skipped a beat. A deep voice spoke in my ear.

CHAPTER TWENTY-ONE
REAL TALK

"Congratulations, Tia."

"Martez," I asked completely bowled over. "It can't be," I said as I spun around in his arms. "Hold on Tye." I hugged Martez tight. "You're here… Thank you darlin'," I all but shouted.

"Nikki said that I would find you either in the kitchen or out by the grill."

"I'm on the phone. Wash your hands and make a plate. I'll be out in a little bit," I said, putting the phone back up to my ear. "I'm sorry, Sweetness."

"Sweetness..." Martez reapeated, a little bit too loudly. I smiled, shaking my head. I remebered that tact was never a strong point of Martez.

"Shut up, Martez," I hissed, glaring at him, and pretending to be angry.

Martez nudged me out of his way by thrusting his pelvis at me. He washed his hands quickly enough. Then he took his time making his plate.

"I can call you back if you are busy," Tyrique offered, slightly insulted.

"I'm not busy. One of the guests can't seem to mind his own damn business. You'd think he'd just get his food and go sit down, but not everybody has manners."

"Who is Martez, Tia?"

"He ain't nobody."

"Nobody," Martez interjected loudly. "Tia, you know I'm your real baby daddy."

"Shut up Martez. Don't make me cut you." I picked up a paring knife and pointed it at him. "Say another word if you want to." I returned my attention to Tyrique. "I'm soo sorry, but no one can control him. Mama dropped him on his head when he was born."

"Oh, so he's your brother?"

"No, but our mothers are best friends. He was born at our house. My mother delivered him during a snow storm. We grew up just as close as if we were twins. He was born first. My mother went into labor the next day, after the snow plows cleared the road. Anyway, I didn't expect him to be here today."

"Why not?"

"He lives in California."

"Don't be telling all my business," Martez said, and I stabbed him. "Ouch," he howled.

"Did you really stab him?" Tyrique asked.

"Yes, it's not the first time. Unfortunately, it won't be the last."

"Well, seeing as you are busy, I'll see you later."

I turned my back to Martez then I said, "I am not busy."

"I'll talk to you later, Tia."

"Okay. Do you want me to make a plate for you?"

"I'll get one when I get there. See ya later."

"Bye."

I hung up the phone. I faced Martez, glowered up at him and

stabbed him again.

"Ouch Tia, that hurts," he pouted.

"Good," I shouted. I tip-toed up and kissed his pouting rose-pink lips.

Martez was male model beautiful with a running back's body, and a magnum XL dick. He stood over six feet tall. He had natural strawberry blond hair, hazel-green eyes, and dimples. He was my freckle-faced Adonis. He and I had a secret that absolutely no one knew about. We were each other's first. We were fourteen years old and curious. We continued our sinfully clandestine liaison for a little over a year. He was my original homey lover friend and the reason I had always preferred that type of relationship above all others. I never had a boyfriend that lasted. I never really wanted to get married. Until Jack, I had never been faithful to any man. Although I was faithful to Jack the longest, in the end I still cheated on him.

Martez and I had been feeling each other up since we were too young to know why. We shared our first kiss when we were three, at our birthday party. We took baths together when no one else was home. He was my very best friend in the whole world. I knew he would never hurt me and to this day he never has. He was angry when I got pregnant. I was sixteen and stupid.

"Who is your Sweetness, Tia," Martez asked.

"None of your damn business," I stated haughtily. It was all I could do not to laugh.

"Tia?"

"What?"

Martez smiled at me before asking, "Can I have a proper kiss now?"

"Yes, of course."

Martez opened his arms to me. He gathered me up in a loving embrace. As our bodies came in full contact, we kissed. Our kisses had always been affectionate and very French. I ended the kiss. I looked up at him and smiled.

"Hmm! Hello there lovely, lovely Tia."

"Hello there bad, bad Martez."

"Tia, we were bad together."

"I was only fourteen. I didn't know enough back then to be bad."

"How much do you know now?"

"Not enough to get down with the likes of you," I said as I pushed away from him.

"What?"

"You had too much dick for me when we were just entering puberty. I can only imagine how much dick you've got now. There's no way in hell I'm going to let you ruin me for everybody else. You're the reason I had to start dating grown ass men in the first place."

"Little ol' me?"

"Yes. You left me, and took all that with you," I said, pointing to his crotch.

"I had no choice," he said defensively.

"I know. How have you been? No, scratch that. What the hell are you doing here?"

"A little birdie told me that old man, Jack finally left. So I came out here to make sure that you were doing alright."

"Thank you." I stepped closer to him, tiptoed up and kissed him once more. He wrapped his arms around me. He held me tight, so very, very tight. "I'll always love you, Martez."

"I love you, Tia. I always have and I always will."

I teared up. For the first time in months my heart hurt. I stepped out of his embrace and turned my back to him. I couldn't let him see me cry; he understood that about me.

"Go on outside with everybody else, please," I said, and my voice cracked a little bit.

"Okay, Tia."

I went to the sink. I splashed some cold water on my face. Once I was presentable I reentered the living room. Just as I was walking in from the kitchen, Tyrique walked in from the foyer, to my surprise.

"Hi," I greeted Tyrique as I walked in direction. "Who let you in?"

"One of the kids," he said as he walked towards me. "How are you doing, pretty lady?"

"I'm doing fine, thank ya. How are you, Sweetness?"

"You look good, Tia," he said lustfully. "Real good, Baabay..."

"Why thank ya." Just when we were getting close enough to kiss, I saw my father sitting on the couch. Although he was watching the game, there was no way in hell I was going to kiss Tyrique right then. I grabbed Tyrique by the hand. He looked confused. I enlightened him posthaste. "Let me introduce you to my father."

"Your daddy is here?" he whispered.

"Yes. Mama is out of town." I let go of Tyrique's hand. "Pop this is Tyrique, Tyrique this is my father Mr. Sylvester Beal."

Once I introduced them, I kept on walking through to the backyard. The two of them exchanged greetings. Before I could get the arcadia door opened, Tyrique was right behind me.

"Who is that sleeping in the lounger?"

"Linda, she's been laying there since three. She claims to have a bellyache but I think she just ate too much."

"Now that's a big girl."

"Stop that Tye, she's unhappy."

We stepped out. The moment my feet touched the ground my brother, Sylver, stood up, grabbed me up in a tight hug, and kissed my cheek.

"Congratulations, Tee-Tee."

"Thank you, baby," I sang. All of a sudden I felt mischievous. Once my brother let me go, I turned to Tyrique and said, "Let me introduce you to my other lover."

My brother extended his hand. "Hello, I'm Wednesday."

Tyrique shook my brother's hand as he stated, "Just don't get your day wrong, dog."

"Damn," Sylver said as he laughed. He was obviously shocked.

"I'm just saying," Tyrique continued. His cool demeanor was void of any cordiality. "If it's not Wednesday…"

I interjected immediately as my brother was the only man smiling. I did not want things to get out of hand. "I'm just kidding Tye. This is my baby brother Sylver. Sylver I am very pleased to introduce you to my Tyrique."

Tyrique looked at me and smiled before shaking my brother's hand again. At that point my brother was cracking up laughing. Tyrique began to laugh too.

"Damn, Tee-Tee, he was making sure I didn't get my day wrong." Sylver chuckled as he said, "I said Wednesday, but here I am on a Sunday."

"I was just sayin', you know," Tyrique said, still laughing.

"Let me show you some ID so if I see you again, but it ain't Wednesday, there won't be a problem. I'm Sylvester Beal the third, but my friends and family call me Sylver."

My brother flipped out his military ID which sparked their friendship.

"I believe you. You don't have to show no ID," Tyrique looked at my brother's ID anyway. "Oh so you are Navy?"

"Yeah! Navy, inactive reserve, I just got out a couple of years ago."

"I'm Air Force."

"My father and uncle were Air Force."

My brother took over introducing Tyrique to everyone else, including Martez. I sat outside for a while enjoying the ambiance of my party. I watched my brother and my lover interact. I watched the women go crazy over Martez. I watched the children play on the trampoline and swing set.

My heart was content. I thought, this is the way life is supposed to be. I am happy today. My children don't seem any worse for wear after yesterday's fiasco with their father. I couldn't have asked for a better outcome. Jack is not here to ruin it.

I excused myself to the bathroom. Just when I exited Martez grabbed me by the hand and pulled me into one of the bedrooms.

"You scared the shit out of me, Martez," I chastised

"Meet me at my hotel tonight. I'm in room one seventy one; our month and our year. You can't possibly forget."

"Which hotel?"

"Here's your room key."

"Okay. Can we stop playing cloak and dagger now?"

"What would you rather play? Catch a girl get a girl?"

"Martez behave or I won't come see you. I have a friend here. I don't want to offend him so will you please stop playing, at least for now?"

"Who, young Tyrique?" he asked sarcastically. "Friend not lover, hmm…?"

"I won't discuss this now. Let's go."

I returned to the party, however, Martez did not. He stopped to talk to my father. Martez invited him for a ride. As I headed out the back door he took my daddy and went out the front.

"Hey Sylver, where are Pop and Martez off to?" I asked.

"The store to get some more dranky-dranks," he said good-humoredly.

"Okay." I noticed that Linda had not joined the party, she was parked right next to Tyrique. I called out to her. "Linda, I see you are up. How's your stomach feeling?"

"I'm all right now."

"I'm glad to hear it." So you have a miracle cure within fifteen minutes of Tyrique getting here? I could be wrong but I doubt it. "Tye, are you hungry?"

"I could eat."

"Well, come on in the kitchen with me. Wash your hands. I'll make your plate."

Tyrique got up but before we could get into the house, my loving brother commented, "Oh snap. She's making your plate? Are ya in looove Tee-Tee?"

I just kept on walking. Tyrique and I were the only people in the house.

"Are you in love, Tia?"

"Are you in love, Tyrique?"

Neither one of us answered the burning question. I opened the stove. I took out the chicken, beef ribs, pork ribs, and the hot links. I placed each container down on the counter one by one. I folded back the foil so that he could see the food. He stood next to me.

"What you got, Miss Tia?"

"What you want."

"You…"

"Okay, tell me what you want to eat."

"You…"

"That has calories."

"Just make me a plate. I'm not picky."

"You want some potato salad?"

"No I don't like that."

"But you are not picky? Let's start with some meat. You want some chicken, ribs, or a hot link?"

"Yeah, load it up."

"You want any spaghetti, baked beans, corn on the cob, salad, or any green beans?"

"Naw, I'm good."

"I've got some macaroni and cheese, homemade."

"I'll take some of that."

"Right."

He sat at the kitchen counter and ate as I put away the food.

"Tia?"

"Yes?"

"Where's your car? I saw your truck, but I didn't see the car out front."

"It's in the garage."

"What, for the party?"

"No. I'm hiding it from Jack. He tried to take it this morning."

He put down his fork, picked up his napkin, and wiped his hands.

"Come here."

"Where are we going?"

"I want to show you my truck."

"Your truck, the SUV?" I asked.

"Yeah, I finally got it out of the shop yesterday. You want to see it?"

"Sure."

He took me by the hand and led me out to his vehicle. His truck was nice, even though it was green. He opened the door and extended his hand.

"Get on in, have a seat."

"Okay."

"You know that you can take it home with you if you need to. You have children. You need to have a vehicle."

"Really?"

"Yes."

"You'll switch cars with me?"

"Hell yeah," he stated emphatically.

"What if something awful happens to your truck?"

"It's insured."

"Oh thank you, Sweetness," I shouted out happily.

"Anything for you Baabay," he said sweetly as he took me into his arms.

We shared a kiss. Afterwards, he scooted the seat closer to the steering wheel until my feet could reach the pedals. He proceeded to show me where all of the gadgets were, and how to work the remote to the stereo. We returned to the party.

The evening was absolutely fabulous. Everyone was proud of me and wished me well. After the party Tyrique helped with the clean up before he drove away in my car. He was the last person that wasn't family, to leave, or so he thought. As the party wound down Martez kept out of sight. I knew he was still there, as he would never leave without saying goodbye. My family members had questions starting with my brother.

"Tia?"

"Yes?" I answered as I retrieved the loratab from my purse.

"How old is Tyrique?"

"I'd like to know the answer to that question as well," Martez said.

"Twenty-three... Why?"

"You are Stifler's mom," Sylver joked.

"Who?" I asked as I reached for my cocktail.

"The lady at the end of that pie movie, you know the older woman who sleeps with her son's classmate?"

"I am not," I stated calmly after washing my pills down with a little tequila sunrise.

Everybody busted out laughing.

"I'm sorry Tia, but I just could not help it," Sylver said, still laughing.

"I'm leaving," I said as I flashed the peace sign.

"She threw up them deuces y'all," Martez added. "I'm a get on out of here too. Tia, do you need me to walk you out?"

"No thank you." I raised my glass. "I still need to finish my drink."

"All right, good night y'all. It was nice seeing every one again."

I headed out thirty minutes later. I was glad that Linda had already taken my children home. She and the children left the party before ten p.m. The girls had school the next day and Linda was starting her first day of work. I knew that ending my special night with Martez would make a wonderful night glorious. I rang his phone once to let him know that I was on my way. I smiled at the inspiration of his room number, our month and our year.

CHAPTER TWENTY-TWO
HOT PURSUIT

When I arrived Martez was waiting for me in the lobby. We shared our usual hug and kiss. He escorted me to his room.

"What's going on Tia?"

"I'm thinking, divorce," I said flatly.

"What happened?"

"He walked out."

"There is more to this story than what you are telling me."

I waited until after the elevator doors closed to answer. "I might have leukemia Martez."

"Tia…" Martez cried out soulfully as he gathered me to him. His emotional display touched my heart.

"Calm down, my love. I don't know anything yet. I'm going through the testing right now. And, I don't want to talk about it."

"I'm here for you, Tia. I have always been there for you."

"Please stop."

"Okay. What's with Jack?"

"Jack cheated on me one month after the car accident. He is still cheating now. Once he found out that I might have a blood cancer he told me to do whatever it took to make myself happy, that he would not stand in my way. About three months after that he walked out."

"You seem so calm."

"I'm not the victim anymore. I stopped being the martyr when I started writing the novel."

"Why didn't you call me when everything started going wrong?"

"I couldn't tell you how bad it was. I couldn't tell anyone what he did to me. I still cannot bring myself to talk about it. Writing the book was therapeutic however many things were left out. The story is a good girl gone bad romance with a hero saving her in the end."

Martez held me close as we walked to the room. Once inside he fixed a couple of drinks. We disrobed and relaxed under the covers.

"What did he do to you, Tia?"

"I was abused." I said as I turned my back to him. I lay with my head on his shoulder as I held on tight to his arm. "Jack tortured me. If I didn't do what he wanted he would purposefully hurt my injured areas. I was raped, sodomized, and left dirty. He fed me like a dog… He tossed food onto the bed once a day and left me there alone. All I had to eat for two months was vending machine food: honey buns, cold cut sandwiches, granola bars, and such." Although my voice was calm, my tears streamed over his arm. "I crawled on the floor just to use the bathroom. I sat on the side of the tub and bathed with a toilet brush wrapped in a face towel and rinsed with a large cup. Little did I know that crawling around was making me stronger until one day I went to climb back into the bed and it did not hurt. I stood up and took a step. I started physical therapy shortly thereafter. I started writing the book two months later."

"That explains Tyrique," Marquez said, rolling onto his side, and tucking me in closer. He handed me a tissue before whispering, "And what did young Tyrique do wrong?"

"He is keeping secrets."

"How can I help?"

"You being you helps," I said, facing him. I looked into his eyes before I said, "No matter what, no matter who."

"No matter who, no matter what," Martez replied wholeheartedly.

"Ever since we were just children…"

"I've had your back since the day you were born."

"Yeah…" I smiled.

"Let's try with each other."

"No."

"Why not?"

"We are too young."

"What?"

"I still have a lot of play in me and so do you."

"What does that have to do with anything?"

"Well, let's go back in time for a moment. I had a boyfriend and you had a girlfriend when we decided to try sex for the first time with each other. We cheated on them and didn't think a damn thing about it. The best thing about us is the fact that we love each other unconditionally. We understand one another."

"Yes, but if we decided to make a life together…"

"Stop. I already know what will happen. We would be happy with one another for a while but then one of us would meet someone intriguing. You or I would come home and tell the other one. Because we have been homey lover friends for almost twenty years one of us would assume the other one must understand, not realizing that the one being told goodbye has fallen in love. In other words, one of us would get hurt."

"Tia, don't say that."

"Why, because you know it's true?" He didn't respond. He looked away. I reached up and cupped his face in my hands turning his face towards me again. I smiled wantonly as I spoke. "I'll let you ruin me with that big ole dick of yours tonight as long as you don't ask me for tomorrow... Sixteen years is a very long time."

"Tia?"

"I know you agree."

"I have never loved anyone the way I love you."

"And I have never loved anyone the way I love you." I kissed his lips before continuing. "Martez let me ask you this... Who can I turn to if you are the one who hurts me? Better yet, who can you turn to if I am the one who hurts you? Who do we have if we don't have one another? You have to remember, I gave my fidelity for fifteen years. I'm not looking for that again, at least not right now. I want to play!"

Martez and I remained the closest of friends over the years. We shared each other's special moments. We stood by one another through the good times, and the bad. He was there when both of my children were born and he was in attendance at my wedding. I was there for him when his mother died of a heart attack. He came to see me the day after my car accident. He had always been there whenever I needed him or even just wanted him to be. I had always been there for him as well. I could never risk losing him, ever.

"Tell me about young Tyrique."

"Young Tyrique was my belated birthday gift to myself. However we have not had sex since the day before Jack moved out."

"Say what?"

"Like I said, he is keeping secrets. No call, no show for days," I sighed. "I like the way by body reacts to his."

"I could make you cum, Tia."

"Let me see whatchu're working with."

"Okay," Martez said before he pulled back the covers. "Touch it, Tia."

"Okay," I agreed, but before I could his dick grew long and hard.

"Hot damn," I exclaimed. "That's a whole lot of dick." I was in shock, eyes locked, mouth wide open.

"So are we going to get busy now?"

"Hell naw!"

"I know you want to." Martez looked at me the same way he use to when we were kids. His eyes said simply, I want you Tia. "I can see it in your eyes."

He was right, I wanted him too. I wanted to get lost in his unconditional love. As long as Martez was alive I never had to face anything alone.

"Well…" I smiled up at him. "We can play around but I am not going to… Where the hell would I put it all?"

"You go'n play with me Tia?"

"We go'n play with each other just like we use to."

"I've never watched you cum, Tia."

"I was too young back then," I said, wrapping my fingers around the shaft of his dick. "I've watched you cum, many times."

"I want to make you cum Tia."

"I want to let you Martez."

When we play we get down right freaky with it; nothing is left untouched. That night was no different. He picked me up, and took me to the bathroom. We thoroughly washed one another. I kneeled in front of him and sucked the hell out of his dick as water ran down his body. I wanted him to cum in my mouth however he would not cum. He picked me up and carried me off to his bed soaking wet. He took his time and licked every once of water off of my flesh. He swirled his tongue around the kiss of my ass coaxing it. He slid two fingers into my anus as he tongue fucked my pussy.

He had definitely honed his skills over the years. I came for him over and over again. I enjoyed myself. I wanted him to fuck me. I was almost desperate to feel his monolithic dick stretch me pussy. However I hesitated. But then I decided to enjoy our moment while it lasted. I licked his balls before gently taking them into my mouth suckling them one by one. I bathed his scrotum and anus with my tongue. I slathered his cock until he screamed out for me to stop. I continued at my task slowly, methodically, until his trembling body relented. Martez cried out as he came.

On my back, my hands tucked under my head, I was ready. He turned onto his side, facing me. He placed a hand on my belly, slid it down slowly until it reached destination. He began stroking my pussy in nice circular motions.

"Mm-m, daaamn Martez! You have learned a thing or two over the years."

"Me? You are the one Tia! You know…"

"Well…"

"I see that you are one of those rare vixens who can cum over and over again. That's nice to know. I can have some real fun with you. You won't dry up."

"I've never dried up with you. Have I?"

"No but you didn't cum either. You would get all creamy but you never had an orgasm."

"Yes, I remember that. I still have those sometimes. I use to call it my pleasure wave."

"Pleasure wave?"

"Yes, there is a wave of pleasure that goes through my body but not enough to give me an orgasm. It takes a build up for that. It's like my body is saying, hmm that feels good."

"Tia, remember our first time?"

"Hmm-hmm, I do."

"Don't you want to know if I still feel the same to you or better?"

"This was nice but I am not going to sleep with you tonight. I have to go"

"Touch it Tia."

"I just finished doing a hell of a lot more than touching it Martez, no means no."

"I can feel you gearing up to cum."

"No I'm not."

"Oh really now?"

"Ooh stop that!!"

"You know what, Tia I'm gon' do just that."

"Good."

He stopped. I had to close my eyes. I could not believe he actually stopped. I needed to calm down. I was lost in thought for a moment, breathe Tia, just breathe, I kept saying to myself. That was too much dick for me to be fuckin' with anyway. Damn! I wanted to cum again, just one more for the road. Martez was being mean to me. He hadn't change in all of these years. He was still my bad-bad Tez. Oh! Oh! Oh!

"Martez," I called out. I looked at him. "What are you doing?"

"Nothin'."

"Don't do that Tez."

"I'm go'n get a little bit of this tonight."

"Tez!"

"I'm not penetrating you. I'm just playing. Didn't you say that we could play Tia?"

"You are being so unfair," I purred as I wrapped my legs around him. "You know damn well what you're doing."

"I'm just rubbing around a little bit. I have on a condom. What?"

"You ain't right Tez."

"I know Tia. May I have you now?"

"Just keep doin' that right there. I'm, I'm cuming baby! Oh! Ooh! Ah yes!"

"Tia?"

"I win you loose. Now I've got to go."

"Tia! Don't make me take it," he joked.

"You wouldn't," I imitated shock.

"Oh yeah! I would. Right about now I'm really thinking that I should."

"Go on and getcha self some pussy then," I said as I allowed my legs to flop down on the bed.

"Really Tia?" Martez asked uncertain. "You know I would never…"

"Yes really and yes I know… Don't hurt me with that big ol' thing."

"I won't hurtcha, Tia. Just tell me if it gets to be too much for you to take, and I'll slow my roll."

"Let's just start off slow, and then see where we end up."

"Okay, Tia." He pressed the head of his dick into my flesh. "How small is your pussy?"

"Very…"

Martez started off slowly for all of about the first two minutes, after which he lost his damn mind on me. That's all I can say. He was the bomb when we were children but that night he was all that and a hell of a lot more. He fucked me like no other before or after. My pussy opened up to him, welcomed him, enjoyed him, and came for him happily. We were sexing it up doggy style when the force of his orgasm sent us both crashing onto the mattress.

"You haven't called me Tez in years," Martez said, after catching his breath.

"I haven't considered having sex with you in years," I replied still winded.

"I thought so… I knew that I had you when you called me Tez. You know for a crippled lady, you out performed just about every woman I've been with and that's saying a lot."

"Just think, I'm not at my best and I'm over thirty. I used to be way better than that."

"How the hell could you get better than that? That right there was down right aerobic. What the hell else did you use to do?"

I explained it in all the glorified details. He silently listened with patience before he finally said, "Well damn! I missed out on all that?"

"Yes Tez, you sure did. But we can do that last little thing now."

"You gon' let me?"

"Yes."

I was on my stomach with my legs slightly parted. Martez straddled my thighs. He licked the pucker of my ass again and then tongue fucked it until my anus began drawing him in. He pressed the head of his dick against my asshole. He added pressure little by little. I was completely relaxed yet excited. Martez rubbed spit all over my anus coating it, making everything nice and slick.

"Stroke your clit, Tia. Cum for me again."

"Help me?"

More pressure was added as he reached for my clit. He rocked his body back and forth enticing my rectum to open up to him. He fucked my ass slowly, gliding his dick into my anal canal inch by inch until every inch was inside of my body. He worked my anus until the bed was soaked with cum. I loved every minute of it…

"This is the way you and Jack use to get down?" Martez asked seconds after he came. "I fuck your ass and your pussy cums?"

"Yes long ago but not anymore, and yes. After my accident, my body hurt too much. Jack could care less. We tried anal sex a few times the year we married, but he would never take his time. I told him it was against my beliefs, and never allowed it again. When he started raping me he added a little sodomy from time to time for good measure."

"Jack will pay for that… And the young Tyrique?"

"It took time for me to get used to what I do now, and I must admit that Tye was very patient with me. Sometimes after we were all done my body would hurt like hell. I would be painfully aware of every injury that I sustained. Although I've tried to hide it, he knows. He plies me with enough liquor for the pain to go away."

"I thought that the liquor comes first."

"With us the liquor came first, during, and after. He loved it when I enjoyed him."

"He is possessive and protective when it comes to you Tia. Has he ever?"

"Never ever, just you and Jack," I said emphatically. "You were my first sexual everything and he was my husband."

"Do you love him?"

"Yes, but you know me, I'm not in love. I wasn't going to let him get too close."

"Why are you speaking in past tense?"

"I broke up with him two weeks ago come Tuesday."

"He wasn't acting like that at the barbeque."

"I know."

"Be careful because that man has an agenda. He wants you and he is not going to stop until he gets you."

"Don't say that. I need to be free. We were on the cusp of being more. We both admitted that we cared for one another but then he tripped, he fucked it all up. All I need is a lover, someone who I can enjoy without all that emotional bullshit."

"Tia baby, you deserve to be happy and in love."

"I know but I want to be single, happy and in lust. I want to have hot passionate sex with no strings attached. After all, my children are almost grown. Thinking of children, I have got to go."

"You're not go'n stay the night with me?" Martez asked.

"Not tonight baby. When are you leaving?"

"Six, I have to be at work by nine."

"If I stayed we would not get any sleep just like when we were back home, in St. Louis," I said.

"I still can't believe that nobody knew."

"I wouldn't have been able to stay over and help you babysit if they had a clue. We must have had sex over five hundred times in just under a year and a half. From our fourteenth birthday up until the day you left."

"Well if you really want to count it all out, we had sex four hundred and fifty five days out of seventeen months, twice a day minimum, all night when you helped me babysit, and God help us over the weekends. It's a wonder that you never got pregnant."

"What's with you and counting?"

"You were all that I thought about. I only had girlfriends for cover."

"Yeah and they didn't last long either."

"That's because I only had sex with them when you were on your period."

"Why are we talking about this now, Tez?"

"I don't care what I have to talk about to keep you here. I want to make sure I get to sex you up again one more time tonight."

"All you had to do was just say so."

I didn't make it home until after three in the morning. I spent the following week exercising my pussy muscles everyday several times a day as I reminisced about Martez. I planned to visit California and soon.

CHAPTER TWENTY-THREE
ENVY

My family planned a Sunday brunch at Nicole's house the subsequent Sunday to welcome my mother home. Everybody was there including Linda, Tammy, and her children. Although my mother extended her trip at the last minute the party continued. We ate well, talked, and laughed. The party began winding down some time after two in the afternoon. Tammy and her children left first. Linda was on her way out of the door when Tyrique called me. She had her hand on the door knob opening the door as I answered my phone. The minute Linda heard me greet Tyrique she shut the door. I took notice right away.

"Hello, pretty lady."

"I'm surprised my phone rang, I'm at Nikki's."

"What ch'all doin'?"

"Having Sunday brunch, you know bacon, sausage, ham, eggs, biscuits, hash browns—the works. Oh and we are drinking champagne, mimosas, and fuzzy navels."

"Oh so you're drinking? I'll be right there."

I don't know if my phone lost its reception or if he just hung up but, the call ended. Linda was still standing there at the door.

"Were you waiting on something Linda?"

"I was going to ask you if you wanted me to take the girls with me."

"No they're fine. They are playing in the family room with their cousins so…"

"I was just saying, if Tyrique is coming over here. Well, I know you don't want your children around someone you're dating."

"I'm not dating Tyrique, we're friends. My children met him as my friend last weekend along with everyone else at the party. There's no problem with his coming over here, especially seeing as he is Jerome's friend too."

"I can stay so that it's more like a get together than a foursome."

"Thank you Linda that would be great."

Linda reentered in the great room; she sat at the dining table and waited quietly. I returned to the kitchen. I had been puzzled by Linda's behavior as of late however in that moment the pieces immediately began to come together. Her misdeeds flashed through my mind's eye. An ugly picture took form, number six of the seven deadly sins, envy. I realized sadly, I was her friend but she was not mine. I resolved to keep a close eye on her. Twenty minutes later the door bell rang. I answered smiling.

"Hello, Sweetness," I greeted Tyrique.

"Hello, Pretty Lady."

"Did you drive my girl?"

"I sure did. I thought that you just might miss her by now."

"I do miss her."

"We'll go for a ride later."

"Why thank you. Come on in. Are you hungry?"

"Hell yeah," he said.

Our small talk continued as he followed me to the kitchen. Linda stared as we walked by. I peeked back over his shoulder just before we entered the kitchen. Linda's eyes were fixated on Tyrique. Her nostrils flared. Her ample bosoms heaved. I saw her lick her lips just before we disappeared into the kitchen.

"You have a fan," I said to Tyrique as he washed his hands.

"Yeah, I meant to talk to you about that."

"We'll talk later, during our ride." I reached for a plate. "Do you want everything?"

"Yes."

"The sausage is beef smoked sausage."

"I still want everything." He crooned, speaking every word just so.

I stopped. I looked into his eyes. "To eat," I asked.

His lusty gaze spoke volumes yet he said, "Yep."

"You are so nasty."

"I just asked for something to eat."

"Come on now, Tye."

I smiled as I shook my head in total disbelief. I took him by the hand, and lead him around the kitchen island.

"Do you want a mimosa?"

"I don't know what they taste like."

"It's champagne with orange juice. Here try mine."

He took a sip and instantly made a face. Then Tyrique said, "No thank ya, I don't like that."

Jerome walked into the kitchen. He went straight to the refrigerator.

"How about a fuzzy navel?" I offered.

His expression asked, "What are you trying to do to me?" But he didn't respond. "Here dog, have a beer," Jerome offered.

"Beer is not a brunch beverage, gentlemen," I chided.

They both laughed. Tyrique accepted the beverage with a smile of relief.

"Nikki tried to get me to drink one of those frou-frou drinks too. I didn't like it either. I'll stick to beer," Jerome said.

"Yeah..." Tyrique agreed.

"We are getting ready to put in a movie."

"Chick flick?"

"Naw man. When it comes down to it Nikki and Tia only possess three truly girly things about them."

"I know man, being a good mother and being good in the kitchen are two of them."

They laughed.

"Oh really now? What's number three?" I asked boldly.

"It sure as hell ain't keeping y'all's mouth shut," Jerome said as he darted out of the kitchen.

"I know what it is," Tyrique stated as he gathered me in a warm embrace.

"I know you do." I all but purred. "Let's go, our movie is starting."

Nikki, Jerome, Tyrique, and I relaxed on the living room couch, an L-shaped burgundy leather over stuffed sectional with two recliners and a queen sized pullout bed. Nikki and Jerome were at one end and Tyrique and I were on the other.

"Linda, are you going to sit way over there or are you going to come over here with us?" I asked.

"I'm fine over here," she responded tartly.

"Okay."

We watched a couple of shoot em up action movies. We laughed and commented throughout, comfortably enjoying one another's company. It was after six when Tyrique got up and stretched. He pulled me up.

"I'm hungry. What about you?" Tyrique asked.

"I could use a bite to eat," I said.

"Come on."

"Where are we going?"

"To the store to get something to eat."

"Okay." As Tyrique drove to the store he began laughing. "What's so funny?"

"What's with your friend?"

I laughed a little bit before I replied, "What do you mean?"

"Didn't you say that she was a lot of fun and that you two were partying all over town?"

"Yes. What?"

"She just seems… She ain't the type. You are."

I cracked up laughing. "I'm what?"

"You have been dragging that poor girl all over town, from club to club, to bars and house parties. Does she always just sit there and stare at people like that?"

I laughed so hard I could barely breathe. I almost slobbered. Tyrique laughed with me.

"I must admit, the first week was a lot of fun. She tried to hold her own but after she fucked one of my friends for money, I just kind of gave up."

"What?"

"She asked for a hundred dollars. He said that he could give her the eighty he had on him. She agreed. He went on to say that he could give her forty for the night but he needed the other forty back. Again she agreed."

"Say what?"

"Now mind you he was joking but since she agreed…"

"How did you find out?"

"He called me the next day laughing his ass off."

"Does she know you know?"

"Hell yeah," I replied. It doesn't matter anymore. I don't go out that much these days."

"Why not?" Tyrique asked.

"Jack's gone. I have no reason to run off now."

"Really?"

"Yes, really."

"She tried cozying up to me at your party."

"You don't say…"

"She was laying up like a beached whale when I walked in. There were more than enough men at the party. Two brotha's tried to holla but she shot em down."

"Wow. She was on full. She ate before anyone arrived and parked her ass in that recliner. She even got a nap in."

"Watch her."

"Trust me, I am," I sighed. "I have known this woman for almost twenty years. If I didn't have so much going on this little revelation would have broken my heart."

"What are you going to do?"

"Let her get on her feet as I promised."

"You are a good woman, Tia."

Tyrique bought more than enough crab legs and shrimp for everyone. He commandeered the kitchen. While we waited for dinner we relaxed in the living room, old school R&B music in the background. Lighthearted conversation was enjoyed by all, except for Linda. She remained in the same seat at the dining table alone, closed off. I prepared two plates of freshly steamed Cajon seasoned crab legs with melted butter.

"Hey Linda, I made you a plate," I said, smiling kindly.

"I'm not hungry," she stated sourly.

Her statement caught me by surprise. Conversation stopped immediately. I stood there for a few seconds longer. I looked around the room. All eyes were on Linda. I gave Linda a quick nod. I smiled brightly as I held the steaming dishes high.

"Who's ready to eat?" I asked as I walked into the living area.

The children took their plates down the hall to the family room. The four of us took our meal in the living room. We gathered around the coffee table and dug in.

"Tyrique, dog this is so good. I mean damn man," Jerome said. "You're showing me up. Nikki's gonna expect me to be in the kitchen cooking."

Tyrique smiled.

"Relax Jerome. My sister already knows that you cannot cook. That's why I did the barbequing last Sunday."

"That's cold, Tia."

"I know Jerome, but it's the truth nonetheless."

"Tia, dear sister, could you please leave my man alone," added Nicole.

"I'll keep her busy," Tyrique said. "Eat up Baabay, you're gonna need the energy."

"We are having a leisurely evening. What on earth would I need energy for?"

Tyrique bit into a crab leg unnecessarily hard, showing his teeth. He winked at me. He broke open the crab's crust, licked his lips, and wiggled his eyebrows at me. Little did we know, Linda watched on absorbedly.

"Oh I can think of a thing or two," Tyrique said.

"Should I do my stretches now?" I asked.

"Ya gotta stay flexible."

"Can y'all keep all that nasty talk to a minimum? Jerome and I are trying to eat," Nicole interjected.

"They ain't sayin' nothin' that we ain't go'n be doin' after they leave," Jerome stated.

"Jerome," Nicole yelled as she swatted him.

"We're all grown sister dear. Don't pretend that you don't do a few freaky things every now and again."

Nikki grinned. She cracked open her crab leg, slid out a big piece, then plopped all into her mouth. She slowly licked the butter off of her fingers one by one. Jerome's eyes locked on her.

"Damn," he shouted. "It's time for y'all to go!"

"Shut up Jerome. We ain't going nowhere," I said.

The next thing I knew every morsel of food turned into to a sexual innuendo. From the way we bit into the crab shell and sucked out the tender meat, to the way we ate our shrimp was down right erotic. We were lost.

"Um, is there any more crab legs left?" Linda asked abruptly.

The spell was broken. I responded to her without looking her way. My voice was anything but friendly. Linda started towards the kitchen before she asked for a helping. I looked to Tyrique, he answered. Linda made herself a plate. She returned to her seat.

"I can see that you all don't know how to eat crab legs properly." Linda announced in a self-aggrandizing manner. We stopped and looked at her, shocked. Ironically she believed we looked to her for instruction. She continued on. She spoke with a condescendingly tutorial tone. "This is how you are supposed to eat crab legs, properly." We were stuck. We looked back and forth one to the other and then back at her again. Tyrique spoke up first.

"I don't need to be taught how to eat, especially by you. We are in private company trying to enjoy ourselves, if you don't mind."

"I'm just saying that you don't crack the shell with your teeth or dig the meat out with your fingers, that's all." Linda pressed on.

"Well Linda, I like what Tyrique was doing with his fingers and his teeth." I turned my attention to Tyrique. He turned his attention back to me. "I liked the way he licked his fingers, and the way he licked his lips, instead of using a napkin. As a matter of a fact I like every barbaric thing that he has said and done since the day that we met." Tyrique and I kissed. We licked the butter off of each other's lips.

"Yes, Tia is right. Just the sight of Jerome licking all of the flavor off of the shrimp before sinking his teeth into the tender meat just made me want to do things," Nicole said before she turned to Jerome.

"Not to mention the way Nikki slid that thick piece of crab meat into her lovely mouth," Jerome summed up.

Nicole snapped a crab leg properly and slid the meat out whole.

"You mean like this Jerome?"

The meat was too long to fit into Nikki's mouth. Jerome bit into the part that hung out. They kissed passionately.

"We have got to stop all of this before the children come in." I said laughing. "Let's finish our food so we can watch the last movie. I have to get my children home and in bed for school tomorrow."

After we called it a night I walked Tyrique out. He gathered me into a warm embrace and kissed me soundly before saying goodnight. Just as he was getting into my car Linda brought my girls outside. He waved goodbye to us as he drove away. We got into his truck. I immediately labeled Linda a black snake. Protecting my children from the reality of my situation was paramount. They had never seen me with any man other than their father. As long as they are minors that will never change. I looked at Linda and she seemed very pleased with herself. I smiled.

"I cannot believe how well tonight went," I said. "I'm so happy to have such a loving family and good friends in my life. Let's listen to some music."

I played love songs all of the way home. I smiled as I sang along. My girls joined in however Linda did not. Her expression was sour. I thought about everything. Linda was supposed to be my oldest and dearest friend. I tried to teach her a little etiquette yet she called me a bujjee white girl, claimed she was keeping it real, and stated that she would never change. I am not bourgeoisie. I have manners. How can a woman who eats a spoon of ice cream like she is trying to suck cum out of a dick teach anyone how to eat? My children begged me to eat in the play room so they would not have to witness her stuff her mouth full and chew like a cow, sound effects and all.

After the fiasco at the Biltmore bistro, no one has ever asked her out to eat in public again. She was loud as hell. She ordered the waiters around as if they were her personal servants, get me this get me that. She sent her food back three time, each time she stated brazenly that the waiter was going to earn every dime of his tip. I could not understand how hard she wanted him to work for four dollars. She asked to taste the food of the other members of our dinner party, reached across the table on more than one occasion knocking over wine, condiment bottle, and she all but slapped the center piece off of the table. But even with all of that, nothing was worse than watching her eat. Her mouth was already big, she did not have to stuff it full as well.

I was actually thankful that she ate before anyone else arrived to my party. A pig wouldn't welcome her to dinner. Oh Lord, please forgive me. Of course she's a little jealous. She just lost everything. Why did she have to try to involve my children? One minute sooner and that would have been that. She has a job. She will be gone soon.

I called Tyrique five days later, Friday early evening. I accepted an invitation to a networking event the following Saturday. I wanted to drive my car. I missed my shiny red GT and I wanted to show her off.

"Hello?" a woman answered.

"Hi, may I speak to Tyrique?"

"Who's calling?"

"Tia."

"He's not here can I take a message?"

"Just tell him that I need the car tomorrow."

"What car?"

"The pretty red sports car he's been driving."

"That's your car?"

"Yes."

"He said that his truck is in the shop"

"It was. Now, I have it."

"What?" she screeched. Her anger flared. She yelled, "Did you know that he has a girlfriend?"

"And I have a husband," I stated dispassionately. "What's your point?"

She was speechless. I patiently waited for her to respond. I hated women who blamed other women for their cheating men. I never understood what they hoped to accomplish. After all the man was in the wrong.

"Well," she began almost a minute later, "did you know that I have spent over three hundred dollars on him since we've been together, including this cell phone service that you are calling him on?"

"Really," I said melodiously, "I hate to tell you this sweetie but, he's driving around in my thirty-five thousand car. Your funky little three hundred dollars ain't shit. Keep spending, good luck."

That took the wind right out of her sails. "I love him," she sobbed.

"If he is giving everything to me yet taking from you, then you are your worst enemy, not me." I ended the call. "Aw, poor stinky got his phone repossessed," I said out loud, and I laughed. "I knew he was hiding something."

CHAPTER TWENTY-FOUR
NOT THE WHOLE TRUTH

I spent the remainder of my Friday evening with my children. Linda had taken to holding up in her room. After dinner Jack picked the girls up for the weekend. I decided to go to bed early. Moments after I relaxed in bed and turned on the nightly news, Nicole called.

"Hello Nikki."

"Hello there Tia," she said uncommonly amused.

"What's going on with ya Nikki?"

"That's what I called to find out about you."

"What do you mean?"

"You will never guess who just left my house just now."

"Who?"

"Tyrique!"

"What?"

"Yeah!"

"What did he come over there for?"

"He said that he was looking for you. He said that he went to the club, but you were not there, and that he couldn't remember exactly where you lived."

"He never knew. What was so important? He could have called."

"No he couldn't. He said that he tried to call you but he couldn't get the last four numbers right. He lost his cell phone."

"Really?"

"Yeah, girl. You should have seen him. He was stuttering and scratching his head like something was really wrong."

"Did you give him my number?"

"Yeah."

"Oh okay, I wonder what's wrong."

"Whatever it was it really had him going."

"What do you mean?"

"I'm telling you, you should have seen that man. He looked ruff. He said that he was sorry for stopping by so late. He asked if I had seen you today. Then he said he lost his phone along with your number. He said he really needed to talk to you."

"Hold on, Nikki I'm getting a call." I took a quick peek. "Unavailable, that's probably him right now. I'll call you back tomorrow and let you know what's what."

"Okay then."

"Good night, Nikki. Thanks."

"You are welcome, good night."

I clicked over. "Hello?"

"Tia," Tyrique sounded kind of stressed.

"Hello Sweetness."

"Did anyone call you today?"

"No, but I spoke to your girlfriend today. I was the one who called. She answered your cell phone."

"Damn."

"What's wrong?"

"What did she say?"

I recited every detail of the conversation. Tyrique actually sounded relieved. He happily questioned me about a few details, admittedly shocked by my candor. I told him that it would be hypocritical to be mad about a little girlfriend when I had a husband.

He took a big breath in relief before speaking again. "Thank you, Tia."

"You know, you could have told me, that way I wouldn't have been caught off guard."

"You sure as hell handled it well."

"Not really. I hurt her feelings. She couldn't say a word after I said that shit to her. I wouldn't have been so cold had I known."

"First of all she's my ex. Secondly, after what she pulled tonight, she deserved her feelings to be hurt."

"It sounds like you had a ruff night."

"I did. I lost my phone at the club Thursday night, so I called her and asked her to stop the service until I got off of work. That way no one would be able to run up the bill and I could get a new phone later on that night."

"Okay."

"Instead of her stopping the service she had all of my calls forwarded to her phone."

"How?"

"We got the phones together back when we were dating. After we broke up, I told her I'd still pay my bill if she let me keep the service. She didn't seem to have a problem with it because she had a contract and she didn't want to be stuck with cancellation charges."

"Okay, so what happened?"

"After a while my calls started coming in. She answered every last one of them. Today she got out the bill and started calling people."

"Say what?"

"Oh yeah! I called her after I got off of work today so that we could go and get a new phone, she was too busy yesterday. She said that she was at her mother's house. She asked me to come and pick her up, I said no problem. She was doing me a favor. She seemed so cool about it too."

"Really?"

"She played me good."

"What happened next?"

"I didn't even go home and change. I went straight over to her mother's house to pick her up. I knocked on the door, her mother answered, I went in and all of my exes were there."

"Say what?"

"There was a room full of women that were all angry at me."

"Please tell me that you are kidding."

"I wish I was, but I'm not."

"What did you do?"

"Well, they all started talking at once, saying I did this or that. When I was able to get a word in I simply said, 'we dated, now it's over, so get over it,' then I tried to leave."

"Tried?"

"Her mother was blocking the door."

"How did you get out?"

"I told her, don't make me have to move you. She moved. As I was leaving, ol' girl yelled out, 'I spoke to Tia!' All I could say was, damn. I didn't know what she had said to you or what to expect when I talked to you again."

"Well after what I said to her she wasn't about to ask me to that little get together. There are two sides to each and every story. And... I'm an amazingly calm person."

"That's a good thing."

"Not always. Calm people can be very dangerous."

"Ya don't say?"

"It's true, but I'd have to have good reason. I can't see where you did anything wrong, at least not by what you've told me. It sounds to me like you need some cheering up. I remember you asking me if I knew how to cook some gumbo. Do you still have a taste for it?"

"Hell yeah!"

"I'll tell you what, I'll cook you some gumbo tomorrow and bring it over to you for lunch. You sound tired as hell so, why don't you get some sleep and I'll see you tomorrow."

"Oh Tia, Baabay you are definitely one of a kind."

"I know. Goodnight, Sweetness."

"Goodnight, Pretty Lady."

The next morning I got up and went to the farmer's market for fresh vegetables and herbs. I purchased fresh crab and shrimp from the fish market. I went to the grocery store for the filé seasoning, stewed tomatoes, smoked sausage, a box of instant rice and chicken broth. It took me an hour to prep, an hour of hands on cooking, and then four more hours of simmering. During the final hour I took a shower, styled my hair and applied makeup. I fragranced with Georgia peach scented after bath splash and lotion. I dressed as a friend, save for my sexy underwear. After I was all ready, I took the pot out to the truck and called Tyrique just before I started the engine.

"Hello there, Pretty Lady."

"Hello, Sweetness. Da gumbo is ready," I said in my best Cajon accent.

"Come on."

"I'm coming."

When I pulled in I saw Tyrique standing outside. He was not smiling. He looked a bit apprehensive as he opened my door. I jumped out of the truck. I smiled a big toothy smile. I greeted him cheerfully. He smiled and immediately wrapped his arms around me. Tyrique held me a little bit too tight however I didn't mind. He kissed me soundly.

"Ah! It's good to see you," Tyrique said.

"There is a big pot of gumbo in the front seat. Could you get it for me?"

"Yeah!"

"Don't shut my door. I have to get the rice."

Once we were inside Tyrique looked at me a bit strangely as if he thought that I would go crazy since I was in his house. I laughed a little bit as I shook my head. He visibly relaxed. I followed him to the kitchen.

"You really made all of this for me?"

"No, I made some of it for you but you get firsts. Take as much as the biggest bowl or pot you've got can hold."

"Aw you go'n make me think that I'm special."

"You're special all right. I need a pot to make the rice in."

"Is there anything else that you need?" he asked as he handed me a pot.

"No, you can go sit down. I'll start the water and join you shortly."

"Okay."

I joined him in the living room where he sat on the couch watching a standup comedy video. I took my usual spot in the big chair. We watched and laughed for a good ten minutes before I got up. The minute I moved, his eyes were on me. I giggled and I shook my head as I walked out of the room. When I returned Tyrique had an inquisitive look on his face.

"I just put the rice in and set the timer on the stove. We can eat in about five minutes."

"Oh okay."

The buzzer sounded. I got up and fluffed the rice. "Do you want to eat out of bowls or plates?" I asked.

"Bowls are fine."

"Where are they?"

"Right there to your left."

I opened the cabinet. "Oh okay."

The very instant I placed the two bowls on the counter I was spun around. Caught off guard, I took in a huge gasp of air. I wondered how the hell he got from the couch over to the kitchen so fast. Tyrique grabbed a hold of me. He kissed me passionately. His hands seemed to be everywhere all at once. I couldn't even think. Lost in frenzy, pawing at one another like dressed monkeys, we ripped at each other's clothes. Freed garment flew through the air. The rice went flying off of the stove. Impassioned beyond all rational thought, nothing short of a house fire could have stopped us. Caught up in a vortex of wild sexual energy, he took me right there in the kitchen. He fucked with unabridged passion—hard—primal—all consuming. The stove jumped around like an unbalanced washing machine. He sexed me up again in the bedroom exerting us both to the point of collapsing. We rested for some time before either one of us was able to move. I bathed. He wiped. By the time I returned to the kitchen, not only was the kitchen clean but new rice had been made and Tyrique was dishing up our bowls.

"Well, well, well lookey there. You have been busy. Was I really gone that long or are you really that good around the kitchen?"

"Do ya really have to ask how good I am in the kitchen?"

"Naw…" I sauntered over to him. "I do believe I know just how good you are." I kissed his lips. "You are excellent," I purred.

"Why thank ya. You Tia, Baabay, are a bad ass woman!"

"Well I try to be a good girl but it never works out when I'm with you."

"There's no need to try to be good around me, no need at all."

"Stop that before something else gets knocked onto the floor. I'm already hungry. If we start this up again I'll be down right famished."

"Go into the living room. I got the food."

"Alright..." I sang.

"I love it when you say that."

We ate our meal in a comfortable silence as we watched another comedy show.

"Oh, I am stuffed," I announced.

"I'm getting seconds." Tyrique paused the movie before looking into my eyes. "I can't believe what happened yesterday," Tyrique stated

"Well Sweetness, it's in the past so let it go. Enjoy today."

"Oh I'm enjoying a lot about today."

"So am I."

"This here gumbo is really good Tia. It's on point."

"Why thank ya."

"Tia," his was tone serious.

"Yes Tyrique?"

"Thank you."

"You are so very welcome, Sweetness."

His thank you carried more meaning than he could have ever put into words. He smiled at me. It seemed to give him great comfort to know that I understood him so completely and accepted him just as he was. He remained content in my company knowing he was not judged. Just as the movie ended my cell phone rang. I looked at the call screen. It was Tammy.

"Hey!"

"Hey, busy?"

"I'm having lunch."

"Two things."

"What's up?"

"The thing for tonight is cancelled but we have been invited to a house party."

"What time?"

"Can you be ready around eight?"

"I sure can."

"Are you with Tyrique?"

"Yes."

"Bye girl."

"Bye."

Tyrique looked at me curiously, however I didn't notice until my mouth was full. I looked at him. My expression asked, 'What?'

"I'm not keeping you am I?" Tyrique asked.

I swallowed my food, smiled, and said, "No."

"Tia?"

"Tye?"

"You go'n make me ask?"

"That was Tammy on the phone. The event that was planned tonight was cancelled but we were invited to a house party. I have to be ready to go by eight, which means she's driving. I won't need the car until tomorrow for Mother's Day."

You have got to be kidding me, I mused. My thoughts must have been clear on my face. Tyrique smiled a sheepish smile. He followed his smile with a very simple statement, just checking. I laughed.

"I'm not the one who got caught. Ain't nobody answering my phone and according to the latest information, my car is on a car lot across town."

"Not everybody is as crafty as you."

"You like my craftiness?"

"Yes I do."

"Just checking…"

Tyrique and I spent about an hour together the next day. Mother's day was not a good day for him. His mother died when he was a young boy. I had to meet my mother, sisters, cousin, and sister-in-law for our annual mother's day outing. We were going to see an impersonations show at the casino. Nicole's car was not fit to drive long distances. I agreed to pick her up. After my visit with Tyrique I started out to Nicole's house. Not even two minutes after I left Tyrique's house my cell phone rang.

"Hello?"

"Hello there Tia."

"What's wrong Sylver?"

"My wife ain't going, so Mama and Rachel need a ride too."

"What?"

"I'm sorry T."

"How the hell am I supposed to pick them up in my little bitty car?"

"Don't you have ol' boy's truck?"

"No!"

"Can't you go get it?"

"I can't stand y'all."

I hung up on my brother, and called Tye. He answered right away.

"Hello pretty lady."

"Hi."

"What's wrong?"

"Can you bring the truck around?"

"What happened?"

"I'll explain when I see you, just bring it around please?"

As soon as I was done talking to Tyrique, my sister Nikki called. As I spoke my body animated in anger. I parked my car in front of Tyrique's community clubhouse and let the windows up. I did not want to cause a scene. Tyrique pulled up beside me. I exited the car still talking. "Get off my phone, I'll be there shortly." My entire demeanor conveyed my anger. I looked at Tyrique however I could not adjust my mood. "Here." I said as I handed Tyrique my keys.

"Damn, who pissed you off? I have never seen you mad."

"Family can do that to you."

"Call me later. I want to know how your day is going."

"Okay, can I have the keys please?"

"The truck is running, Tia."

"Oh damn! I'm sorry. I'll calm down later. Right about now I just can't seem to."

"What's wrong, Tia?"

"All I wanted was to drive my car for Mother's Day. I enjoyed it for all of two minutes before my family ruined that for me."

"How?"

"At the last minute my brother's wife cancelled which means that Mama and my cousin Rachel don't have a ride. I was told that I had to pick them up in your truck of course, seeing as I have access to it and all."

"You are more than welcome to use it."

"Thank you Sweetness, however that's not the point." Tyrique hugged me before escorting me to the driver's side of his truck. He helped me in, kissed my cheek, and closed the door. I let down the window. "Thank you again Tye."

"Don't forget to call me later."

"I won't forget."

"Come back and see me tonight if it's not too late."

"Okay."

CHAPTER TWENTY-FOUR
MOTHER'S DAY

After I picked everyone up and we were on our way, I was still in a mood. My mother tried her best to cheer me up. All I wanted to do was listen to my music, take the drive, and calm down. I did a good job of blocking everyone out however I had no choice but to respond to my mother.

"Tia I don't know why you are so mad," mother stated.

"All I wanted to do was drive my own car today. I miss my girl."

"Well why didn't you?"

"Because all of you needed a ride..."

"Well why didn't you just take your car and the truck?"

"You know Mama, I've got some good pussy but I don't think that it's that damn good. I can just see me now, 'Tyrique, I need my car and your truck. I'm gon' let one of the women in my family drive your truck because they need a ride. That way I can drive my car and be happy. You don't have a life or any plans today because I'm busy with my family and there's no way you'd ever make plans without me, so you don't need your truck, now do you?"

"Well what can he possibly have to do today? It is Mother's Day,"

NAKED CONFESSIONS

she said.

"I don't care if he was sitting around scratching his balls, it's not right to leave someone stranded. Especially someone that has been kind enough to give me his vehicle no questions asked, no payment needed and take care of mine, including offering to make my payments."

Mama didn't say a word, but Nikki sure did. She said, "You are throwing boulders, Tia. You threw a quarry full at your own mother, and on Mother's Day too."

"I asked all of y'all to leave me alone one by one as you got into the truck. I told you all that I was very unhappy to be inconvenienced this way. If I could just take this drive to the casino in peace then I would be alright. But nooo, you all are selfish and impertinent, y'all think it's funny and to make matters worse none of you will leave me alone about it."

"Tia, you have a man that's willing to give you a truck, not just any truck but a nice SUV. Why are you so mad?"

"Let me put this simply so that all of you women can understand. This truck is not mine and because of the jackass that I'm married to I had to give my car away. The one day that I thought I'd be able to drive what belongs to me, you people made it impossible. So can y'all please just let me finish driving in peace?"

"We have to pick up Irene," Mama said.

"Yes ma'am."

I was originally told that my oldest sister was going to meet us at the casino. We were supposed to call her once we got to the loop for directions. It was a forty-five minute drive to my older sister's house and then another thirty minutes to the casino. My oldest sister was ready and standing outside smiling when we pulled up. She opened my door.

"Get out, Tia," Irene ordered.

"What?"

"You don't know how to get there so I'm driving."

I put the truck in park, took off my seatbelt, and got out. I mumbled under my breath. "Fuck all y'all."

"I heard that, Tia, don't make me tell Mama," Irene said, laughing.

"Yeah Tia, get in the back because I'm not moving," Nicole added, laughing.

I did not reply. I sat in the back next to my cousin Rachel and stared out of the window. For the life of me I could not understand why they were all getting such a kick out of playing their little game. I could not believe it.

"I don't know why you are so mad Tia, we are all together and that's all that should matter," Irene stated.

Nikki answered for me. "She wanted to drive her own car. She was throwing boulders at Mama earlier."

"What? On Mother's Day... Tia!" Irene's faux shock was all too obvious.

"Oh yeah, she told mama that her good pussy got her this truck," Nicole added.

"All I asked her was why didn't she take her car and the truck. Hell if you are busy doin' it why not get all that you can? After all it's just for the night," Mama chimed in.

That got me. I spoke up quickly, and said, "The night, what do you mean for the night? We are going to see one show and that's it. I'm taking y'all home after the show."

They all laughed including my cousin.

"No. Who told you that?" Irene spoke up. "We have the whole evening planned. We are hanging out at the casino. The show starts at seven. We are having dinner afterwards and then you can run off to your young man. I've got your keys and you ain't getting them back until we are all ready to go. We all know you will sneak off."

"I hate y'all, hate, hate, hate!"

"Tia, now that's not nice." Irene pressed on.

NAKED CONFESSIONS

I flipped her off.

"Why are y'all doin' this to me? All of y'all seem to be taking some perverse pleasure in not letting me do what I want to do."

"It's Mother's Day!" they all said together.

Nicole looked over her shoulder at me. She smiled before she began speaking. "Tia, you are spoiled. You're the only woman I know who went from her husband taking care of her to her young lover taking over where the husband left off, within a matter of hours."

"It wasn't a matter of hours. Yes, he gave me his truck but I really wanted to drive my car today. I hate having to compromise. That is my car. What would y'all have done if I didn't have this truck? Oh nevermind, it doesn't matter. We have the truck and we are on our way."

"Exactly!" the ladies said in tandem.

"I just think that it's unfair to me."

The impersonation show was really good. By the end of the second act I was in a better mood. I called Tyrique. He was happy to know that I was in better spirits. Although it was a brief conversation our words were passionate. I looked forward to seeing him again after the Mother's Day festivities were over.

Once we were seated to dinner one hour turned into two. I knew I would not be making it back to Tyrique's house that night. I simply put the idea out of my mind. By the time we were done with dinner it was past ten o'clock at night. We all got into the truck in the same spots as when we came. Irene put the truck in reverse however it didn't move.

"Tia you have transition problems," Irene announced.

"What?" I asked.

"The truck won't move."

"Before we panic, let's see if we have any fluid in the back. Open the hood and the back please."

We were very industrious women, well rounded. Not only did we know how to diagnose mechanical problems, we knew how to fix them, most of the time, or at least jimmy rig it until we could get it fixed. Irene got out with me, mind you we were dressed up in beautiful after five attire. She went to the front of the truck, while I went to the back.

"We are in luck! There's a half of a bottle of transmission fluid left," I announced.

"Tia!" Irene shouted.

I trotted to the front of the truck wearing four inch heels. "What's wrong?"

"Look, you have a severe leak."

"Damn!"

"I'll call him right now." He answered right away. "Hello Baabay!"

"Hi. What the hell is wrong with your transmission?"

"Are you stuck?"

"Hopefully not, however you have a serious problem. There's a puddle of transmission fluid on the ground and the truck won't go in reverse. I'm more than an hour away from you. I have all of the ladies with me."

"I just got everything fixed. Maybe a hose is loose." I cracked up laughing. That was exactly what I needed to lighten up my mood, especially in that situation. "What's so funny?"

"The transmission doesn't have a hose. If you just got it fixed, you probably just have a gasket that didn't seal properly."

"Okay then, I don't know a damn thang about transmissions."

"I do. It's a minor problem. I'll go to the nearest gas station and get a few bottles of fluid. Don't worry, I'll be straight until you can get a shop appointment."

"Call me if I need to come and get you."

"I will."

"I'm serious, I'll come take all of you home two at a time if I have to."

"Me last?"

"Oh yes!"

"Good. Goodnight Tye."

"I'm not going to sleep until you tell me that you made it home safely."

"I'll call you the minute I get there."

"Make sure that you do."

"Yes sir."

We barely made it to the gas station. The truck drove very badly, jerking all the way. Happily we made it, laughing all the way. I went in and bought all of the transmission fluid they had. I asked the attendant for a stepladder. I did not want to balance on the front tire wearing pumps again. There I was standing in ruby red high heels bent over under the hood with my ass high in the air. All I could do was balance, pour, and laugh to myself as I did what I had to do. When I was done, I righted myself, and stepped off of the ladder. The moment I turned around I noticed that every man at the gas station was staring, I smiled. I dropped everyone off and went on home. I called Tyrique after I got into my house, it was just after midnight.

"Hey pretty lady, you home?" He sounded tired.

"Yes, Sweetness. Goodnight."

"Goodnight."

I fell asleep laying sideways on my bed clothes and all. The next morning just after nine Tyrique called me. I wasn't up yet. I spoke in a deep morning cracking voice.

"Hello Sweetness."

"Aw Baabay, are you still sleep."

"Not anymore."

"Good morning, pretty lady."

"Good morning, what's goin on witcha this early in the morning?"

"I called the transmission place. You can drop the truck off if you would like or I can come by after work and do it."

"I'll do it. Where do I have to go?"

He gave me the name and address of the place. It was a good thirty minutes away from my house.

"You really don't mind Tia?"

"No, not at all. I'll call Irene and have her meet me there."

"Sounds like you already have it all worked out."

"I'm very efficient. I'm go'n be stranded for a few days while it is in the shop, hmm?"

"I can bring you your car if you need it."

"If I need something I'll call you."

Everything went smoothly. I put the truck in the shop. Had lunch with my sister Irene, after which she drove me home. There was nothing much to do without wheels. I just hung out at the house. The next night Tyrique came to my house for the first time. I needed to run some errands. The last stop was close to Nicole's house. We visited for a short while.

On the ride home I slowly unzipped Tyrique's pants.

"Should I pull over," he asked quickly.

"No," I replied sweetly. I reached inside and fondled his dick for a little while.

"I can pull over." He put click on the right signal.

"No," I said more firmly as I looked into his eyes. I stroked his dick until my hand grew wet with precum. "Please turn off that blinker." I freed his dick from his pants. "Concentrate on the road Tye." I slowly licked and sucked the head. He almost swerved off of the road, twice. I giggled as I tucked his dick back into his pants.

"Tia I've never…"

"I see," I sang.

The next day was my wedding anniversary. I really did not want to be alone. I thought it would be a good idea if Tyrique helped to cheer me up.

"So, what are you doing tomorrow Tye?"

"Just working."

"Can you save some time for me?"

"Yeah, what's going on?"

"I'll tell you when I see you tomorrow."

Tyrique drove me home. He came in for a little while. We ate lunch together. The next day he called to confirm our plans for later on that evening. Shortly thereafter the shop called. His truck was ready. The gasket that did not seal properly just as I suspected, there was no charge. Nicole drove me to pick up the truck. She attempted to question me about the nature of my relationship with Tyrique however I was not forthcoming.

It was after six when I finished readying myself for the evening. I had expected Tyrique's call. I attempted to check my messages to see if I missed his call however, the call did not go through. I called my cell phone from the house phone only to learn that the service had been disconnected. I called my service provider. Jack cancelled the service. I reinstated my service and added a security code. I used my home phone to call Tyrique. He was still at work and having a bad day; the call was brief. He called me back thirty minutes later.

"Hello Sweetness."

"Hey Tia."

"Ooh your day is going badly."

"You don't know the half of it."

"Well if you can't make it tonight just call me."

"I'll be there."

"Okay, I'll wait for you at JD's."

"What's wrong with your phone?"

"Jack turned it off but it should be back on any minute now."

"Oh, okay. I have to go but I'll call you later on tonight."

"All right."

"Bye, Baabay."

"Bye."

I did not hear from him that night or the next. By Friday morning I had reached my limit.

CHAPTER TWENTY-SIX
HAVE A GOOD DAY

I called. I got voicemail. "Give me back my shit, today." I said very calmly. I went on with my day as usual. As an unknown author I was challenged to find ways to promote my book. I received an email from Tammy, an invitation to an all male review the following month. As I looked at the pictures of the sexy men and read their bios, an idea popped into my mind. I called their manager. I inquired about booth space. He informed me that the only vendors were in the sex toy and movie industry. I was determined to get my way. He offered a small table at a discounted booth price. I made the arrangements. I was happy.

Later on that evening while I prepared dinner, Tyrique called.

"Hello."

"Tia?"

"What time can we do the exchange?"

He let out a breath, and said, "I'll be home by seven." He sounded as if he just gave up all hope.

"Okay, call me when you get there, bye," I said then hung up the phone.

He called me at seven sharp. "I'm home."

"Okay, bye."

I took my time eating. I decided to do the dishes. I watched my favorite television show. At eight thirty Tyrique called me again.

"Hello."

"Hey Tia, are you coming?"

"I'll be there in a little bit."

I arrived around nine. When I pulled in he was outside. He did not look happy at all. I exited the truck carrying his belongings, the things I wanted to give back. My face was the void of expression.

"Tia?"

"Here are your keys, CDs and DVDs," I said coldly. He took the items, however, he did not hand over my keys. He used my remote to unlock the door. He opened it. I got in. He handed me my keys. I looked into his eyes. He silently pleaded for a chance to explain however I could not allow him to speak. "Good bye," I said flatly.

I closed my car door, started my engine, turned my music up high, and pealed out. I was less than a mile down the road when I noticed his garage opener was still on my visor. Although we had exchanged cars many times Tyrique had never left anything behind. Mother's Day immediately came to mind. I knew it was a setup. I pulled off of the road and stared at it lost in thought. Fuck him, man. I'm not going back. I'm not going to his door. I am not getting pulled in again. I'm done with being disappointed.

Tyrique called not even an hour after I got back home. The moment I saw it was him I smiled. However I could not allow my smile to resound in my voice. I attempted to sound sleepy instead.

"Hello."

"Tia, its Tyrique."

"What can I do for you?"

"I didn't wake you up did I?"

"No. Is there something that you needed?"

"I think I left my garage door opener in your car. Did you see it?"

"Where would it be?"

"Either on the seat or the visor."

"Let me go check." I took the time to get out of my bed. I walked all the way to my car, open the door, took a look, and close the door, letting him hold the line and listen all the while. "Yes, it's in there."

"Can you hold on to it for me? I'll come over tomorrow after work to pick it up."

"Okay."

"Thank you."

"Good night."

I laughed to myself as I thought, good one, round two is tomorrow. I'll be just as cold and distant. Tyrique called me just after three in the afternoon. I gave him a bit of false hope by sounding cheerful.

"Hello."

"Hey Tia, I'm off work now. I was hoping to stop by."

"Okay, I'm at home, come on."

"I'll be there in fifteen minutes."

"Ha, ha, ha okay," I said, before ending the call. He arrived not even ten minutes later. He called to tell me he was in my driveway. I told him I wasn't dressed. I asked him to come to the door. I opened the door wearing his red football jersey. I handed him my keys and said, "It's exactly where you left it." I smiled. Tyrique was beyond shocked. He stared at me for the longest moment. He took the keys turned and walked away. I shut the door and lay down on the couch. Shortly thereafter he rang my door bell. "Now it's time to gut punch his ass," I murmured. I smiled as I sashayed towards the door.

I opened the door just enough to reach out and get my keys. I stole a look at him as he handed them back. Total disbelief vividly radiated on his face. He turned, as a soldier would, and marched away, head held high, shoulders straight. I waited until he was halfway down my drive before I stepped out of my house and called out to him. He stopped. He turned to face me.

"Come here, baby," I beckoned. He all but ran back to me. I had my arms out to him. He gathered me up like I was his lifesaver. I whispered in his ear. "Have a nice life."

He stiffened. He stepped away from me; looked directly into my eyes. His determination was vivid in the set of his jaw. I stood strong. I didn't turn away. The wanton look in my eyes silently dared him to take me. I dared him to do something, anything other that just walk away. I thought if I pushed the envelope he would respond. I was wrong. He stood there looking at me for a moment longer.

"Have a good day, Tia," he replied coolly.

His head dropped as he turned and walked away. I watched him. I stood there at my door until I heard him get into his truck. Everything in me wanted to call him back. I wanted to run after him but my feet would not move. My pride held me still. Once I heard him start the engine I stepped back into my house and closed the door. I wanted to cry but something about his last words negated that notion. I believed in my heart it was not over. I smiled as I stretched out on the couch. The next thing I knew my front door swung open startling me. I sprung up off of the couch. "Stupid wind, I thought I shut that better," I said as I started for the door.

"You really should learn to lock your door, Tia," Tyrique said as he reentered my house.

"What the…" I was flabbergasted and flummoxed.

I raced towards the foyer just as Tyrique slammed the door shut. Our eyes locked. I froze. Every fiber of his being was filled with intent: every breath, every step. He moved towards me swiftly. By the time my mind had processed the situation he had me. Tyrique flung me around and threw me up against the front door, all in one smooth motion. Palms flat, I caught myself before my face smashed against the wooden surface. I tried to get away however he used his body to hold me still. As he pressed me up against the door I heard him unzip his pants and tear open a condom. My body grew restless. I was so excited. I did not want to say a word for fear that the spell would be broken. He wielded his power over me. He took complete control.

He drove his dick into my pussy like a power driver. He was rough and unrelenting. I loved every minute of it. His every thrust sent shock waves of delight coursing through my body. The angle of his dick stimulated my g-spot perfectly. Cum ran down my legs in streams—pure orgasmic excellence. I could barely stand. After he released me I slid slowly down the door. He caught me. He lifted me up, carried me into the living room and laid me on the couch. He kissed my cheek gently before he turned and walked out of my door. All I could do was just lay there. Two days later I was checking my email when Tyrique chimed in. He said hello and asked how life was treating me. The conversation was trite, polite at best. That was the extent of our relationship.

Saturday night, I was home alone. My children were enjoying a weekend at their uncle's house. Linda was on a date. I did not want to be alone. I called my brother-in-law.

"Hello?"

"Hey Don."

"Hey Tia, what's going on?"

"Can you do me a favor?"

"Whatcha need?"

"Call your brother for me please."

"What's wrong Tia?"

"Our anniversary was five days ago and I guess I miss him. Tell him that I need my husband tonight. Will you do that for me please?"

"Yeah Tia, I'll call him for you."

"Thank you, Don."

Within an hour I got a call from a blocked line. "Hello?"

"You called?"

"Yes."

"What do you want?"

"Some meaningless sex."

"What?"

"You heard me."

"I'll be there in an hour."

That conversation was the dawn of a great affair. I never imagined one could have an affair with one's own husband, nevertheless I did. All I had to do was make it fun and impersonal. We met at hotels at odd times of the day both during the week and on the weekends. It was the most exciting time in our marriage; although it didn't last long. Jack labored in vain under a misperception, the aspiration of winning me back. When it became clear that I was not interested, Jack's true colors began to shine through.

It was the middle of June. I had my first official book signing scheduled at a male strip show. The male strippers loved me. They used me as a prop in the last act, which was exciting. Before they took their final bow they introduced me and my book. While the dancers took their final bows one by one, I set up my book display in a booth in the atrium. I earned over a thousand dollars that night. After the book signing I received invites to several summer parties. I began having the time of my life. My children spent most of the summer with their father. I was free as a bird. It was a very electrifying existence.

Although I thought about Tyrique everyday I did not dwell. I refused to allow my looming feelings to interrupt my everyday life. Most nights I was too tired by the time I got home to even change my clothes; there were no sleepless nights. Every now and again Jack would stop by and slip into my bed. I really did not mind as he was familiar, comfortable. In my mind it

NAKED CONFESSIONS

was just sex, taking Jack as my lover did not impede my filing for divorce. I simply no longer had the desire to be anyone's wife.

On July first I checked my emails. Tyrique chimed in. Apparently he had tried to call. I gave him my new phone number. He called immediately. He began the conversation with I miss you. After the pleasantries he announced that he had a newborn son. I immediately thought, that explains a lot. I wondered why he could not tell me the truth long ago. I congratulated him. The child was a month old and named T'avion.

"Oh what a lovely name, I'll bet he is just as handsome as his father."

"You're just saying that, but thanks for making me smile."

"Anytime, Sweetness."

"When can I see you again, Tia?"

"Whenever you'd like."

"Well it has to be soon because I'm about to leave the country."

"What? When? Where are you going?"

"I'm going to Korea next month."

"Damn!"

"I want to spend as much time with you as possible before I go."

"Okay, but I'm going to Atlanta for a wedding."

"When?"

"I leave on the thirteenth."

"When will you be back?"

"I'll be back on the twentieth."

"Oh okay."

"What are you doing for the Fourth of July?"

"I don't have any plans. What about you Tia?"

"I don't have my children so I'm free. There are a few barbeques I've been invited to. You can tag along if you'd like."

"That sounds good."

Something in his response sounded a little bit off. I decided not to hold him to his word. Nicole and I took an early Sunday morning flight to Atlanta. The groom, Jordan, met us at the hotel. The affair between Nicole and Jordan had been going on since they were freshmen in high school. His engagement was not a hindrance. I found myself locked in the bathroom within an hour of arriving. After my shower the door would not open. Thirty minutes later they let me out. Jerome met up with us the following Wednesday. He immediately knew that something was going on between Nicole and Jordan. His heart broke into a million pieces. Jerome confronted Jordan at the bachelor party to no avail. He confronted Nicole the moment we returned from the bachelorette party. He had no luck. She pretended to be too drunk to comprehend English. Everywhere Jerome turned he was fed lies, including me. Nicole and Jerome's relationship ended shortly there after—less than one week after we returned home.

Surprisingly Jack picked me up from the airport. He greeted me as would a loving husband. He loaded my luggage and helped Nicole with her luggage as well. He was all smiles, happiness and joy. I was at a loss for words, dumbfounded. Nothing Jack did made any sense, until I got home.

"Welcome home, Tia."

"Thank you, Jack."

"Are you hungry or thirsty? Can I get you anything?"

"No thank you. What's this all about?"

"I did a lot of thinking while you were gone Tia."

"Really, about what?"

"Us."

"Why?"

"After you served me with the divorce papers I just started thinking."

"And?"

"And I think that we should try again."

"Try what again?"

"Being a family."

"What?"

"I missed you while you were gone. I want you back Tia."

"We tried that last month Jack. I've been trying with you for fifteen years. It never works out. I filed for divorce because I realized it never will. We were never meant to be."

"I know how you feel. It took the realization that you had finally given up on us to make me see what I was giving up."

"Too bad."

"Why do you have to be so cold?"

"I'm not being cold. I'm being realistic. There's no way in hell I'm going to take you back now. I don't mind sleeping with you whenever the mood strikes me but I don't want you as my husband. You hurt me. You cheated on me. You turned your back on me when I needed you the most. I cannot spend the rest of my life with a person like that. The best we can ever be is friends."

"Well I moved back home and I'm not moving back out until the judge tells me that I have to."

"Okay, so that's what it is. You got kicked out of whereever you were."

"No, I left."

"Whatever. I can't have sex with you if you are living with me."

He got mad instantly. "What?" he bellowed.

"You heard me. No sex at all and I'll fight you tooth and nail if you try to take some pussy anyway. You can't have your cake and eat it too. It was different when you stopped by from time to time. I enjoyed making you cheat on your new woman, however living with you as man and wife again, oh hell no."

"Who were you fucking in Atlanta?"

"Nobody."

I turned away from him, gathered my purse and keys, and left the house. I got into my car and sped away thinking, what the hell else can happen now?

Two weeks later I was out and about with my home girl Tammy and Uncle Ralph. Ralph Long is a very good friend who we met the year before. We call him Uncle Ralph because he is over fifty yet he is still fun to party with. We were doing a little bit of parking lot pimping at the after hours lounge when, lo and behold, Tyrique happened by. I caught him out of the corner of my eye walking my way. I looked. It can't be…

"Tyrique?"

He smiled as he mimicked me. "Tia?"

I immediately started his way. The minute I got close enough to him he gathered me in his arms and planted a hell of a kiss on me. The kiss was so hot and lasted so long that people started to comment as they walked by. We stepped away from one another.

"Oh, Tia baby," he shouted. "Damn, I have missed you."

"I've missed you too. What are you doing in my neck of the woods?"

"I heard about this place so I thought I'd check it out. Who are you here with?"

"Tammy and Uncle Ralph."

"Uncle Ralph?"

"He is a friend. Let me introduce you."

I made the introductions before relaxing against the car. The men shook hands. Tyrique turned his attentions back to me.

"Come here, Pretty Lady," Tyrique invited.

I smiled, tempting Tyrique with my eyes, the moment I took just one step in his direction. He grabbed a hold of me again. The next thing I knew I was bent backwards over the top of Ralph's trunk. Tyrique and I were going at it like fiends. We were bad, very very bad. He picked me up and sat on top of the trunk. I wrapped my legs around his torso. He massaged my breasts as we passionately kissed. His forward momentum did not stop until I lay flat on the truck of the car. He gripped my hips as he kissed his way down my neck. A desirous moan escaped me.

"Day-um!" Tammy and Ralph commented together.

We stopped. Tyrique righted himself and pulled me up as well. I slid down off of the car. My head down, I straightened out my clothes.

"Look at what you got me doing," Tyrique accused.

"What," I asked as my head snapped in his direction. "What I've got you doing?" I smiled at the irony. "No you didn't just blame me, damn it."

I don't know what came over me but for some reason I spread my legs slowly as I licked my lips at Tyrique. I gave him my very best come hither look and it worked. He mobbed me again. He jumped me like it was the thing to do. Just as fast as he jumped me he let me go. It was as if he kept loosing his mind and then finding himself again.

"Tia, where are you parked?" Tyrique asked.

"I'm in the truck today," I pointed to my pickup which was parked three spaces away, "right there."

"Let's go."

He pulled me by the hand as he started towards my truck. I looked back towards Tammy, who looked shocked.

"Bye Tammy," I shouted.

"Have fun, girl," she replied.

CHAPTER TWENTY-SEVEN
TAKE ME

I handed Tyrique my keys as he opened up the passenger door for me. Once I was seated, he slid his hand between my legs, and massaged my pussy while he kissed me.

"Hmm! This right here is still mine," Tyrique stated.

"Yes, it is, Sweetness. You know it is," I agreed.

He drove to the nearest hotel and secured a room by the hour. It was seedy, vibrating bed seedy, perfect for a quick fuck hello. The foreplay was maddening. Tyrique savored my pussy. He licked it thoroughly — greedily — drinking my juices. We fucked like it was mating season in the rainforest. The vibrating bed added an interesting twist. We did not just stop after that night. He came to my house the following Tuesday for some hot passionate sex, an early dinner, some more hot passionate sex, a movie and a quick fuck goodbye.

The next night I went to his house. We lay intertwined catching our breath after a pre-dinner quickie.

"When will your divorce be final?" Tyrique asked.

"I'm not sure yet but I now live in a happier home."

"What ever happened to your home girl Linda?"

"I don't talk to her anymore."

"What? What happened?"

"Linda tried her best to ruin my life. She told Jack that I had your truck. She said that she did not know a man who would give his SUV to a woman without expecting something in return. She went on to offer him revenge sex. She had no idea I had returned home and witnessed her whole display. I waited quietly for Jack to accept, but he wasn't interested. I could have killed two birds with one stone. I kicked her out of my house and took my truck back."

"What?"

"Oh yes, she was that jealous. I didn't make a big scene. I just simply told her that she needed to find another place to live because she had worn out her welcome."

"Damn, what kind of woman is she?"

"Linda is a jealous, petty bitch. She even tried picking on my children."

"How?"

"My oldest daughter has a perfect apple bottom shape. Linda stood in the mirror trying to get her EFG sized breasts lifted as high as she could one night when she was preparing for a date. My daughter watched her curiously. Linda grabbed both of her breasts and looked at my fifteen year old child. She said, 'You have a lot of growing to do to get to this size,' and grinned triumphantly."

"Damn, that's foul."

"No worries. My daughter walked down the hall and into the bathroom. She called Linda's name, backed up just enough for her butt to stick out of the bathroom door and said, 'You will never have one of these,' and laughed."

"Oh da-a-mn," Tyrique hooted. "Her ass is flat."

"Indeed. She had the nerve to yell at me about my child being disrespectful. I was laughing too hard to even respond."

"So, how are your girls?"

"They are doing well. They'll be starting school soon. I have two daughters in high school. How's your little man?"

"He's getting big."

The following afternoon he was at my house again. I made a large pot of gumbo for lunch. I settled him in the living room and started a Bond movie. I went to the kitchen, got our food, and returned. We looked at each other and smiled contently before bowing our heads in silent prayer. After we watched about an hour of the movie, Tyrique pressed pause, jumped up out of the blue, and snatched me out of my seat.

"I've been polite long enough."

"Well damn!"

Tyrique kissed me quickly, spun me around, snatched my pants down then pushed me forward onto my couch. He stood behind me kissing my neck as he put on his condom. He entered my body without preamble in one thrilling thrust. His sexing me was all I could take. Actually it was a little bit more than I could take, truth be told, but I was brave, loud, but brave. I called out his name over and over again. I gripped the couch. I hit the wall. Hell, I even bit a throw pillow. My juices washed out of my body like an everglade. His body quaked. He cried out my name as he came.

After we showered and dressed we finished watching the movie. Three hours had passed. It was time for his departure. We fucked again at the door. He didn't bother cleaning up after. He simply pulled up his pants and walked out. The following Friday I was at his house. We lay in bed. Tyrique stroked my hair as we watched a movie together. It was as if no time had passed between us. After a while he began to speak.

"Tia, this will never be over. You are mine. Boy have I missed you. There are so many things that I love about you. I enjoy you so much."

"I will be your Tia for as long as you want me to be. Until you marry. What I don't understand is why you won't be my Tyrique as well. If I'm so much fun why don't you enjoy me? If I'm so easy to be with, why don't you seek out my company? If I'm so lovable, why don't you love me? What the hell are you holding back for?"

"You are married."

"I was married when you met me. I didn't keep that a secret."

"I didn't care for you then like I do now. I can't let myself fall too deeply in love with you when you belong to another man."

"So why don't you let me go?"

"I can't do that either. You might as well stop trying to run from me because it ain't gone work. I ain't going no where and neither are you. "

"What about South Korea?"

"That's postponed."

"So what the hell am I supposed to do?"

"Do what you got to do, Tia. I'll be right here."

"So I'm supposed to see you, talk to you, cook for you, and fuck you whenever the mood strikes you but I can't ask for your company?" He just looked at me. "Why can't we just be good friends? I'll talk to you, come visit you, cook for you, you know, share your company without the sex."

Although his gaze asked, 'You have got to be kidding me, right?' Tyrique said, "No Tia."

"I cannot take this. I can't keep having hot passionate sex with you every once in a blue moon and then just sit and wait for your call. Every time you lay me down all I want to do is do it again. Whenever I leave here I miss you. I look forward to seeing you again. You just… You make me feel so…I can't do this man. We need to be just friends."

"No."

I looked up at him and frowned as I thought, no? We will see about that.

"Don't make me act the fool, Tia. I'll come to your house, and tell your husband to send you on out. If you try to run from me I will act very badly."

"What?"

I got out of the bed, straightened out my clothes, and walked out of the room. He followed me.

"For now I'm willing to wait, but if you don't come to me when I call you I will come and get you. I've never let you pull away from me before so what makes you think that I'm going to let you go now?"

"Tyrique?"

"No, Tia. If you decide that you want to be mad, like you have so many times before, I'll give you some time to get over it, but not too much time."

All I could do was stare. I was lost in thought remembering all of the times that I had had enough of his shit and told him goodbye. From the first time to right at that moment I had never realized that he had a master plan.

"Tia, do you want something to drink?"

"Yeah Tyrique, that's just what I need right now."

"Brandy?" he asked as he retrieved a glass from the bar.

"Sure, I'll drink heavily then drive on home."

"I'll take you to your sister's. You can come back and get your car later on tonight or tomorrow."

Tyrique poured brandy as if it was iced tea. He handed me the glass. I glared into his eyes and drank half of the smooth rich spirit down at once. I turned away from him and walked over to the couch.

"No, Tia. Go back to the room."

I stopped, my head bowed. I was bowled over. I faced him, glowering as I thought, you have got some big ass balls if you think you can just say all of this shit to me and I'll just obey—I mean damn. I looked him up and down as I asked, "What?"

"Don't make me come over there and get you."

No the fuck he didn't! He's got life twisted. Yeah right. I eyed him. I took another sip of my drink as I turned and started towards the couch. However before I could make it his hands were on me. He took my drink out of my hand and placed it on the end table. He wrapped one of his arms around me from behind, reached down between my legs and grabbed a hold of my pussy, catching my clit. I took in a sharp breath.

"This here is mine, ya heard me?"

He turned me so that I was facing him and gathered me up in his arms. I was a bit startled but not afraid. He bent me back as far as I could go. I defiantly looked into his eyes as I thought, fuck you damn it. My pussy is mine. I ain't scared of you.

"If you've got something on your mind, Tia, say it out loud."

"Fuck you damn it! My pussy is mine, not yours. I ain't scared of you Tyrique."

"Really?"

"Really!"

"We will see about that. Struggle if you want to, just don't hurt yourself trying to fight me."

Oh damn! He was pressing forward, pushing me backwards to his bedroom. I tried not to go, alas, I was off kilter. I had no leverage to stop him and nothing to grab a hold of slow him down. I reached and grabbed for the door jam but all that did was pause him for a second or two. He reached out and gently removed my hand as he proceeded to the bed.

"Stop fighting me, Tia. All you gon' do is hurt yourself."

"You gon' have to take it. I'm not gon' give it to you. I really would like to see how you gon' get me on that bed," I said, mentally preparing for a fight.

"What? You know I can pick you up."

Tyrique's swift actions left me defenseless. I was landing on the bed before I had realized I had been lifted. He was on top of me in a flash. My mind raced. Oh damn! I am all hemmed up. Why the hell did I wear this today? Because you wanted to seduce him. I bet you never thought you'd end up fighting now, did ya? I wouldn't exactly say that I was fighting because I hadn't been able to do a damn thing to him yet. Oh just let me get one of my hands free so that I can slap the shit out of his ass just once. It's time for me to cheat.

"Ouch! Tyrique you are hurting me."

He released his hold just enough for me to get the leverage that I needed. I flipped him clean off that bed. I wrestled in high school. I was so proud of myself. I smiled brightly thinking, hehehe! I bet that you didn't expect that, now did ya? He landed on his feet. Before I could get off the bed he grabbed my ankle. I mean damn, that man was quick. He pulled me to the edge of the bed.

"I won't fall for that again," Tyrique calmly stated.

Oooh he was mad. The thought flashed in my mind, almost making me laugh. Tyrique held my leg as he began pulling my panties off. I made the mistake of kicking. He caught my other leg. He trapped them, pressing them against his chest with is arm. He looked very triumphant as he kneeled on the bed spreading my legs. I tried to swing at him however he just caught my arms by the wrist effortlessly, and continued. The moment that his torso was past my knees I clamped my thighs on him. I had amazingly strong legs. I use to leg press two hundred pounds, three times a week, before my accident. Although they were not as strong as they used to be, they were still powerful. I squeezed as hard as I could. I concentrated hard. He could not move forward or backwards. Tyrique was stuck for as long as I could hold him there. It was my turn to be triumphant.

"Oh so you really want to fight me?" Tyrique asked rhetorically. I smiled, which pissed him off a little bit. He continued, "See, I thought you knew you could not win. I could've sworn you were being difficult just for the hell of it. All right Tia..."

He put my wrists together holding them with one hand. The minute he thought he had me under control I snaked one free and pinched his nipple. I held on tight until he grabbed my wrist again. I could not help but laugh a deep throaty laugh. I looked at him and smiled a very taunting smile.

"I always knew you were willful but what you don't know is, so am I and I never lose," he announced.

He put my wrists together and grabbed them with one hand again, but this time he held on very, very tight. I struggled. I closed my eyes and tried with all of my might to get free of him, however I could not. I felt his fingers on my pussy. He pinched my clitoris hard. I gasped. I gasped again. I came. My knee jerk reaction gave him all of the slippery wet access he needed. His dick was inside of me before I could recover.

"Oh shit, Tyrique!" I exclaimed.

"Um-hmm. I told you this right here is mine," he shouted.

"Fine," I yelled. "Take it."

He was vigorous yet thorough. The sensations of his sex rocketing throughout my body hurled me into a mind numbing cloud of passion and pleasure. I had no inclination to fight. I waded through a lascivious tailspin of orgasmic nirvana. He fucked me as if he was branding my pussy, "Property of Tyrique,'" and when he was done all I could do was hold my pussy tight and look at him. "Damn," was the only word that came to mind.

He gathered me in his arms, tucking me close. He rolled so that I lay on top of him. He hugged me tight, oh so tight, for what seemed like forever. Thoughts began to enter my mind one by one. I have known for quite some time that I'm yours Tyrique, yet I didn't want to admit it to myself ever again. However, after tonight I can no longer deny it. What am I going to do? What else can I do? He won't let me go. Whoa, did he say that he can't let himself fall too deeply in love with me? He is in love with me? No.

I need to get the hell out of here. I need to go home.

I tried to get up. I needed to take a shower and leave. Tyrique would not allow me. He held me tight. We fell asleep that way. I woke up about an hour later, he was still sleeping. I slowly slid out from under his arms, quietly gathered up my clothes, and tippy toed into the living room. I dressed, without taking a shower, and showed myself out.

On the drive home I was still deep in thought. I would not allow myself to think about his love for me. I needed to focus on breaking free. I did not know what he meant when he said that he would act bad. I wondered what he could possibly do. If he showed up at my house I could always tell Jack that he was a lunatic, a stalker who must have followed me home from the club. What we had was not love. It was chemistry—hot, passionate, desirous, orgasmic, mind-blowing sex—nothing more nothing less. I needed a plan. I needed to call my sister.

"Hello?"

"Hey Nikki girl."

"Hi Tia, what's goin' on girl?"

"I need some help."

"What's wrong?"

"I need to figure out how to kill a bird with a stone."

"A bird… with…. a stone?"

"Yeah."

Nicole laughed. "A bird with a stone? You need to kill…a…bird with a…stone?"

"Yeah!"

"Now, I've heard of killing two birds with a stone, but you actually need to kill a bird with a stone," she laughed so hard her voice squeaked.

"It's a shifty ass bird. Damn it!"

"Who? Tyrique?"

"Yes, who else?"

"How many times have you tried to break up with him?"

"Five."

"Well, maybe you need more than one stone."

"Naw, I just need a really big stone."

"That's still funny, a bird with a stone."

"Let it go, Nikki. Please. I really need your help. I have feelings for Tyrique that I have not been able to get past. I try to be strong and keep my distance but he keeps showing up in my life or… I get all weak and call him."

"So what are you going to do?"

"I don't know. Hell, if I knew what to do I wouldn't have called you for help. Are you going to help me figure this out or what?"

"Well, I really don't know what to tell you Tia. I mean you have already broken up with him, a few times, but he keeps seeking you out so, you know, I guess that you have to get creative. Hell, tell him that you are going back to your husband."

"I tried that and he didn't believe me. He said I wouldn't react to him the way I do if I was still in love with my husband. Not only that, he said he is willing to wait the four years for my girls to be grown. He told me that this is only the beginning. He told me that I was going with him when he gets re-stationed."

"Well damn Tia! Give up on trying to get rid of him and just take it one day at a time. You never know, the answer may just come out of waiting him out. There's no way that he can know, for four years, that you are still sleeping with Jack and still hangin' there."

"It has been a year already, yet, he has not faltered. All he has is a little over three years left. I've tried to put some distance between us but every time I try, I fail miserably."

"I don't even know what to tell you."

"I'll figure out something."

"Well let me know if you come up with something that I can help you with."

"Okay Nikki, bye."

"Bye Tia."

I asked myself why. Why did I let that man into my life? The answers came flooding into my mind. He seemed to be exactly what I needed at the time. He was someone to play with, someone to make me feel whole, not crippled. He wanted me and I loved being wanted. I needed to be wanted. I needed the excitement, to feel alive. After all, the doctors told me I was slowly bleeding to death. They just did not know which cancer was stealing my blood. I was vulnerable, emotionally at the lowest point of my life.

Cheating husband and permanent physical disability combined with facing cancer, I was down for the count. My own husband didn't even care if I lived or died. I just needed to have someone hold me make me feel good. In my opinion there's no better feeling than passion, the pure ecstasy of making love, but I couldn't have that. I settled for hot passionate sex and multiple orgasms. Now I'm no longer facing lymphoma or myloma, my body is stronger. Although I still have my challenges, I'm so much better than I was eleven months ago. The problem is, I have feelings for Tyrique and he has feelings for me that can't go anywhere. I wish I never met him.

I pulled into my driveway. I sat up straight and smiled. "Nikki's right, I have the perfect plan."

CHAPTER TWENTY-NINE
FRUSTRATING SAGA

I decided to stay breezy and busy. Every time Tyrique called me I was somewhere doing something with someone, but not just any someone, family. Although I ignored his calls, I sent text messages apologizing for being busy. I did not want to be tracked while I went out at night, therefore I stopped driving. Weeks passed. My plan worked perfectly, or so I thought.

One night I partied with Nikki, doing my level best to cheer her up. The breakup with Jerome left her feeling blue. We sat in a booth close to the dance floor. She spotted Tyrique, and pointed in his direction. I did not see him at first. I panned the crowd. I spotted him heading towards the bar. I all but leaped out of my seat. I strutted across the dance floor and walked straight up to him. His back was to me. I touched his arm to get his attention. I smiled up at him.

"Hey," I said happily.

"Hey Tia, let me get my drink."

"Do what you got to do," I replied.

Tyrique stepped away. I was a bit put off by his greeting. On the other hand, I was free to do as I wished. I fancied play. I saw my friend

David sitting with his back to the bar, David Franks was a forty year old hard bodied mechanic with dark chocolate skin and ice gray eyes. As I approached, he looked my way. I smiled at him. He opened his arms to me. I walked up and stood between his legs. He pulled me closer.

"Hello Tia. Baby girl, you are looking good tonight." David said.

"Hey David baby, how you doin'?"

"Give me my hug, girl."

I leaned in closer. My body touched his, groin to groin. We hugged for longer than would be considered friendly. I remained in his embrace while we talked.

"Are you being bad tonight?" David asked.

"Yeees, very bad," I purred.

"Well you know I'm horny, right?"

"That sounds like a personal problem, bye."

I smiled at him as I stepped back. I turned to walk away, however I stopped when I saw Tyrique walking towards me, our eyes locked. I smiled as I waited for him to reach me. He collided into me, grabbed a hold of me and pressed me to him.

"Who you here with?" Tyrique asked.

"My sister."

"Where y'all at?"

"Right over there." I pointed out our table. "I'm gon' go back to my seat now. I'll talk to you later."

I turned and walked away. As I was walking to my seat I caught the eye of several men. One in particular, a young man who could have easily been a Chico DeBarge double, blatantly stared. By the look of him, he could not have been older than twenty-one. He was pretty. I smiled at him appreciatively as my eyes said, I see you looking at me young sexy. I winked at him as I passed by. I took my seat. Percy, a man that Nicole had seen out from time to time had joined our table.

"You look mighty happy," Percy complimented.

I smiled a little brighter. Percy looked away from me. I followed his gaze. Tyrique approached. I scooted over. He stayed next to me for a little while. He laughed and talked to Nicole and Percy all the while stroking my pussy. I came in the palm of his hand. Tyrique closed his hand into a tight fist and excused himself to the bar. When he got back he stood by the DJ's booth. I was unaware that the pretty yella boy kept an eye on me. Within five minutes of Tyrique's departure he approached.

"Hello," the pretty-yella boy greeted me.

"Hi," I replied sweetly.

"Would you like to dance?"

"Sure." I took his hand and followed him to the dance floor. As we danced we introduced ourselves. His name was Dominique.

"Is that your man?" he asked.

"Who?"

"The brotha who was sitting next to you."

"No."

"Maybe you should tell him that."

Dominique nodded his head and looked to his right. I looked over my left shoulder and there Tyrique was standing next to me. He looked furious. I stopped dancing. I looked up at Dominique and smiled.

"I have to go now," I stated simply.

Dominique smiled back at me, and said, "No hard feelings."

I waved goodbye as I was taken, by the arm, back to my seat. Tyrique sat me down and then went back to his spot standing in front of the DJ's booth. He watched me. I immediately thought, I am not going to behave. I'm going to act as bad as I possibly can tonight—every time you turn your back. And I did just that. He could not go to the bar or even to the bathroom without coming back to find me dancing with someone. The moment I saw him coming, I ran back to my seat. This went on for most of the night. Dominique asked me to dance again. I danced, moving my body like a snake. I closed my eyes and let the music take control.

"Tia," Tyrique bellowed.

"Oh shit," I cried out startled.

I went quietly. Actually I laughed all the way. He found me a seat, and sat with me.

"Why do you keep getting up?" Tyrique asked perturbed.

"I was asked to dance," I replied honestly—ersatz innocence—saccharine sweet.

"You were told to sit down."

"I don't remember my father being here tonight."

"Don't get up again."

"Well damn. I guess I should find a way to occupy myself seeing as I have to just sit here." I looked into his eyes as I slipped my hand down his pants. "Hmm, now that's better."

He followed suit. That night he posed for a picture of himself at the club. He gave it to me before I left. He looked unhappy I thought, damn! I need another chance. I sent a text while I was at the club asking if he wanted gumbo. He replied, yes, right away. I asked, carry out or delivery? He replied, IDK what time will the gumbo be ready? I let it go. I text messaged him the following evening at six. I let him know that the gumbo was ready. He messaged me back saying he would have to take delivery the next day. His little man had an emergency. The next morning I went on about my day as usual. Tyrique text messaged me at ten thirty asking for gumbo delivery. I called. He asked again very nicely. I agreed. He said that he could really use a hug. I told him that I would be on my way shortly.

I showered and dressed in a hat, t-shirt, and jeans. I prepared a plate of gumbo and rice for my sister's new boyfriend, packed a gallon bowl filled with gumbo and one filled with rice. I text messaged Tyrique, I'm on my way. I arrived within ten minutes. I carried the plate with me to the door. I knocked. He opened smiling.

"Hi." I said.

He looked at me. He looked at the little plate and then over my shoulder for a moment. He smiled. He did not say hello nor did he take the plate. I could not help but to giggle a little bit.

"This is enough gumbo for you isn't it?" I asked, holding the plate higher.

"Oh yeah, I'm just glad you brought me some. Come on in."

Still he did not accept the plate. I walked on past him and into the kitchen. I put the plate in the refrigerator. Just as I did he smacked my ass. I quickly turned and smiled at him. I went into the living room and took a seat on the couch. He remained in the kitchen. I kept my seat for about a minute. I returned to the kitchen.

"I can't stay baby. Give me a hug. I have to go," I said.

He wrapped his arms around me right away, and asked, "Can you come back after you go to your sister's house?"

"No."

"You can't come back?" he asked seriously.

"I'm just kidding. I can stay for a while."

"Here's my keys, your gumbo is in the car. That little plate is for my sister's boyfriend."

He smiled a really big smile, took the keys, and left. His enthusiasm tickled me. I sat watching a comedy show as I waited for him to come back in. He returned smiling brightly and carrying the two big bowls. I laughed out loud. He looked over to me, he was pleased.

"Now this right here is what I'm talkin' about!" Tyrique exclaimed.

"Come on now Tye, you know damn well I wouldn't just give you that little bitty plate."

"I was hopin' not."

"Yeah, tried to play it off but you not taking the plate from me was a dead give away You generally take whatever's in my hand and put it down, so that you can get your hands on me."

He laughed as he sat next to me on the couch. We looked at each other and smiled before turning our attention to the television. He invited me to his bedroom. Mindful of my physical condition, he wanted me to be comfortable. We spent the afternoon together lying across his bed watching football.

The following day I attended Tammy's birthday party. We partied hard. I woke the next morning to find a very attractive nineteen year old young man sleeping on my bosom. I thanked God that I was fully dressed.

I drove home laughing all the way. I remembered stealing that young man from his little stuck-up girlfriend, an atypical Black-American princess. I never liked those types of girls. I told her boldly, "I did not grow up as a princess however I am a conquering queen," and then threatened to break her jaw if she did not get out of my face. Holding my weight while I learned to walk on my own again gave me amazing upper body strength and very nice biceps. She backed off quickly. I loved every minute of it. Almost everyone who slept over found a reason to enter the room the next morning while we lay together, save for Tammy. I loved Tammy. She had a live and let live outlook on life. I turned up my music and hit the gas as I entered the highway. Tyrique called moments later.

"Hey, Pretty Lady."

"Hello, Sweetness."

"How was the party?"

"It was off the hook. I haven't even made it home yet."

"Damn you must have had a really good time."

"Hell yeah, I was drunk off my ass, man."

"Well, I'm not mad at you. Were ya able to keep your clothes on?"

"Lookey here, the only occasions I have ever had trouble keeping my clothes on were when you are around, drunk or sober as a bug. All you had to do was look at me and my clothes flew off."

"Come on over here so that I can look atcha then."

"Okay, I'll be there in about five minutes."

"Five minutes? Where are you?"

"I'm driving on the highway to my home. I'm about a mile from your exit right now."

"I'll leave the door unlocked, just come on in."

"Well all right..."

We had sex that morning. I wasn't impressed. That was the last time I saw him for over a month. He called to check up on me from time to time. My birthday came and went. I celebrated in Las Vegas with Martez, Tammy, Nicole, and Percy. We partied very, very hard. Tyrique called me to wish me a happy birthday. I woke the next day and, amazingly, without a hangover. Martez had taken the liberty of ordering room service. I so enjoyed breakfast in bed.

"What are you hiding from me, Tia?" Martez asked, out of the blue.

I placed my fork down. My eyes filled with tears. I whispered, "I'm dying."

"But you said..." Martez began mystified.

"I did not lie to you. I don't have leukemia or any other blood cancer. A tumor, the size of a grapefruit, is sucking out my blood like a vampire."

"How long have you known?" Martez asked with a frown. "No, wait, you knew you were still losing blood all along. Why the hell did you hide that from me?"

"I hid it from everyone," I cried. "I need to fight. I cannot do that effectively while dwelling on the fact that no one cares but you and my daddy." My heartache became unbearable. I relented. Sorrow engulfed me. My resolve fell away. I crashed. I wept uncontrollably. My tears fell like spring rain as I clung to Martez. "Please don't be angry at me," I begged.

"This has been the most difficult journey of my life." I looked into his eyes. "I am doing the best that I can."

"What about your children?" he asked as he gathered me into his arms.

"I have been the best, most attentive mother ever. They are in high school now." Talking about my children calmed my heart. "I don't get to spend as much time with them as I would like, however I am very supportive and understanding. My children adore me. They both did a school paper naming me has their hero because of the way I battled to walk again. I thank God for that. I refuse to steal their happiness."

"And Jack?"

"He has no idea."

"What did the doctors say?"

"I am scheduled for surgery April first."

"I will be there."

"Thank you."

"Stop keeping secrets," he demanded before smiling. Then he said, "I'm your only secret."

"Yes sir."

Martez held me tight. We made love, slowly, all day and all night long. I loved having Martez to rely on, he was my rock. Saying goodbye to him was bittersweet. I hated that he lived so far away. I wished to God that things were different. Alas, I could not escape my reality, no matter how hard I tried. I returned home. I climbed into my bed and cried myself to sleep. Weeks passed, nothing and no one could lift me up out of my state of woe. I put on a happy face whenever my children were with me. I cherished every moment with my beautiful babies as if it was my last.

My liaison with Tyrique had developed into a nice friendship. He was still my happy place. I had gotten into the habit of cooking gumbo from time to time. It took hours to prepare, thus served as an excellent pastime. I called Tyrique, packed a large bowl full and headed over. The moment I saw him again I immediately missed the way things were between us.

"Come on in, and have a seat, Tia, so we can talk."

"Oh, we go'n talk," I said jokingly, although he was serious.

"Tia?" He took a seat at the table. "Lets catch up."

I sat across from him. "So what do you want to talk about Tye?"

"Tell me about how you've been. How are the girls?"

"I'm fine. The girls are doing well. Did you just get back from the gym?"

"Nah, I was at the park playing some ball." All of a sudden he got up, went into the bathroom and turned on the shower.

I spoke a little bit louder, "Oh okay. I can leave so you can get all cleaned up."

"That's okay. Come on in the bathroom with me. You can have a seat and talk to me while I shower."

I laughed, and said, "You are kidding, right?"

He poked his head out of the bathroom door. "Come on. We're friends now aren't we?"

"All right..."

I went into the bathroom, placed the toilet lid down, and took a seat. He undressed in front of me. My desire reflected in my eyes. He smiled as he stepped into the shower. He spoke to me as if everything was completely normal.

"So tell me more about your big birthday bash, Tia."

"All right, we partied everyday from the New Year's Eve to January thirty-first."

"You had a thirty-two day party?"

"Well, my birthday portion of it didn't start until the first so I actually had a thirty-one day birthday party. There was something to do everyday of those thirty-one days including the week I spent in Vegas."

"You were there for a week?"

"Yeah," I said enthusiastically.

"Your birthday was on a Friday. I thought you were just going for the weekend."

"No, when I party I do it up right."

"Did you get any birthday sex?"

"No, but I was too busy to even care," I lied, Martez immediately came to mind. "I never came back to my room sober enough to even change my clothes before bed. Hell, there was this one time that I even passed out on the floor after stumbling into my suite."

"Damn!"

"Lookey here, I couldn't even walk up a flight of stairs. I took the elevator to the second floor everyday and one time I got lost."

He cracked up laughing before he asked, "How do you get lost going to the second floor?"

"By pushing the wrong button. I went the wrong way after I got off of the elevator and ended up on different elevators. Once I did find the right floor, I forgot my room number all together."

"What?"

"It was funny as all get out. I had to call Nikki just to find my room. Thank God for speed dial."

"Where were you?"

"Two doors down. My sister stepped out of her room and there I was to the left of her room instead of to the right."

"You have got to be kidding."

"Nope, I'm not kidding at all. As a matter of a fact, at the time, I was actually shocked at how fast she found me. I did not realize she had just walked out of her room. She told me the next day. Anyway, I told her I couldn't find my room because I could not remember the number." Tyrique laughed so hard he made me laugh too. Moments later, I was able to continue on with my story. "She took me over to my room and helped me with my key, laughing the whole time of course. She told me to go to bed and then shut my door. I leaned down to take my boots off but my head started spinning. I sat on the floor. I woke the next morning holding one boot."

Tyrique laughed uncontrollably. I peeked behind the curtain to look into his eyes. I wanted us to share the moment of laughter together.

"Ah, Tia… You know you need help, right?"

"Yes Tyrique, I know." The water splashed on me. I squealed as I quickly closed the curtain.

"I'm sorry."

"I'm okay."

"You know you can always join me, if you'd like. I need some help washing my back anyway."

"Well, I am feeling kind of dirty."

We bathed together, washing each other's backs. It was nice. He left me to finish up. I exited the shower. I searched for a towel.

"Tye!"

He appeared like magic. "Here's a towel."

"Thank you."

"You really don't need to get that dry."

"What?"

"Come here."

"What?"

He took me by the hand as he led me to his bedroom. The room was illuminated by candle light. Candles were everywhere, it was beautiful. I looked into his eyes. I smiled lovingly.

"I need you, Tyrique."

"You have me, Tia."

I was overjoyed to be in Tyrique's arms again. I was face to face with my mortality, in the fight of my life. As time passed the rate of my blood loss increased. I was tired all of the time. I was not sure if I would die before my divorce was final or if I'd survive and be granted my freedom. I did not have leukemia, lymphoma, or myloma as previously prognosticated. I had a tumor that was growing fast, slowly bleeding me to death. However in the moments I spent with Tyrique none of that ugliness mattered. He was my happy place. A few weeks later, he was my Valentine.

I told no one about my health, save for Martez. I smiled happily as I told my father that I did not have any of the blood cancers which I had been tested for over the previous year. No one in my family helped me when Jack was abusing me. My father was the only person who kept up with my testing schedule. No one else, not even my own mother offered one word of support or even asked how I was doing. I chose to keep the tumor a secret because I simply could not cope with the idea of no one caring and I could not put my father's life at risk as I tried to save my own. They gave me a year, and in that time I tried my best to live it up.

April fourteenth, I opened my eyes, I was alive. I looked around the recovery room. The only face I saw belonged to Martez. He gathered me into his arms as he cried in relief. He stayed with me from registration to release. He took me to his hotel and tucked me into bed. He held me tight.

"You stopped breathing on the operating table, Tia," Martez said, his voice filled with emotion. "Your doctor was very angry when he told me. He said you gave up."

"Are you serious?" I asked.

"Yes. He told me that less than a minute after you went under, you took a deep breath, sighed in relief and then your heart stopped."

I immediately understood why, and said, "I happily let go because I was no longer in pain."

"Why only in death, Tia? Why not live a happy pain free life?"

"You're absolutely right Martez."

Ninety days later, I was happily divorced. Martez remained my best friend forever. Tyrique became nothing more than a character in my book, a New York Times bestseller.

WHERE HIP HOP LITERATURE BEGINS

AUGUSTUS PUBLISHING

LOVE & A GANGSTA
ERICK S GRAY

**UNBELIEVABLE: THE LIFE
DEATH AND AFTER LIFE OF
THE NOTORIOUS B.I.G**
CHEO HODARI COKER

HARD WHITE
SHANNON HOLMES

Inspirational, Graphic, True stories... Hip Hop Literature... Teen lit, Hood Erotica, Street literature, urban gangsta drama, our titles interlace action, crime, and fast life clashing with the harsh realities of life on the streets. Augustus Publishing brings a vast array of exciting titles. Sometimes raw and dripping with gritty ghetto realism... Often revealing the high price of street life.

AUGUSTUSPUBLISHING.COM

FOR BOOK STORE ORDERS CONTACT:
PUBLISHERS GROUP WEST | WWW.PGW.COM
CUSTOMER SERVICE 800-788-3123

nook amazonkindle

READ ALL OUR BOOK ON YOUR COMPUTER, TABLET,
SMART PHONE OR OTHER MOBILE DEVICES

DEAD AND STINKIN'
STEPHEN HEWETT

A GOOD DAY TO DIE
JAMES HENDRICKS

WHEN LOVE TURNS TO HATE
SHARRON DOYLE

**IF IT AIN'T ONE THING
IT'S ANOTHER**
SHARRON DOYLE

WOMAN'S CRY
VANESSA MARTIR

BLACKOUT
JERRY LaMOTHE
ANTHONY WHYTE

HUSTLE HARD
BLAINE MARTIN

A BOOGIE DOWN STORY
KEISHA SEIGNIOUS

CRAVE ALL LOSE ALL
ERICK S GRAY

LOVE AND A GANGSTA
ERICK S GRAY

AMERICA'S SOUL
ERICK S GRAY

SPOT RUSHERS
BRANDON McCALLA

**THIN LINE:
A CHILD'S EYE NEVER LIES**
ANTHONY WHYTE

NAKED CONFESSIONS
TRACEE A. HANNA

PURE BRONX
MARK NAISON PhD
MELISSA CASTILLO-GARSOW

**IT CAN HAPPEN
IN A MINUTE**
S.M. JOHNSON

HARD WHITE
SHANNON HOLMES
ANTHONY WHYTE

STREET CHIC
ANTHONY WHYTE

BOOTY CALL *69
ERICK S GRAY

POWER OF THE P
JAMES HENDRICKS

STREETS OF NEW YORK VOL. 1
ERICK S GRAY, ANTHONY WHYTE
MARK ANTHONY, SHANNON HOLMES

STREETS OF NEW YORK VOL. 2
ERICK S GRAY, ANTHONY WHYTE
MARK ANTHONY, K'WAN

STREETS OF NEW YORK VOL. 3
ERICK S GRAY, ANTHONY WHYTE
MARK ANTHONY, TREASURE BLUE

SMUT CENTRAL
BRANDON McCALLA

GHETTO GIRLS
ANTHONY WHYTE

GHETTO GIRLS TOO
ANTHONY WHYTE

**GHETTO GIRLS 3:
500 HOOD**
ANTHONY WHYTE

**GHETTO GIRLS IV:
YOUNG LUV**
ANTHONY WHYTE

**GHETO GIRLS 5:
TOUGHER THAN DICE**
ANTHONY WHYTE

**GHETO GIRLS 6:
BACK IN THE DAYS**
ANTHONY WHYTE

LIPSTICK DIARIES
CRYSTAL LACEY WINSLOW
VARIOUS FEMALE AUTHORS

LIPSTICK DIARIES 2
WAHIDA CLARK
VARIOUS FEMALE AUTHORS

SAINT AUGUSTINE'S

Childhood

GARRY WILLS

SAINT AUGUSTINE'S
Childhood

Confessiones Book One

CONTINUUM
London • New York

First published in Great Britain in 2001 by
Continuum
The Tower Building
11 York Road
London SE1 7NX
www.continuumbooks.com

First published in the United
States of America in 2001 by
Penguin Putnam Inc.,
375 Hudson Street, New York,
New York 10014, USA.

BRITISH LIBRARY CATALOGUING-IN-PUBLICATION DATA
A Catalogue record for this book is available from
the British Library.
ISBN 0-8264-5690-1 (Continuum)
ISBN 0-670-03001-5 (Viking Penguin)

LIBRARY OF CONGRESS CATALOGING-IN-PUBLICATION DATA
Augustine, Saint, Bishop of Hippo.
    [Confessiones. Liber 1. English]
    Saint Augustine's childhood : Confessiones: Book One / [commentary by]
  Garry Wills.
      p. cm.
    ISBN 0-670-03001-5
    1. Augustine, Saint, Bishop of Hippo—Childhood and youth.   2. Christian
  saints—Algeria—Hippo (Extinct city)—Biography.   I. Wills, Garry, 1934–
  II. Title.
  BR65.A6 E5 2001c
  270.2'092—dc21
[B]   2001017987

This book is printed on acid-free paper.

Printed in the United States of America
Set in Aldus with Phaistos display and MT Arabesque Ornaments
Designed by Carla Bolte

TO MY OWN GODSENDS

John, Garry, Lydia

CONTENTS

Key to Brief Citations

Boldface numerals in square brackets **[1]** refer to paragraphs in Book One of *The Testimony*.

comm. refers to the Commentary on Book One.

O, with volume and page (O 2.52–56), refers to James J. O'Donnell, *Augustine, "Confessions"* (Oxford, 1992).

T, with book and paragraph number (T 10.5), refers to books of *The Testimony* other than Book One.

I translate all Scripture texts from the Latin versions Augustine used. The Psalms are numbered as in the Vulgate bible and in the Douay-Rheims Catholic translation of them.

FOREWORD

It may seem odd to devote a whole volume to one short chapter ("Book") in a not very long work, Augustine's *Confessiones*—though it will not surprise classicists, who are used to separate texts (with commentary) of the various "books" of Homer's epics, or of Virgil's *Aeneid*. I, at least, am not likely to feel uncomfortable with this format, since I wrote a book of over 272 pages on a speech of only 272 words, the Gettysburg Address. And there are reasons to think readers may need more sympathetic exposition of Augustine than of Lincoln, who is closer to us in both geography and time. The American president's world cannot possibly look as exotic as Augustine's African environment and late-antique thought patterns. Besides, the first book of the *Confessiones* (which, for reasons later given, I shall be translating as *The Testimony*) offers special challenges to line-by-line attention. It is a famous source of later controversy in philosophy and theology. It is also, in ways the reader first encountering it may not expect, a source of information for one of the most important relationships in Augustine's life. The book is largely about his son.

Book One covers the first two of the six ages of man into which Augustine divided every human life that ran its full span. Of the first stage, infancy, he remembers nothing, while the most important aspect of the second stage, learning to talk, he remembers accomplishing, though he says that only later did he find out how he had done it. That would seem to give him little to work with in a book covering one period that he does not remember and another period that he did not understand. For both ages, he says, he relies not on direct autobiographical reminiscence but on close observation of other infants: "I have learned that babies act this way, from the ones I had occasion to observe, who, without having known me [as an infant], taught me more about myself than the nurses who did know me"[8]. The most obvious and immediate object of such scrutiny—a scrutiny he kept up at close quarters over a long period of time—was the son he found himself unwillingly saddled with when he was a graduate student. He would soon come to love and even admire this talented youth, who was fated to die when he was seventeen, his father's age at his birth. Called Godsend (*A-Deo-Datus*), the boy elicited this proud statement while he was still alive: "His talent, if a father's fondness deceives me not, is full of promise" (*Happiness in This Life* 1.6). Recalling the time when father and son were baptized together (Godsend was fifteen, Augustine thirty-three), the Bishop of Hippo wrote:

> We made the boy Godsend one of our company [as catechumens], a product of my sinful flesh but of your beneficent creation. He was only fifteen, but in talent he was forging ahead of many older scholars. I testify to your great gifts in him, my Lord God, the creator of everything, able to shape a form out of our deformities—for I had no part in him but my sin, and the

very fact that we had nursed him on your teachings was at your prompting, none other's—it is to your gifts, then, that I bear testimony. In that book of mine called *The Teacher*, he converses with me. You are my witness that all the ideas attributed to my partner in that dialogue were actually his, though he was only sixteen at the time. I had many other experiences of his preternatural ability—it was such that it stunned me, and who could have wrought such marvels but you? Shortly after, you ended his life on earth, but I look back on his life with assurance, with no misgivings about his boyhood or youth—or, if it had come to that, his maturity (T 9.14).

The words "we had nursed him on your teachings" show that Augustine, like his own father, left the boy's religious training to his Catholic mother. This was a providential arrangement, he states, since the boy came to baptism as the culmination of long Catholic training. Augustine had experienced the first stages of such training, but broke it off in his own adolescence.

The dialogue with Godsend, *The Teacher*, was taken down by scribes a decade or so before Augustine wrote the first book of *The Testimony*. That he had the dialogue in mind, and his son's brilliant learning of language, is apparent from the way he returns to the earlier work's themes and very terms when describing how children learn language (see, for instance, **[13]**). The importance of the dialogue for a correct interpretation of Book One of *The Testimony* can be seen from the most famous attack on Book One. Ludwig Wittgenstein, in the prominent opening passage of his *Philosophical Investigations*, convicts Augustine of a simplistic view of language. But later scholars have demonstrated that Wittgenstein did not understand Augustine's position, which was spelled out more fully in *The Teacher*, and then referred to only briefly in *The Testimony*. Wittgenstein, despite his obvious interest in Augustine's theory of language, seems never to have read the principal source for it, *The Teacher*.

Some scholars have come to realize that Augustine's approach has important similarities to the linguistic school founded by Noam Chomsky, and to laboratory work still being done with children in the various stages of language acquisition. Augustine's startling contention is that no one taught him language. That is the position Chomsky takes—in, for instance, *The Architecture of Language* (Oxford University Press, 2000), page 6:

> [Language acquisition] is also called "learning," but that is a pretty misleading term because it seems more like growth processes than anything that is properly called "learning." You put a child in a situation where the right stimulation is around and acquisition of language is something that happens to the child.

So important is *The Teacher* to a correct reading of Book One (see *comm.* [13]) that I print a new translation of the dialogue in an appendix. My frequent references to the dialogue can thus be consulted in their original context, and those interested in the relation of Augustine to his son will have access to its best expression.

ACKNOWLEDGMENTS

I am grateful to Peter Brown and James O'Donnell for their valuable correspondence on Augustinian issues. Also to my editor, Carolyn Carlson, and her assistant, Lucia Watson. My agent, Andrew Wylie, and his assistant, Zoe Pagnamenta, are ever watchful.

PART I

Introduction

1. The Man and His Book

Augustine was born in the era of Late Antiquity, that now much-studied period when the Roman empire was widespread, officially Christian, and not fully aware of the end that was looming for it. Born (354) in an obscure corner of this imperial structure—in the North African town of Thagaste (now part of Algeria)—Augustine, like his parents, thought that the empire offered him a vast staircase he could climb by rhetorical skill (the general coin of achievement and influence) backed by well-cultivated patronage. His father Patrick was a modest landholder and minor Roman official; his mother Monnica was probably from Berber stock and may have been illiterate, though she had a natural shrewdness to match her Christian piety. Their son was sent off, from age twelve to sixteen, to live in a neighboring town (Madaurus) for his early literary training. When he returned to Thagaste, his father could not afford to give him the crucial equivalent of graduate school in rhetoric. But Romanian, a Thagaste millionaire with wide connections in the empire, made Augustine his protégé, and after a year of mild hell-raising in Thagaste, Augustine went on to complete his studies in Carthage. He probably took with him a young woman he fell in love with in Thagaste, a woman he would live with for the next fifteen years—"and with her alone, since I kept faith with her bed" (T 4.2). This stable relationship is far from the picture of a sexually promiscuous youth presented by those who have not read Augustine carefully.

Soon after his arrival in Carthage, Augustine's partner bore their first and only child. Augustine admits that the baby was born because he did not take contraceptive measures—which he obviously observed for the rest of his years with the boy's mother. Friends in the Manichaean sect, a fashionable though forbidden religion in the Christian empire, helped Augustine find patronage in Rome, which he reached in 383, at the age of twenty-nine. Within a year, his brilliance was rewarded with appointment as court orator to the young emperor Valentinian II in his western capital of Milan. While in Milan, Augustine met another influential group of thinkers, this time Christian Neoplatonists, and he was soon converted to their philosophical and ascetic tenets. The ideals of this group made him give up his plan to marry into wealth and position, a step he had prepared for by separating himself from his son's mother. But the ties of the flesh were still too great for him to throw them off entirely, and he took a second mistress for a short time. He was unable to break away from her until he had undergone a series of conversion attempts. These reached their crisis in a garden, where he heard an accidental chant that broke down his resistance to grace. He, his son, and some of the protégés he had acquired were baptized on Easter Day, 387, by Ambrose, the charismatic bishop of Milan.

Returned to his African home of Thagaste, Augustine and

his friends planned to found a philosophical monastery for Christian intellectual-ascetics, where Augustine would write an encyclopedic series of works defining Christian humanism. His son was initially part of this community, though he died soon after its formation. Since Augustine was still known in Africa for his earlier defenses of Manichaeism, he wrote some pamphlets denouncing that doctrine. This conflict with Manichaeans laid the basis for a new kind of fame. That fame led Catholics in the harbor town of Hippo, where he chanced to be staying, to demand that he accept ordination as their priest. Since this was the normal way to recruit clergy at the time, and Christians were not normally allowed to hold themselves exempt from such a call, Augustine reluctantly gave up his preferred life of study and prayer and writing, to become a priest at age thirty-seven and a bishop four years later.

He would spend almost forty years, from age thirty-seven to his death at seventy-six, ministering to his small flock at Hippo. He never again left Africa, though he engaged in theological controversy with figures throughout the empire. He addressed topical issues in his flood of letters, sermons, and pamphlets. Early in his tenure as bishop he tried to escape the demanding routine of such occasional writings. This led him, as the fourth century was ending, to undertake three major works not tied to specific controversies—*The Testimony* (begun in 397), *The Trinity* (begun in 400), and *First Meanings in Genesis* (begun in 401). Finishing and polishing these works was his great project of the new century. They introduced "psychological" readings into the mysteries of the Creation and the Trinity.

Only the monumental *City of God,* completed in Augustine's last decades, can compete with the spiritual depths explored in the three central masterpieces of his life, of which *The Testimony* was the inaugural work.

2. *The Book's Genre*

The Testimony is commonly called an autobiography, even "the first autobiography." But that raises expectations, or imposes restrictions, the work cannot support. Autobiography professes to satisfy the expected audience's curiosity about a person's life. But over and over Augustine fails to supply even basic information about himself, or about the events and people that shaped him. We learn that his mother died (though how and of what we are not told), that his son died (though not exactly when or how, or who was present at his death—including, very likely, his mother). His sister is not mentioned, though we know he was close to her, since she superintended a convent annexed to his monastery. He mentions his brother, though not that brother's son, who became a member of his monastery. The family's property dealings are left out. We learn nothing of the officials he dealt with at Valentinian's court, or of the Christian community he came to know in Rome as a recent convert. The man who most influenced his crucial conversion to Neoplatonism, Mallius Theodore, is not even named in *The Testimony.* From his close and intimate circle of Manichaean friends in Carthage, not a single name is recorded. The list could go on.

As surprising as the omissions are the things Augustine includes. Half of Book Two is given over to a youthful theft of pears. Much of Book Three is spent on the death of a nameless friend, while the loss of his beloved son is referred to in just a sentence. There are long disquisitions on time and memory, and—most surprising for those who consider this an autobiography—the last three books do not even mention events in Augustine's life, but comment on the opening of Genesis and on the mystery of the Trinity. If we are to assume that the work has some principle of unity, it is clearly not an autobiographical principle. The work leaves too many things out, and brings too many things in, that offend against that principle.

It may be objected that other famous autobiographies include or exclude much of the subject's life. Henry Adams, in *The Education of Henry Adams*, does not mention his wife or her tragic death. John Henry Newman, in his *Apologia pro vita sua*, does not mention important relations with his brother or his sister. In fact these, along with Rousseau's *Confessions*, are often compared with *The Testimony* as "thesis" biographies—works that use the author's life to argue a certain point of view. Adams uses his baffled attempts at education to argue that the historiography of the United States is in practice unknowable, and he ends with a discussion of potential laws in history. Rousseau argues that his life exemplifies innocence partially corrupted by society, in answer to a "conspiracy" of those accusing him of monstrous behavior. Newman argues that his religious positions were developed consistently, against those accusing him of holding a series of dishonest views. The intended audience, in each case, is made up of those interested in such charges and countercharges. That audience cannot rightly complain if things irrelevant to the book's purpose are omitted or downplayed.

In all three cases, the audience is clearly indicated. Rousseau addresses those who have entertained the attacks on him by *philosophes* as important as David Hume. Newman tells us that he addresses the charges of Charles Kingsley, answering anyone who believes in those charges. Adams admits that his book, privately printed under no author's name, is for a narrow circle of Americans capable of entertaining his dark views. None of these men addresses humankind in general. They have specific people in mind, and they speak directly to them. Augustine, by contrast, does not address any human person. He has an audience of one—God. The entire book is a prayer to him—a point he keeps before his (and our) mind by frequent apostrophe to "Lord" or "God" or "Lord God" or "God my Lord." His language often has the form of liturgical incantation, and the narrative is arranged according to his theological concepts. When he reflects on the fact that his prayer is being taken down by scribes (T 10.3–6), it is only to remark that all men's testimony to God (by word or act) is observable by others, for their own edification, disgust, or self-examination. In *The Teacher* 2, he notes that those who recite psalms in church are praying to God, though they are also reminding each other of God's role in their life. "My heart's fellow will love in me what you, Lord, tell us is lovable, deplore in me what you tell us is deplorable" (T 10.5).

It is hard to take seriously enough the nature of the book as prayer. This sets it off from autobiographies, and answers the principal objections made to it, those having to do with its structure, veracity, and unity.

Structure. Augustine used a patristic Christian scheme of human life to compare the ages of man with the days of Creation and the eras of history (O 2.52–56). There were six of each, and each member in one series reflected the corresponding part of the other two series. Here is the list of them, with the days of Creation placed centrally, since they were the controlling concepts for Augustine (who wrote five extended commentaries on them, including the one in *The Testimony*):

Ages of Man	*Creation*	*History*
1. Infantia (pre-verbal)	Light	Adam to Noah
2. Pueritia (speaking)	Sky/Earth	Noah to Abraham
3. Adulescentia (15–30)	Vegetation	Abraham to David
4. Juventus (30–45)	Galaxy	David to Babylon
5. Maturitas (45–60)	Fish	Babylon to Christ
6. Senectus (60–)	Animals/Man	Christ to End

This is not the place to go into all the parallels that stimulated Augustine's imagination over the years. But the first two ages clearly provided the structure for Book One, the work we are considering. What divides and defines these early periods is speech—the lack of it in infancy (*in-fans* means "not speaking," and Augustine plays constantly on that etymology), and the acquiring of it in childhood *(pueritia)*. Day One of the Creation brings an unarticulated light into existence, and Day Two articulates earth and sky by dividing them. In the same way, Augustine has the radiance of being, even as an infant (see *comm.* at [12]) and learns to articulate his desires as a child [13]. These stages agree with the historical epochs since infancy "is wiped from our memory as by the obliterating Flood" (*Literal Meanings* 1.35), and in the second period the Jews were unable to beget their own people (as Abraham's descendants would, ibid., 36).

The Testimony will clearly mark the point at which Augustine enters the third age (T 2.1), and the fourth age (T 7.1). But since he is still in that fourth stage as he writes, he cannot discuss, as yet, the final two periods. Instead, he anticipates the "seventh day," when God rested on the Sabbath. Since the Sabbath signified, for him and his fellow Christians, the final state after time ends, when the saved soul will contemplate the Trinity, his final three books directly meditate on the days of Creation and their expression of the nature of the Trinity. James O'Donnell has traced the ways trinitarian images run through all the earlier books, with their multiple triads, leading up to the final books' completion (O 2.46–51). In Book One, for instance, the triads of the following passage reflect (a) qualities

of the Trinity, followed by (b) distorted images of those qualities pursued in sin, followed by (c) responses to those qualities
by the devout: "I sought joy, glory, and truth, not in him but in
things he made, in myself and other creatures, thus sliding off
toward pain, dejection, and error. Still I thank you, you my delight, my pride, my trust . . ."**[31]**. "Augustine interpreted his
life by a textual tradition" (O 2.53).

Veracity. One of the perennial problems in discussion of *The
Testimony* is that Augustine "remembers" his life before and
soon after his conversion in ways that conflict with the record
he left behind in writings from those years. His early letters
and reported dialogues give an authentic picture of his intellectual development that he does not even try to reproduce in *The
Testimony*, where (for instance) the influence of Neoplatonist
teachers like Mallius Theodore is drastically downplayed and
the importance of Ambrose vastly exaggerated. But Augustine
is not trying to tell us what "really" happened according to our
historiographical standards, nor does he want to "clean up" the
record in earthly terms. His prayer is a meditation on the action of grace in his life, now acknowledged in ways that he did
not always recognize at the time. He is interested in patterns
that emerge only in testimony to what God was telling him,
despite his resistance or misperception, obstacles from which
he is still wrestling free with God's help. For him this is the
true story, God's story that he has lived through, moving from
blindness toward light. That the pattern corresponds with

God's revelation in Creation and in history just proves that it is grace he is describing, his own participation in the divine drama of salvation.

Unity. The unity of the book—the norms for inclusion and exclusion of material, the progress to a climax in the final three books—becomes obvious once we understand its organizing principle as one of prayer. Augustine does not "all of a sudden" start talking of Genesis and the Trinity in Books Eleven through Thirteen. He has been talking of them all through the earlier books, not only in terms of the days of Creation, but in the way he discusses representative moments. When his father sees him in the baths and knows that he can beget a child (T 2.6), this not only marks the beginning of Augustine's third age *(adulescentia),* capable of procreation. Rather, since he is "clothed" *(indutum)* in nakedness, this recalls Adam's discovery of his own nudity in Genesis, when he felt the need to clothe himself, and it will be contrasted with the spiritual "bath" of baptism by which Augustine heeds the call to be clothed *(induite)* in Christ.

Other events, too, "re-enact" Genesis. The theft of the forbidden pears in Book Two is deliberately recounted in ways that refer to Adam's eating of the forbidden apple—as the dialogue with Monnica in Book Nine, reaching back toward Eden, indicates a partial healing of Augustine's fallen spiritual state. The death of the friend in Book Four makes Augustine compare his envy of the friend's relationship with God to Cain's anger when Abel's sacrifice pleases God. Tracing the presence of many other "Genesis moments" is not necessary here. What matters for Book One is the way the Creation of the whole universe is implicit in the creation of Augustine's petty self—which can, nonetheless, not be called petty because God made and is remaking him—and the way God drew him through the waywardness of boyhood, just as he drew a refractory people through the early books of Jewish Scripture. The unity of the book is the unity Augustine discovers in himself as a reflection of God's unity: "I preserved myself—by an echo of your mysterious oneness, out of which I came to be—as I maintained a single control over everything my senses delivered to me"**[31]**.

3. The Book's Title

Transliterating (rather than translating) *Confessiones* into English as *The Confessions* has the misleading result of suggesting that the book is an autobiography, that Augustine is recounting his sins like someone going into a modern church confessional and spending days there. But confessionals did not exist in Augustine's time, nor anything like the modern sacrament of penance. *Confessio,* moreover, was not primarily self-accusation but any kind of "corroborating" testimony (*con-fiteri* is, etymologically, "to speak with," and Augustine had the rhetorician's love of etymology). Augustine testifies to God as the stars do by their beauty—*pulchritudo eorum confessio eorum* (*Sermon* 241.1). The pagan author Apuleius (also from Africa) said that her jewels "confess" (confirm the status of) the grand dame (*Golden Ass* 2.2). Augustine testifies *(confiteor)* that time is measurable (T 11.33)—one of many uses where sin is not at issue. "The tribes of Israel go up to the Temple to testify *(confiteri)* to God's name" (*Explaining the Psalms* 121.8). Even the devils testify to God's power by their opposition to it (*Interpreting John's Letter* 10.1), as do heretics (ibid., 6.12).

For Augustine, then, testimony *(confessio)* is speech that acknowledges the power and claims of God: "This it is to testify [*confiteri*], to speak out what the heart holds true. If the tongue and the heart are at odds, you are reciting, not testifying" (*Interpreting John's Gospel* 26.2). The proof that *confessio* does not speak only of sin is the fact that the sinless Jesus "confesses" to the Father at Matthew 11.25.

> "I will confess the justice of the Lord" [Psalm 7.18]. This cannot be confessing to sin, since it is said by the one [David as prophetic type of Jesus] who just denied most truthfully that there is "evil in what my hands do" [Psalm 7.3]. This is a testimony to God's justice, the kind that praises God. . . . There can be no admission of sin when the Lord says, "I testify [*confiteor*] to you, Father, Lord of heaven and earth, because you have concealed these things from the learned and revealed them to the lowly [Matthew 11.25]. Ecclesiasticus [39.19–21] puts it the same way: "Testify [*confitemini*] to the Lord for all his works, and your testimony shall make this affirmation: 'All the Lord's works are of the highest good.' " . . . So, after saying "I will testify to the Lord," lest we think he was confessing sin, the

Psalmist adds, at the end, "And I shall sing the Lord's name as the most high." Singing is characterized by joy, not by the sadness sin requires (*Explaining the Psalms* 7.18).

The deepest kind of testimony is the cry of the Spirit in the heart of the believer, drawing a person into the inner conversation of the Trinity. This is the prayer of the Christian community: "As the Spirit gave them an inner testimony to Christ, they spread the testimony themselves" (Sermon 94.2). To *confiteri* is to "speak with" the Spirit to the Father, as well as to speak with a knowledge of one's own willed distance from God in sin. The title of the book thus answers the opening query of the book, how can a mere mortal dare to praise God? He cannot do so unless God himself speaks within the believer through grace and the Spirit. "May my God cry through my soul, your truth assuring me . . ."[22]. One of Augustine's favorite Pauline passages is Romans 10.10: "When the heart believed that we were whole, the mouth testified [*confessionem fecimus*] that we were saved." Though Augustine testifies to his sinful state, he testifies to much else in the book he called a testimony.

4. The Book's Style

The style of *The Testimony* is extraordinarily intimate, a quality derived from its prayer form. Augustine is not preaching outward to others, praising or reproaching them, arguing with any human audience. He is allowing others to eavesdrop on his inner colloquy with God. Because he is praying, he uses the invocations he knows best and uses most, not only in public liturgies but in his private meditations. Scripture phrases are woven throughout his language, not interrupting it but serving as a remembered music that plays along with and through his deepest expressions of emotion. It is hard to indicate the extent of this reliance on Scripture verses without suggesting a chopped-up text. I indicate the most recognizable lines with single quotation marks in my translation, but this should not draw attention away from the flow of words that seamlessly incorporates all biblical echoes.

In this respect, the normal punctuation of the text observed in translations can be inadequate to the stream of consciousness that Augustine achieves, to the long-breathing arcs of his prayer. He often uses a phrase at or near the beginning of such an arc, and then echoes it toward the close. Such members should not be put in different sentences, as Chadwick does in his creditable translation. Thus he translates the second sentence in the opening paragraph of Book One as two sentences:

> Man, a little piece of your creation, desires to praise you, a human 'bearing his mortality with him,' carrying with him the witness of sin, and the witness that you 'resist the proud.' Nevertheless, to praise you is the desire of man, a little piece of your creation.

Augustine is not so choppy:

Yet man, a mere segment of what you made, strives to appraise you—man, 'confined by a nature that must die,' confined by this evidence of his sin, the evidence that you rebuff the over-weening, yet man would still appraise you, this mere segment of what you made.

When Augustine launches a thought with a phrase and then repeats it to round off the thought, the unity of movement should be preserved. Here is Chadwick, using five sentences:

Who reminds me of the sin of my infancy? For 'none is pure from sin before you, not even an infant of one day upon the earth.' Who reminds me? Any tiny child now, for I see in that child what I do not remember in myself. What sin did I then have?

This is all one question:

Who is there to remind me of my sin before I spoke?—'no one being clear of sin, not a speechless child with but a day upon this earth'—who will remind me, will any (even the tiniest) baby help me observe what I do not remember myself, will it show me what sin I was committing at that age? **[11]**.

The biblical text Augustine uses most often—the ostinato to his prayer—is the Book of Psalms. The psalms were the staple of church services he presided over—they were used in hymns, readings, and sermons, ready at hand in Augustine's memory to be quoted, paraphrased, or alluded to. They are admirably suited to the prayer form of *The Testimony*. The unit of verse in Hebrew poetry is the couplet that states a theme in two different ways:

> Great is the Lord's power to act
> and his knowing goes beyond measure [Psalm 146.2].

These sighing replications are the overlapping units that determine much of the rhythm of thought in Augustine's prayer. And such couplets are a perfect bridge to the rhetorical devices that were second nature to Augustine, which also moved in doublets—antithesis, chiastic pairs, isocolons, and similar devices: You "honor debts without owing, cancel debts without losing"[4].

5. The Book's Imagery

The Bible also encouraged Augustine to think in images. For him, God is fountain, light, vine, cup of plenty, bread, sky, and other concrete symbols. He knew that God is knowable only in veiled approximations and paradoxical formulations. Though Scripture calls him an angry and a jealous God, Augustine cautions that these are economical expressions suited to human limits. He must add, therefore, that God is "loving, yet not inflamed; jealous, yet not disturbed; regretful, without remorse; angry, without intemperance"[4]. All these are images, not the reality—though they are as close as we can come to certain aspects of reality. The habit of using images is so strong with Augustine that when he uses a symbolic term, it often colors the whole passage where he made it explicit. When Job's language of challenging God to a trial is renounced at [5], Augustine nonetheless goes on to talk of pleading before an implied court in the first sentences of [6].

Scriptural imagery opened a vast interior landscape for Augustine, a geography of the soul where the sower sows seeds, rocky soil resists truth, mountains of belief stand firm, seas are swept with peril, paths divagate or plunge downward or climb up. The most common images in Book One are those connected with paths and with water. The path images are probably the most pervasive throughout Augustine's writing. They reach from the Jewish idiom for "paths of righteousness" and "by-paths of the wicked" to the New Testament message that "I am Path, and Truth, and Life" (John 14.6). Christianity itself is "the Path" in Acts of the Apostles. Augustine associates the Neoplatonic path down from the One and the path back up to It with the prodigal son's travel away from his father and his return [28]. In Book One, he equates moral wanderings from God's straight path with Aeneas's "strayings" [22]. All dark and tangled and thicket-obstructed ways are images of his psychic aberrations: "You drew me from my vicious bypaths, outdazzling with your allure the attractions that misled me, so that I may love you more worthily, hang on to your hand with a whole heart's energy, as you 'carry me out of trial to the final goal' " [24].

The other common image is of water—the stormy seas of worldly converse [13], the wild waves of temptation [18], the stream of Society **[26]** which one must ride over on the plank of the Cross, the dissolving waters at odds with the shaping waters of baptism.

Perhaps the most important image used in Book One is the treatment of language as an act of mental parturition. This reflects Augustine's rejection of the idea that the mind is a passive tabula on which external things are printed. Book One anticipates aspects of Noam Chomsky's "generative grammar." This generative power is, for Augustine, the action of God within the mind, "the vital principle breeding depth of thought out of my intelligence"**[21]**. "I went into labor to deliver my thoughts . . . and in their ears I completed the parturition of what I felt within me"**[23]**. This generation, of course, reflects God's fertile action within the child, "the power that breeds depth of thought out of my intelligence"**[21]**.

6. The Book's Rhetoric

Though Augustine knows how little human language can do to reach God, he does not therefore abandon the rhetorical skills he had acquired so painstakingly. Only the best is good enough for God, however inadequate it might be. We should stretch ourselves, to the extent of our ability, to express our yearning and need for him **[4]**. No one could be more scathing than Augustine in attacking rhetoric as "phrase peddling" **[22]** for gain or flattery or seduction. But he did not have the modern prejudice that artful language is of necessity insincere or nonauthentic language. He knew that Scripture itself is highly artful, full of poetry, imagery, antithesis, and paradox. Some of these devices are essential to religious speech itself—God can only be approached by way of paradox and image. The couplet form of the Psalms and other poems is built on antithesis, and tends toward the balancing of speech members *(cola)*.

> *Antithesis.* This, says Gilliam Clark, "is Augustine's favorite technique, if 'technique' is the right word: antithesis is so frequent in all his writing that it seems rather to be the way he thinks." One of the most important antitheses for him is *intus-foris,* "within-without," deployed through Book One as through all his thought. God and the self are within. The world and others are without. Language is the bridge between the two, capable of enriching what is *intus* or of dispersing it. The infant ("pre-verbal") thrashes about to find words for his demands because those without cannot otherwise perceive what is within him. Other regular antitheses are those of God and creature, soul and body, word and act, their elements chiming against each other on every page.

> *Chiasmus.* A special form of antithesis—antithesis compounded, as it were, and "criss-crossed"—is that which bunches two identical elements in the middle and puts two others on the outside. One might print the former in capitals to bring out the construction. A simple case is at **[13]**, describing the ramble-scramble of a child's futile attempts at communication—"my *noises* RANDOM and RANDOM

flailing" *(vocibus VARIIS et VARIIS membrorum motibus)*. More complex patterns show up constantly: "so long as he *finds* in love what he does not FIGURE OUT, instead of FIGURING IT OUT without *finding* you"[10]. Augustine discovered this figure everywhere in the Psalms.

> I have *sought* your COUNTENANCE,
> it is your COUNTENANCE, Lord, I shall *seek* [28].

Paradox. Since God does not fit into our minds or words or categories, the proper way to speak of him is in contravention of our categories—as in the long string of paradoxes in [4]. But the allure of false values is also expressed in paradoxes throughout the book—"this dying life, or should I call it living death"[7], "to sate insatiable yearnings for penurious wealth and infamous fame"[19].

Alliteration. The patterning of consonants gives point to epigrams or satirical definitions. When Augustine says that a violent baby is *tantillus puer et tantus peccator* [19], it is not enough to translate (as Chadwick does) "so tiny a child, so great a sinner," since the interlocking *t* and *p* give a bite of self-satire to the paradox. We need similarly interwoven consonants in English: "little in size, large in sin." Again, when he writes *conturbata matris carnis meae* [17], the folding in of the sounds on each other, expressing the maternal bond, demands something like "the mournful bearer of my mortal body." The play of sounds in *pauca quae poteram qualia poteram* [8] calls for "the best of my little (and little availing) ability." Alliteration often adds point to other rhetorical devices, as with *vocibus VARIIS et VARIIS* in the chiasmus mentioned above.

Polyptoton. A figure that comes easily to inflected languages is the juxtaposition of the same word in various cases or forms—*misericors misero,* "merciful to me needing mercy"**[9]**, *mecum meorum meaque diligentia,* "care be taken of myself by me and mine"**[18]**. Or: *miserius misero non miserante,* "more pitiful than a pitiable man without pity"**[21]**. The play on strategically placed *omnia* and *omnibus* in **[13]**, backed up by the chiming *valerem . . . volebam . . . volebam,* makes fun of the baby's demand for instant wish fulfillment. So *nec valerem quae volebam nec quibus volebam omnibus* should be: "for want of getting each thing I wanted from each person I wanted."

Colometry. Much of the power of Augustine's flow of language comes from the artful varying of the lengths of his sentences' members *(cola).* A good example is the interplay of various grammatical structures and phrase lengths in the tour-de-force sentence on God at **[4]**. This ranges from climactically lengthening the members to interjecting *isocola* (exactly equal phrases): *reddis debita nulla debens, donas debita nulla perdens* is not only an isocolon, but a paradox involving alliteration and homoeoteleuton (similar endings to successive cola). Thus: "honor debts without owing, cancel debts without losing." The tricolon at **[9]** rises to a crescendo: with God are "the certain causes of contingent outcomes, the unchanging origins that abide through all that changes, the eternal rationale of all irrational things that pass away." The way God endows a baby with its faculties has the same effect [12]: "how you articulate its sensory apparatus; fit limb to limb, giving beauty to its form; and coordinate all its instincts of self-preservation as a single thing." The interrelationship of verbal technique and theology comes out when repeated tricola refer to aspects of the Trinity.

7. Translating the Book

It will be seen from the above examples that I think the form and force of Augustine's language should be replicated, so far as possible, in an English translation. This is often neglected in translations of prose, though some effort is made to give the effect of form when translating poetry. Augustine's language is as highly wrought a thing as many poems. It is very much aware of its own artistic aspirations. His training as a rhetorician made this inevitable. His skill at turning this secular discipline to sacred uses makes his text dramatic. A translator's aim should be to find some English way of approximating *what* he was saying and *how* he was saying it.

One must be careful, of course, when searching for the modern *way* to say what Augustine said, to retain *what* he said. One might argue, for instance, that if he were alive today he would use gender-neutral language. Maybe, but only if living now made him change his mind about male primacy, and not just the form of his expression. We cannot "educate" him to our values, but must keep to the historical limits of his outlook. Thus "he" will embrace the whole race in this translation. In the same way, we cannot attribute to him less idiosyncratic theories of physical sensation [12], or the language of modern science. Even when he sounds most modern, as in his view of newborn children's mental activity, that cannot be divorced from the theological rationale that underlay his view—i.e., the way the mind (he held) reflects God's generation of the Verbum in the Trinity. Nor can his theology—e.g., on sin, hell, and the devil—be softened to fit modern tastes. It is his whole world that must be brought over into our tongue.

At times Augustine plays so constantly on the etymology of a word that this must be kept foremost in the translation. He was always aware for instance of the literal meaning of *in-fans,* "non-speaking." This led him in his Christmas sermons to pun on the fact that the Christ child was also the Word of God—an "infant Verbum," a wordless Word. So I use "the speechless stage," not "infancy," throughout the translation—which is clumsy, but less so than parentheses pointing up the sense wherever needed.

Problems of tone arise constantly. Augustine's language can be racy, but his attitude is reverent in this long prayer. Self-abnegation should not become bathos. Satire should not become undignified. When he uses a diminutive like *mulierculae* ("little women") of his nurses *considered as witnesses,* the dismissive note should be struck, but not exaggerated. I call them "gossips" where Henry Chadwick gives us "weak women." It is not lack of strength that is being singled out, but lack of authority as witnesses. Chadwick translates the same word simply as "wives" at T 6.24, where the diminutive means something more like "homebodies" in their opposition to a philosophical commune (see *comm.* [10]). When searching for the right word in an author with the self-conscious artistry of Augustine, the shading of each word, the weighting of it, must be taken into account.

PART II

The Testimony: Book One

Notes

L1 *vast]* Psalm 47.2: "Vast is the Lord, and to be praised as such." *Valde* is "as strongly," i.e., validly, appropriately, as opposed to the Vulgate *nimis* (excessively). Vast is quantitative here, not qualitative, setting up the "size" comparison between Augustine and the Lord *(comm.)*.

L2 *what you do]* *Virtus* is Augustine's principle of action.

L2 *beyond assaying]* Psalm 146.5: "Great is the Lord's power to act, his knowing goes beyond measure [*numerus*]." *Numerus* was associated by Augustine with the Second Person of the Trinity (the Verbum), the principle of form *(comm.)*.

L3 *strives to appraise]* Man is trying *(vult)* to do what he cannot adequately do. To praise is to fit the right approbation to its object, as part of the language of adequacy throughout this passage *(comm.)*. In English, both "praise" and "appraise" mean to "set a price on." The point here is that God is priceless.

L4 *confined]* 2 Corinthians 4.10: "moving within his mortality." This movable prison inhibits the effort to praise God adequately.

L5 *rebuff]* Proverbs 3.34: "God rebuffs the overweening, but favors the lowly."

L8 *tilted toward you]* For Augustine's cosmology of "gravitation" in this passage, see *comm.*

L15 *how shall people call]* Romans 10.13–14: "Who calls on the Lord will be saved—but how can they call on one they do not recognize; how recognize without hearing of him; how hear without being told, and who will tell unless sent to do so?" *(comm.)*.

L19 *seeking him they find]* Matthew 7.7: "Seek and you will find."

I. How to Begin?

1. 'Vast are you, Lord, and as vast should be your praise'—
'vast what you do; what you know beyond assaying.' Yet man,
a mere segment of what you made, strives to appraise you—
man, 'confined by a nature that must die,' confined by this evidence of his sin, the evidence that you rebuff the overweening,
yet man would still appraise you, this mere segment of what
you made. You prompt us yourself to find satisfaction in appraising you, since you made us tilted toward you, and our
heart is unstable until stabilized in you.

Then help me, Lord, to recognize and understand what
comes first, to call for you before appraising you, or to recognize you before calling for you. Yet how can one call for what
one does not recognize? Without such recognition, one could
be calling for something else. Or is calling for you itself the
way to recognize you? Yes, 'how shall people call for one they
do not believe exists? And how are they to believe it exists if
no one proclaims it?'

Still, 'those who seek the Lord shall appraise him,' for by
seeking him they find, and by finding they appraise. I shall seek
you then, Lord, by calling for you, call for you by believing you
exist; for you have been proclaimed to us, and it is my belief in
you that calls out to you—the faith that is your gift to me,

L1 *by the humanity*]   By the descent to humble station *(humilitatem)*, with reference to Philippians 2.7–8.

L2 *mission of proclaiming*]   The previous clause shows that the bringing of the good news was a concomitant of the Incarnation. God's Word is the one teacher/preacher. See *The Teacher.*

L11 *has no claim*]   Taking *inferi* as possessive genitive, "I do not belong to it."

L12 *if I do go down*]   Psalm 138.8: "Go I down to hell, yet there are you."

L15 *from whom*]   Romans 11.36: "From him, through him, in him are all things."

L19 *God who has said, 'I fill . . .'*]   Joel 2.23, 24: "The heavens I fill, and the earth."

L27 *Spirit is poured*]   Acts 2.17: "My Spirit over all flesh shall be poured out."

which you breathed into me by the humanity your Son assumed, taking up his mission of proclaiming you.

2. Yet how shall I call for my God, the God who is my Lord, when it is precisely to me I am calling him when I call, and what in me is large enough for God to enter? How can he who made heaven and earth come into me? Is there anything in me that can hold you? Can even heaven and earth, which you made, and in which you made me, hold you? Or, since nothing that is can exist without you, do all things that exist hold you?

And since I too exist, how can I ask you to come to me, who would not exist if you were not already in me? Hell has no claim on me, not yet; and even there, you are present—so 'if I *do* go down to hell, there are you.' Thus I would not exist, my God, could not exist at all, were you not already in me. Rather, I could not be, were I not in you, 'from whom, through whom, in whom are all things.' Assuredly that is so, Lord, that is so.

Where *to* can I, already in you, call you to come? And where *from* would you be coming? Where *to* could I retire, outside heaven and earth, for God to come there to me, my God who has said, 'I fill heaven and earth'? 3. Since, then, you fill heaven and earth, do they contain you? Or do you fill them, with a surplus of you left over, beyond their containing? Then where, once heaven and earth are filled, does the overflow of you go? Do you, who contain all things, need no container because what you fill is filled by your containing *it*? Any receptacle containing you cannot confine you—were it broken, you would not spill out of it. When your Spirit is poured out upon us, you do not fall down but lift up, you are not scattered out, but gather in.

L8 *What other Lord]*   Psalm 17.32: "For who is God but the Lord, and who is God but our God?"

L10 *hidden far]*   Augustine, *City of God* 1.29: "God at our side in hiding—yet, without moving, remote."

L13 *age the proud]*   Job 9.5: "who ages mountains away insensibly."

L16 *jealous]*   Joel 2.18: "the Lord is a jealous Lord." Augustine is countering Manichaean criticism of the Jewish Scriptures as attributing unworthy acts and feelings to God, who is said to feel these emotions by analogy with human reactions, though they are not strictly true of him.

L17 *regretful]*   Genesis 6.6–7: "The Lord regretted his making man."

L17 *angry]*   Exodus 4.14: "The Lord was angry at Moses."

L26 *say the most]*   Here and elsewhere in Augustine, *loquaces* are Manichaeans quick to criticize. He called himself, in his Manichaean days, "inflated and verbose in the debates of so-called scholars" (*The Need to Believe* 2); *(comm.)*.

L27 *find stability]*   *adquiescere,* a reference back to the unstable *(inquietum)* heart of **[1]**.

L28 *make it drunk]*   Ambrose, Hymn 1.7.23–26: "Drink we in joy, soberly drunk in the Spirit." *Testimony* 5.23: "soberly drunk on your Vine."

But in filling all things, do you fill them with all of you? Or since all things cannot hold all of you, do they each hold its own part of you—all of them the same part, or each its own part, larger or smaller as they are large or small? Can there, then, be a larger or smaller part of you? Are you not entire everywhere, though nothing can hold the entire you?

4. Then what are you, God—what, I inquire, but simply God the Lord? 'What other Lord is Lord, what other God but God?'—highest, best, most powerful, all-powerfulest, most merciful yet most just, hidden far away yet very near, most beautiful yet most strong, most fixed yet most elusive, change-less in changing all things; neither young nor old, you give youth back to all things yet 'age the proud away insensibly'; ac-tive always, always at rest, you acquire without lacking, you support, fill, and protect; create, raise, and complete; seeking, though you have all; loving, yet not inflamed, jealous, yet not disturbed; regretful, without remorse; angry, without intem-perance; you change event without a change of plan; acquiring what is at hand without having lost; never in need, yet happy at gain; receiving, without exacting interest on what is owed you; overpaid to be put in debt, yet none pay you with anything you did not, in the first place, give; you honor debts without owing, cancel debts without losing. And what, with all this, have I said, my God, my life holy and sweet to me, what can anyone say when speaking of you? Yet we must say something when those who say the most are saying nothing.

5. Who will help me find stability in you, help you come into my heart, to make it drunk with you, oblivious of my ills

L8 *I am your rescue*]   Psalm 34.3: "Tell my soul, 'I am your rescue.' "

L11 *Hide not*]   Psalm 26.9: "Hide not your countenance from me."

L11 *die into you*]   Colossians 3.3: "For you have died, and your life is hidden away with Christ in God."

L13 *too cramped*]   Isaiah 49.20: "Too cramped is this place, make it wide enough for me to dwell in it." Augustine in his commentary on Psalm 100.4: "Our inner dwelling place is our heart."

L16 *inmost sins*]   Psalm 18.13–14: "Who knows his own sins? From my own secret acts cleanse me, and save your servant from others." The interpretation of this verse in the translation is taken from Augustine's consistent statements of its meaning—e.g., in *Free Will* 3.29: "Sin has two springs, one from one's own conception, the other from external persuasion."

L19 *anticipated*]   *Pro-locutus sum.*

L19 *freed my heart*]   Psalm 31.5: "You have freed me of sin's iniquity."

L20 *take you into court*]   Jeremiah 2.29: "Would you contend with me in court?"

L21 *iniquity*]   Psalm 26.12: "Iniquity is lying to itself."

L22 *If you arraign*]   Psalm 129.3: "If you keep record of our crimes, Lord—Lord, who will stand cleared? Do not take your servant to court, since no one alive can be acquitted under your scrutiny."

L25 *earth and ash*]   Genesis 18.27: "Shall I, a thing of earth and ash, address my Lord?"

L27 *mock me*]   Psalm 2.4: "With laughter from his heavens he will mock them."

and hugging all my good to me, the good you are? Why do you matter so much to me?—pity me enough to let me say. Why, indeed, do I matter so much to you that my loving you is something you require, that you should be angry and threaten me with heavy punishments if I love not? Then can my not loving you be a slight thing? No, it cannot, to my sorrow! Tell me by your acts of mercy, God my Lord, what you are to me. Tell my soul, 'I am your rescue.' Tell me in a way that I may hear. My heart is all ears for it, Lord. Open them and tell my soul, 'I am your rescue.' I shall rush toward those words and lay hold on them. 'Hide not your countenance from me.' Let me die into you lest I die away from your countenance.

6.   My soul is 'too cramped for you to enter it—widen it out.' It is in disrepair—restore it. It is filthy in your sight, I admit and recognize this, but who is to sanitize it? To whom before you should I call out, 'Cleanse me of my inmost sins, and outward promptings fend off from your servant'? I believe in you and that is why, you know Lord, I address you. Have I not anticipated accusation of my own sins, 'and you freed my heart of impiety'? I do not 'take you into court,' you who are Truth. I would not deceive myself, not let 'my iniquity tell itself a lie,' so I go not to court with you. 'If you arraign our sins, Lord—Lord, who can stand the indictment'?

7.   Yet let me enter my appeal before your mercy, let me, 'a thing of earth and ash,' appeal to you, since I enter my plea before your mercy, not before a fellow man, who might well mock me. Or do you, in fact, mock me? But even if you do, you will change your mood and pity me.

L19 *inner and outer]*   Augustine's usual distinction between *intus* and *foris*. God's activity informs not only Augustine's weighing of what the senses deliver to his internal forum, but the initial sensing itself. This is a first sounding of the theme that he learns only from God, even as a struggling infant.

L22 *began to smile]*   Virgil, *Eclogues* 4.60. *Incipe, parve puer, risu cognoscere matrem.* "Smile early knowledge at your mother, child."

II. In-Fans (Speechless)

What would I plead with you, Lord, but my ignorance of whence I came into this dying life, or should I call it living death? I know not whence I came, only that your merciful sustenance kept me alive when I did, as I learned from the parents who gave me flesh—the father from whom, the mother in whom, you made me (but not my memory) begin in time. It was your sustenance I drew from fleshly milk, since neither my mother nor nurses were filling their own breasts with it. You yourself dispensed this baby food through them, following the pattern, the gracious providence, you have embedded deep in nature. You provided that I should wish for no more than was supplied, and that those supplying it should wish to give me what you gave them. The wish to supply me came from the natural instinct you planted deep in them, so that doing me good did them good, a good they did not provide themselves but passed on from you, the source of all good, my God, my rescue at every stage.

This I came to reflect on only later, heeding the persistent call you issued through the inner and outer faculties you blessed me with, but then I knew only how to suck, to sleep when soothed, to cry when my body vexed me—this I knew, no more. 8. In time I began to smile, only in my sleep at first,

L6 *inside me]* The persistent contrast of *intus* and *foris.*

L8 *signal out]* Using "signs something like what I desired." The interplay of body language and the verbal system is a key to Augustine's analysis of children's learning in *The Teacher.* The infant is trying to use a body language it understands imperfectly in order to create its own verbal language *(comm.).*

L21 *causes . . . origins . . . rationale]* The key terms in a climactic tricolon (Introduction).

L23 *rationale]* For Augustine, God's fixed forms *(rationes eternae)* caused the unfolding forms *(rationes seminales)* of temporal succession.

and later when awake—so it was said of me, and I believed it, since we observe the same thing in other babies, though I do not remember it of myself. Gradually I became aware of my surroundings, and wished to express my demands to those who could comply with them; but I could not, since the demands were inside me, and outside were their fulfillers, who had no faculty for entering my mind. So I worked my limbs and voice energetically, trying to signal out something like my demands, to the best of my little (and little availing) ability. Then, when I was frustrated—because I was not understood or was demanding something harmful—I threw a tantrum because adults did not obey a child, free people were not my slaves. So I inflicted on them my revenge of wailing. I have learned that babies act this way, from the ones I had occasion to observe, who, without having known me [as an infant], taught me more about myself than the nurses who did know me.

9.   See then how I lived on when my speechless stage had died away—unlike you, who live on always, with nothing of you dying away, since before all ages began, before everything that can be called before, you are, and are the God and Lord of all that you created, and in you are the certain causes of contingent outcomes, the unchanging origins that abide through all that changes, the eternal rationale for all irrational things that pass away.

Tell me, your supplicant, Lord, merciful to one needing mercy, tell me whether my speechless stage occurred after some other stage of me had died away. Was it just the time I spent in my mother's body—for I came to be told of that, too,

L1 *pregnant women*] He is, of course, referring primarily to his partner's pregnancy with their son, Godsend.

L1 *something before*] Augustine was an agnostic about the soul's origin, but did not believe in any pre-existence of the soul that evaded solidarity with Adam *(comm.)*.

L11 *gossips*] Diminutive *mulierculae,* stressing the flimsiness of Augustine's evidence for his own earliest existence, not the unworthiness of women *(comm.)*.

L12 *existence . . . life . . . signaling*] an echo of the Trinity—*esse, vivere, intelligere*—in the child's basic gifts.

L22 *years never run out*] Psalm 101.28: "You are the same, and your years do not run out."

and observed pregnant women myself. But was there something before that, my delight, my God? Was I, anywhere, anyone? I have no one who might tell me that—neither father nor mother, nor anyone claiming experience of such a stage, nor any memory of my own. Or do you smile, to mock me as I ask, you who tell me to praise you for what I know, and testify to that?   10.   I can bear you testimony, Lord of heaven and earth, returning praise to you for my origin and speechless days, though I remember it not, because you let man learn of his infancy from analogy with other infants, if not from women gossips who were there.

[So even without remembering] I was already in existence and had life, and I was striving, while still (just barely) speechless, to find a way of signaling my own meanings out to others. Where could such a creature come from, Lord, but you? Can any such have framed itself, or found a conduit through which existence and life could stream into him from some other source than you, for whom existing is not one thing, living another, since you are perfect existence, perfect life? Perfect you are, beyond all change, and today does not reach its end in you, yet it does end in you, since all days are in you, nor could they have a course of transit not defined by you. But your years never run out, your years are a single today; and our days, no matter how many—not only our own but those of all before us—run their course through your today, are brought into being in it, find their identity in it; and days still to come shall run their course through it, with their own being and identity, while you alone are identical with yourself, so every tomorrow

L6 *sad for sinner*]   Isaiah 1.4: "How sad it is for a sinning race of men, a people deep in iniquity."

L9 *no one being clean*]   Job 14.4–5: "Who can be clean of all foulness? Not a single one, so long as he shall live a single day on earth."

L27 *flailing away*]   The child's desperation to speak was repeated, for Augustine, when he came back to the church desperate for truth: "Dehydrated and weakened by lack of nourishment, I sought the church's breasts with a wild abandon, flailing at them with deep sobs and groans, wringing out a flow that would restore me from my plight" (*The Need to Believe* 2).

to come, every yesterday gone, is made in your today. What does it matter if one fails to figure this out? Let such a one be content to say, "How could this be?"—so long as he finds in love what he does not figure out, instead of figuring it out without finding you.

11.   Pay me heed, God. When one says "How sad it is for the sinner," God takes pity, since he made the sinner (without making the sin). Who is there to remind me of my sin before I spoke?—'no one being clean of sin, not a speechless child with but a day upon this earth'—who will remind me, will any (even the tiniest) baby serve for me to observe what I do not remember of myself, will it show me what sin I was committing at that age? Was it sin to work my mouth toward the nipple as I cried? If I did that now, working my mouth not toward the nipple but after food proper to my present state, I would be derided and properly reproached. But though my behavior then deserved reproach, I would not have understood if anyone issued it, the reproach would have had no effect, either from social pressure or personal acceptance. As we grow up, we root out and relinquish such behavior. (People, I observe, when sorting out bad things to reject, do not knowingly throw out the good instead.)

Or is this behavior allowable in terms of a baby's age—to demand with tears what would harm it; to throw a tantrum when not obeyed by servants and adults, by his own parents, by any bystanders (however wise) not knuckling under to its whim; flailing away to hurt (if he could) those who dare disobey his own self-harming ukase? The harmlessness of babes

L4 *sudden pallor]*　For a memory of Godsend in this passage, see *comm.*

L14 *sensory apparatus . . . beauty to its form . . . self-preservation]*　An echo of the Trinity in the human body.

L18 *testimony of song]*　Psalm 9.1–2: "Good it is to testify to the Lord, and sing to your name, you most high."

L21 *oneness . . . beauty . . . law]*　Another trinitarian reference.

is in their body's effect, not their mind's intent. With my own eyes I was a present witness at what we have all observed, a tiny thing's fierce competitiveness—how, though he could not speak, he made himself clear by his sudden pallor and the sour contortion of his features at a rival for the nipple. Mothers and nurses claim they can check the tantrum by some trick of their trade, treating as harmless a baby's effort to deprive another of the one food it depends on, though the milk flows abundantly for both. We put up with the tantrum, not because it does not matter, or matters little, but because the baby will grow out of it—as we see from the fact that no one will put up with such behavior in an adult.

12. You God, who are my Lord, give life to the baby when you give it a body—we see how you articulate its sensory apparatus; fit limb to limb, giving beauty to its form; and coordinate all its instincts for self-preservation as a single thing. It is your will that I appraise all this, pay you, the highest of things, my testimony of song to your name, since this in itself, had you done nothing more for the baby, shows that you are all-powerful and kind, that no one else could do what you do—could, from your oneness, give each thing its degree of being; from your beauty give it shapeliness; from your law give it its rank in the creation.

Such, Lord, was the period when I was alive though I do not remember being so, a period for which I have taken on trust what others told me, or have guessed at my own behavior from analogy with other babies. However persuasive such analogy may be, I hesitate to count that period as part of my life in this

L2 *conceived in evil]* Psalm 50.7: "For I was conceived, you see, in evil, and my mother sheltered a sinful me in her womb."

world, since it is as wrapped in a darkness beyond recall as was the period I spent in my mother's womb—and if 'I was conceived in evil, and my mother sheltered a sinful me in her womb,' where, my God, I ask you, where, my Lord, was I, your servant, ever free from sin? Beyond that I say nothing of a time with which I recall not the faintest connection.

L9 *All by myself]* The emphatic *ego ipse.* Augustine is not excluding *God's* teaching role, of course, as his next words indicate—God gave him the brain he is using "by myself." But the assertion of independence from human teachers is the key to this whole passage, just as it is the central idea of *The Teacher*; *(comm.).*

L13 *began . . . to pull in]* The manuscripts' variant reading *prensabam*—"I was beginning [imperfect tense] to grab"—is preferable, as the unexpected word *(lectio difficilior)*, to a copyist's tamer *pensabam*, "I began to ponder" *(comm.).*

L14 *people named something]* *The Teacher* 33: "When the word [head] was said again and again, I began to take notice of it and to figure out where in conversation it was being used, until I connected the sound with something already familiar to me from sight."

L14 *named something]* Emphasis on *thing*—which led Wittgenstein to think naming things was all that the learning of language involved for Augustine *(comm.).*

L20 *miming actions]* Literally, "motion of other members [than the face]." In *The Teacher*, Augustine finds a whole language in the mime's art.

III. Childhood (Speaking)

13.   What but childhood could I enter by advance beyond my speechless stage? Or is it better to say that childhood entered me, displacing the speechless stage? Yet my speechlessness did not depart—where else could it have gone?—though it was no longer with me. As soon as I began speaking, I could no longer be speechless, but a speaking child. I remember speaking, though I learned only later *how* I came to speak. It was not by the teaching of my elders, arranging words in some prescribed order, as when I learned grammar. All by myself, using the brain you gave me, my God, for want of getting each thing I wanted from each person I wanted, when my screams, my noises random and random flailing of limbs, did not convey the desires within me, I began to use my memory to pull in what I desired. Whenever people named something, and used the same inflections when indicating that thing with their bodies, I would take note and store in memory the fact that they made the same sound when they wanted to indicate that thing. It was clear they wanted to do this from the physical action that is a body language for all humans—facial expressions, glances, or miming actions that, linked with vocal inflections, convey an intention to get or retain, repel or evade something. The words I heard, used in their right way in different grammatical

L2 *wrestling my mouth*]   Modern observers have recorded the way babies try out and master various sounds in their "nonsense" cooings.

L5 *shaped . . . pressures*]   The language system of Society may not be able to give understanding, but it can corrupt the heart, and in that sense "teach" bad ways.

L18 *people who prayed*]   A glimpse of Augustine's boyhood in the context of his local church—he always said he *returned* to the church, rather than discovered it later in life.

L25 *not yielding*]   Literally, "not to my lack of perception." The translation follows Augustine's understanding of Psalm 21.3: "Cry though I will, my God, you heed me not by day, nor answer at night by leading me to false values, not true ones."

settings, and recurring over time, I steadily accumulated and, wrestling my mouth around these sounds, I expressed what I wanted. With these tools for enunciating what I wanted, I plunged deeper into the storm-tossed lives of those around me, where I was shaped by my parents' direction and the pressures of my elders.

14. God, you who are my God, what pitiable things, things that made me ridiculous, did I undergo when the goal marked out for me as a boy was to follow advice that would make me a success, would give me an orator's facility for gaining human fame and a wealth that deludes its slaves. For this was I sent to school and taught grammar; and though I could not see what use there was in that, I was beaten for not being eager in its pursuit—a custom praised by our elders, since men living long ago laid out the painful course we must be forced down, adding more to the work and suffering that was already our lot as sons of Adam.

But I came across, as well, people who prayed to you, and they made me, in my small way, aware of you as a vague high being beyond my sensible experience, one who could, nonetheless, hear me out and bring me help. Thus, even as a child, I ventured on prayer to you as my support, my place of shelter. Tongue-tied words I faltered out, using my small voice with no small intensity, to be spared being beaten in class; and when you did not grant me my prayer (not yielding to my false values), my elders, including my parents, laughed off my beatings, not wishing me ill, though a large and weighty ill the beatings were for me.

ʟ5 *and to laugh*]   The variant *deridens* for *diligens,* since the two groups (martyrs and parents) are compared in terms of their contempt for suffering, not of their love for others *(comm.).* The martyrs have a right to mock, and do not, while the parents have no right to mock, and do.

ʟ8 *lack . . . lack . . . lack*]   *minus . . . minus . . . minus . . . deerat.* The play on various senses of "lack" undercuts the melodrama of comparison between his schoolboy beatings and the martyrs' sufferings. He did not lack a martyr-sized fear, though it arose simply from a lack of study. The beatings could have been avoided, easily, if he had just done his homework.

ʟ14 gain . . . *game*]   The original pun is *nugae . . . negotia.*

15.   Is there, Lord, anyone so brave, so resolute from love of you (aside from mere natural obduracy), is there, I say, anyone so steeled by love for you as to make light of the rack and tearing instruments and other tools of torture (things people all over the earth beg with great terror to escape) and to laugh at those stricken with terror at the tortures as much as parents made light of the torments we children underwent from our teachers? I did not lack any of the panic, or lack any desperation in begging to escape blows—though it was only my lack of attention to reading and writing and performing the assignments given me that was to blame. I had no excuse from lack of memory or talent, which you made sufficient for my age; I simply loved games more, and I was disciplined by those who had their own games (since *gain* is the game of adults). So children's games are punished by their elders, and no one gets worked up for the punished, the punishers, or both, unless some calculater of advantage should *approve* my being beaten for a child's games since the games slowed my rapid advance in the education I could use for viler games. Who, in these terms, was worse—my teacher, who writhed with bitter envy when caught in a solecism by a fellow pedant, or I, when I resented losing my ball game to a fellow player?

16.   This is not said to deny my sin, Lord, you who both correct and create all things in nature, but can only correct [not create] sins—it was a sin to defy the edicts of my parents and those teachers, since I later put to higher use the education those people, from whatever motive of their own, made me acquire. I did not disobey them to do something better, but from a

L1 *fantastic tales*]   Not pagan myths but, as the surrounding phrases show, tales of athletic glory in the games. Augustine was a fan of sports celebrities, like a modern boy collecting baseball cards—except that the games had an expressly religious aspect in his day, with vestiges of pagan sacrifice. At T 10.57 and *Order in the Universe* 1.25, Augustine admits to his early fascination with the games, one he helped his friend Alypius to overcome (T 8.13).

L12 *taught about the eternal life*]   Another glimpse of the degree to which the boy Augustine was an active participant in his local church, where the priest would seem to have taken the position Augustine later did, urging the baptism of children—which Augustine's mother opposed in any case but imminent death. This is one of the places where Augustine criticizes his mother *(comm.)*.

love of games—I longed for lofty triumphs and fantastic tales that tickled my ears and made them itch for more, making my eyes sparkle bright and ever brighter with excitement at the public games, the play of adults. Those who put on such shows are clothed with a high dignity that parents wish for their children; and they gladly let those children be beaten if attending shows hinders their education, which can gain for them the status to put on shows themselves. Look on all this, Lord, with a forgiving eye, and free us now that we call on you, freeing as well those who do not call yet, that they may call and you may free them.

17.   Already in my boyhood I was taught about the eternal life promised us through the Lord's lowliness reaching down to our haughtiness—I was signed already with his cross, seasoned with his salt, when I left the womb of my mother, who turned fervently to you. And you saw, Lord, how I, while still a boy, almost died from a sudden attack of chest fever— you saw, Lord and guardian, with what emotion and belief, with what reliance on my own mother and the mother of us all, your church, I begged for baptism in Christ your son. The mournful bearer of my mortal body cared more, from her pure heart's faith in you, to deliver me into eternal life than she had to bear me into this one. She made quick arrangements for the rites of my ablution in the saving mysteries, with my testimony to you, Lord Jesus, for forgiveness of my sins. Only, instantly, I recovered—so my cleansing was put off, on the assumption that I would surely be tainted as I grew up, and

L20 *myself by me and by mine*]   Polyptoton (Introduction), descriptive of all the cares folding in upon the newly baptized child of Augustine's hypothesis.

L24 *my mother . . . preferred*]   Relapsing after her panic during his illness.

L25 *waters' workings*]   Literally, "in those [waters] by which I would be wrought," *per eos [fluctus] unde formarer.*

L25 *already reshaped*]   Literally, "already the prototype" [of a newborn Christian]. Augustine is contrasting the flood of temptation working on his soft clay with the hard shape his clay might have taken from the different waters of baptism.

the taint, after such a cleansing, would be greater and more perilous.

I already had faith, then, as did my mother and all our household, except my father, who, though he was not yet a believer himself, did not deny me the protection of my mother's devotion, that I should believe in Christ. She made it a point to say that you, not he, were my father, my God, and you helped her in this way to prevail over her husband, staying subservient to him though superior to him, since in this she was obeying your demands.

18.   This is my request, God: I would know, if you will let me, why I was put off, why not baptized; was it for my own good to be given free rein to sin for a while, or was I not, in fact, given free rein? Why even now is it everywhere dinned into our ears, when this or that class of men is discussed, that we should "Let him carry on, since he is not yet baptized," when we do not say about physical health, "Let him further damage his body, since he is not yet given his health." How much better would it have been for me to be healed on the spot, so that care might be taken of myself by me and by mine, that the healing given my soul should be preserved in your preserving ways who gave it—how much better indeed. But mighty storm-waves, and many, were foreseen rolling over me after my childhood, and my mother, understanding this, preferred to commit to the waters' workings my unshaped clay rather than a self already reshaped.

L11 *our every hair*]   Matthew 10.30: "a count is kept of every hair on your head."

L13 *so little in size*]   See Introduction for the alliteration.

IV. Schooling

19.   Yet even before my testing time as a young man, even in my childhood, I resisted education and despised those pressing it upon me, though they pressed anyway, and good was done me though I myself did no good. I would have learned nothing if it had not been forced on me, and no one deserves credit for what is forced on him, though the thing itself be creditable. Nor did those forcing me deserve any credit, since the credit is all yours, my God. They did not realize—as they forced learning on me to sate insatiable yearnings for penurious wealth and infamous fame—what different uses I would make of it. But you, 'who keep count of our every hair,' put to my use the useless efforts of those forcing me to learn, and used my resistance, which merited the beatings, as a punishment for me, so little in size, so large in sin. Thus you get the credit for those who earned no credit for what they did to me, and I got the punishment I deserved for resisting what they were doing, for what you have decreed is fulfilled when sin becomes the soul's own punishment of itself.

20.   Why I loathed Greek lessons, when I was plunged into them at an early age, I have not to this day been able to fathom. I took fondly to Latin, not indeed from my first tutors but from those called teachers of literature. The basic reading,

L3 *fleshly whims]* Literally, "because I was flesh and a wind wandering off and not returning," adapting Psalm 77.39: "He remembered they were flesh, a wind that strays off without returning." Augustine is striking the theme of wandering thoughts that leads into Aeneas's wanderings in the next sentence.

L10 *astray myself]* Augustine's omnipresent path imagery (see Introduction) identifies his own straying with the travels of Aeneas.

L14 *pitiful . . . pitiable . . . pity]* More polyptoton (Introduction), for which the inflected Latin allows greater variety of forms: *miserius misero non miserante.*

L18 *breeding depth of thought]* Literally, "wedding my intellect to the seat [breast] of reflection," in order to produce the intellectual offspring of that reflection, a recurrence to Augustine's striking view of thought as parturition, the generation of an inner *Verbum.* God is the vital principle *(virtus)* working through this cross-fertilization—a variant on Augustine's more normal identification of God as the *light* that makes intellection possible.

L23 *exploring with the sword]* Virgil, *Aeneid* 6.457: "You were dead, having by sword explored your utmost doom."

L25 *to earth returning]* Genesis 3.19: "Sprung of earth, to earth you shall return."

writing, and numbering in Latin I considered as dull and irk-
some as any aspect of my Greek lessons—the explanation of
which must be sin and the aimless life of 'fleshly whims that
stray off without returning.'

Actually, the basic lessons were the more valuable ones, just
because they went by rule, letting me acquire and retain the
ability I still hold to read any book I come across, or to write
exactly what I want to say—things more useful than the strayings of some Aeneas that I was forced to memorize while for-
getting that I was astray myself, better certainly than my tears
for the perished Dido, who killed herself from love, while I, the
truly pitiful one, was dry-eyed to my perishing, my God, from
loss of you.

21.   Who is more pitiful than a pitiable man without pity
for himself—one who weeps for Dido, dead because she loved
Aeneas, but not for himself, dead because he failed to love
you, God, my heart's enlightener, the feeder of my soul's inner
hunger, the vital principle breeding depth of thought out of
my intelligence? I [not Aeneas] was the abandoner, the faith-
less lover, and my faithlessness earned the world's "Bravo!
Bravo!"—since love of the world is abandonment of you, and
the world cries "Bravo! Bravo!" to keep its own in line. For all
this I had no tears, only tears for Dido, 'exploring with the
sword her utmost doom.' So I, in flight from you, explored the
utmost depths of your creation, 'earthy and to earth returning.'
If I had been forbidden to read this tale, I would have lamented
the loss of what made me lament, so crazed are those who think

L8 *veils of honor*]   Entry drapes were signs of dignity, for teachers and others. See Augustine's *Sermon* 51.4.5: "The more honored the man inside, the more drapes hang at his house's entry."

L9 *phrase peddlers or purchasers*]   *venditores grammaticae vel emptores.* Augustine uses the term "phrase salesman" *(venditor verborum)* to mock his own role as court orator in Milan (T 9.13).

L27 *Creusa herself ghosting*]   Virgil, *Aeneid* 2.772: "sad trace of Creusa herself's ghost."

belles lettres nobler than the rudiments of reading and writing I had to learn.

22. Now, however, may my God cry through my soul, your truth assuring me "That is not the case, not at all—basic learning was far better." Assuredly I am readier to forget, now, the strayings of Aeneas and all his sort than to lose my ability to read and write. Ceremonial draperies are hung at the school door, but they are not so much veils of honor for the esoteric as blinds for the erroneous. And let no phrase peddlers or purchasers scorn me, an escapee from their thrall, while I give you my soul's willing testimony, since I accept the correction of my strayings, I long to tread your righteous ways. If I should confront them with the straightforward question whether the poet spoke true when he claimed that Aeneas went to Carthage once upon a time, the uneducated will admit they do not know, while the educated admit it is not true. But if I ask how to spell Aeneas' name, all those who know how to read will give the right answer, honoring the agreed-on conventions that establish the alphabet. Similarly, if I ask what would make life less bearable, to forget how to read or write or to forget those poetic imaginings, we know what anyone in his sound mind will say. So it was sinful of me to prefer airy trifles to the solider rudiments—or, more accurately, to loathe the latter and love the former. The singsong "one and one make two, two and two make four" was detestable to me, but sweet were the visions of absurdity—the wooden horse cargoed with men, Troy in flames, and "Creusa herself ghosting by."

L15 *labor to deliver*]   In Augustine's "language obstetrics," the child performs his own mental delivery, using as instruments words not specifically aimed at assisting him (e.g., tutors' conscious instruction), but words encountered "higgledy-piggledy." Using this material, the child is able to deliver the offspring of his brain, expressing his own inmost needs, to the external world (his listeners' ears) *(comm.)*.

L25 *Hear, Lord*]   Psalm 60.2: "Hear, Lord, my cry to you."

L28 *vicious bypaths*]   One of the most extended uses of Augustine's "path imagery" (Introduction).

23. Then why did I loathe Greek literature, which has tunes for the same kind of tale? Homer knew how to weave the same spells, just as pleasantly trivial, yet he repelled me as a boy. I suppose Greek boys would feel the same about Virgil, if they were forced to con him as I conned Homer. It is hard, very hard, to pick up a foreign language—for me, this dashed with bitterness all the sweet Greek nonsense. I was ignorant of the words, and violent threats and acts were used to make me learn them. Once, admittedly, still in my speechless state, I knew no Latin words either. Yet I applied myself to learning them, without intimidation or coercion, surrounded as I was by nurses who coaxed, adults who laughed, and others fond of playing with a child. The Latin words were learned without others' punitive insistence that I learn. From my own heart's need I went into labor to deliver my thoughts, which I could not have done without a stock of words, picked up not just from tutors but from anyone who spoke with me, and in their ears I completed the parturition of what I felt within me. Unfettered inquisitiveness, it is clear, teaches better than do intimidating assignments—which assignments, nonetheless, chasten random inquisitiveness within rules, your rules, God, imposed even in the beatings of teachers, as in the trials of martyrs, those healing pains that draw us back from the sickly pleasures that might drift us off from you.

24. 'Hear, Lord, my cry to you,' lest my soul prove too weak for your discipline, lest I prove too weak to bear testimony to all your merciful dealings with me, by which you drew me from my vicious bypaths, outdazzling with your

L3 *carry me]* 1 Corinthians 1.8: "He will be your strength all the way to the goal."

allure the attractions that misled me, so that I may love you more worthily, hang on to your hand with a whole heart's energy, as you 'carry me out of trial to the final goal.' You see, Lord, my king and God, I would use whatever I learned as a child for your service, whatever I speak or write or enumerate—since you disciplined me when I was learning trifles, and have forgiven me the sin of taking my delight in them; for I learned some useful words even from trifles (though I might have learned them from less trivial sources, as is the safer way for children to proceed).

L1 *Society*]   *Mos* (Custom) is the personified way life is lived in common, which carries people in a flood of multiplying practices—like the passed-on habit of beating a child, or the "storm" of general conversation at **[13]** or the storm-waves of temptation at **[18]**. Here Augustine moves into the final section of Book One, describing how conformation to the world, thrust upon him by his sinful fellow children of Adam, deformed God's gifts in him.

L4 *the Wood*]   Augustine regularly refers to Christ's cross as a plank to cling to in the flood of human sin (O 2.86).

L8 *gowned*]   Literally, "wearing rhetors' hoods."

L9 *breathes the same court air*]   Literally, "of the same dust" (of the public arena).

L15 *hellish river*]   What Augustine has against the school system is that it sets the patterns of socialization that trap people in blind efforts at respect—a respect to be derived from actions shameful in themselves. Even adultery is not the product of mere lust but of expectations set up by peers and superiors' pressures—the point of the passage on Terence that follows.

V. Conforming to a Deforming Society

25.   Cursed be you, Society, onstreaming—who can stand
against your tide never stemmed, your torrent carrying Eve's
sons out to the vast sea's peril, where even those who ride on
the Wood barely survive? Was it not from you, Society, that I
learned how Jove is both thunderer and adulterer? He could
not really be both, but he was portrayed as both, so that real
adultery could be indulged with fictitious thunder serving as its
pimp. What gowned rhetorician can take it seriously when his
fellow, who breathes the same court air, says: 'Homer in his fictions made gods behave like humans, but I prefer for humans
to behave like gods'? Well, in fact, Homer did create fictions
precisely to give divine sanction to human vice, so vice would
not seem vicious, and those indulging it could claim to be following the example of gods on high, not of lowliest men.

26.   Into you, you hellish river, men's children are thrown,
to learn such things for a price, and a great ceremony is made
when they display what they have learned in the forum, the
very place where the teachers' state fees, superadded to the private fees, are posted. And the river, pounding against these
rocks, roars out: 'This is the reward for learning literature, for
acquiring the eloquence needed to plead persuasively and argue well'—as if we could never have encountered the phrases

L2 *Terence*]   In the comedy *The Eunuch* (161 B.C.E.), lines 583–91. The words referred to by Augustine are italicized:

> While she was sitting in her room, she viewed
> A mural in which Jove himself pursued
> A maid, ejaculating *showered gold*
> Into her *lap*—for me, example old
> Of just what I was up to in disguise.
> He too arrived as man, to *trick* her eyes.
> If ev'n this god, who thumps *heaven's temples* so
> With crashing noise, showers also down so low,
> Can lowly I not follow where he goes?
> You bet, and have great fun, too, heaven knows.

Augustine's departures from known texts show that he quotes from schoolboy memory—an example of the tainting of the young mind he is describing.

L14 *choice and precious vessels*]   Acts 9.15: "a vessel of choice." Proverbs 20.15: "a precious vessel."

L25 *fending off*]   Virgil, *Aeneid* 1.38: "Nor can I fend Troy's king from Italy."

'showered gold' or 'lap' or 'trick' or 'heaven's temples,' or other words put together in one place by Terence, if he had not put on stage a vile young man taking Jove as a model for his act of rape. The man gazes on a mural presenting the device by which Jove tricked a woman, ejaculating himself as showered gold into her lap. Just see how the youth works up his lust, as if by heavenly injunction:

> If ev'n this god, who thumps heaven's temples so
> With crashing noise, showers also down so low,
> Can lowly I not follow where he goes?—
> You bet, and have great fun, too, heaven knows.

Vocabulary is surely not acquired more readily by means of obscenity, but *this* vocabulary makes obscene acts more accept-able. I indict not the words, which are 'choice and precious ves-sels' in themselves, but the wine of error poured into them by teachers drunk with it, who beat us if we do not drink with them, and we cannot appeal to any sober arbiter—not that I did not drink it gladly, my God, I recall that fact clearly before your gaze, I was wretch enough to enjoy it. That, indeed, is why I was said to be a promising child.

27.   Let me say, my God, something of the talent, your gift, that I dissipated on various forms of nonsense. I was called to a contest that destabilized my mind between praise hoped for and embarrassment or a beating feared: I had to recite the speech of Juno as she raged in anguish over not 'fending off Troy's king from Italy.' I had learned that no Juno ever said that, but we were compelled to follow poetical strayings into

L7 *drifted smoke]* Literally, "smoke and wind," like *fama fumi,* "reported smoke" at *The Need to Believe* 36, or *vendere fumum,* "selling smoke" in Martial (4.5.7).

L10 *heart's young tendrils]* John 15.4: "The tendril bears no fruit if separated from the vine; nor can you if you are separated from me, since I am the vine, you the tendril."

L11 *rotten prey]* Virgil, *Georgics* 2.60: "The [untended] vine yields only birds' prey of rotten grapes."

L19 *long patient]* Psalm 85.15: "long patient, very merciful, and true."

L23 *whose heart tells]* Psalm 26.8–9: "My heart has told you, 'I have sought your countenance, your countenance, Lord, I shall long for.' "

L27 *younger son]* The parable of the prodigal son, at Luke 15.11–32, is a structural model for *The Testimony* (O 2.95–97); *(comm.).*

L28 *horses or chariots]* Plotinus, *The Nines* 1.6.8, describing descent from the One and the need to return to It: "Let us fly back to the homeland . . . by what vehicle of escape? We do not need to walk . . . nor to employ a chariot-and-team, nor any kind of boat." This is a passage often echoed in Augustine, and it ties in with the departure and return of the prodigal son (O 2.95); *(comm.).*

unreality, paraphrasing in prose what was set down in verse. The child who best adapted the emotions of rage and anguish to the status of the imaginary queen, fitly decking her thoughts out in words, was given the prize.

What of value was it to me, my God, my true life, that my recital was praised beyond the multitude of my fellows in age and study? What was this but drifted smoke? Was there no other way to develop my talent and my speaking voice? Honoring you, giving honor to the words of your scripture, would have 'trellised up my heart's young tendrils,' not raveling them out in vain exercises to be 'the rotten prey of birds.' So many ways we find to honor the dark angels.

28. It is not surprising that I was swept along in folly away from you, my God, and wandered abroad, when the role models I was given were ashamed if they were caught describing their own good behavior in ungraceful or ungrammatical terms, but luxuriated in men's praise if they could describe their vicious acts in choice words well fitted together, flowing with easy and elegant phrases. Do you Lord, 'long patient, very merciful and true,' look on all this in silence? And will your silence never end? Already you are drawing from such an immense abyss the soul that longs for you, that thirsts to be satisfied by you, whose heart tells you, 'I have sought your countenance, it is your countenance, Lord, I shall seek,' for to be far off from your countenance is to be in a murk of feelings. It is not by walking or by any locomotion that one moves off from you or comes back to you—the younger son of the parable did not call for 'horses or chariots or ships, nor soar off on

L18 *Treat another*]   Matthew 7.12: "Treat another as you would be treated yourself."

L20 *housed on your heights*]   Isaiah 33.5: "Lofty is the Lord, housed on heights."

L27 *I, wretch*]   The last three paragraphs report the deformation Society wrought upon Augustine's youth, tarnishing the gifts God gave him.

visible wings, nor trudge along on foot,' when in a distant land he prodigally wasted what you, mild father, had given him on departure. Mild when he left, you were milder when he came back destitute. To be in a lustful murk of feeling, therefore, is what being far off from your countenance means.

29. Look on, Lord God, and, as you look, with patience look at how carefully men's sons honor earlier speakers' conventional arrangements of letters and syllables, while they neglect your eternal arrangement for eternal salvation—so that if one who is taught or teaches the rules of speech should, against the norm of pronunciation, drop the *h* before 'human being,' he is more censured by human beings than if he, a human being, should, against your rule of love, hate any other fellow being—as if another human being could hurt him more than does the hate he directs at that human being, or as if a man could inflict on a foe some wound greater than he inflicts on his own heart by letting it hate. The rules of grammar are not as deeply inscribed as the morality of scripture, which says: 'Treat another as you would be treated.' How hidden you are, God, 'housed on your heights,' who alone are great, cloaking in penal darkness all criminal desires, when you look on while a would-be champion orator stands before a judge, with a crowd looking on, and lashes his opponent with a boundless hate, yet is cautious not to say something ungrammatical, like 'between he'—and he does not care that the rhetorical storm he is working up may sweep his victim off from life.

30. I, wretch, was even as a child abandoned to Society, left at the edge of the arena where I was to contend, where I was

L5 *swept off*] Psalm 30.23: "I said in my anguish, 'I am swept off from the gaze of your face.' "

L10 *ludicrous clumsiness*] Literally, "with a ludicrous wobbling [instability, *inquietudine*] to imitate [plays]." The fact that the bias toward plays is a perversion of the imbalance of the *cor inquietum* toward God **[1]** is underlined by the triad of charms inverting the claims of the Trinity: games-plays-imitate.

L27 *Heaven's kingdom*] Matthew 19.14: "Allow the children to approach me, since heaven's kingdom is for the like of these."

more afraid of committing a solecism than concerned, if I did so, with my envy at any who did *not* commit it. I tell you this, and testify, my God, that this kind of praise was what I sought from those whose approval was my goal in life. I did not realize in what a maelstrom of ugliness 'I was being swept off from your gaze.' What could be fouler than the way I earned disapproval even from the worldly with my endless lies told to pedagogue, to teachers, to parents, so I could indulge my love of games, my passion for trivial plays, for re-enacting them with ludicrous clumsiness.

I also sneaked food from my parents' cupboard or table, to pamper myself or to give to others, who exacted this price for letting me share their delight in the games they played. And, once in the game, I often maneuvered to overcome others by devious means, overcome myself by a blind urge to win—yet I was a stickler for the rules, too, and savagely denounced any other's infraction of them I uncovered, even when it was the very infraction I was guilty of; while if *I* was caught out and denounced, I would throw a fit rather than admit it.

Is this the innocence of children—how can it be, I ask you, Lord, how can it, my God? Is it not a natural progression, from one stage of life to the succeeding ones, to move from playing for nuts and balls and sparrows, under pedagogues and teachers, to playing for gold, estates, and slaves, under governors and kings, and to move from beatings in school to criminal sentences? You, then, praised nothing but a child's small stature, as a symbol of humility, dear king, when you said 'Heaven's kingdom is for the like of these.'

L5 *a single control*]   A return to the mystery of each animate thing's unitary action through all its parts *(comm.)*.

L16 *joy, glory, and truth*]   This first triad goes with the two that immediately succeed it, showing the Trinity under three aspects, as truly seen, as falsely sought, and as rewarding the seeker:

joy	pain	delight
glory	dejection	pride
truth	error	trust

The whole of Book One is implicit in this sentence, which counterpoises the essential goodness of Augustine's self as received from God with the counterbias of Adam's sin and Society's deformations. The latter tugged him away from God even before he realized how they conscripted him into the world's system of sin.

31.   I must, however, still give thanks to you, Lord, highest and best maker and ruler of this universe, had you given me only the life of a child; for during that time I existed, I experienced sensation, I preserved myself—by an echo of your mysterious oneness, out of which I came to be—as I maintained a single control over everything my senses delivered to me, and my first slight hold upon slight truths gave me satisfaction. I tried to avoid fallacies, my memory developed, I learned to wield words, I was shaped by friendship, I shunned being hurt or losing hope or being fooled. What, in this animate life of mine, was not admirable, worthy of praise? All of these were your gifts, God, I did not endow myself with any of them—and the sum of these good things was myself. My maker is good in himself, and my only good, and I hold him high for all the good that was in me even as a boy. Only sin was my own, when I sought joy, glory, and truth not in him but in things he made, in myself and other creatures, thus sliding off toward pain, dejection, and error. Still I thank you, you my delight, my pride, my trust—I thank you, my God, for your gifts to me, may you preserve them, thus preserving me, so that everything you gave me may grow and be improved, and I shall be with you, whose gift it is that I exist.

PART III

Commentary

༼ଈ✿ଈ༽

I. How to Begin?

1. The originality of Augustine's work is marked from the outset. It is different not only from other people's books, but from his own: "No other work of his begins with direct address to God" (O 2.8). Though that points us in the right direction—that Augustine is writing a prayer, not an autobiography—this exordium is also unlike any normal beginning of prayer in the classical era. Suppliants addressed deity by a title or titles that gave them some specific claim on the god. Diana of Ephesus will hear her clients if (and because) they are Ephesians, or because they come to worship in her cult shrine at Ephesus, or because they share some attribute of her cult (as virgins, for instance, or hunters). Zeus the Protector of Guests (Philoxenos) will avenge wronged guests as a proof his own prerogative. The more titles one can claim as appropriate for one's plea, the greater leverage is exerted on the god.

Was this form of prayer ruled out for Augustine because of its pagan roots? Not quite. The Jewish Scripture he uses speaks in terms of the Covenant to "the God of our fathers," to the God of the Promises made to Abraham and Moses. There is even a trace of such thinking in the New Testament prayer par excellence, which calls on "Our Father" by a double claim, as Father of the Jewish ancestors and as Father of Jesus. Even the prayer's spatial invocation ("the One in the heavens"—*ho en tois ouranois*, Matthew 6.9) supplants reference to cult places by appeal to a trans-cult *place.*

Nothing of that tradition is appropriate for *The Testimony.* The old prayer form approached the god by limiting deity to a place, or a role, or a compact by which it was bound. But Augustine asserts that God is beyond all limit, beyond any obligation we can impose on him, any privilege we can assert. We humans have, in the legal sense, "no standing" with him. We cannot control what we cannot measure, even to praise. This is a prayer that has to forswear everything, even the claims of prayer. So here is the first of the endless paradoxes about *The Testimony*: it is a prayer that does not begin like a prayer. And a second paradox follows immediately: it begins, instead, as that least likely thing for such an intimate (almost private) book— an oration. Though Augustine cannot appeal to a cult title or place or function for his opening, he does turn to the tricks of his own rhetorical profession.

To assert one's *aporia* (paralysis) before an imposing (if not impossible) task, to plead one's shortcomings ("unaccustomed as I am . . ."), to ask for undeserved help from one's audience— that is the classical orator's "preemption of sympathy" *(captatio benevolentiae).* Is such an artificial device, stilted and often insincere, out of place in a prayer addressed to God? It does, at first, seem so. Even while he is saying that he has no claim upon the deity, Augustine uses a topos meant to "captivate" the divine audience, bind it to the speaker. But Augustine makes of the maneuver a startlingly new thing, seeing that what is

rigged or hyperbolical when used in the forum, or in human
law courts, has a depth of literal meaning when directed at
the audience from which Augustine most needs a hearing, but
which he can least command. Here is *aporia* indeed—God is
laudabilis, worthy of praise; but no one is worthy enough to
praise him. Augustine avoids the Vulgate reading of the Psalm
he quotes in his opening line, though he had used that reading
in *Explaining the Psalms* (95.4), where God deserves praise
nimis, "exceedingly," not *valde,* "strongly [enough]." Since
valde is simply a contraction of *valide,* it means validly or adequately. It is absurd, in Augustine's view, to think God can be
praised excessively, or beyond his merits. He cannot even
be praised (by us) inadequately, or below his merits. Though
God deserves praise equal to his vastness, we are in no position
to deliver it. His wisdom, we are told, is beyond appreciation
(numerus).

Numerus had a powerful technical (and mystical) meaning
for Augustine in just the period when he wrote this opening.
Over the years he had already formed his cosmology around a
favorite verse in the book of Wisdom (11.21), to which he gave
a trinitarian interpretation (O 2.293–95): "You have ordered
all things by measure [*mensura*] and number [*numerus*] and
weight [*pondus*]." Much as he had cited this line before, he
gave it special attention in the years around 400, when he was
using it to explore the profundities of the creation narrative in
Genesis. That meditation was carried on in three overlapping
works of the period, *The Testimony, Literal Meanings in Genesis,* and *The Trinity.* All three terms of the Wisdom verse are

used in the opening paragraph of *The Testimony*, where the explicit doctrine of *Literal Meanings* sets the implicit framework of this prayer's opening.

In *Literal Meanings* 4.3–4, Augustine asks whether God is number, and answers that he is not number himself, but is beyond number—just as he is beyond measure and weight. These three principles of order are also principles of limit—limiting, specifically, extension and form and stability. Since God does not have limits, he cannot be ordered by these principles, though he emanates the principles for ordering others. He is Numbering, but not numbered—that is the sense of Augustine's *non est numerus* in the second line of *The Testimony*. God is "Measure without measure, Number without number, and Weight without weight" (*Literal Meanings* 4.3).

What Augustine says in *The Testimony*, quoting Psalm 146, is that God's wisdom *(sapientia)* has no number. Number in these works of ca. 400 is the principle of form, of music, of beauty, of words, as well as of wisdom. It is the way the One is articulated in the many. Computing *numerus* is not at issue here, so much as *appreciating* the principle of beauty and order. Computation belongs better to *mensura,* the first term in the book of Wisdom, which establishes each thing's extent of being. Though *mensura* is not, like *numerus,* expressly mentioned in the opening paragraph of Book One, it is present in the way the text contrasts the vastness of God and his creation with Augustine's own limited segment *(portio)* of the whole. Setting the degrees of existence, the limits of each *portio,* is the act of the creating First Person of the Trinity. Since Augustine is thinking in this context of extent, *Magnus,* the first word of the book, should not be translated "great," since that can refer to nobility or other qualities, while the problem of the opening paragraphs is that there is no match between Augustine's insignificant *portio* in relation to the vastness of God and his creation.

The third term from the Wisdom verse is weight *(pondus)*, which is referred to in these words of *The Testimony*'s first paragraph: "Our heart is unstable [*inquietum*] until stabilized [*donec requiescat*] in you." The ancient principle of "gravity" described each physical thing's "restlessness" so long as it was kept from reaching its natural level in the variously dense texture of the physical world. This natural place was determined by the mixture, in anything, of the aspiring or light elements (fire and air) with the thick or lapsing elements (earth and water). Push oil down in water, it will "gravitate" up, since it has important traces of fire in it. In this system, "weight" does not respond, as in the Newtonian universe, to a uniform drag of everything downward to a center. It manifests multiple pulls of things up, away, or down, to differentiated levels. So in modern terms "weight" is a misleading translation for *pondus.* We are talking of a thing's natural "level." Augustine often referred to this system, spelling it out for his congregation in *Explaining the Psalms* 29.2.10:

A thing's natural level [*pondus*] is a kind of urgency [*impetus*] making it strive [*conare*] toward its proper place. That is its level. Pick up a stone, you are affected by its natural level. It presses down on your hand, since it wants to be where it belongs. If you would see what it wants, pull your hand away. It falls to the ground, and is stabilized [*quiescit*] on the ground. It follows its tendency, and finds its proper place. Its level is its unwilled energy [*motus*], without any life or sensation. Other things strive upward. If you pour water over oil, it sinks to the bottom by its own level [*pondere*]. It wants its own place, it wants to be in order with respect to other things, since oil is above water in the order of nature. Until it achieves that order, it has an unstable [*inquietus*] energy. On the contrary, if you pour oil under water—as, let us say, a flask of oil falls overboard into the water, into the ocean or the sea, and breaks—the oil will not just passively lie there. . . .

From analogy with this physical system Augustine creates a psychological gravity of the Spirit as an attractive force drawing souls to their proper level: "My level is my love—wherever I am tugged, it is the thing tugging me" (T 13.10). Augustine wrote in his book *Music*: "Satisfaction [*delectatio*—compare "You prompt us yourself to find satisfaction," *delectet*] is the natural level of the soul. It is what puts the soul in order— 'Where your treasury is, there will your heart be' [Matthew 6.21]." This drag on the heart, this *pondus*, is associated with the Third Person of the Trinity through the third term in Wisdom 11.21. The corruptible human body tends downward, but "our [spiritual] heart is unstable until stabilized in you." This spiritual gravity acts against natural gravity (which the Spirit also establishes in the universe). That is how God has made us biased, or unbalanced, *ad te.*

The whole of Wisdom's cosmological scheme, then, is present in the opening lines of *The Testimony*, dwarfing Augustine, making his effort at prayer seem doomed. He is an insignificant part of a whole he cannot measure, understand, or control. How can he praise, when fitting tribute to its object is an act of appraisal, and God is too great to be appraised? The unknowability of God is brought home to Augustine in the lack of a cult title by which to call on him. There is no ritual beginning of prayer here, no controlling invocation. "How can one call for what one does not recognize?" But where man is helpless, God himself takes the initiative, lowering his own level to man's. The Spirit may make the human heart aspire up, but that is not sufficient unless the Son "ascends down" into the lowliness *(humilitas)* of the Incarnation, turning the whole concept of levels topsy-turvy. The incarnate Son is the Word and the bringer of the Word, the praying human who will make possible a praying humanity, breaking up the *aporia* that paralyzed the whole praying project. Augustine's topos, his *captatio,* cannot really pre-empt the sympathy of his divine audience, but the Son has pre-empted Augustine's call by his antecedent response. The call does not elicit response. In fact, the response is what makes the call possible, grace enabling one to seek for grace.

2. As Augustine has no cult title to call on, he has no cult place, no *pou sto*, no where-to-stand. "Where *to* can I, already in you, call you to come?" Yet paradoxically, while he has no place where he might call God to a meeting, he also has no place where he might escape him, or avoid meeting him—not even if, like the Psalmist, he descends to the abyss. Even there, so long as anything exists, it is as a result of God's existence, and is ordered by its own kind of *mensura, numerus,* and *pondus.* One cannot step away from God in order to face toward him. We are in him, and he in us, "deeper in me than I am in me" (*intimior intimo meo,* T 3.11). We cannot call to us the already there.

3. The mystery of God's continuing act of creation in everything created means that God is everywhere, yet contained nowhere—a circle whose center is everywhere and circumference nowhere. The quandary here is what Augustine described in *Faith and Creed* 7: "God has no opposite. If asked for the opposite of white, we would say black; for the opposite of hot, we would say cold; of swift, slow; and so on. But if asked for the opposite of What Is, we can only answer: what is not." The *aporia* just deepens: God is both too far from Augustine and too close to be addressed—too high above, and too deep within. No wonder this prayer opens with a string of unanswerable questions.

4. Augustine has admitted that there is no cult title that compels or even identifies God—"what are you, God—what,

I inquire, but simply God the Lord?" (a question, not an invocation). But then he gives a series of "titles" that are self-canceling, paradoxes that state what God is not. He takes a series of terms from Scripture that are obviously not true in a literal sense. These are the very terms that had led him to mock Jewish Scripture in his Manichaean days (T 3.13–18), and he told Manichaeans after his conversion that orthodox Christians did not take them literally: "The object of our religion is not a God who repents, who is jealous, needy, or cruel, who takes delight in the sacrifice of human or animal blood" (*Catholics' and Manichaeans' Moral Codes* 1.10.16). Yet the terms are undoubtedly present in Scripture, so God must have wanted them there. Augustine says they are the half of a paradox that we must complete: "loving, *yet* not inflamed; jealous, *yet* not disturbed; regretful, *without* remorse; angry, *without* intemperance." These are what Newman called "economies"— ways of moving us closer to the truth without being able literally to state it. Terms like "father" and "son" are not literally true of the Trinity, but are paradoxes of this sort: "Father, *yet* not pre-existing his 'offspring'; Son, *yet* coeval with his 'sire.' " Paradox is a way of knowing by admitting what you do not know.

O'Donnell thinks that the Manichaean objection to these terms is what leads Augustine to end the paragraph with a swipe at *loquaces* (a nice frog-croak of a word)—"those who say the most" while meaning the least. He describes one Manichaean controversialist as "one who, to put it gently, has given the slightest consideration to the things he most likes to talk

about" (*The Pragmatism of Belief* 3). But in adding that everyone must say something about God, Augustine is denying that
there is an intellectual "means test" for praying to God. We
must pray as best we can; but we are all, even the most sophis-
ticated, using baby talk when we speak of God.

5.   This paragraph "unpacks" the last sentence of the preced-
ing one, where it was asserted that we *must* speak of and to
God. He requires it without "needing" it, by a gratuitous entry
into a relationship of love with us, one that we can reject but
not ignore. It is literally a "life or death" matter to us. If we
deny that love, we die to its rich world; and bodily death is
nothing compared with that. Augustine, *Sermon* 231.3.3: "One
who has not died and risen [in Christ] may live on but he lives
evilly—and if evilly, not really living. Let him die, lest he die.
How can he die lest he die? By undergoing conversion lest he
undergo damnation."

6.   By admitting his unworthiness even to pray, Augustine
"throws himself on the mercy of the court." He has admitted
the indictment before it is served *(pro-locutus sum)*.

II. In-Fans (Speechless)

7. For Augustine, the in-fans, the non-speaker, is a mystery. He cannot remember being one, and of course he left no spoken words from his time as a non-speaker. Since memory and language are, for him, the intertwined principles of identity, how can he say that he had any identity that is unremembered and unspeaking, that *that* he was really he? Memory is the link between the present instant and every lived instant that preceded it. Break that link, and what continuity can there be with a former self, one known only from others' reports (gossips in his nursery) or from the supposition that he must have been what other infants seem to be? Furthermore, language was formed by the use of memory [8]—that is one reason the in-fans does not speak—and remembered things are often summoned up in connection with words (*Teacher* 1). Take away both memory and language, and Augustine finds no difference between the infant state and the time he spent in the womb—or even some earlier time than that, if there was one [9].

Augustine will say in [13] that the child recalls earlier uses of the same word and connects them with the objects being referred to. The storing of such memories obviously begins in infancy, to accumulate a store or backlog to call on—so by not remembering his infancy Augustine does not remember such remembering, a thing that will puzzle him later on (T 10). But how can one not remember remembering? What is memory good for if it cannot even retain itself? The scale of this problem can be seen from the fact that Augustine, at the end of **[14]**, just gives up trying to solve it.

8.   Augustine's observation of his son and other infants made him marvel at the active, striving, acquiring energies of the child. Here was no tabula rasa to take an impression from the activity of others. His child grabs at the world and pulls large parts of it into himself. This picture is confirmed by a large modern body of ingenious experiments on the actions and responses of neonates, infants, toddlers—and even of the unborn, who now respond to experiments in the womb. I list just three books from the flourishing literature, each of which sums up other researchers' findings:

Steven Pinker, *The Language Instinct* (Harper/Perennial, 1994).
Ann B. Barnet and Richard J. Barnet, *The Youngest Minds* (Simon & Schuster, 1998).
Alison Gopnik, Andrew N. Meltzoff, and Patricia K. Kuhl, *The Scientist in the Crib* (William Morrow and Company, 1999).

What Augustine first notices about the infant's activities is its smile at its mother. Folklore cynicism has recently held that this is just a twisting of the mouth to ease the escape of gas, a kind of silent burp, but researchers find that it is one of the earliest manifestations of a sign language that precedes verbal expression and is an occasion for it—as Augustine will assert

([13]; *Teacher* [36]). Augustine no doubt recalled his favorite secular author's wonderful line, *Incipe, parve puer, risu cognoscere matrem* (Virgil, *Eclogues* 4.60), where the smile itself seems to have a cognitive power. Gopnik et al. (28–29) demonstrate that evolution (Augustine would say God) has rigged this early transmission of meaning by giving the newborn's eyes a focus of one foot—just the distance to the face of a nursing mother. The Barnets (p. 45) sum up further research on the encounter:

> Each mother-and-infant pair interacts in its own subtly different way, but the choreography is essentially the same: the meeting of eyes, the movements toward each other, the facial expressions and postures of the head and body changing ever so slightly to mirror the other. Child psychiatrists sometimes call this delicate and lovely expressiveness "attunement."

Augustine will describe the large attunements that made possible his easy acquisition of language as a child: "surrounded by nurses who coaxed, adults who laughed, and others fond of playing with a child" [23].

It is only within this primal communications system that the infant's anger at not getting the response he wants is explicable. He already knows that a response is possible, and resents it when the smiling mother does not pick him up, expose her nipple, or rock him when he wants it. Personal anger focuses as early as does the recognition of other persons. Gopnik et al. (p. 24) sum up their findings:

> The new research in developmental psychology tells us that
> quite literally from the moment we first see other people, we
> see them as people. To be a person is to have a mind as well as a
> body, an inside as well as an outside. To see someone as a person
> is to see a face, not a mask; a "thou," not an "it." We arrive in the
> world with a set of profound assumptions about how other peo-
> ple are like us and how we are like other people.

Augustine knew that from his own "experiments"—by watching Godsend, his son.

9. Augustine worries again the problem of how he came to
exist without knowing he existed, in a sequence lost to him but
obviously taking place in the timely unfolding of God's time-
less rationale. Then, in a playful recasting of the child's smiling encounter *(ridere)* with the mother, he wonders if God
smiles in gentle mockery *(inrides)* at his thrashing about for a
meaning that is beyond him. The child's *aporia* is repeated in
Augustine's testimony to his present incomprehension.

10. The diminutive *mulierculae* ("little women") is dismissive, not of women as such, but of the weight of their evidence,
since Augustine is stressing how slender are his proofs of anything about his infancy. Elsewhere, describing things we cannot
know by direct evidence, he writes that we have nothing but
faith in others' reports about the identity of our parents (*The
Pragmatism of Belief* 26): "There is no way to reason our way
to this. We have to take the mother's word for who the father is,

yet we cannot take the mother's own word—but that of mid-wives or nurses or servants—for who the mother is, since the mother herself can be deceived if the wet nurse gives her a different child after spiriting hers away."

The same kind of dismissiveness for a specific reason can be found in the only other use of *mulierculae* in *The Testimony* (6.24), where Augustine's earnest young Neoplatonist friends were prevented from forming an ascetic philosophical community because some had already established domestic arrangements with *mulierculae*—which has the force, here, of "homebodies." This, too, refers not to the inferiority of women as such (though Augustine, like most of his contemporaries, believed they were inferior), but to their lack of a philosophical turn. Monnica, to Augustine's surprise, showed a philosophical gift when she was finally admitted to the conversations of his circle at Cassiciacum.

11. In describing infant tantrums, Augustine dwells especially on one scene, which becomes for him almost as much the model of motiveless malignity as his theft of the pears would be in Book Two. The scene is one he clearly witnessed, and it depends on the African practice of using wet nurses. He has already told us [7] that he was suckled by his mother (at first) and by nurses—always used in the plural. He must have followed the same practice with his own son and seen him, or one of his peers, as they suckled at one of the wet nurse's nipples, push an infant away from her other nipple (this is the force of the word *con*-lactoneum, *fellow*-suckling). This was not done

out of hunger—the angry child was being fed, and Augustine told us in [7] that God supplies milk to fit the need. The baby could not be realizing that his nipple might run out if the other one were suckled. Augustine emphasizes that this is a real event: "With my own eyes I was a present witness [*Vidi ego et expertus sum*] of a tiny thing's fierce competitiveness."

The details are vivid and specific: "Though he could not speak, he made himself clear by his sudden pallor and the sour contortion of his features." The adjective *amaro* (sour) means he is screwing up his face as at the taste of something bitter. Compare the way Cain's "face is contorted" by envy of his brother Abel at Genesis 4.6, referred to by Augustine as the expression of envy (T 4.9). The infant at the nipple is not quite Cain slaying Abel, but he is trying in his feeble way to do something similar, "to deprive another of the one food it depends on." As with the case of the pears, Augustine is not looking at what later moralists would call "parvity of matter," but at the intent. The infant is clearly trying to harm another infant for no good reason—as the infant tries to harm adults when he does not get his way, "to hurt (if he could) those who dare disobey his own self-harming ukase."

The modern reader will, of course, think Augustine is too hard on infants, demonstrating his general pessimism and his specific preoccupation with "original sin." But we are thinking mainly in terms of morals, while his concern might more properly be called metaphysical. He is not trying to indict the child but to ponder the origin of evil. He has said, and he will repeat, that everything was good about the way he was brought into being. God himself formed him, framed the marvelous circuitry of his perceptive apparatus [12], providentially supplied the very milk in his nurses' breasts [7]—yet here is something not-good on the scene. Excusable perhaps, given that it is just an infant acting. But the behavior in itself is not good, as Augustine proves by showing that it would be condemned if indulged by those without extenuating youth. He is not concerned with blaming the child but with explaining how bad behavior can occur in a good universe. The child's case puts the mystery in its starkest terms, as Graham Greene realized in his tales of perverse children. G. K. Chesterton argued in the same way when he said that original sin becomes easier to understand at the moment when, on a long summer's afternoon, bored children begin to torture the cat.

Evil, for Augustine, is a lack, a gap in the good universe caused not by its creator but by a free will that can choose the lesser good in defiance of the higher; opening up, as it were, a crevice between one good and another, affording a glimpse into the abyss of the non-good, the anti-being. This makes the gears slip, causes a disconnect or slippage between what should be and what is. Only the human will can do this, and *Mos* (Custom), the solidarity of the willing human community, has made it occur as a general phenomenon after Adam's fall. That is what is happening in the nursery as Augustine watches.

For the modern reader, who believes in evolution, the baby's strivings are part of the general competitive struggle to survive, one that will be refined with success, moving from brute struggling to more intellectual efforts at mastery. Progress is from the lower to the higher. But Augustine believed that all creation is from God and was good in itself to begin with. Non-good behavior could only come about by defection from an original *bonum*, a motion from the higher to the lower—until God should check the downward spiral by his redemptive mission in Jesus. Accepting his own unremembered but undoubted sin as an infant, Augustine expresses the need for such redemption from the general perversity of fallen human beings. That perversity is best established if it can be found in even the most "innocent" condition of infancy. If universally good behavior is not found there, where can it be found? "Nowhere outside Christ" is Augustine's proclamation in his prayer.

12.   Augustine re-emphasizes that the child lives in creation where everything God made is good, beginning with himself. His own body is a miracle, and Augustine singles out three aspects of it reflective of the Trinity that created it—his sensory system, his physical organization, and a superintending unity. First, "how you articulate *(instruxisti)* its sensory apparatus." *Instruo* was said of arranging complex items like battle formations. The wonder of sensation was especially impressive to Augustine, since he thought external pressures on the body were not the source of sensation. He held that the inferior cannot determine the superior, that the body cannot dictate to the soul. He compared the external world's action to knocking on the portals of the senses, which the soul must open to emerge and seize the sensation. The soul itself acts, apprehending sights, sounds, smells, et cetera. The soul acts instantaneously,

shooting out (e.g.) its rays to distant visibles ("Open your eye and you are there," *Sermon* 277.10). The soul is entirely present in its every act of sensations ("entire in each"), and it creates the internal image of external things by a reflection of God's creative power (*The Trinity* 16.2).

So powerful is the soul's active power of imaging things, its ability to mold an inner reality, that Augustine wondered at this creativity even in sinful misuses of it (*Trinity* 11.2.7): "I recall hearing from a man that he could ordinarily hold in thought such a solid and, as it were, tangible image of a woman's body that he felt as if he were in intercourse with her, to the point of ejaculation, so strong is the power of the soul's imaging over the body—it can shift the body around, the way the body shifts the hanging of a cloak by its motions, making the cloak conform to its contours." However man misuses this mental control of the body through the instruments of the senses, it remains a miraculous dispensation for Augustine. We shall hear in the next paragraph how a baby "grabs" *(prendere)* the sound of a word, a perfect instance of the *active* power of sensation that Augustine admired.

In a second endowment of the child, God "fits limb to limb" (*compingere,* from *pangere,* means to glue things into each other), giving beauty to its form. The symmetry and beauty of the human body was a prime example for Augustine of "number," the attribute of the Second Person of the Trinity. Here "number" means the harmonious relationship of part to part, making the body "numerous" *(numerosum),* while especially beautiful bodies are *numerosiora* (*Music* 6.4.7). Indeed, Augustine says that the beauty of the body transcends even its adaptation to the requirements of survival (*Trinity* 22.24):

> Entirely apart from the body's operational equipment, the coherence of all its parts is so proportionate *(numerosa)*, and their responsiveness to each other is so beautiful, that one cannot say whether form or function ranked first in the composition of it. . . . But since no component (at least of those visible enough to be judged unerringly) is so devoted to useful function as to exclude beauty, and some have beauty without function, I think it is easy to see that splendor was preferred to utility. The need for utility will pass, the time will come when we shall take delight simply in each other's beauty, with no taint of lust—to the glory of the Creator, as the Psalmist says [104.1]: 'You clothed us in beauty as a testimony *(confessionem)* to you.'

This "testimony" of beauty shows how one-sided are old notions of *The Testimony* as mainly concerned with sin. Throughout the book, Augustine is testifying as well to God's gifts, wonders, and grace.

The third endowment of the baby is a coordinating unity in all its different components' actions, the binding together in love that is a prerogative of the Third Person of the Trinity. The organic oneness of any living thing made Augustine marvel even at the lower animals (*True Religion* 77):

> I could descant in all candor on the glories of the worm, when I look at its iridescence, its perfect corporeal rotundity, its interaction of end with middle, middle with end, each contributing

to a thrust toward oneness in this lowest of things, so that there is no part that does not answer to another part harmoniously. And what of the principle of life effervescing its melodious order through this body?—its rhythmic activation of the whole, its quest for that which serves its life, its triumph over or revulsion from what threatens it, its reference of all things to a normative center of self-preservation, bearing witness more striking than the body's to the creative unity that upholds all things in nature?

One interesting thing about this passage is the way it seems to grant some validity to the evolutionary struggle ("its triumph over or revulsion from what threatens it")—a hint conveyed elsewhere as well (*Order in the Universe* 1.25). But he could justify any person's deliberately harming another—who, is, after all, the image of the Trinity—only in exercises of individual or corporate self-defense.

Augustine moves from the traces of the trinity to the Trinity itself when he celebrates the oneness, and beauty, and law that emanate their energies throughout creation. Only God can "from your oneness, give each thing its degree [*modus*] of being; from your beauty give it shapeliness [*forma*]; from your law [*lex*] give it its rank in creation." This triad is a correlative of the one in Wisdom 11.21 [1]. *Modus* is like *mensura* in delimiting the extent of existence in its various manifestation. *Forma* is like *numerus*, the melodic principle of unity. And *lex* is like *pondus*, the compulsion that assigns each thing its ordered place.

III. Childhood (Speaking)

13.　Since speech distinguishes childhood from pre-verbal (and pre-remembering) infancy, this first paragraph on Augustine's childhood deals directly with the subject of speech, and tells us how Augustine taught himself to talk. Taught *himself*—that is the most surprising assertion of the whole paragraph. Unfortunately, it is the one thing in the paragraph that Wittgenstein, in his 1934 notes of *The Brown Book* (Blackwell, 1972, p. 77), ignores or denies: "Augustine, in describing his learning of language, says that he *was taught* to speak by learning the names of things" [emphasis added]. He goes on to say that Augustine just relates words to physical objects, not to the relationships and structures that make up language, nor to abstractions or actions: "It is clear that whoever says this has in mind the way in which a child learns such words as 'man,' 'sugar,' 'table,' etc. He does not primarily think of such words as 'today,' 'not,' 'but,' 'perhaps.' " In his better-known passage, opening the *Philosophical Investigations* (Anscombe translation, Blackwell, 1968, p. 2): "Augustine does not speak of there being any difference between kinds of words. If you describe the learning of language in this way you are, I believe, thinking primarily of nouns like 'table,' 'chair,' 'bread,' and of people's names, and only secondarily of the names of certain actions and properties." This, Wittgenstein says, is not so much teaching as "training," as one does dogs, by pointing to things and making a sound ("ostension").

But if Wittgenstein had bothered to look at *The Teacher*, he could not have said that Augustine "does not speak of there being any difference between kinds of words." Augustine did not restrict himself to words like "table," but asked his son to give the meaning of words exactly like those Wittgenstein said he excluded. The modern philosopher wonders what Augustine would make of "not" and "but." Augustine asked Godsend to explain "nothing" and "from" at *The Teacher* 3–4, and "if" at (9), as well as to distinguish "because" from "if" at (16). He clearly saw the need to go beyond "ostensive" language (pointing to a table)—and this in a dialogue that precedes *The Testimony* and that he says at the end of his life he still agrees with.

Yet one does not have to appeal to *The Teacher* to see that Wittgenstein is distorting what is in Book One of *The Testimony*. First, look at what is said of the process: "These words, used in their right way in different grammatical settings [*variis sententiis locis suis posita*], and recurring over time, I steadily accumulated . . ." To measure the full force of that phrase, we must remember that Latin is an inflected language. Augustine would not have learned *this* word means *that* thing by recognizing a single word, say *tabula* for "table." He would, according to the use of the word in its right place in various sentences, have heard *tabulae, tabulam, tabula, tabulae, tabularum, tabulis,* and *tabulas.* Not only that, if he were to understand them in their various sentences, he would have to grasp the difference between *tabulae* as genitive singular or nominative plural or vocative plural, and the difference between *tabula* as nominative and as ablative, the difference between *tabulis* as dative and as ablative, and so on. And that was just beginning of the connections to be learned along with the words. Pronouns have several roots (*ego* but *mihi*) as well as all those cases. Verbs had even more forms than nouns, including tenses. It seems impossible that these could be learned one by one according to external rules—and it *is* impossible. Augustine, like modern experimenters, denies that they are learned. What the words refer to (the physical table) is pointed out, but the words act according to a system that is not learned but intuited. Wittgenstein said Augustine described the learning of inert single words outside a language system, but Augustine could not have thought in those terms. The Latin words did not exist without their inflections, and the inflections put them inescapably inside a system. Augustine could not store them up and use them outside that system.

In fact, experiments on children show that they do learn words *in their functions*, not apart from them. Given sentences calling for word formations they have not heard and cannot be parroting, children "invent" logical extensions of the forms they have heard (Pinker, p. 276). They have an inbuilt system of their own. The external system is not imported into them; it stimulates and confirms the internal system (while giving some arbitrary material like the names of things to be processed in the system). This is what Chomsky calls a "generative grammar," one developed from within, not imposed from without.

America's greatest classical scholar, Basil Gildersleeve, described something similar when he said that the archaic Greeks knew grammar before the rules of grammar were formulated. They had no grammatical mistakes, just "mispronunciations." The grammatical way of saying things was more *seen* (or heard) than taught. Although we do not have a heavily inflected grammar like Latin, it has been proved that children learn the right way of identifying words when they are spoken in all kinds of different accents and in odd constructions. They recognize them *because* of their connectedness with other words, not despite it.

Each child, according to the Chomskian linguist Steven Pinker, invents its own language, even though it turns out to be everybody else's language too. There is a language system that goes with being human, just as two arms and two legs do. That is the situation we have evolved to. The system can be damaged or developed poorly—or even be missing from the outset—just as arms and legs can. But we no more introject language into the child than we can stick arms or legs on it. They are already there: "The crux of the argument is that complex language is universal because children actually reinvent it, generation after generation—not because they are taught, not because they are generally smart, not because it is useful to them, but because they just can't help it" (Pinker, p. 32).

I said above that there were two things in Book One that should have prevented Wittgenstein from reaching his simplistic view of Augustine's position. The first was the linguistic *embeddedness* of the words Augustine was learning. The second is the semantic system that was stimulating and confirming the innate verbal system—that other language, "body language." This is not just a matter of pointing with one's finger. There is an elaborate enacting process that goes on when people communicate, and especially when they communicate with children. Augustine describes it this way: "facial expressions, glances, or miming actions . . . conveying an intention to get or retain, repel or evade something." This goes far beyond "ostension" of a table. Augustine limns in his words a vast emotional repertoire for indicating not just things but attitudes, actions, desires, judgments, or doubts. I translate as "miming actions" the words "enactment of other body parts [then the face]" because at *The Teacher* 6 he describes actors and ballet dancers who can tell whole stories without using words. In *Christian Culture* (2.3.4) he describes languages that can do without words: "We can, by moves of the head, convey what we want to the eyes alone. Certain gestures of the hand are full of significance, and actors can with their whole body make others understand them, in a conversation of the eyes, while soldiers manipulate flags and battle standards to issue orders from their generals. All of these are the equivalent of an eye language [*verba visibilia*]."

Nor is body language entirely divorced from words. Modern experimenters show how attuned are children to tone of voice, inflection, facial frowns and smiles, and sound patterns of their native tongue—all of these going along with the contents of the word as a kind of *music* of meaning. They even acquire a feel for this music, from their mother's voice, within the womb.

Since this musical language *is* a language, it is good for stimulating or confirming the language system already in the child. To read this language takes an innate skill like that which the verbal system cues.

Augustine shows that, despite all the skill of the mime-dancer, the physical demonstrations are not perspicuous in themselves. The example he uses in *The Teacher* (6) is the person who gets up and walks when asked what the word "walking" means. The demonstration is not sufficient in itself. One might take it to mean that walking is hurrying or lingering, or going far. In fact, unless one *keeps* walking to and over the horizon, it might even mean *stopping* when the walking ends. But this objection applies equally to simple "ostensive" identification of a word as well as demonstration of an act, as Pinker (p. 153) illustrates, using an example from the logician E.V.O. Quine:

> A rabbit scurries by, and a native shouts, "Gavagai!" What does *gavagai* mean? Logically speaking, it needn't be "rabbit." It could refer to that particular mammal, or any member of that species of rabbit (say, *oryctolagus cuniculus*), or any member of that variety of species (say, chinchilla rabbit). It could mean scurrying rabbit, scurrying thing, rabbit plus the ground it scurries upon, or scurrying in general. It could mean footprint-maker, or habitat for rabbit-fleas. It could mean the top half of a rabbit, or rabbit-meat-on-the-hoof, or possessor of at least one rabbit's foot. It could mean anything that is either a rabbit or a Buick. It could mean collection of undetached rabbit parts, or

"Lo! Rabbithood again!" or "It rabbiteth," analogous to "It raineth."

Then how do people take the right meaning out of such inherently ambiguous signaling? By a grasp of the intention of the speaker that reads whole systems as presciently as the internal language system reads words in their relationships. The Barnets (p. 40) put it this way:

> Our ability to communicate also depends on our using and understanding, in differing ways in various cultures and circumstances, the raised eyebrow, the pregnant pause, the shrugged shoulder, the inclined head, the raised hand. We depend upon the concept of symbolic utterance, and on our ability to make use of symbolic utterances, to connect the idea in our heads with the object out there, or to an action, an intention, or a stream of ideas and feelings.

Augustine realized [23] that the ease with which he learned his first language, Latin, came in part from "nurses who coaxed, adults who laughed, and others fond of playing with a child." He generalized this in his pedagogy, saying that one learns best in an atmosphere of love. In *First Instruction* 17 he advises those teaching catechumens to "put ourselves in their affectionate brother's place, or their mother's or father's . . . The more, by the bond of love, we enter into each other's mind, the more even old things become new for us again." And in *Christian Culture* (Preface 12): "Though love unites us in close ties, it would have no channel for souls to flow into each other and mingle unless each were learning from the other." He remembered his companionship with a young Manichaean circle as almost replicating the sign system of the nursery: "Reciprocated love uses such semaphorings—a smile, a glance, a thousand winning acts—to fuse separate sparks into a single glow, no longer many souls, but one" (T 4.17).

But after making a broad argument on the ability of body language to convey meaning, Augustine says that the response to these signals, like that to language in general, is a matter of confirming the interior system that tests and establishes the child's innate language sense. What Chomsky calls an innate language-creating capacity, and Gopnik et al. call a gift perfected by evolution, Augustine calls the inner light given by God to each person coming into the world. In fact, Jerry A. Fodor says that Wittgenstein stumbled on a truth in what he thought of as a criticism of Augustine. Here is *Philosophical Investigations* (pp. 15–16): "Augustine describes the learning of human language as if the child came into a strange country and did not understand the language of the country; that is, as if it already had a language, only not this one. Or again: as if the child could already *think*, only not speak. And 'think' would here mean something like 'talk to itself.' " But Chomsky and others say that the child does have its own internal language for talking to itself (what Pinker calls "mentalese"). Fodor concludes (*The Language of Thought*, Crowell, 1975, p. 64):

So one cannot learn a language unless one has a language. In particular, one cannot learn a first language unless one already has a system capable of representing the predicates in that language *and their extension.* And, on pain of circularity, that system cannot be the language being learned. . . . Wittgenstein apparently takes it that such a view [as Augustine's] is transparently absurd. But the argument that I just sketched suggests, on the contrary, that Augustine was precisely and demonstrably right, and that seeing that he was is prerequisite to any serious attempts to understand how first languages are learned [emphasis in the original].

Language as innate is an evolved faculty for most modern observers (though Chomsky cannot imagine how a process of natural selection could account for it—see his *The Architecture of Language*, pp. 49–50). For Augustine it was part of the "illumination" that God grants each individual, what the Gospel of John (1.9) calls "the light enlightening every man who comes into the world." For Augustine, the mind can no more see truth without this light than the eye can see objects without an external physical light. He applied to the process what his version of Psalm 35.10 said: "By your light we shall see light." In order to think at all, he argued, the mind must generate an internal *verbum*, a mental word, by a process that dimly echoes the eternal generation of the *Verbum* by God the Father (*The Trinity*, 15.20). This mental language resembles (in result, not cause) what Pinker calls the mental language that precedes spoken language in babies. And all understanding of truth takes place through the inner illumination that makes the divine *Verbum* stand warrant for each of our tested and truthful *verba*.

That is why Augustine says that, when it comes to *understanding* any proposition (his definition of knowledge, *scientia*), there can be no external teacher, just the inner one—the point of his dialogue with his son: "You have only one Teacher . . . for you have only one Father in heaven" (Matthew 23.8–9).

According to *The Teacher*, when the child pulls into its mind the conventional (arbitrary) words that others are using for external things, he is acquiring the counters by which he can communicate with others, who have their own "mental language" but need external signals of it. The real learning goes on in that mental language, which comes not from the external world but from God. The external teacher can give information about the arbitrary sign system, or draw attention to a subject—the parallel is with external objects "knocking at the door" for sensation to let it in. Some have compared this external teacher in Augustine to Socrates' conception of himself as an intellectual midwife (Plato, *Theaetetus* 149). But it is important to note the differences between Plato and Augustine on this point. In *Theaetetus*, an important role is that of the maieutic attendant, "Doctor" Socrates. Augustine, by contrast, is a self-deliverer of his thought, divinely pushed from within, not pulled from without: "From my own heart's need I went into labor to deliver . . ."**[23]**. Nor is the knowledge delivered by the child a result of some Platonic memory *(anamnesis)* from a former existence. It comes from God's illumination of the mind *at the moment*. There are many secular objections that can be made to this doctrine, but Wittgenstein's claim that it involves a simplistic view of language is entirely outside the realm being discussed. That is why it is important to read this section of *The Testimony* in conjunction with *The Teacher*.

14. From this paragraph on, Book One finds the child Augustine caught between two groups of adults. One is made up of his teachers, who are driving him on a course of worldly ambition. They want him to be skilled in the rhetorical use of language, but they do not use language to persuade him of the wisdom of their course. They beat him, confessing the weakness of their own persuasive rhetoric. The other group is made up of those who believe in God, and in prayer to him. This refers clearly to the church his mother took him to. Membership in an African church of the time involved very close ties of community, guarded by strict standards of conduct, and by excommunication if those were broken. Among other things, there was a siege mentality caused by competition with the schismatic Donatist churches paired off with Catholic ones. This is the time when Augustine acquired his affection for the very name of Christ (T 4.8), one he missed in later engagements with pagan philosophy and Jewish Scripture (though not with Manichaeism, which honored Christ).

15. Augustine is confused by the way his parents stand between the two groups of adults in his life, the church and his teachers, laughing when he prays to the martyrs (specially honored in Africa after the persecutions there) and supporting the school discipline. The confusion this caused in him may account for the way the paragraph opens with one of the rare

clumsy sentences of *The Testimony*. One may suspect corruption of the text, since it makes no sense as it stands. It is a comparison, of martyrs *so (ita)* disposed *as (quemadmodum)* parents. But (in the best manuscripts) it asks if martyrs so *love* those who fear pain as parents *laugh at* children who fear pain. The *comparanda* do not conform to each other, and the long parenthesis (martyrs facing all pains, others fearing them) are semi-humorous exaggerations of Augustine's own childish fears of being beaten. The point should be that martyrs might have a *right* to laugh at the fearful, but the parents, who are not such heroes in facing pain, do not. That meaning is achieved if we follow the reading of one manuscript, *deridens,* for *diligens.* The last word could have been imported by a confused scribe who remembered that Augustine had just said that his parents "were not wishing me ill." The sense then is: would even heroic bearers of pain think little of the less heroic, as my parents thought of me? The next sentence shows that the hyperbolic parenthesis on suffering is what was mainly on Augustine's mind: *I* was not less afraid than those who trembled at martyrdom. This sentence should determine what the *comparanda* are. The triple play on *minus* in the next sentence shows that there is a note of self-satire, of hyperbolic description, running through both sentences.

Augustine will not let his teachers off the hook. Though he admits he had no right to evade his studies, since he did not do it for any higher purpose (just to indulge his love of games), he turns around and says that the teachers were playing more sinister games. He is angry that they made him fear them so. It was probably the contrast between these terror merchants and the more humane pagan he met in Madauros, Maximus, that first lured Augustine into his adolescent paganism (*Letters* 16, 17). In that case, he resents the fact that the flagellant tutors frightened him away from the faith.

17. The clash between adults over Augustine's future career reached a climax when his lung problems threatened his life. (He would always have some weakness of the lungs, which he later used as an excuse to escape from his court position in Milan.) The equivocation of his parents also reaches a climax. Augustine himself, not his mother, initiates the request for baptism—begs it, not only from his own mother but from "mother church" (another sign of the degree to which he was integrated into the Catholic community's liturgical life as a child). Though his mother anxiously complies while the illness persists, she relapses into the worldly judgment of others as soon as it passes. This is one of several places where he indicates that Monnica was not yet the model of piety that would later be made of her (O 2.308). At T 1.8, for instance, he says that, while living with him in Carthage, she was only in the "out-skirts" of God's favor. His famous tribute to her at T 9.17–37 is a form of funeral tribute, in which, as Samuel Johnson reminds us, one does not speak on oath.

18. It is not surprising that Augustine would take the position as bishop that he was urging on his own congregation—that Christians should be baptized as children and live all their

lives in the church. We would find it hard to regret that he had the great experience of living with a woman he loved and raising a child close to his heart. But one of the things he reproached himself with was the way he drew his loving partner away from the practice of her own faith for so many years. He would never admit that sin should be indulged for the good that might come of it.

IV. Schooling

23. The image of words' internal conception and delivery into the ears of others, already discussed, is spelled out here. It was an image he explored ever more thoroughly, since it showed to Augustine how the structure of the Trinity is reflected in human generation of a *verbum mentis* that is then "born" into the external world. This was not only a type of the Trinity, but of the Incarnation, since God's Word takes on flesh in order to reach humans who will believe in it. As Augustine will put in *The Trinity* 9.12–13:

> We *conceive* a true knowledge of things as an enunciation to
> ourselves, begetting it as an inner word which does not leave us
> when it is delivered by *birth* [to others]. Rather, when we speak
> to others, we join to that inner word either our voice or some
> other material sign, as a kind of physical [incarnated] report of
> what remains in the mind of the speaker even as it conveys
> something similar to the mind of the hearer.... Now this word
> is conceived out of love—love for creatures or for their creator,
> for changeable beings or changeless truth.... But it is born
> when, out of pondering it, we act [or speak] either sinfully or
> virtuously. In this way a union between begetting mind and be-
> gotten word is effected by love, which makes a third member in
> this embrace of things at one with each other but also distinct.

V. Conforming to a Deforming Society

25.   The ways of human Society *(Mos)* play the same role, at the public level, that *Consuetudo* (Habit) does at the private level—see T 8.10, where he describes habit as the chain one forges around oneself. The difficulty of breaking habits is treated in Augustine's *Sermon* 307.5, where he describes how hard it was for him to discontinue his swearing of oaths (against the scriptural prohibition at Matthew 5.33–37). *Mos* is the communal habit that pressures one to internalize it as *consuetudo*. In [26], for instance, the *Mos* that condones the use of Jove's rape as a respected model leads to the *consuetudo* of indulged lust.

26.   For us, the offense of the Terentian passage (if any) would be its sexual naughtiness. But we are not tempted to believe in Jove. Augustine's contemporaries still were. Many then remembered the Emperor Julian's revival of the pagan system in the second half of the century that was ending as Augustine wrote, and modern scholars have shown how thin a veneer was Constantinian Christianity over a world still largely pagan. What bothered Augustine in the play was less its low morals than its delusive religion.

27.   In the fond description of his heart being trellised up around the supporting study of Scripture, Augustine regrets that he was not given the kind of mental formation he outlines and advocates in *Christian Culture* (as Peter Brown calls *De Doctrina Christiana*).

28.   The idea of being far off from God often triggers in Augustine a reminiscence of the prodigal son's going to a "far country." This first reference to the parable of the younger son is followed by other references in *The Testimony*, direct or indirect—so much so that Georg Nicolaus Knauer argued that the entire book is structured around the parable ("Peregrinatio Animae," *Hermes* 85, 1957, pp. 216–46). But this is just one of the many "strayings" that Augustine took from scriptural imagery of paths (see Introduction: The Book's Imagery). What is important in this paragraph is the equation of the son's return to his father with the return of the soul to the One in Plotinus.

30.   This paragraph summarizes the sins of Augustine's boyhood, moving backward in time from the point his narrative has reached. He begins with his most recently acquired faults, the same snobbishness about committing solecisms that he imbibed from his teachers, despite the defiance he showed them in lying to escape their classes—which was done, not from any high principle, but to indulge in plays and games that undermine morals. Going even further back into his boyhood, he recalls how he stole food from his parents' house to bribe playmates into letting him play with them. Then he cheated those

who admitted him into their circle, while hypocritically attacking them for doing the same thing. He was, without knowing it, pre-enacting all the follies and faults that make up secular life, doing for game prizes what adults do for gold. The innocence of children is a myth.

The emphasis on deception in this summary is typical of a man who came to prize truthfulness as the essential virtue for one dealing with a God who is Truth. He *lied* to pedagogue and tutor, to mother and father, when he evaded class or stole food. He lied in two ways with his playfellows, while cheating and while objecting to cheats. As he says, the role models proposed for him were hardly ones to show him how wrong this was. The art of rhetoric, as he was instructed in it, was a way of coloring or distorting truth for advantage. His masters preferred a lie, or any other wrong, to an embarrassing slip in grammar or pronunciation.

31.   Yet the book cannot end, self-centeredly, on what was wrong (i.e., what was his) in Augustine's boyhood. He was, after all, an image of the Trinity. "I existed [*modus*], I experienced sensation [*numerus*], I preserved myself—by an echo of your mysterious oneness [*pondus*]." The book then ends in a swirl of triads: *joy-glory-truth*, played against *pain-dejection-error*, leading to *delight-pride-trust*.

PART IV

Appendix: *The Teacher*

Introduction

This dialogue of Augustine with his sixteen-year-old son Godsend was composed in 389–390 C.E., when the two had returned to Africa after their baptism in Milan. With a small group of friends gathered in his native city of Thagaste, Augustine intended to create a library of Christian knowledge, an encyclopedic project begun in Milan and carried forward in a connected series of dialogues on different topics. The whole project was abandoned when Augustine was compelled to accept priesthood in 391 at Hippo, where his pastoral duties supervened. One reason for Augustine's removal to Hippo may have been the death of his son soon after this dialogue with him was completed. There was no reason for Augustine to superintend the family property now that there would be no heir of his to use it. In fact, family memories with his brother and sister and their children might have been sad in these circumstances. One reason for his returning to Thagaste in the first place might have been to keep his son near his mother, if (as I have argued elsewhere) Thagaste was her hometown, to which she had returned.

Augustine's practice in these early dialogues was to carry on a real discussion, taken down by stenographers, and then to polish the resulting text. He assures us (T 9.14) that all the responses (sensa) made by Godsend in this published work were actually voiced by him in the original conversation. Given Augustine's scrupulous standard of truthfulness, we can assume that he edited Godsend's words very lightly, preserving their point. The result is a wonderful record of the two men's relationship—one of deep mutual respect that did not preclude a joshing familiarity. Godsend does not hesitate to tease his father, cleverly saying that he will answer Augustine's questions without using words when the questions are asked without words (5). When Augustine suggests that the word *nothing* might be meaningless, Godsend says (3) that only a fool would use a meaningless word—so why was Augustine using it? The son wonders (15) whether the father can come up with a master rhetorician to answer their questions—knowing that Augustine is supposed to be the master rhetorician. After Augustine posits a whiz of an intellect to cope with one problem, Godsend says he could as easily posit a whiz to solve another problem they had found unsolvable (32). When the father asks what his son thought of his "entire" speech, Godsend admits that it *was* rather long—in fact, *perpetua* (46). A professor of philosophy tells me that this dialogue is a welcome break from Plato's, where Socrates manipulated intellectual patsies. Two real minds are shown at work in *The Teacher*.

The warmth of the dialogue does not come across in most translations of it, for two reasons—of style and of method. In style, the dialogue imitates those of Cicero, where the inflected Latin leads, even in informal exchanges, to circumlocution, a kind of "structurey" throat-clearing, and delay of the emphatic matter to the end of the sentence. This is not so much a problem in *The Testimony*, where the psalm-couplet style led to parataxis instead of periodicity. But normal Latin uses transitions like *quae cum ita sint*, "if this should be [subjunctive] how things are," where we would use, according to context, pithier conjunctions. Thus when Augustine asks Godsend at the beginning of *The Teacher*, "Why do we talk to each other," the answer in Latin is: *Quantum quidem mihi nunc occurrit, aut docere aut discere*—literally, "Insofar as comes to me at the moment, either to teach or to learn." The punchy *docere . . . discere* is saved for the emphatic spot, after some periphrastic groping. The natural way to say this in English, which favors emphasis at the outset, is: "To teach or be taught—that's my hunch." This is not departing from what was said, it *is* what was said—but as it would be said in English. So in this translation I try to avoid the structurey transitions and pleonasms, informal in the original, that just sound artificial in our idiom.

The *method* that makes this dialogue sound more stilted than natural is what Augustine himself calls its "verbal jousting" technique (31). The preliminary arguments are all limbering-up exercises, in which conclusions are reached, or exceptions allowed, that are canceled later, but not necessarily explicitly. As M. F. Burnyeat writes, in the best commentary on the dialogue: "This bewildering sequence of about-turns shows that Augustine, like Plato often (and Wittgenstein), is determined not to tell us how to read his writings."[1] Yet Augustine explained his method in a work he was completing as he conducted the dialogue with his son, the *Music*. He moves from the outer to the inner, from the physical to the spiritual, devoting the first five books to metrics in song and verse before moving in the last book to the music of the spheres and the beauty of Number in the mind. He explains the transition in 6.1, where he hopes "the reader will understand that this lowly road is not of lowly value—it is, in fact, the one I have trudged along with the weak (being no athlete myself), rather than commit unfledged wings at once to thin air."

In *The Teacher*, Augustine first deals with the sign system of words considered in their taxonomic and external aspect, before moving to the mind's own inner language, by which it tests what it apprehends by the senses. The argument is one long paradox:

> Nothing can be taught but by signs.
> *But:* Signs cannot teach.
> *So:* Nothing can be taught.

Augustine is not denying that we get information from others, but this process is not understanding *(scientia)*, it is trust *(fides)* in the "say-so" of another. It is the difference between taking a teacher's word for it on the solution of a geometry problem and "seeing" it oneself. Thus all our historical knowledge, or knowledge of others' states of mind, is based on acts of faith. He does not deny—how could he?—the importance, even the necessity of faith. In his books *The Pragmatism of Belief (De Utilitate Credendi)* and *Various Subjects (De Diversis Questionaibus,* Number 30), he makes the distinction between necessary means one uses *(uti)* for an end, and the fulfillment *(frui)* of things accepted for their own sake. So faith is a means on this earth to reach the fulfilling vision of God in heaven. (Saint Paul says faith and hope are the means, love the end, at 1 Corinthians 13.13).

Understanding *(scientia)* is a different matter. No one can understand for us. We do that by our innate mental powers, which operate in the light of God's truth. Others can "post a sign" *(admonere)* for us to exercise our understanding on, but—as Burnyeat puts it—this is just "providing an occasion" for our inner powers to operate. Thus when Augustine uses, provisionally, the example of a bird catcher teaching by showing how he operates, we are meant to see the narrowness of the term "teach" in this sense:

> If showing or teaching requires no more than deliberately so acting or arranging things that other people may, if they wish, learn for themselves, then nothing is easier and the bird catcher is a perfectly good teacher. What Augustine is denying when he reaches his conclusion [that humans do not teach each other] is that anyone can do what telling is supposed to do, namely, transmit knowledge to another mind. On that commonsense understanding of "teaching," the bird catcher does not teach.[2]

Burnyeat argues that Augustine has, on his own, arrived at Plato's distinction between "true judgment" and *episteme*, calling them "trust" and *scientia*. *Scientia*, like *episteme*, must be firsthand knowledge, personal, justified by one's own reason:

It is eloquent testimony both to Augustine's philosophical acumen and to the coherence of the Platonic epistemology that Augustine should have been able to reconstruct it, on the basis of a quite new set of arguments, so much better than many who have actually read Plato's dialogues. Whatever is to be said about Adeodatus, of Augustine at least it is true that he learned it for himself, without being taught.[3]

Notes

1. M. F. Burnyeat, "Wittgenstein and Augustine *De Magistro*," Inaugural Address as president of the Aristotelian Society, *Proceedings* 1987, p. 14.
2. Ibid., p. 15.
3. Ibid., p. 22. Though some have compared Augustine's questioning of his son with Socrates' questioning of the slave in *Meno*, Burnyeat notes that Augustine "does not know what questions Socrates put to the slave . . . because he read about the *Meno* in Cicero [but not the *Meno* itself]."

The Teacher

1

Father: Why, in your view, do we talk to each other?

Son: To teach or be taught—that's my hunch.

F I am with you on the first, since we clearly talk in order to teach. But what makes you say we talk in order to be taught?

S Why do we ask questions if not to be taught?

F I suspect that even then we are trying to teach—don't you suppose we teach those we question what we want from them?

S That's true.

F Is it agreed, then, that we talk for no other reason than to teach?

S I don't quite follow that—after all, if talking is just saying words, I find that we do that when singing a song, and since we often sing when alone, with no one there to be taught, I don't see how we can be singing in order to teach.

F I believe there is a way of teaching, and not the least way, that is a recalling—as will come out in the very discussion we are having now. But if you do not yet agree that we are taught when we recall, or that we teach when we remind, I will not dispute this, but I advance the minimal point that two possible reasons for talking are to teach or to remind, either ourselves or others—which we do even when singing, won't you agree?

S Not really. It is not often I sing to remind myself. I do so to enjoy myself.

F I see what you are getting at, but haven't you noticed that the enjoyment of song comes from the windings of the tune, to which words can be supplied or from which they can be removed, marking the difference between singing and talking?[1] Tunes can be played on flutes and harps, and birds sing tunes, and we too can make music without words, which can be called tunes but not talk, right?

S Right.

2

F Do you concede, then, that talking has only two functions, for teaching or reminding?

S I might, if it did not occur to me that praying is a way of talking, and surely it is impossible for God to be taught, or to be reminded of anything by us.

F It is for this very reason (I'm sure you realize) that we are instructed to 'pray in our inmost chambers,' a term for our soul's deep recess—because when we ask what we most direly need, God is not waiting to be reminded or taught what that is. One who talks is varying conventional noises to signal the wants within him outward to others. But God is sought and prayed to precisely through our unexpressed

interior wants, by a call within, in the temple whose conse-
cration he desires—you have read, of course, the Apostle
[Paul] saying, 'Do you not see that you are God's temple,
and his Spirit makes his home in you?' Or, elsewhere,
'Christ is found in humanity's depths'? Or do you doubt the
prophet's [David's] words, 'Talk inside your inmost self, and
reform yourself in your bedchamber, where the offering to
be made is a conduct reformed and a trust in God's mercy.'
Where do you suppose the offering of right conduct could
be made but in the temple of the soul, in the bedchamber of
the affections—that is the temple of our offerings, the established place of prayer. That is why talking is not needed
for praying—unless, of course, priests talk, to signal outward their interior message; not that God should hear, but
that men should, who, when they hear, are jointly reminded
of their dependence on God. Do you agree so far?

S Certainly.

F Aren't you bothered that the highest teacher of all, when he
taught followers to pray, gave them specific words [to the
Our Father]—was not this very clearly telling them that
one must talk in order to pray?

S That is not confusing, since he did not teach the words but a
reality behind the words, using words to refer us back to
him, indicating to whom and how we should pray in the inmost chamber of the self—where, as you said, we do our
praying.

F You get the point—I suppose you also realize that, if anyone
says we talk inwardly to ourselves, by thinking of words but

not saying them, this "talking" is nothing but remembering the things the words indicate. By our recurrence to them we bring to mind the realities of which they are the signs.

S I see that, and keep step with you.

3

F We agree, then, that words are signs?

S Of course.

F And can a sign be a sign without something it signifies?

S Clearly not.

F Well, how many words are in this line of Virgil: "If gods decree nothing from High City [Troy] remain . . ."[2]

S Eight.

F Requiring eight signs, right?

S They must.

F I presume you understand what the line is saying?

S Well enough, I suppose.

F Then tell me what each word, separately, signifies.

S Of course I know what *if* means, though I cannot come up with another word for it.

F Do you, then, understand what the word means when you come across it in context?

S *If,* I suppose, indicates indeterminacy, and where can that exist but in the mind?

F That will do for now. What of the other words?

S What can *nothing* mean but what does not exist?

F You may be right, but I hesitate to affirm it because of your earlier assent that every sign must have something it signifies—but what does not exist is not a something. So the third word in this line, since it does not signify a something, must not be a sign; and we must have been in error when we agreed either that every word is a sign, or that each sign has something it signifies.

S You have me on the ropes, I grant; but if a word has nothing it signifies, a man would be a fool to use it—and since you are talking to me, and I do not suspect you of making random noises, but of using words meant to advance my understanding, you would not have pronounced *these* two syllables [no-thing] if they did not signify something. If you chose them to elicit something by their sound in my ears, or to make me recall something, then you must know what I am trying to say, though I cannot formulate it.

F How shall we put it then?—perhaps that the word does not signify a thing that does not exist, but signifies our state of mind when we perceive that it does not exist, or think we perceive it.

S That may be just what I was trying to maintain.

F Well, let's in any case move on or we risk looking silly.

S How so?

F Breaking down because nothing got in our way.

S Embarrassing, all right. I don't see how it happened to us—but it clearly has.

4

F   Perhaps, with God's help, we may untie this knot later on. Meanwhile, go back to Virgil's line, to define the other words in it.

S   Well, the fifth word is *of*, for which I suppose we could substitute *from*.

F   That is not what I was after—that for a familiar word you substitute an equally familiar one with the same meaning (if indeed it does have the same meaning, which we'll stipulate for now). Obviously, if the poet had said "from High City" rather than "of High City," you could have told me that *from* means *of*, since the two are equivalent in your eyes. But I am looking for the one reality, whatever that may be, that these two signify.

S   I think *from* signifies a withdrawal of something from its former place; we say it is "from" there, whether the place no longer exists (as Troy does not in the verse) or whether it does (as we say that traveling merchants in Africa are "from" Rome).

F   Even if I accept your examples (though I could perhaps give a number of counterexamples), you must admit that you are explaining words with other words, signs with other signs— that is, the obvious with the obvious. But I am after the reality signified by these signs.

5

S   You surprise me by not recognizing, or pretending not to recognize, that I simply cannot do what you are asking. We are carrying on this very conversation by words, yet you keep asking me for things that, whatever they are, are *not* words—and you have asked for them in words of your own. If you want answers without words, then ask questions without words.

F   Your point is well taken, yet if I use a word of three syllables, *partition*, and ask what they mean, couldn't you point with your finger, and I would instantly recognize what is meant by the three syllables, though you spoke nothing as you showed me what they meant?

S   Of course that's possible, but only with words for physical objects, and for ones that are here to be pointed at.

F   How about colors—are they physical objects, or aspects of the objects?

S   The latter.

F   Can't we point out colors? And if so, do you think that aspects of physical objects, along with the objects themselves, can be signified without using words so long as they are here?

S   When I said physical objects, I was trying to indicate anything physical—everything, that is, that the body can sense.

F   Look again—isn't there an exception to what you say?

S   Oh yes—I should have said everything visible, not everything physical. I realize that sound, odor, taste, weight, heat, and other things are grasped by the senses, but cannot be identified by pointing at them.

F   Yet you have seen men converse in a way with deaf people merely by gesturing; and the deaf themselves, using nothing but gestures, ask and answer questions, inform others, expressing everything (or almost everything) they wish to. In their case, your sounds and tastes and such, and not visible things alone, are indicated without words. Often, in fact, mimes narrate and explain whole stories without using words.

S   True enough, but still—your mime cannot, any more than I can, show without words what *from* means.

6

F   Perhaps not—but even if he could, whatever he might do to dance out the word's meaning would be just another sign for the thing, not the thing itself. He will still, that is, be indicating one sign with another sign (though not one word with another word)—so that his motions and the word *from* both indicate the same reality [which is neither of them]. And that reality itself, not any sign of it, is what I want to be shown.

S   But how, I ask you, can such a thing be shown?

F   As we showed the partition.

S   But even that could not be shown without a sign, as the course of our argument has made clear—for the finger pointed at the wall is not the wall, but a sign directing one's attention to the wall. So I still do not see how anything can be shown without a sign.

F Well, if I should ask you what *walking* means, and you got up and showed me, wouldn't you be teaching by means of the thing itself, and not by words or other signs?

S I would, and it embarrasses me not to have anticipated a response so obvious, one that suggests at once a million other examples of things that can be shown directly and not by words—eating, for instance, or drinking, sitting, standing, shouting, and so on.

F Well, take another case. If I, having no idea what the word *walking* means, should ask you what it means, and you were already walking when I asked, how would you show me?

S I would keep on walking, but speed my pace, and what I did in response to your question would answer you, and I would not be using anything but the action itself to explain itself.

F Isn't hurrying different from walking? One who walks is not necessarily hurrying, nor does one have to walk at all in order to hurry—we say that one can read or write, or do all kinds of things, in a hurry. So if you just speed up what you are already doing when I ask you what walking is, I might be fooled into thinking that walking means hurrying, since that is what you added to your action.

S Then I admit we cannot show a thing without a sign if we happen to be doing the thing when we are asked. If we do not do something different, but continue what we were doing, the questioner will think we are ignoring him, and he will be insulted. If, however, he asks us to demonstrate an action we can perform on the spot, but don't happen to be performing when he asks, then we can show him what his word means by matching our action to his question, and no words will have been used—unless, of course, he asks me what talking is while we are talking. Then, no matter what I say in order to answer him, I'll have to keep on talking. But no matter how long it takes to make clear what talking means, I shall not be departing from the thing itself, to rely on signs instead of it, since talking is itself the thing at issue.

7

F Neatly put. Are we agreed, then, that a thing can be shown without signs if we can answer a question with a corresponding action (but only if we are not already performing the action), or when we are asked about signs that we *are* making at the moment—for then we can speak on and continue to signify, since speech is itself a sign?

S Agreed.

F When [1] the question is about signs, therefore, it can be answered with signs; but if it is about things that are not signs, it can be answered either [2] with a corresponding action, if that can be performed on the spot, or [3] by drawing attention to the thing with signs.

S So it seems.

F Of these three then, consider first explaining signs with signs. Are words the only signs?

S By no means.

F   When we talk, it seems, we use words either to signify other words or other signs (for when we say "gesture" or "letter," those too are signs, along with the words we use of them), or we use words to signify things that are not signs—as when we say "a rock," a word that is a sign itself but that signifies what is clearly not a sign. This latter category, in which we use words as signs of things that are not signs, takes us astray, since we said we were first considering the signs of signs, and we can establish two kinds of these, namely the signs with which we teach or remind people of [the meaning of] the signs being used, or those that deal with other signs. Is that right?

S   Surely.

8

F   Tell me, then, what physical sense do words address.

S   Hearing.

F   What do gestures address?

S   Sight.

F   What if the words are written down—do they remain words, or become signs of words? If words are, properly speaking, vocal noises that articulate some meaning, and if vocal noises address the sense of hearing, then a written word, which addresses sight, is a sign directed at the eyes for bringing to mind a sign directed at the ears.

S   My view precisely.

F   Do you agree, too, that a noun is the sign of something?

S   I do.

F A sign of what?

S Of an entity that can be named—Romulus, for instance, or Rome, virtue, river, and so on.

F So the four nouns you give signify certain things?

S Of course.

F Is there any difference between the nouns and the things they signify?

S A great difference.

F Namely?

S In the first place, the nouns are signs, the things named are not.

F Could we give the name "signifiables" to the things that can be designated by signs but are not signs themselves, as we call things that can be seen "seeables"—to refer to them more conveniently?[3]

S All right.

F Can your four nouns, which are signs, be signified themselves by other signs?

S I haven't forgotten already that we saw a difference between spoken words and written words, the former signs, the latter signs of signs.

F And what makes them different?

S The written are seeable, the spoken are hearable—why not admit a new term like hearable if we have already used signifiable?

F That's fine with me. But I'm asking if your four nouns can be indicated by different hearable signs, as you said they could by seeable signs.

S Well, as I said a while back that a noun signifies a thing, and gave four examples, that must entail that both "noun" and the four specific nouns, when pronounced aloud, are [different] hearables.

F Then, since both the seeable and the hearable signs are similar as signs, how are they dissimilar?

S One difference is that the word *noun* is a hearable sign of other hearable things, but the four examples are signs of things, not of other signs—though some of the things signified are themselves seeable (like Romulus, Rome, and river), while others are only thinkable (like virtue).

9

F Fine—now, do you accept the definition of *word* as any vocal noise articulated to convey meaning?

S I do.

F So *noun*, since it is a vocal noise with meaning, is itself a word, and when we say that an eloquent man uses fine words, he must be using nouns—as when the slave in Terence tells his master, "Use fine words of me," he might have said "fine nouns."

S He might.

F Then you see that when we pronounce the single syllable "word," we are also pronouncing a noun, and the word is a sign of the noun?

S That follows.

F Then tell me this. You hold, on the one hand, that a word signifies a noun, that a noun can signify a river, and that *river* can signify a visible thing; and you also hold that there is a difference between the seeable thing and the word *river*, which is its sign; and also between that word and *noun*, which is a sign of the sign—but what, precisely, is the difference between the sign for the word *noun* and the sign that the word is?

S I see this difference at least. A thing signified by a word can, it is true, be signified by a noun as well—a noun is a word, but so is river a word. But what is signified by a word is not always signifiable by a noun. The *if*, for instance, at the beginning of the verse you brought up, or the *from*, from which we derived the long mental exercise that has brought us to this point, are both words, but not nouns. And there are many such. Since every noun is a word, but not every word is a noun, I find this difference between them—that a word is the sign of a thing that does not signify other signs; whereas a noun is the sign of a thing that can signify other things.

F As you would say that a horse is an animal, but not every animal is a horse?

S Exactly.

F So the difference between noun and word is the same as between horse and animal [pause]—or do you hold back from making this equation because a *verb* with its tenses (like "I am writing, I wrote," or "I am reading, I read") is also called a word [*verbum*], though it is not a noun?

S That did puzzle me.

F Don't let it. Anything signifying another thing we can call a sign, and words are just one example of that. Military insignia are also signs, but not verbal ones.[4] So if I tell you that, just as every horse is an animal, but not every animal is a horse, every word [*verbum*] is a sign, but not every sign is a word, would you still be puzzled?

S No, I can agree that words in general differ from a noun as animals in general differ from a horse.

10

F Are you just as certain that the three-syllable word *animal*, when we pronounce it, is different from the thing it refers to?

S Yes, I said that—a sign is different from what it signifies.

F Then you hold the corollary that all signs are signs of something other than themselves—as the three syllables we sound out as *animal* are not themselves an animal?

S Certainly not, but when we say "sign," we refer not only to other signs, whatever they may be, but to itself, since sign is a word, and words are signs.

F Doesn't what you say about "sign" apply as well to "word," since when we say that single syllable, we mean whatever is articulated with meaning, and that describes itself as well?

S Yes it does.

F And cannot the same be said of "noun"? For while it refers to nouns of any gender, it is itself a noun of the neuter gender [an "it"], and if I asked you what part of speech it is, could you give any other answer than that it is, itself, a noun?

S None at all.

F So some signs are signs not only of other things but of themselves.

S True.

F Could we say the same thing about the three-syllable word *conjunction*?

S Not quite, since what it *signifies* is not a noun, though *it* is a noun.

11

F You see my point already—that though some signs are interchangeable, the first meaning the second, the second the first, we cannot say the same thing about the three-syllable word *conjunction*—since it denotes words like *if, because, or, since, except, so, therefore,* and the like; and none of them means our three-syllable word, yet it means all of them.

S If that is the case, I would like to know what signs are interchangeable.

F Have you noticed that in using the terms *word* and *noun* we were using two words?

S Certainly.

F And in using them we were using, as well, two nouns?

S That, too.

F Thus a noun can be signified by a word, a word by a noun.

S Exactly.

F Can you say, then, how they differ—apart from their diverse spelling and pronunciation?

S Yes—I just made the point a moment ago. When we say

word, we mean any vocal noise that conveys a meaning. Thus every noun, and even the word *noun* itself, when we pronounce it, is a word; but not every word is a noun, even though any word, including *word*, is a noun when we pronounce it.

12

F If someone claimed that every noun is a word, and every word a noun, could you find some difference between them, apart from the sound of the letters in each?

S I doubt that I could, or that there would be any other difference.

F Even if every vocal noise with any meaning were both a word and a noun, but designated a word for one use and a noun for another, would there still be no difference?

S Not that I can see.

F Yet you will admit that all colored things are seeable, and all seeable things colored, yet the two words are different and have different meanings?

S Yes.

F How if, in the same way, though every word is a noun, and every noun a word, whether considered as two words or two nouns, they should still have different meanings?

S I suppose that could be, though I don't see how—no doubt you will explain.

F You admit, of course, that if any vocal noise, one conveying meaning, is pronounced by the lips, it whirs in the ears to be heard, and stirs memory to be known?

S Clearly.

F So two different operations occur when we say any word.

S They do.

F What if the very names of these two should be derived from this difference, *word* from "whirred" and *noun* from "known," so that the first is rightly named for the ear, the second for the mind?[5]

13

S I will concede that, if you first prove that every word is a noun.

F You remember from your grammar lessons that a pronoun is what takes the place of a noun, giving it a briefer designation? Isn't that the definition you had to recite for your schoolmaster: "A pronoun is that part of speech which takes the place of a noun, expressing the same thing as the noun does, but more briefly"?

S Yes, an excellent definition.

F Then it follows that, by this definition, pronouns can exist only with reference to their nouns, of which alone they can take the place. When we say this man, the king himself, the same woman, this gold, or that silver, the words *this, himself, the same, this,* and *that* are pronouns, while the words *man, king, woman, gold,* and *silver* are the nouns, which have a fuller meaning than their pronouns.

S I see that, yes.

F Give me, then, a few conjunctions.

S All right—*and, moreover, but, yet.*

F Haven't you made a mistake? Aren't those nouns?

S Certainly not.

F So when I asked "Aren't those," was my grammar wrong?

S Not at all—and *touché* for showing me how they have to be nouns, to be called "those" in the sentence. But I still have misgivings. Without denying that you used "those" correctly, since the conjunctions can, I admit, be nouns, nonetheless "those" may be properly used because it implies "those *words*," and if you ask me what part of speech "words" are, I say *it* is a noun. Use of the pronoun for noun is proper because it *implies* the noun.

14

F Clever, but a fallacy. To escape it, follow me closely—if I can succeed in making it clear. To handle words with words is to interweave them like interlaced fingers: rubbing them together makes it hard to tell, except by each finger on its own, which is doing the itching and which the scratching.

S After that comparison I am *really* paying attention.

F Then (to invoke the authority that stands highest with us) when Paul the Apostle says, "With Christ there is no Is and is not, only an Is" [2 Corinthians 1.19], I doubt that we are to think the two letters of "Is" *are* Christ, but he is what the two syllables stand for.[6]

S Clearly.

F So when the Apostle says "With Christ there is an Is," that is equivalent to saying "What is *called* an Is was with Christ." If he had said, "There is power in Christ," that would be equivalent to "What is called power is in Christ." The two syllables we pronounce as "power" are not in Christ, what the syllables stand for is in him.

S I see that.

F Then you must see that there is no difference between saying "what is *called* power" and "what is *named* power."

S None at all.

F And no more difference in saying "what is called an Is" and "what is named an Is."

S I see that too.

F So you know where we are going?

S Not quite.

F You don't deny that a thing's name is its noun.

S Yes, that's obvious.

F Then Is is a noun when it names him.

S Inescapably.

F Yet if I had asked you what part of speech *is* is, you would, I think, have told me it is a verb, not a noun, though now we are discovering it is a noun.

S You have me there.

F Then the other parts of speech must also be nouns, by this line of reasoning.

S Yes, considered only as signifiers. But if you ask about the signified things they refer to, as named by them, what can I say, but that they name different parts of speech and not nouns, however your argument tries to make them nouns?

15

F Does it bother you that someone might argue that the apostle Paul has a command of reality but not of verbal usage, so that the basis for our demonstration is less solid than we proposed, and that Paul was sound in his living and teaching but not necessarily in his command of language when he said, "With him is an Is"—remember that he himself admitted he was "not gifted in speaking" [2 Corinthians 11.6]. Could you mount an answer?

S I am not ready for him myself, but I hope you can call on some champion arguer who will do what you have in mind.

F But can't reason alone, without appeal to authority, show that all parts of speech are signs of something; and if signified by them, then named by them; and if named by them, then named with a noun—something true not only of our language but of others, since it is obvious that if you ask *what* Greeks use for our "who," they would answer *tis;* if what they use for "wish," the answer is *thelein;* if for "written down," it is *gegrammenon;* for "and" it is *kai,* for "from" *apo,* for "alas," it is *oi*—and so on through all parts of speech which I have referred to, rightly asking *what,* which could only be done if a *noun* is demanded. That is why Paul spoke accurately and we can uphold him without calling on any verbal champions—is there anything they could add to make our position any firmer?

16

But if someone too weak of mind or strong of will should resist this reasoning, and demand some super-lexicographer to lay down the law of of verbal usage, what greater Latinist could there be than Cicero? He, in the famed Verrine speeches, called "among" a noun, though it is a preposition in grammar. Perhaps I misunderstand the passage, and I or another will later advance a different interpretation of it—but this much, I think, none can deny: masters of grammar teach that a complete sentence (what Cicero calls a proposition) contains a *subject* asserted or denied by a *verb*, and they correctly say that when the verb is in the third person, the subject must be in the nominative case—so that if I say "The man is sitting" or "The horse is running," you will recognize that I have formed two propositions.

S   Surely.

F   And you can distinguish the two sentences' subjects, man and horse, as well as what they were doing, as shown in the verbs—sitting in the one case, running in the other.

S   Yes.

F   So if I said "is sitting" or "is running," you would rightly inquire of me who or what was doing these things, and I would answer either a man, or a horse, or some animal, or whatever, anything to join the verb and complete a statement, an affirmation or a denial.

S   Right.

F   Take it a stage further, and imagine we are looking at something far off, unable to see whether it is an animal or a rock or whatever, and I said to you, "That must be an animal, since it is a man," wouldn't I just be babbling?

S In that particular case, of course. But it would not be babbling to say, "That must be an animal if it is a man."

F You make the right distinction—your *if* is right in my view as well as yours, and my *because* is wrong for both of us.

S We are agreed.

F Did I use complete sentences when I said "*if* is right" and "*because* is wrong"?

S Yes.

F Then give me the sentences' subjects and verbs.

S The verbs are "is" in "is right" and "is wrong," which leaves "if" and "because" as the nouns.

F Thus proving that the two conjunctions are also nouns.

S Entirely.

F Can you use the same method on your own to show that all other parts of speech are nouns?

S I can.

17

F Moving on, then, tell me whether you would equate nouns and *terms*, just as we have equated nouns and words.

S They do seem the same, apart from their syllables' different sound.

F That's good enough for now, though some *do* find a difference in their meaning. In any case, as you have noticed, we are now dealing with signs that signify each other, without any distinction except for different pronunciation of their sounds, and we say that each can signify other parts of speech as well.

S I don't get that.

F Do you get this—that noun means term and term means noun; that the two do not differ except in pronunciation, so far as a noun is a noun; but that they do differ insofar as a noun is a grammatical part of speech [and term is not]?

S Oh. Yes.

F That is all I mean by word and term signifying each other.

18

S That is clear enough, but I still wonder what you meant by saying that they can "signify other parts of speech as well."

F Didn't our argument show that all parts of speech can be called either nouns or terms, and both words will refer to them all?

S It did.

F How about "noun" considered as the sound of a single syllable, what would you call it if I asked? Wouldn't you answer that it is itself a noun?

S Of course.

F But when we call a conjunction by its three-syllable name, that noun does not include the thing it signifies.

S I can see that.

F That is why I said that a noun signifies not only itself but the other parts of speech as well—and *term* acts the same.

S Clear enough—and now it comes to me that *noun* can be either general or specific, but *term* is not one of the grammatical parts of speech, so this sets it apart from *noun*, along with their difference in sound.

F How about *noun* and *onoma?* Does anything set them apart but the fact that one is in our language and the other in Greek?

S Nothing that I can see.

F So we end up with four kinds of signs—signs that mean themselves; signs that mean each other; signs that refer to the same thing; and signs that have no difference but their pronunciation—the latter we have just turned up, and the first three we said could be understood as either nouns or words.

S That covers it.

19

F Would you run over, then, what we have established so far?

S I can try. First we spent some time inquiring why we talk to each other, and we answered, either to teach someone or to recall something; that when we ask a question, it is to teach another what we want; that when we are singing only for our own enjoyment, we are not talking as such; that in prayers addressed to God (who, we realize, cannot be informed or reminded of anything), we use words only to remind ourselves or so that others may be reminded or informed by us.

Then, after it was agreed that words are nothing but signs, and that what does not mean something beyond itself is not a sign, you presented me with a verse, and asked me to give, if I could, the meaning for each separate word. It runs, "If gods decree nothing from High City remain," and though the fourth word is familiar and clear, we could not determine what it means. When I observed that we could not be using it without a point, but must mean to convey something by it, you said that it might indicate the attitude of mind when one expects to find that a thing exists but finds instead (or thinks he finds) that it does not exist. But then you put off with a pun any probing of this mystery (whatever it may be), saving it for another time—do you think I have forgotten you still owe me that explanation?

While I was trying to state the meaning of the fifth word [from], you pressed me not to explain one word by its synonym but to show the thing it signifies. When I said that could not be done in an exchange of words, we turned to things that can be shown a questioner by pointing at them—I thought these would all be physical objects, but we agreed that it meant all seeable things. From this we moved somehow or other to deaf people and mimes, who could indicate by bodily signs not only all seeable things, but many other things as well—in fact, almost everything we describe with words—though we agreed that even such bodily actions make up a system of signs.

Then we returned to the inquiry whether things represented by signs could be presented without signs, since even the act of pointing, to a partition or a color or anything seeable, is itself a sign. Here I made the mistake of saying that such a signless answer cannot be given, though at length we worked it out that one can answer a question with an action if we are not performing the act while being questioned, and can then perform it as the answer. But even here there is an exception—talking, since we can tell a questioner what talking is even while we continue to talk, a matter easily enough put in words.

20

So we were now agreeing that there are signs representing other signs, signs signifying things that are not signs, and even things we can signify without signs—by action in response to a question. The first one we went into more thoroughly and it emerged that some signs cannot be signified by the sign they signify, as is the case with the trisyllable *conjunction*. But other signs can, as when we say *sign* we signify *word*, and vice versa, since signs and words are each of them both sign and word.

But in this category of signs that signify each other, some do so as equivalents, others as nonequivalent, and a third group as identical with each other. For when we pronounce the monosyllable *sign* we refer to everything it can signify and to everything that signifies it. But when we say *word*, that is not a sign of all other signs, but only of vocal noises shaped to convey meaning. Thus, though the monosyllable *word* and the monosyllable *sign* can refer to each other, *sign* has greater scope than does *word*, one monosyllable covering more than the other one does.

But word and noun, in their widest use, are to some

extent equivalent—our discussion showed that all parts of speech can be nouns, since pronouns can refer to them, proving they are the names for something—and, besides, they can all be made the subject of a sentence by addition of a verb to them. Still, though noun and word are to some extent equivalent, in that each word is a noun, each noun a word, yet they are not exact equivalents—in fact, it is highly probable, according to our exchange, that they have different etymologies, word coming from "whirred" in the ear, noun from "known" in the mind—that is why, when we want to lodge a thing in our inner mind, we properly ask what its name is, and only rarely what its word sounds like.

There are, finally, signs not only nearly equivalent but entirely identical, differing only in their pronunciation, like noun and [Greek] *onoma.* Oh, and one thing I almost forgot—the thing in this category I had not seen: that when signs signify each other, each signifies itself as well as other things. This is as much as I can remember. Since I think your order of exposition was logical and clear, you will judge whether my account of it was as well arranged.

21

F You remember everything I was asking for—in fact, I admit that I understand better, after your summary, things we were trying to dig out of their dark crannies by study and conversation.[7] But it is hard to say, at this point, what goal we are moving toward through this labyrinth. I hope you don't think we are just playing intellectual games, diverting ourselves from important matters with childish quibbles of little or no practical import. Or if you suspect that our discussion is laboring to bring forth something worthy, you must by now have wanted to know what it is, or to get some hint of it. I want to assure you I did not start this discussion to make low puns. We may be having some fun while we are at it, but not of a sort to be despised as childish, since these are not trivial or indifferent things we are weighing. I am trying to prove there is a life that is blessed, one (moreover) that is eternal, which we might achieve if God (who is Truth) assists our feeble steps in ways that suit them, and I hope you won't think I started such a journey from an inappropriate point, not looking to things themselves but to their signs. Do you see that I am leading you into the subject, not with light games but with limbering-up exercises for the mind, to equip us not only for breathing the rare bright air of the blessed life but for making our home in it?[8]

S   Forge on, as before—I don't think anything you say or do is trivial.

22

F   Go back, then, to a thing that is signified by a sign but is not itself a sign. And first tell me whether the masculine is masculine.[9]

S   Now I fear you *are* playing games with me.

F   How?

S   By seriously asking whether the masculine is masculine.

F   Would you still think I am playing games if I ask you

whether the first syllable of that word is *mas,* the second *cu,* the third *line?*

F   Yes.

F   Yet you would not deny that the three syllables, taken together, mean masculine?

S   Who could?

F   And what if I ask are *you* those three syllables?

S   Oh, I see where you are going—no, I am not.

F   Then tell me, so you will not think I am playing games with you.

S   You want me to say I am not masculine.

F   Why not, since you have granted all the premises to the question?

S   I cannot say what I think until I learn from you whether your question was whether I am the *three syllables* or the *thing* they signify.

F   It was for you to say which question you are answering. If my query could be taken two ways, you should have recognized that fact, and asked which was at issue before you responded.

S   Why should the two senses bother me, since I would answer both the same way—whether we are talking about the three syllables of the word, or the real thing the word refers to, masculine is masculine in either case.

F   True enough—but why did you take the word *masculine* in two senses, but not the rest of my sentence?

S   What makes you think I did that?

F Well, first of all, if you thought my first question only sounded out three syllables, you should not have answered me at all, under the opinion that I was not even asking a question [just making three sounds]. But when I put the three syllables in a context, asking "whether the masculine is masculine," the context made you think not of the three-syllable sign, but of what it signifies—as is clear from the promptitude with which you assumed you knew the answer to the question.

S That's right.

F Then why did you take only the single word as both a sound and as a sign?

S But now let me take the word in its context, as dealing only with what it signifies. Let us agree that we cannot hold discourse at all unless our minds are directed by the sound of words to the things they indicate. Show me then, how I was tricked by a line of argument leading to the conclusion that I am not masculine.

F Instead, I'll repeat my questions, so you can see for yourself where you went astray.

S All right.

23

F I won't repeat the opening question, since you have already answered it. But consider this point more accurately—does the syllable *mas* refer to anything beyond itself, or the syllable *cu*, or the syllable *line?*

S   None that I see at the moment.

F   But when you put them together, the masculine comes into being.

S   Not at all, for we agreed, and did so on good footing, that we should treat signs in terms of the *things* they refer to, and affirm or deny what is said of *them*, but those three syllables, taken separately, do not signify anything and have to be treated merely as sounds.

F   You take the position, then, on the basis of principle, that answers to questions should address only what the words refer to [not the words themselves]?

S   Provided we are dealing with compete words [not just syllables], I do not see what other position could be taken.

F   Then I would like to hear you refute the man who used the common joke to argue that a lion came out of his opponent's mouth. Having asked the man whether what we say comes out of our mouth, and won agreement on that, he easily maneuvered him into saying *lion,* and then began to fleer and insist that, having admitted that whatever we say comes out of our mouth, and that he undeniably did say lion, the good fellow spewed out a bad beast.

S   Refuting such a buffoon would be no trouble at all. I just deny his premise, that whatever we say comes out of our mouth. We speak to signify something, and the signified thing does not come from our mouth, only its sign—unless a sign is precisely what we are signifying, as we said before.

24

F The fellow would be no match for you. But still—how do you answer me when I ask is *masculine* an adjective?

S It is.

F Then I must see an adjective when I look at you?

S No.

F Need I draw the conclusion?

S Please don't. I admitted that I am not masculine when I answered you that masculine is an adjective. But I thought it was our understanding that we should affirm or deny what is said according to what it refers to.

F Yet even your mistaking my question was instructive. You were confused by the very way our mind works. If I should ask you, "What is masculine," you could answer "a gender"; but if I asked what part of speech is masculine, the only correct answer you could give is "an adjective." Thus since masculine is both a gender and an adjective, the first answer addresses what is signified, the second addresses the sign. Whoever, then, asks whether masculine is an adjective, I would have to say yes, since he has made it clear that he is considering the word precisely as a sign. But if, instead, he asks simply what is masculine, it is even easier to answer him—if he makes no distinction between sign and thing signified, asking simply what is masculine, the mind inclines naturally, by the structure of language itself, to what the three syllables signify, and there is no appropriate response except to say *gender*, or even to give a complete definition, as "one of the two divisions of sexual animals." Do you agree?

S Entirely. But if, nonetheless, we grant that masculine is also an adjective, how do we escape the uncomfortable claim that we are not masculine?

F How otherwise than by showing that the answer did not fit the terms of the question as asked? Or if the questioner insists on an answer in terms of the sign [not the thing itself], why should I be bothered in admitting that I am not three syllables, which is all he means by masculine?

S That is all true, but why, in that case, is it annoying to hear, "You are not masculine," when all I am admitting is that I am not three syllables?

F Because it is hard not to refer the three syllables as they are being spoken to the thing they signify, so natural is it in most cases for the mind to go immediately to their significance.

S That must be the case.

25

F Now I ask you to concede that what is signified is more to be esteemed than is its sign. A thing that exists for the sake of something else is of necessity inferior to that other thing, is it not?

S I'm not sure. *Ordure*, for instance, is a word worthier than what it refers to. What repels us it not the sound of the word, since it is, with a slight change, the same as *order*— but think of the vast difference between the things signified.[10] So I would never attribute to the sign what we find offensive in the signified, but would prefer the former, affecting our ears, to the latter, affecting our noses.

F You are quick on the uptake. But are you really denying that signs are inferior to the things they signify?

S That's my opinion.

F Then why do you think men bothered to create a word for such a vile and contemptible thing? Or do you think it was wrong of them to do so?

S I cannot call them wrong or right, since I do not know what they had in mind.

F Do you know why you, at least, use the word?

S Of course—because I use this sign to teach or remind another, when I address him, what I think he should learn or remember.

F And the knowledge or remembrance, made possible only by this word, is that not worthier than the word itself?

S Admittedly the knowledge is better than the word, but the word is still better than the thing.

26

F Going back to my general rule, even if not everything is to be preferred to its sign, it remains true that everything that exists for the sake of something else is inferior to that something else. The knowledge of *ordure,* for the sake of which the word was created, is just as superior to the word as the thing itself, according to your claim, is inferior to the word. We say that knowledge conveyed is superior to the word conveying it because the word was created for the knowledge, not the knowledge for the word. Thus when a certain glutton—a "belly worshiper," as the Apostle would put it [Romans 16.18]—said that he lived in order to eat, a more disciplined man replied in disgust, "Better, rather, to eat in order to live." Yet both men were applying the same norm. The first disgusted the other because he thought so little of his life as to make it exist only to gratify his belly, having no other reason for living than to eat. And the other man deserves praise simply for reversing the rank of things, affirming that we eat to live rather than live to eat.

In the same way, if some talkative lover of his own voice should say, "I teach others in order to talk with them," you (or any person not dull to the real worth of things) might respond, "Talking in order to teach is surely better, sir." If these things are true, and you know they are, how can you deny that words are less important than the things for which we employ the words; that this use of words is itself preferable to the words themselves; that words exist only for their usefulness; and that their usefulness is for teaching. The test that makes teaching better than talking is the same that makes talking better than words. For knowing is better than the words by which one knows. If you have anything to counter this, I would like to hear it.

27

S I go along with you when you say that knowing is better than the words by which we know, but I do not know if that justifies your more general claim that anything that exists for the sake of another thing is necessarily inferior to it.

F Let's probe that matter further when we have more time. What you have admitted so far is sufficient for my present point, since you grant that knowledge of reality is worthier than knowledge of its sign. Then knowledge of the former should be preferred to knowledge of the latter, should it not?

S When did I grant that knowledge of the signified is not only better than knowledge of the sign but than the sign itself? That is what I would be conceding if I agreed with your last statement. What if the name of ordure is not only better than the thing, but knowledge of the name is better than knowledge of the thing, though the name is inferior to knowledge of the name? There are, after all, four things in play—the name, the thing named, knowledge of the name, and knowledge of the thing. If the first is superior to the second, why should the third not also be superior to the fourth—or be its equal if not its superior?

28

F The way you not only remember what you conceded, but defend each of your positions, is admirable, I concede. But even you, I bet, must realize that the monosyllable *sin* is, as we pronounce it, better than what it stands for; yet knowing about the word is not as important as knowing about sin. Admittedly, of the four things you list for our consideration—the name, the thing named, knowledge of the name, and knowledge of the thing—the first is justly thought superior to the second. When Persius, for instance, uses sin in a poem [3.32], calling a person "by sin dumb-founded," the word *sin* does not make the poem sinful but gives it in fact a certain elegance. But when the reality symbolized by the word is found in a person [not a poem], it makes him sinful. So the third of your four items is not [as you say] superior to the fourth, but inferior to it. Knowing about the word *sin* is not as important as knowing about sin.

S Would you still prefer such knowledge when it makes men miserable? Didn't Persius himself say [3.35–38] that the agony of men who know all the sins they cannot escape is greater than any inflicted by a tyrant or by their own evil cravings?

F By that line of argument, knowing the name of virtue would be superior to knowing virtue itself, since knowing virtue without having it is a torture—is indeed the very one Persius wished upon tyrants.

S God keep me from so crazed a view. Now I see that knowledge itself is not to be blamed [for the sinner's suffering], since the highest moral discipline enlightens our soul with it, but that those should be called most wretched—I think Persius really meant this—who are so subject to sin that not even healing knowledge can help them.

F You put the matter well. But what care we how Persius is to be interpreted? We are not accountable in such grave matters to poetic sentiment. And it is no simple matter to sort out what forms of knowledge are preferable. It is hard enough to have reached our present position—namely, that knowledge of a signified is superior to its sign, though it may not be superior to *knowledge* of its sign. So let us go farther and deeper into our earlier discussion of things that can be shown without signs but by enactment, as we saw in the case of walking, sitting, and the like.

S Oh yes, I remember.

29

F Do you think all the actions we might perform in answer to a question reveal a thing without the use of signs, or do some fail to do that?

S Mulling it over, I cannot now find a single thing demonstrable without a symbol—unless perhaps talking, or the act of explaining when that is what is asked for. For I see that any act performed in answer to a question cannot of itself show what is being asked for. If someone, to take our earlier example, asks me what walking is, when I am not doing anything, or doing something else, were I to walk at once, trying to show him what he asked about, how do I know he will not take the *distance* I walk as the answer to his question, and be misled by that interpretation, so he thinks that someone going farther than I did, or less far, is therefore not walking? And what I say about this word holds true for all the things I thought could be demonstrated without a symbol—with the two possible exceptions I brought up.

30

F Fair enough so far. [But about those two things,] would you say talking is different from teaching?

S They must be—if they were the same, no one could teach without talking. But since we can teach by signs other than words, who can doubt that they differ?

F Do teaching and signifying mean the same thing?

S I believe so.

F If it were claimed that we make signs in order to teach, would you agree?

S Surely.

F So if one, on the contrary, said that we teach in order to make signs, wouldn't the general rule we reached be enough to refute him?

S Yes.

F And since we use signs in order to teach, not vice versa, teaching must be something different from making signs.

S That's right—I was wrong to equate them.

F Then answer this: when one teaches what teaching is, does he do this with signs or in some other way?

S How else?

F Then you were wrong as well when you said, earlier, that if one asked what teaching is, that could be taught without using signs. Now we see that this is impossible, since you have admitted that making signs and teaching are distinct things. If, as it appears, they differ, and teaching cannot be demonstrated without using signs, then teaching cannot be demonstrated by itself, as you said. So nothing at all can be demonstrated by itself, except for speaking—and since it *is* a sign, then *nothing* can be demonstrated without a sign.

S I see no flaw in that.

31

F We have established, then, that nothing can be taught without signs, and that the knowledge which is conveyed by the signs is worthier than the signs—though it is possible that some of the things signified are not superior to their signs.

S So it seems.

F Does it seem to you that we have taken a wind-about journey to a trivial objective? For ever since we began this verbal jousting, which has gone on so long, we have been working to discover three things only—whether anything can be taught without signs; whether signs are to be preferred to what they signify; and whether the knowledge of the signified is preferable to its sign. But I would like to raise this fourth brief point with you—whether what we have discovered so far you can affirm as beyond question.

S I would hope we gained some certitude through paths so dubious and difficult, but something about your question troubles me, and makes me leery of a confident reply. I suspect you would not have asked me if you did not have something in reserve to spring on me; and the very complexity of such matters eludes my grasp of them as a whole and keeps me from giving an assured answer, for fear that something lurks in their depths that my mind, for all its effort, has not reached.

F   I welcome your wariness, as evidence that you are not rash in your judgments—which can help you preserve a certain equanimity. For some uneasiness is almost inevitable when things we have been quick to accept as certain, are, by logical challenge, shaken to their foundations—wrenched, as it were, right out of our grasp. In proportion as it is safe to accept arguments well framed and tested, it is perilous to entertain unexamined propositions as if they were established—or else, when we see things undermined that we believed firmly built and permanent, we may develop a dislike or distrust of reason itself, as if there were no way of giving a sure consent even to the most evident truths.

32

Despite all that, let us rethink your withholding of consent to what we have so far concluded. I put it to you thus: if one unacquainted with the art of snaring birds, which is done with twigs and birdlime, should meet a bird catcher along the way, one outfitted with all the tools of his trade but not plying them at the moment, just walking along— suppose the observer should quicken his pace, puzzling out to himself what such strange equipment might mean, until the bird catcher, noticing the man's curiosity and wanting to demonstrate his skill, deploys his limed reeds, his rod, and his hawk when a little bird presents itself, using them to immobilize, manipulate, and bag the prize. Hasn't he taught the onlooker what he wanted to know, enacting the answer without any signs?

S I suspect we have the same problem we encountered in the case of a question about walking—and, besides, I doubt that the whole art of bird catching could be demonstrated by your example.

F Let's make it simple by stipulating that the observer in the example is so quick at understanding as to see the whole bird-catching art from this one display of it. For my contention it is enough that, in some cases (though not all), some men (though not all) might learn in this way without any signs being used.

S Then I would just stipulate a man so quick at understanding as to recognize the whole art of walking from the taking of a few steps.

F Stipulate away—I balk not at what you say, but welcome it, since it means that we have discovered together that some things can be demonstrated without the use of signs, and that our earlier conclusion that nothing can be demonstrated without signs was false—and not because one or two examples can be cited of such demonstration without signs, but because thousands can. Why, after all, should that surprise us? Putting aside the performances to be seen in any number of theaters, where actions are performed without the use of signs, what about the sun, streaming light over all things and luminously clothing them, or the moon and stars, the earth and the sea with all things bred in them, are they not revealed to us simply as we look at them, God and nature supplying them to our view?

33

We may in fact discover, if we press the matter closely, that nothing is demonstrated by its own signs. If a sign is shown to me before I know what it signifies, it can reveal nothing to me. But if I do know beforehand, what has it demonstrated on its own? When I read in the book of Daniel [3.94] that "their *sarabarae* were immune to harm," the word *sarabarae* means nothing to me. If someone suggests to me that the word refers to some kind of headgear, is he teaching me what head means, or what gear means? I already knew those things. And I did not learn them just because someone called them that, but when I saw them for myself. When the monosyllable pronounced as "head" first stirred in my ears, it meant as little to me as when I first heard or read *"sarabarae."* But when the word was said again and again, I began to take notice of it and to figure out where in conversation it was being used, until I connected the sound with something already familiar to me from sight. Before I made that connection, "head" was just a sound. It became a sign to me only when I recognized the *thing* it signified—so I learned not from the sign of the thing but from the sight of it. In this way, a sign is more to be learned from its object than the object is from it.

34

For a clearer grasp on the matter, suppose this case: we have just heard for the first time someone say "head." Since we do not know whether this sound is simply a noise or the sign of something, we ask what "head" is—remember, we are not yet asking *what* it signifies, but *whether* it signifies, which we cannot be sure of so long as we wonder whether it is a sign in the first place—and at this point someone points to the head. Seeing the thing, we learn that what we heard was a sign, a thing we could not have known earlier. There are two things involved in its being a sign, its sound and its sense, and the sound does not strike us as a sign but as a stirring in the ears, while its sense becomes apparent only as a sight—of the thing it symbolizes. The pointing of the finger cannot signify anything but the thing at which it is pointed, since it is not pointing to another sign but to the actual part of the body called its head. So the pointing does not give me knowledge of the head, which I already had, nor of the sign, at which it is not pointing.

The pointing, in fact, is not very important in itself, since it is more a sign of indicating than of the thing indicated—like the imperative "See!" with which we sometimes accompany our pointing, in case one sign of indication does not suffice. What I am trying to bring home to you, as best I can, is that we are not taught by the signs we call words. Rather, as I told you, the force of a word—that is, the meaning connected with its sound—we learn from the signified reality, which we already knew, rather than learning the reality from what signifies it.

35

Now what I said about the head applies also to gear, and to numberless other things I could cite. Yet my knowing these things would not, of itself, make me understand *sarabarae*. If someone were to describe what *sarabarae* are like by tracing one in the air or on a page, I will not say that he does not teach me (though, given some time, I could maintain that) but, more important for our present purpose, I maintain only that he did not teach me by words. Still, if we are both in the presence of *sarabarae* and he says, "See! *Sarabarae*," I would learn something I did not know before, not by any words that were said, but rather by looking at the thing, from the sight of which I learn and remember what the word refers to. For in learning about that thing, I did not rely on someone else's words but on my own eyes— though I may have relied on words to tell me what to look at, after which I saw it by myself.

36

The most, then, that can be said for the scope of words is that they afford us an occasion for examining something, but they do not demonstrate it to our understanding.[11] One who would really teach must bring before my eyes, or some other bodily sense, or the mind itself, that which I want to know. From words we learn nothing but other words, or rather their sound and accent. Since a word is by definition a sign, a word I hear is not even a word for me until I know what is signified by it.

So it is only from knowledge of the things they signify that words become signs, while from the sound of words alone we do not even know that they are words. We learn nothing new from words we already know, and we cannot testify to new knowledge from those we do not know until we learn what it is they signify, which is established not by the hearing of the sounds that carry them but from knowledge of the things they symbolize. The soundest rule, then, the whole summary of truth with regard to words, is that we either know what they signify or we do not. If we know that already, we are not taught it but remember it; and if we do not know that, then we cannot remember it, but may perhaps be directed to seek it.

37

You might say that we cannot truly understand *sara-burae*, the sound of whose name is all we now have in mind, unless we can visualize what it is, and we cannot know more about the word [than its sound] until we know about the headgear itself. Yet we recognize that the three young men [who wore the headgear in the book of Daniel] overcame the ruler and his fire by their faith and piety, sang praise to God, and earned praise even from their foe—and what but words taught us this? I answer that we already had stored in our mind what every one of those words symbolizes. I already knew what three young men are, and a furnace, and a fire, and a ruler, and what it is to be burnt by fire, and everything else conveyed by those words.

But the words Ananias, Azarias, and Misael are as strange to me as ever *sarabarae* was. And for knowing them the words themselves were no help, and could not be. That everything contained in scripture happened as it did in history is something that I rather believe than know—a distinction recognized by those we believe in, since the prophet Isaiah said [7.9] "Unless you believe, you will not understand." He could not have written that unless he understood the distinction. What I understand, I believe as well; though what I believe I do not necessarily understand. I know I need to believe some things I do not know—need, for instance, to believe the story of the three young men. Even where I cannot know, then, I need to believe without knowing.

38

As for all the things we do understand, we do not derive them from a speaker sounding words exterior to us, but from listening to the interior truth that informs our mind, however much words may provide us an occasion to consult that truth. The one we listen to there is the one who teaches us, the changeless power of God and his Wisdom never ending. Every creature that reasons is listening to him, but he responds according to each person's disposition toward him, as accepting or resisting him. If error occurs, it is not because there is no [interior] truth for us to listen to, just as our eyes do not deceive us for lack of an exterior light by which we should be seeing things. We realize that we must seek that light if we are to behold things according to our physical capacity.

39

Now if we interpret colors by means of light, and other things we sense by the world's physical elements, and the sensations themselves by the soul that uses them as intermediaries, then we must interpret intelligible things by our mind's interior truth—and what could better illustrate the fact that from words in themselves we learn nothing than does the sensation of their sound in our ears? For everything we perceive is perceived either by physical sensation or mental apprehension, giving us either sensible things or intelligible ones—or, as our Christian writers would prefer, objects either carnal or spiritual. If we are questioned about the former, we can answer if the question involves things present to our senses—if, for instance, we are looking at a new moon when asked about its position or phases. If the questioner does not himself see the moon, he has to take my word for it—or, more frequently, refuse to do so. In any case, he does not really learn the facts unless he sees them for himself—in which case, not the sound of the words but the sight of the thing informs his own senses. As far as the words go, they are the same whether one is seeing or not seeing what they describe.

But when we are asked about things not present to our senses now, but perceived by our senses at some prior time, then we are no longer describing things perceived as we speak, but images of them received by our senses in the past and now stored away in our memory. And since we are no longer considering the things themselves, but something they are not, I do not know how we can continue to call our answer a true one unless we admit that we are reporting not what we see or perceive, but what we remember to have seen or perceived. Such images, filed away in the archives of memory, are like documents recording past experiences, and if we scrutinize and report them honestly, we are not lying. Still, they are our own inner documents. If one hearing my report has experienced the same things himself, by his own present sensation, then he learns nothing from my words, but recognizes the same reality he had stored up his own record of. But if he has not experienced the same reality himself, then we must admit that he does not have his own understanding of the thing but a mere trust in my words.

40

If, however, we are dealing with things we perceive in the intellect, using our understanding and reason, then we speak of things perceived directly by the inner light of truth, which enlightens and fertilizes what we have called the interior self. And our listener, if he too perceives them with his own inner and innocent eye, knows what I am describing by his own vision of it, not by my words. In that case, even though I should speak true and he accept it as true, I teach him nothing. He learns not from my words but from the realities themselves, revealed to him by God's action within him. What could be odder than for him to think he was learning from my words what he could have told a questioner before I ever spoke to him?

When, as often happens, a man denies something when first asked about it, and then has to affirm it under harder questioning, this comes from his own weak inner vision, which kept him from submitting the whole matter to truth's inner light. And he is led beyond the part he sees if one asks him about all the parts that make up the matter he had not seen clearly as a whole. And even if words are used to help him on, the words themselves do not teach him, though they afford an occasion for him to consult the inner truth from which he must learn.

If, for instance, I were to ask you (in keeping with our subject) if nothing can be taught by words, the question might seem silly if you were not up to seeing the problem in its entirety. I would be obliged, in that case, to frame my questions in such a way as to direct your talents to what your interior teacher is telling you. And if I were to ask you, "How did you learn to speak the truth when I was questioning you, and to be firm in it, and to say you know that you know it," you might tell me that I was teaching you. But then I would take you a step further, and ask you this: If I told you I saw a man flying, would those words be as convincing to you as if you heard me say that wise men deserve more respect than fools? Naturally, you would say no, telling me you do not believe what I said about flying, and even if you did believe it you would not know it, the way you are certain of the truths you listed. Surely that is enough to make you see that my words taught you nothing—neither when I said I saw a man flying, of which you said you could know nothing, nor when I said about wise men what you knew perfectly well on your own. Indeed, asked about these two points [entirely apart form my words], you would have been prompt to say that the first was unknowable, and the second was readily known.

You would thus have reached the point of admitting on a full view a thing you had denied on a partial view, having put all the elements of the problem together in a clear and certain way to reach this conclusion: Whenever we talk, the one who hears us either does not know whether what we say is true, or does know that it is false, or he knows that it is true. In the first case, he has belief or opinion or doubt; in the second, opposition or denial; in the third, affirmation—and in none of these cases is the hearer being taught. In the first case, he has not grasped a truth from my words, in the second he knows my words are false, and in the third he already knows what I was saying and could have affirmed it without hearing me at all.

41

If this is so, then where inward understanding is at issue, it does no good to hear about another's understanding unless one has the same understanding on one's own—except in cases where *trust* is relied on for the period when one cannot reach understanding. But anyone who is able to reach his own perception is a learner in his internal forum, and a judge of those addressing him in the external forum, or at least a judge of what any person says, since he often understands what is being said though the speaker himself does not. Imagine, for instance, that a man who believes with Epicurus that the soul is mortal should cite sounder persons' arguments in favor of its immortality, and his listener, who has greater spiritual discernment, sees that the words he is citing are true. The speaker, then, who is speaking truths he is unaware of, or rather things he is sure are false—can we say that he is teaching others what he does not know himself? He is, after all, using the same arguments that those who believe in them would use.

42

We can no longer, therefore, claim even this minimal role for words, that at least they express the speaker's views, since he may not realize what he is saying—or in fact he may be lying or misleading others, in which case he is not only failing to express his views, but actually using words to falsify them. I do not deny that some try to express their views in truthful words, even go as it were on oath for their veracity, and they might be believed if we could exclude liars from the process. But we also know from experience that words, our own as well as others', often fail to reflect the speaker's thoughts. I believe two of the ways this can happen are, first, when one recites words familiar to memory and often repeated, while thinking of something entirely different (for instance, while singing a psalm); or, second, by accident, when ill-considered words slip out that misrepresent what one really intended to say, and the signs of things we have in mind are not conveyed to the listener. The opposite of this occurs with the liar, who is extremely conscious of what he is saying. Even if we cannot tell when a liar is telling the truth, we can be sure that he is conveying what he means to—unless one of those two kinds of inadvertence should happen even to him. If one objects that these ways of misleading are uncommon and easily recognized, I have little trouble with that, even though the misdirection often goes unrecognized, and I have often enough been fooled by it.

43

A different category altogether, a common one, the cause of endless wrangling and misunderstanding, involves the person who does express his views, at least for himself and his own coterie, though his words do not have the same meaning for any other who hears them, or for that man's company. Someone might say, for instance, that some animals are brighter than human beings, a proposition we cannot accept, and which we vigorously denounce as false and corrupting—while all the time he just meant that some animals are brighter in color, not in intellect. He was not lying, nor confused in his own mind, nor thinking something different from what he was saying, nor reciting by mindless rote, nor mispeaking by accident. He is merely expressing his thought with a word whose meaning we do not share with him. We would agree with him at once if we could read his mind, which remains closed to us, though he has spoken accurately about what he is thinking.

Some say this problem can be solved by careful definition—in this case, for instance, by defining what one means by brightness. They say that will make it clear that one is wrangling over words, not things. Even if I should accept that, there are few men who can make accurate definitions. And there are, besides, theoretical difficulties about the act of defining, which this is not the time for us to entertain, even if I knew (and I don't) how to resolve them.

44

Another problem I pass by is the frequency with which we conduct energetic disputes over words imperfectly heard, though we think we heard them clearly. Not long ago I told you a certain word means "mercy" in Punic, but you said you had heard from those better acquainted with the language that it means "piety." I doubted that, and said you must have forgotten what you were given as the meaning, since I had heard what you said as "faith"—even though you were close to me as you spoke, and the words do not sound at all alike. For some time I thought you did not know what you were saying, when it was really I who did not know what you were saying. If I had heard you properly, it would not have seemed odd for the Punic language to use the same word for both mercy and faith. This is not an isolated occurrence, but I shall, as I said, pass it by, lest I seem to be convicting words themselves of their users' carelessness or mere defect of hearing. But the cases I mentioned earlier are more troublesome, where we cannot understand what the speaker has in mind, even though he voices it with perfect diction and in the Latin language we share with him.

45

But even if I stipulate that it is possible, when we recognize words being spoken, that a speaker's views can be ascertained from those words, does that mean that we ascertain the *truth* of those views, which is what we are concerned with? Do teachers advertise that they verbally transmit their own acts of understanding, or the truths of their discipline, for students to receive and retain? What father sends a child to school with the silly aim of finding out what the teacher's understanding is? Rather, when all subjects, even those concerning virtue and wisdom, have been expounded by those who profess them, then students, if they are really to be called that, investigate within themselves whether what they are hearing is true, strenuously putting it to the test of their own interior truth. That is the point at which they learn. And when they reach an inner conviction of truth, they praise their teachers, not realizing that, even if the teachers knew what they were saying, the praise rightly belongs to the taught ones not the ones who taught. Men make the mistake of calling others their teachers when they are no such thing, since there is a near-simultaneity between what is said and what is understood, and where inner assent follows so quickly on outer discussion they think the latter caused the former.

46

We may, God willing, get around later on to a general consideration of the use of words—properly undertaken, that is a major project. My only caution for now is that you not ascribe to them greater power than belongs to them. We should resolve to bring reasoned understanding, not mere pious acceptance, to the text given us by divine authority, that we should call no man our teacher, since 'the single teacher of all men is he who dwells in heaven' [Matthew 23.10]. The meaning of the words 'in heaven' he will himself teach us, who provides us the external occasion, through others' words, to submit to his internal schooling. Knowing and loving him make up the blessed life, which all say they want to attain, though few can feel assured that they have found it.

Tell me, finally, what you made of this whole speech to

you. If you found any truth in what I said, you can assure anyone who asks that you already knew it, down to the finest points—which shows that you realize who was really teaching you. It was not I, though you were responding to things I said. But if you found no truth at all in my words, then no one taught you—not he, and not I. Not I, because there is nothing that I can teach. And not he, because there was nothing that you learned.

S By the occasion your words provided, I have learned that words can do no more than provide such an occasion for learning; that words cannot even tell us much about the thoughts of those using them; and that their truth is to be established only by our internal teacher, who provides external words only as an occasion for me to love him more ardently, with his help, and learn in proportion as I love.

As for your speech, it *was* a long one, though I am glad of that, since you anticipated and removed objections I was ready to make, leaving out no point I would have raised, and each thing I learned from my own internal oracle corresponded with your words.

Notes

1. Windings of the tune: *modulationem quandam*. In *Music 5*, Augustine says that *modulare* means to arrange the intervals in pitch and tempo.
2. Augustine artfully chooses a line, from his vast repertoire of remembered Virgilian verses, that begins with three tricky words—*Si nihil ex*—just the kind Wittgenstein said Augustine overlooked in his theory of language (see *comm.* [13]). Godsend has to take them

in order. The translation cannot keep these words at the head of the verse, unless I resort to some periphrasis that would involve more words than eight. So Godsend takes the words out of order in the translation.

3. Since Godsend is about to say that *audibilia* is an odd form ("hearable"), its parallel *visibilia* should be formed to match it.

4. Deaf "signing" and military standards are Augustine's regular examples of nonverbal symbol systems—see *Christian Culture* 2.3.4, cited in *comm.* **[8]**. For the importance of sign language to the study of modern linguistics, see Noam Chomsky, *The Architecture of Language* (Oxford University Press, 2000), pp. 9, 50–52, 66.

5. The etymologies are as forced in the Latin, and more like puns than serious arguments, an important clue to the "jousting" nature of this part of the dialogue, its "limbering up" part. "Whir" is *verberare*, "impinge"—since Augustine thought hearing resulted from a stir in the fine air of the ear, which the soul went out to "seize." The *noun-know* pun *(nomen-nosco)* is not equally absurd; it has some linguistic basis.

6. Augustine's Latin Bible misrepresented the original Greek, which said "yes and no" where he read "is and is not."

7. Augustine, with his view of conversation with others as a stimulant to the internal teacher, says that one often learns by teaching others—see *Christian Culture*, Preface 12 and *comm.* **[13]**.

8. Compare *Music* 6.1.

9. Augustine asks whether "man is man," but the later breaking of the word into syllables makes it impossible to use a monosyllable in the translation, or an equivalent like "human" since one of its syllables, *man*, is a word in itself. Masculine is the closest I could come in English. *Mas* is *male* in Latin, but I am using the *English* word in the translation.

10. The pun *ordure-order* is, in Latin, *coenum-coelum* (excrement-heaven).

11. "Afford an occasion" is the meaning Burnyeat finds in *admonere*.